Mrs Wallace J. Lamb
1948

THE FIRE BALLOON

THE FIRE BALLOON

RUTH MOORE

William Morrow & Company, Publishers

* fjl *

Acknowledgment is made
to Henry Holt & Company, Inc.,
for permission to quote from A SHROPSHIRE LAD,
by A. E. Housman.

For Eleanor Mayo

PART ONE

July, 1941

Drift down to earth, bright dream, and fly no more:
The stars were lovely, but their trails are higher.
Come home to earth, and on its horny floor
Put by your wings of thistledown and fire.
Lighter than ashes, softer than a cloud,
Fall from the blazing orbit where you spun,
For you are beautiful and you are proud
No more among the planets of the sun.
There are the hills, their echoing arches, there
The lawns and lanes of earth, the stony coast;
What flies too far in high and cloudless air
In time comes home, a secret and a ghost,
Where low beneath the towering stars is spread
A gravecloth for the bright and lovely dead.

THE hours between six and eight on Fourth of July night were the longest ever known. Supper was over and the dishes done, and now there was nothing to do but wait until it got dark enough for the fireworks. Sit in the hammock, so as not to muss the best white dress with the picot holes and the crisp blue ribbon sash, until it was time to go down to Mr. Beacon's.

Weeks ago, when Theoline had started looking forward, the

Fourth had seemed like a small round dot, red-colored and far away, at the end of a long tunnel of days. Through the days, though, there had always been something to do to make the time go fast.

She could finger her six packs of firecrackers and the soft sticks of punk, being careful not to break any; she could close her eyes and imagine the bright bang, the red paper shattering, the satisfactory, muffled "*plonk!*" inside the tin can, the can flying as high as the house.

She could spend time figuring how to get even with Wesley, because her six packs of firecrackers had suddenly become five, and she knew he had taken one. It was mean of him. He had six packs of his own and a box of six-inch salutes as well. He always had more than she did. She still had that bone to pick with him; she meant to pick it, too. You couldn't pin anything on Wes, you never could, but you knew what you knew.

The days had gone by somehow and now they were time past. All at once this morning, it was the Fourth. She had known almost before she was awake, because at daylight Pa had let off both barrels of his shotgun to usher in the great day. For a moment it seemed as if the walls of the world had crashed down; then she knew.

To dress and get out on the hill with her firecrackers before Wesley was what she had to do, and she did it, pulling on only her dress over her underdrawers. All Wes ever had to put on was his overalls but a girl's things were different. He always beat her dressing. This morning he didn't. He was sleepy. She was out on the cold wet grass, barefooted, opening up her first pack, before he was even out of bed.

If only she could have been let alone to set off her own firecrackers, the day might not have gone bad. She had looked forward so long, having over in her mind how wonderful the Fourth would be, that now it seemed like something she had to do by herself, slowly and keeping her mind on it, tasting every minute. She tore off the bright red paper and the tearing sound was rich and satisfactory. She unbraided the twist of gray fuse that held the firecrackers together. She lit a stick of punk. It caught slowly because the night's damp was still in it; but presently it sent up a clear blue thread of smoke into the still air.

The sun was coming up. Timothy and lace grass on the hillside were bowed down with dew so heavy it made the whole field look gray. The first red firecracker she threw must have hit a dewdrop, for it sizzled and went out; but the next one went off with the bang she had hoped for and sent a shower of bright sparkling drops into the air.

But now here came Wes, with his nose turned up at any bang she might make, and his first six-inch salute blasted a hole in the morning. To meet it, she set off a whole pack at once, but little firecrackers made only thin, popping sounds now. Wes had the seat pocket of his overalls carelessly stuffed with red packs; he pulled one out and lit it, and she knew by the way he grinned at her that it had been hers. And now here came Jimmy and Joe. They were only four and five, too young to be trusted alone with their own firecrackers, but they were crazy wild to have some, lying in wait and creeping up to grab. Theoline had to watch every minute to keep things out of reach of the small snatching hands. Impossible now to light a cracker, hold it, throw it and watch it go off. You lit it and threw it and swung around to smack a small brother out of the way.

Little firecrackers would hardly stir a tin can off the ground. It just bounced and fell over. But a six-inch salute would flatten one and send it high into the air.

Theoline's insides started to churn with nervousness and frustration. She knew that churning feeling well; it meant she was going to get mad. She didn't want to get mad on the Fourth of July; so finally she gave up, just lit her last two packs whole one after the other. Then she went back to the house and sat down on the piazza steps.

Ma had got Jacky, the baby, dressed and fed and had put her out on the piazza to play. Or maybe you couldn't say that

Jacky was playing. She never played like other babies did. Jacky had Something The Matter with Her. Theoline had no idea what it could be. All she knew was what she had heard Ma say to Pa one time when she thought no one was listening.

"I guess we'll have to give up, Syl, and admit that Jacky's got Something The Matter with Her."

Jacky was quite a big baby now. She was almost three, but she was still creeping, not walking, and instead of getting around underfoot, she would just sit still most of the time, poking her finger into a patch of sunlight, maybe, and taking it out again. She was doing that now, sitting on the piazza in her bright blue romper suit, smiling softly to herself.

On the steps, Theoline said under her breath, I hate the Fourth of July, and instantly in her mind she was far, far away from the place where the Fourth of July was. She was a beautiful little princess, the only child of the king and queen in a palace over the sea. It was Christmas, and standing by a window in the great palace throne room was a marvelous tree, full of packages, large and small. The little princess was lovely in her golden robes. She was just opening a velvet box and taking out a diamond ring. It was the first package she had opened and there were many to come.

The king in his jeweled crown was there, with his arm around the queen. He was saying, "Queen, I'm so glad we never gave our darling any little brothers and sisters, because we love her so much there isn't any love or any Christmas presents to spare."

That'll learn that old Fourth of July, Theoline said between her teeth.

She heard a slight crunching noise, and looking down, saw that Jacky had crept over beside her and was eating a stick of her punk. It was her best stick, the longest one, and now it was broken. She slapped Jacky.

Gram Sarah came past the end of the piazza just in time to see. She let out an outraged squawk, made a swipe at Theo and missed, and gathered the wailing Jacky to her bosom.

"You little limb of the divil!" she said. "Hittin a poor defenseless baby!" Her voice changed to a croon. "Nev-er mind, Gram Sarah's baby. Gram Sarah'll take care of her."

From a safe distance, Theoline thumbed her nose at Gram Sarah and vanished into the lilac bush.

"You better hide!" Gram Sarah shrieked. "I git my hands on you . . . Phoebe! *Phoe-beee!* You come out here and tend to this cussid little heathen. I never in all my life . . . !"

So that meant a spanking for Theoline and spending the rest of the morning up in her room. She didn't know as she cared. It was just about what you might expect of a day like the Fourth of July. She cried until her bottom stopped stinging, and then she began to think about Mr. Beacon's fireworks. Maybe the day would save itself after all.

Mr. Beacon was summer people who brought his family to Granite Hook every year, where he owned a "cottage" down by the shore. Nobody ever called it anything but a "summer cottage," but it was a great big house, much as fifteen rooms, set out on the shore away from the village, the way the summer cottages were. You got to it by going down a long white gravel drive, which led between gardens of bright flowers, green lawns and big leafy trees. You went there, quite often, because Mrs. Beacon liked to have you and Wes come to play with their two kids, Felix and Jane. On the Fourth of July, Mr. Beacon always invited some of the village people to come down and sit on the big front porch which looked out over the water, and see the fireworks which he'd brought from Boston. It was quite an honor to be one of the families that Mr. Beacon invited.

In the city where he lived, Mr. Beacon had another great rich house, and his kids had playthings like nothing you ever saw in your life. Here, Felix and Jane, who were ten and eleven, just the age of Theoline and Wesley, had doll houses and water wings, and tennis rackets and hundreds and hundreds of clothes and dresses. And look at all the money Mr. Beacon spent for fireworks!

Fireworks were expensive, anyone could tell you that. Wes had a skyrocket to set off tonight; it had cost a dollar. Ma had scolded him for throwing away so much on it. Theoline herself had paid fifty cents for her Roman candle. But Mr. Beacon, they said, had as many as twenty skyrockets and who knew how many Roman candles. He had pinwheels and scenes in fire and sky-bombs with colored stars. And this year, they said, he was going to have a real fire balloon.

Theoline had no idea what the fire balloon was, but she had heard people talk about it as if it were something wonderful. It was filled with heated air, they said, kept hot by some kind of a long-burning chemical, and it soared into the air until it went out of sight.

There's only a few of them in the whole world, Theoline told herself, leaning out her bedroom window, trying to imagine the dark night sky and the fire balloon in it, and we're going to see one.

Probably, now she'd got into trouble, they'd give Wes her Roman candle to set off. Anyway, it would be something hateful Gram Sarah would think of as punishment and put Ma up to. It wasn't worth your life to sass Gram Sarah. She always got back at you five times over.

But even if they don't let me go down to Mr. Beacon's tonight, they can't stop me seeing the fire balloon. I can watch it, I can see it when it rises up over the woods. I can watch all the fireworks from my bedroom window.

But Ma had called her downstairs at dinnertime and nothing more was said. Theo had got all over, anyway, imagining that Ma was so mean. It was only when you were mad, you felt madder thinking everybody was cruel to you. And now here she was, all dressed up and waiting for it to be dark enough for the fireworks, and for them all to go down to Mr. Beacon's. One thing, Uncle Morgan and Gram Sarah hadn't been invited.

Uncle Morgan lived at Gram Sarah's house. She didn't think she liked him any better than she did Gram Sarah. He was always saying, "Now, you kids clear out. I'm busy."

Wesley came out on the piazza with his skyrocket. He was going to take it down and set it off in Mr. Beacon's skyrocket cradle. Wes wasn't dressed up. He had on his same old overalls, only they were clean and ironed. He was going to help Mr. Beacon and Felix set off the fireworks.

Of course nobody asked *her* to help set off fireworks. She was a girl, a "little lady." She was supposed to stay on the piazza with Jane, that dope, and all the big ladies and go "Oo!" and "Ah!" at what the menfolks were doing. Well, all right, she would. But nobody but her was going to set off her Roman candle. She had it here in the hammock with her now. Its handle was damp and beginning to crumble a little where she had held it tightly in her hand.

Wesley laid his skyrocket down on the step, carefully, and went back through the screen door for something. He should have known better, but he, too, was a little bemused by looking forward to the fireworks. Theoline waited until the door had slammed shut behind him. Then she reached down from the hammock and quickly and smoothly twisted the fuse out of the rocket. She took the fuse between her thumb and finger and snapped it into the syringa bush.

Wesley came back and sat down to wait. He didn't notice anything. After a moment, he wiggled. Waiting was hard for him, too. To pass the time, he twisted his head over his shoulder and made a sissy face at Theo in her best dress in the hammock.

"Mama's little lady," he remarked in mincing tones.

But Theo didn't even bother to make a face back at him.

"Guess this rocket isn't any good, Wes," boomed Mr. Beacon. He was a big man, expansive, in a suit of white cotton duck. When the fireworks went off, creating colored lights, the same colored sweat shone on his cheeks and on the polished dome of his bald head. He was working hard, harder than he was used to with his hands, setting off the fireworks, stooping down a lot, which was a chore for a man with a big stomach.

"What's the matter with it?" Wesley's voice was high, the way it got when he was excited or disappointed. Mr. Beacon had promised him he could light the fuse on his own rocket.

"Fuse gone out of it," the big man said. "But never mind. I've got lots more."

"But I wanted to light one," Wesley said. He sounded ready to cry. "I wanted to light *mine*."

"Better not fool with it. Likely to explode on the ground." Mr. Beacon picked up the rocket, broke it across his knee. "Mustn't take chances, with all these ladies around. Come on, stand back now, let's see what this funny thing is."

Wesley moved away, his face a mask of disappointment. From the hammock on the Beacon piazza, another mask, very bright-eyed, looked out; but its expression was one of demure disinterestedness.

The "funny thing" was a waterfall of green fire which poured down for a long moment, turning faces and hands to a corpse-like pallor, making the smooth grass of the Beacons' front lawn almost white. Nasturtiums in a big round bed changed to white ghosts of nasturtiums. Black shadows of the men and boys slashed across the lawn, the darkness withdrew for a long way, the stars in the sky winked out into black velvet. A magic green river carved itself out of the night, held steady and faded away, with a dying hiss of red hot wire. For a moment it was dark, as if you had your eyes closed; then, slowly, the outlines of things began to come back again.

It was not a dark night. The western sky, behind the woods, still glowed a little with light from the sunset. The water in front of the Beacon house, which faced east, was luminescent and polished like the inside of a shell. There was no wind, not even a breeze. The air seemed to hang motionless, though it was not heavy, and there was no sign of storm. Over the sea, a star hung big and bright, as if it were not very far away. The fireworks put it out, but it always came back; in the still water it made a long, sharp, silver bar.

"Well," Mr. Beacon said at last. He fumbled around in the

last of the cartons, from which he had been taking the fireworks. "I guess that's the works." He paused for his pun to be appreciated. "There isn't a thing left but this fire balloon, and it may not amount to much. It works with a chemical, a new thing just developed this year, and I hope it functions." He lifted out what seemed to be a flat, limp, gray bag.

In the hammock, Theoline caught her breath. That thing *couldn't* be the fire balloon. Why, it was nothing! It looked like an old dirty stocking. She let her breath go softly, so as not to be noticed by anyone.

Don't let them see that you are disappointed. The fireworks have been lovely, Mr. Beacon. The pinwheels. The rockets. The green fire. Niagara Falls. Lovely. Be polite and don't let *them* see. Enough of them, as it is, think you are a horrid little girl, who doesn't appreciate what is done for her.

But Mr. Beacon was doing things to the flat gray bag. He was working around it with a strange, dull-looking light, that seemed to glow rather than to burn; and the bag was acting in a queer way for anything so dead. It seemed to come alive, rising up from the ground with little jerks all by itself, starting to shine with a lovely light. You could hear a sound, too, a hissing. As you watched, you saw something you had never seen before, nor ever expected to see. You saw ugliness, under your very eyes, grow beautiful.

The bag grew and grew and shone and shone. It was a perfect globe now, luminous, two feet across, rising up under Mr. Beacon's hand and tugging to be free.

Oh, let it go, don't hold it! See, it wants to go. It mustn't stay held, when it wants so to go! Theoline watched it, and something in her chest seemed to grow and shine with it.

Then Mr. Beacon stepped back and let it out of his hand. It shot into the air, going up, growing smaller. When it seemed to be about as big as a full moon, it stopped, then, slowly and majestically, began to move out over the water. It went out over the ocean and hovered there.

"Well!" Mr. Beacon said. He sounded surprised. "That's

certainly an odd thing. I never saw anything like that before. You'd think it would keep on moving, go up or down."

Someone on the piazza said, "There must be some kind of air pocket out there, holding it still."

They *would* talk. The grownups would talk, and out on the lawn among the shards of the fireworks, Wesley and Felix were starting a wrestling match. Mr. Beacon came up on the piazza, dusting his hands. He put one hand under Theo's chin and turned her face up to his. His fingers smelled like the inside of an old shotgun shell.

"Well," he boomed heartily. "Here's a little girl who enjoyed the fireworks, all right. Look at those eyes. Just like stars!"

She mumbled, "Yes, thank you, Mr. Beacon," but that was as far as politeness would carry her. She twisted her chin out of his hand, put down her head and charged out of the hammock. She struck the ground running and headed for home. She heard behind her Mr. Beacon's annoyed exclamation, and Ma called out, "Theo! You come back here!" Wes yelled excitedly, "Hey, look, Felix! She's forgot her Roman candle!"

But she kept on and did not stop until she was at home, upstairs in her bedroom and taking off the white dress with the blue sash. Sweat was coming out from the run in the warm night. She hurried to get the dress off before she spoiled it.

She put on her nightgown and stood in the window, feeling the air cool her skin a little. Out over the sea, the fire balloon still hovered, moving slightly up and down, with a gliding motion, softly colored and shining. It was not a thing that belonged to anyone else, nor ever could. It was the last package opened from the Christmas tree of the little princess; the ultimate, finest thing bought from the limitless purses of a king and queen.

"Oh," she whispered, the sound on her mouth only a soft stirring of her breath. "My fire balloon. My lovely fire balloon."

And as she watched, she saw the light dim down, flicker and stop shining, and over the water the luminous globe vanish into darkness.

PART TWO

April, 1947

THE queer light from the sunrise woke Gram Sarah out of a sound sleep. For a minute she was bewildered, trying to think how on earth her white bedspread could have turned itself pink overnight. Then she sat up and saw through the window the clouds in the eastern sky.

"For heb'n sake!" she said, blinking. "If I ever in all my life see anything look so stinkin mean."

The clouds weren't even honest red, they were off-pink and

streaky magenta, shading to purplish black. Here and there, a sullen, smoky bulge was edged with hot cerise almost too bright to look at. Down low was a ruddled swirl of bricky red, the color of old iron rusted under water, and below that, a streak of clear salmon-tinted sky.

"My lord," Gram said aloud. "Looks like a cancer. Looks like Mat Dawes's fancy petunias." She closed her eyes, trying to think of her own garden as it would come up this spring full of perennial blue and white and yellow, but the after-image of the outrageous sky blanked out everything else, and presently she popped them open again. "Humph!" she said. "I wouldn't plant them petunias on my grave."

The light grew as she watched, turning the spruces in the pasture to flat black paper cutouts, spreading a lush glow over the wintered stubble in the field.

"I spose the's them that thinks that's pretty," Gram muttered. "And I'll hev t' hear all day what a lovely sunrise we hed this mornin. Well, all it means t' me is, a storm's comin."

She shivered, not alone with the chill of the spring morning in the room. She hated storms. Even before she had been alone, when Ernest and the children were alive, and the living ones home, she had thought of a storm as the last thing God made up before he set the world a-goin.

Storms laid waste to property and changed the face of things. In summer, they beat down flower beds and ruined the vegetable garden. In fall, they blew apples off the trees. If there were a slack place in shingles or around chimney flashings, the rain was sure to find it, and that meant wet plaster and rotten wood somewhere—more things going to pieces in an old house that had enough to stand up to anyway. Change took place, and plenty of it, in the slow and natural course of time. There was no need to take, say, a tree that had been growing for a hundred years and crash it down in a single night, as if time and growing didn't mean a thing.

Gram Sarah lay back against the pillow, but the light now

was too bright to sleep against. Besides, the thought of the coming weather made her restless.

"Four o'clock," she said. "I might's well say my prayers and be up and doin. It ain't a mite of use tryin t' git my sleep out, with that nasty mess a-glarin in my winder. And I want You to know, God," she went on, sliding smoothly into her devotions, "I'm a good mind not to say no prayers at all today."

Living alone so long, Gram Sarah hardly knew now when she talked aloud to herself, but when she prayed she raised her voice to make a distinction.

"I spose You're a-rarin back t' let go a gale," she said. "All right, but git it over. Last time, You let it go on for pret-nigh a week. If You'll recall, You raised the devil. You blowed off my gutter and You knocked six bricks off'n my ell-chimbley. It warn't no actions for a Lovin Father, if You ask me. Don't bust up no more fish boats 'n lobster traps 'n You have to. I spose You always know what You're a-doin, but sometimes I doubt it. Amen."

She scrambled out of bed, shivering in earnest as she laid aside her long-sleeved nightgown and began to dress herself from the neat pile of clothes folded on her bedside chair. She pulled on a knitted cotton shirt and gasped as the cold steel of her corsets clutched her skinny body.

"If men wore cossets," she told the air in front of her indignantly, "the'd be some way thought up to have em warm in the mornin."

The light in the kitchen was uglier, if anything, than the pink reflection in the bedroom. Its atmosphere was dim and purplish. She rattled the covers off the range, stuffed in newspapers and kindling, doused the whole with kerosene and stood back with a grunt of satisfaction as the fire began to thunder up the chimney. From the pump by the sink, she filled the teakettle and set it on to boil. Then, warmed by the fire and the thought of coffee to come, she opened her back door and stood on the step, breathing deeply the cold morning air. It felt, she was bound to say, better than it looked, like a singed cat.

The back door faced south toward the village and a wide sweep of island-studded sea. Only a finger of the savage color in the east stretched up over the house. Low down on the southern horizon some small pale rose clouds were beginning to fade with the coming sun, but the sky in the south was baby blue, the water pearly, darkened here and there by a short-lived breeze.

Gram sniffed up at the sky. "You ain't foolin nobody," she said. "I know *You*."

Today might be fine, but that didn't signify about tonight and tomorrow. As sure as she was livin, the fog would be in tighter than a tick before noon. The storm had served notice. Now folks could batten down and make ready.

Gram Sarah glanced along the houses in the village. There were not many of them—twenty-five or so, set down at random on a wide hillside that sloped gradually to the row of ramshackle fish houses and landing places along the shore. They were square-set and sturdy, most of them with long, low kitchen-and-woodshed ells, each ending in an ample barn. Most were neatly kept, painted white with green trim. Some were badly weathered and scaled; and one shone with a paint job so new it dazzled the eye. This belonged to Mat Dawes, Gram Sarah's next-door neighbor. Mat's father, Uncle Wheat Salisbury, who lived with her, had had her house painted white; but to Gram Sarah's eternal disgust, the new trim, not traditional dark green, was a brilliant electric blue. It gave her a turn every time she saw it, and for a while after the job was done, she'd kept her window shades pulled down on the side of her house that looked toward Mat's.

The houses looked as if they had been where they were for a very long time, their gables rearing up like the jut of so many stubborn chins. They needed to be stubborn, for the village faced east. Every easterly that rocked in from the North Atlantic rooted them deeper into their foundations. The hillside was weathered down in places to the essential granite, which thrust out, blunt-nosed in pastures and hay fields, along the bumpy macadam road, often in somebody's very dooryard, where children played on it and considered the rugged ledges a blessing. It was poorly thought of, however, by anyone who tried to farm. Fields everywhere were bounded by stone walls which grew higher every year. For no matter how clean a man picked up his vegetable patch, next spring's plowing was sure to turn up another crop of rocks.

As the old saying went, there was some land that the rocks *grew* on.

At the top of the hill, thick woodland began behind the houses, spruces and alders, yellow birch and beech, stretching away west to the state highway and north to Bellport, eight miles away. A tough, steep little brook ran down the slope paralleling the country road that connected with the highway. Hardhack Brook, it was called, after the next-to-indestructible brushy weed that grew thick along its banks. Because it was spring-fed, Hardhack Brook always had a trickle of water, even in the driest seasons.

The woodland was handy for firewood and nearly everyone who didn't burn oil, had a woodlot there; but what good was a windbreak on the west'ard side of town? It broke the back of the cold northwesters in winter, that was all. The old busters, the southerlies and the northeasters, made up out over the ocean; they might sweep a thousand miles without a check, and the first thing they hit would be this knot of houses, pinched on the bare hillside between the water and the woods.

The narrow point called Granite Hook sheltered the foreshore from the sea, its low massive claw, curled in a near-circle, all that made a harbor possible below this village. But so far as the wind was concerned, The Hook might just as well not have been there.

Gram Sarah hated the storms. She also got a good deal of satisfaction out of them and out of the bleak land. To stand such weather, in such a place, took a specially tough-minded and enduring breed of people—at least, she felt so. In fact, early settlers had had a reputation for austerity, up and down the coast villages. Carter's Landing had been the original name of the place, after one of these hard-hided old pioneers. It was one of them, who, in disgust during a prolonged series of hard times, gave it the nickname of Scratch Corner.

To Gram Sarah, it was still Scratch Corner, and if you had lived to be over eighty there, as she had, without dying, or starving, or freezing to death, you could take considerable credit.

Some summer people, led by the Beacons, who had wanted a nice-sounding address, had succeeded in getting the post office officially changed to Granite Hook. Gram Sarah had fought the movement, tooth and nail.

In the village, chimney smoke had thinned down, showing that people had been up for a while. Most of the men would be hustling off to shift lobster traps out of shallow water and to snug things in down around the shore. But from her son Sylvanus's chimney, at the southern end of the village, the smoke was heavy and tumbling from a just-built fire. As she looked, his back door opened, and a black, two-legged dot emerged, moving slowly down the hill in front of his house.

Gram Sarah's eyes sharpened and her mouth closed with a snap. She reached around the doorjamb and took from its rack an ancient leather-bound spyglass, as big around and as long as her arm. Pulled out and focused, it nearly doubled its length and was awkward to handle, but she had long ago devised means. Low down on the doorframe, she had nailed a stout wooden hook to cradle its heavy end. Then, sitting comfortably on her chair in the doorway she could hold the eyepiece to her spectacles and sweep the village.

The spyglass might be old—Ernest, her husband, had used it for years at sea—but it was a good one. She could make out Sylvanus's easy ambling walk, the graceful slouch of his shoulders, his big hands on the bales of the water buckets.

"Sylvanus Sewell!" she said. "You ain't gone out hauling today!"

Sylvanus was headed for the well. He had on his rubber boots, so he must be planning, at least, to go down to the shore later on, and he had on the brown pants Gram Sarah'd brought home last week to patch the seat of, trying to ease some of the work off Phoebe, Sylvanus's wife. As he tipped back the well-curb cover and bent over to hook a bucket on the rope, Gram Sarah saw with satisfaction the large, workmanlike double patches she had sewed on, of a lighter material than the pants because she hadn't had an exact match.

"Sylvanus Sewell!" she said. "The way your womenfolks work for you and them five kids, it seems to me you might at least *try!*"

Sylvanus, unmoved, went on drawing water. She watched him lift the buckets, go back up the hill and bump the toe of his boot against the door for someone to open up, so he wouldn't have to set a bucket down. She did her best to see who opened the door for him, but it merely swung and closed behind him.

"It was Jacky," she decided. "Them other ranicks wouldn't be up to open the door for their father."

After she'd had her breakfast, she'd go down and get Jacky to come up and stay with her till the storm was over. Jacky wouldn't be any help—you couldn't make her understand what you wanted done, of course—but there, she'd be lots of company and she loved to stay with Grammy.

"It's the God's cryin shame they wun't let her stay with me all the time. She'd be a lot better off than she is now, turned loose amongst them howlin wild Injuns." Gram Sarah's craggy face, with its sunken cheeks and its hard promontory of a nose, softened a shade. "Poor little thing," she said. "Gram's poor plagued little baby."

Briskly, she swung the spyglass along the line of houses to see if anybody were out yet. Few were, but in the side yard of her house, Mat Dawes was hanging up a washing.

"Up early, ain't you?" Gram Sarah said. "Maybe you think them clo'es'll git dry before 't rains."

Uncle Wheat Salisbury was out, spading among his straggled flower beds. He looked humped over, this morning, and he moved with painful care. He had been a big man and he was still, though nothing like so stout as when he had skippered coasting vessels from Lunenberg to Boston. His wide shoulders had sagged and his flesh had shrunk on his bones; he was seventy. He went lobstering now, though there were some days when he couldn't go out to haul, never admitting that he felt too lame, but always saying he had something more urgent to do ashore. Not that it mattered whether he hauled or not—he had money put by from his sailing days.

Gram Sarah gave a sharp little click with her tongue. "Bones hurt, don't they, Wheat? Bad weather comin. And I guess that ain't all that's the matter with you. You was lucky, this year, you made it up over March hill. I'll live t' see you buried, even if you have gut money put by." Humph! Far as that went, she had money put by herself.

Around the house in the middle of the village, where her youngest son Morgan lived with his new wife, there was no sign of life, not even a drift of smoke from the chimney. But no need to ask where Morgan was. By now he would be shifting traps offshore. Morgan wasn't one to get caught in bad weather with his traps in shallow water for the heavy seas to smash against the ledges.

"Nothin don't ketch *him* nappin," Gram Sarah told herself proudly. "But I bet he et a cold breakfast. By the looks of things, that mewly Emly ain't up yit." She trained the spyglass on Morgan and Emily's upstairs bedroom window, but the white panes sent back only a pale reflection to her eye. "Humph!" Gram Sarah said. "The little Southern lady of all!" She sniffed and slowly folded in the spyglass.

From the kitchen she could hear the comfortable thump of water boiling in the teakettle. "Well, coffee!" she said, and went in, dropping the glass on its brackets as she went by.

Gram Sarah took her food to the kitchen table and sat down heartily to eat. It tasted good and the world brightened around her.

Let's see. She'd have to batten the tie-up window—no sense in havin it blow open in the middle of the night and half-drowned the cow, the way it had last time. It might be a good idea to nail some slats across the windows in the hen pen, too. A pity she'd took them off, thinkin the bad winter storms was all done. She'd have to throw in a good lot of dry wood, just in case it rained for a long time. You never could tell about a storm this time of year—might be nuthin, might be a wet spell for two weeks. There was that leak in the ceiling of the woodshed chamber—she couldn't remember whether she'd left the bucket under it to catch the drip.

"It'll be one awful job," she said, contemplating it with anticipation. "My Lord, I do hate a storm. Everything comin all of a heap!"

Gram Sarah jumped up from the kitchen table and tumbled her breakfast dishes into the dishpan. She'd wash them later on. Outdoors work first—you could always wash dishes. She'd have to milk the cow and let her out, and feed the hens, and then, before she did one other thing, she was going to take time and go down and fetch Jacky.

"If I'm goin to have to work my fingers to the bone, I'm go'n t' have some pleasant company while I do it."

The sun, she saw when she turned the cow out through the pasture bars, was coming up clear.

"Git along, you old besom," she told the cow, giving her a companionable slap on the rump as she went by.

The cow went at once to a patch of green wet grass, thrust her nose into it and began to eat with rich, tearing sounds.

Gram Sarah set off down the road to Sylvanus's. There was still no smoke coming from Morgan's chimney. Maybe she'd just better look in as she went by.

Morgan would have gone before daylight, of course—he had his traps to tend, and this year, he was going to build a herring weir as well. Going to hire men to help him, too, she thought with pride. It was about time one of the Sewellses amounted to something again. None of them had been worth a picked coot, not since the time Papa Jasper had owned the vessel; but now it looked like Morgan was going to be the one. Not Sylvanus, nor any of his tribe.

Too much mixed blood in em, Gram Sarah said to herself. Too much Sewell. Too much Carter.

Sylvanus and Morgan were the last of her brood of ten children. The others were all dead so long ago that she scarcely remembered her grief over their dying young. Once it had been almost a byword in the town how unlucky with their children she and Ernest were. Red-cheeked and healthy every one of them, but if a diphtheria or a typhoid epidemic came along, you could count on it, people said, it would take one or two of the Sewell kids. Sammy, the oldest, had died of pneumonia the year before Sylvanus was born, leaving the house, at last, empty of children, and she and Ernest couldn't stand it. They'd tried hard for Sylvanus. She'd almost died having him, too, after so many, and she forty; she'd thought, Now he's surely the last one. But in his crib, when he was a day old, the Sewell stuck out on Sylvanus like a rash. Even bottom up he was Ernest Sewell all over again. I'll try again if it kills me, she'd said to herself. It had taken her twelve years, but then, just at her turns, and the very winter Ernest was drowned at sea, she'd surprised everybody and had Morgan.

And Morgan, he was pure Hutchins, like her own folks. She knew for a fact that he had cleared a thousand dollars lobstering and trawling, since he'd come home from the Navy last November. Made him almost four thousand dollars in the bank, what with his Navy pay that he'd kept, and what he'd saved before. He had showed her the bankbook. Nothing close-mouthed about him. Sylvanus never peeped about anything he'd made, but there, it couldn't be a cent over what he'd needed to keep things going. Morgan had some of his in the

Postal Savings, too, just in case the bank should go bust sometime.

You'd have thought, his first year out of the Navy, he'd need a little time to get his hand back in, but not Morgan. He'd taken right a-holt of the fishing again, just like Papa Jasper would have done. Born with a fishhook in his mouth, that's what he was.

Gram Sarah didn't doubt, though, that Morgan'd made a bad mistake marrying that Emly. She wished she'd had some say about it, but he'd met her in Savannah, Georgia, while he was in the Navy. Couldn't even wait to get home; or the way *she* told it, her folks wouldn't let her go with him until he was married. Maybe he wasn't to blame, for when a boy's been on a ship a long time, any little slut could catch him. And now he couldn't get rid of her, even if he'd wanted to, because she was six months along. Not that he seemed to want to, even though she was such a drag on him, and no use at all when she was in the family way. Morgan ought to have known better. But there, you take a man smart in everything else, and nine times out of ten he'd get mixed up with some slimpsy woman who never got her housework done—that Emly'd spudge around all day in a two-quart dish.

Gram Sarah went up Morgan's back steps, shutting the door loudly behind her, and stopped in horror at the sight of his kitchen. His breakfast things were still on the table. The back of the stove and the sink were piled with dirty dishes. Morgan had not even tried to make coffee in the black, encrusted coffee pot—he had had to use a saucepan, and for his fried eggs a tin pie plate, to which they had stuck. The iron spider was soaking on the stove, half full of a rust-rimmed tan mush, which, Gram Sarah decided, poking into it, was flapjack batter. But what brought her to a full stop and tightened her lips in an outraged thin line, was an egg, which someone had dropped and left to cruddle in its skimmed-over yolk and mashed shell on the soiled linoleum.

"My Lord of Heavens," she breathed, staring at it. "A *whole* egg."

You could always save an egg after you dropped it on the floor if you scooped it right up, and you were a fool if you didn't.

The things in the kitchen were new—Morgan had, in fact, been married not quite a year—and some of them had an expensive prettiness, as if friends with more affection than taste had tried to do something out of the ordinary in the way of wedding presents. The place might have been one where somebody had given up in defeat, as on a battlefield, but Gram Sarah did not see it so. After a moment, she went out through the kitchen door, banging it again, and went, tight-mouthed, down the road to Sylvanus's.

Gram Sarah stalked up the front steps of Sylvanus's house and was brought to a full stop by the storm door which had a faulty catch and was swollen anyway. She rattled the catch and even took two kicks at its bottom panel before Sylvanus, on the inside, could get the door open.

"Well, there, Sylvanus," she greeted him. "You ain't gut your storm door off yet, and it April."

"I plan to," Sylvanus said. "Ain't got around to it. Come in, won't ya, Ma?"

"It's a good thing plans ain't rattlesnakes," she said, regarding him. She went past him into the kitchen, untying her shawl as she came. "Why ain't you out haulin? Morgan's been gone since three-thirty."

"Morg's smarter'n I am, remember?" Sylvanus said. He grinned, seeing at once that his mother was on the warpath. "I got a busted switch on my engine. Had to send away for the part. I was just headed down to the office to see if it come in today's mail."

"Humph!" Gram Sarah grunted. The mail wouldn't be in till around nine, he knew she knew that. She made a beeline across the kitchen and sat down in Sylvanus's big chair behind the stove. Being mad, she had walked too fast down from Morgan's, but she wasn't going to let on that she was puffing. "What you plan to do—sit on the post office steps for two hours till the mail gits in?" she asked acidly.

"It'll be in by the time I git there," Sylvanus said comfortably.

Phoebe, half-turning from the board laid across the kitchen counter, where she was putting together an apple pie, gave him a warning glare, which he met with a bland smile.

"You want anything to the store, Phoebe?" He was looking all over the kitchen for his hat.

"I don't believe so, Syl," Phoebe said. "Unless you might stop by the fish wharf and bring back a haddock for dinner. I ain't got a thing."

"My land, Sylvanus," Gram Sarah said. "You ain't *buyin* haddock!"

Sylvanus, having found his hat hanging on the hook where it was supposed to be, stopped in his easy-going progress toward the door, and regarded her amiably from his great height. He was nearly six-foot-three, with a tremendous spread of shoulder and length of limb, but his big bones were neatly put together, so that he moved compactly and with grace.

"About as cheap's anything, ain't it?" he said. "Meat's out of all reason."

"Be cheaper if you was t' drop a line overboard sometime when you're outside, and ketch one," Gram Sarah said.

"But I ain't outside. My switch's broke," Sylvanus pointed out, with patience. "And Phoebe wants the haddock for dinner."

The look in his eyes was quizzical. Gram Sarah shut her mouth to with a snap. It wasn't any use trying to get under his skin. You try to argue with Sylvanus, and the first thing you knew, he'd be a-talkin to you reasonable, as if you was a little youngone. She ought to know better—his father'd been just exactly like that to the day of his death. But then, she'd never been able to steer clear of him, either.

"You'll rue the day you broke that switch, if you've got any traps in shaller water," she said, sniffing. "You see that sun come up this mornin?"

"Pretty, warn't it?" Sylvanus said. "You notice them little pink clouds?"

"Pink clouds! Oh, I spose they had turned pink, time *you* gut up. I'd just as soon see the devil himself come up, as the sun lookin like that."

"Oh, we're in for a spell of weather, I guess," Sylvanus said cheerfully. "Just about wipe me out, it will, too, if the's any kind of a sea. Every trap I got is right spang in on the Hook." He heaved a long, hollow-sounding sigh. "Morg, now, he's off there this minute shiftin his off into deep water. Well, maybe when he gits through, he'll shift mine."

"Sylvanus," Phoebe said, eyeing him over her shoulder. "You git along now. I'm go'n to need that haddock, and they may all be gone, you wait too long."

The color had risen high in Gram Sarah's bony cheeks. Maybe folks thought Morgan didn't go out of his way to do favors, but how could he, when he had so much on his mind?

"Morgan's gut his own work to do," she began shrilly.

"Ain't he, though?" Sylvanus said. He waved his hand at her and closed the door behind him.

"There now, Marm," Phoebe said. "I'm glad you come. I been wantin you to tell me what ails these molasses cookies." She held out a plate on which four succulent round brown objects rested. "Seems like I can't make cookies right any more. Clisty was in here yesterday, she says she can't either. She thinks it must be the flour. You better have some coffee, too, or you won't be able to git em down."

From the big pot on the stove, Phoebe poured out a rich brew, added copious cream and sugar and set the cup by Gram Sarah's elbow.

For a moment, after Sylvanus had gone out, Gram Sarah had been too mad to speak. That devil, making out with his limber tongue that Morgan was so busy grabbing after every penny that he couldn't stop to do a favor to his brother. She knew, too, that Sylvanus didn't have all his traps in the shallow water off the Hook. No fisherman would be fool enough to do that, and Sylvanus was no fool. All he was doing was making fun of her and Morgan; and if you got mad, he'd look innocent and wonder what in the world he'd said. Gram Sarah champed the cookie in her strong old teeth, and swallowed it down without tasting a speck of it.

After the third one disappeared and Gram Sarah had had a long schloop of coffee, Phoebe said patiently, "What do you make of em, Marm?"

"I'd say," Gram Sarah said, judiciously running her tongue around the inside of her cheek, "that 't was a matter of the shortenin ain't no good."

"Shortenin!" Phoebe said. "I never thought of shortenin."

"Nothin ain't the same since the war," Gram Sarah said. "No knowin what kind of old juice they've mixed in with the lard. They don't care, long's it fills up the package."

"Well, there," Phoebe said, as if a light had dawned. She didn't actually feel that very much was wrong with the cookies, but she had to get Gram Sarah's mind off of Sylvanus somehow, and she knew the old lady dearly loved to criticize another woman's cooking.

That Syl! Phoebe thought. He just can't resist poking her up. He ought to know better. The last time she got mad, she made my life miserable for weeks.

"They do it after all the wars," Gram Sarah said, warming up. "Sand in the sugar, rocks in the yeller-eyed beans, and stick the price up sky high till they clean everybody out of money. Then it's hi-ho-and-starve-to-death till they can start up another war. I seen it happen, many's the time. Pack a fools, don't know nothin, can't learn nothin. And every livin time, it's no percale, and I'd like to know what happens to the percale in time of war. All the politicians, from the President down, must go t' a war dressed up in percale, for the can't none of the rest of us buy any."

"Why, they make grain bags out of it," Phoebe put in, helping out. Thank the Lord, she'd got off of Syl.

"I know it, my Lord, don't that beat all!" Gram swallowed the last of her coffee, tipping her head back heartily to get at the sugar in the bottom of the cup. "Durin the war, I ast the grain man about it, but he didn't know no more'n anyone else. I says to him, 'Joel,' I says, 'how come they can git percale to put chicken feed in, and human beins can't buy none?' He says, 'Why, you're supposed to make your aprons out of the feed bags.' Hah!" Gram Sarah snorted. "My housedresses might git wore down to the bare-nekkid rags, but I'd see the day when I'd wear feed bags. Reminds me of old Aunt Polly Dawes, dead she is now, poor soul, she was so stingy she never would buy herself enough cloth to make dresses or drawers of or like of that, and every time she bent over in them short skirts, you could read *Lay or Bust* acrost her stern. Well, Phoebe, I can't stop, I'll git to talkin. I'm late anyway. Reason I came down, I thought I'd take Jacky up to spend the day with me."

Oh, dear, Phoebe thought. *Now* what'll I do?

Gram Sarah was always coming after Jacky to spend the day, and while Phoebe wouldn't have minded that, the trouble was that Jacky always came home with an upset stomach from all the candy and trash that Gram Sarah stuffed her with. She was a delicate little girl anyway—Phoebe always had to be careful what she gave her to eat, and the doctor always said they might have serious trouble with her digestion, if she got upset too often. Yet, if you refused Gram Sarah, she'd fly right into your hair.

"Well, there," Phoebe said. "I'm real sorry, Marm, but I've got an appointment to take her to the dentist today over in Bellport." She hadn't any such thing, and her blood curdled a little at the idea of such a baldfaced lie. Now she'd have to go to Bellport, she thought irritably.

"The dentist!" Gram Sarah said. "No baby Jacky's age needs

to go to the *dentist*. Them little milk teeth, take hold of one with your apron over your fingers and pick em right out."

"I know. But you know how careful we have to be of Jacky."

"Cost you a bill. Ain't no need of it." Gram Sarah shut her mouth to again. "Well, I better be goin back again. Much as I've gut to do, come down here for nothin . . . I'm late anyway. I stopped in at Morgan's on the way down." Remembering Morgan's kitchen, Gram Sarah began all over again with what she'd planned to say when she came in and got sidetracked with Sylvanus.

"My Lord of Heavens, Phoebe, what a mealy in that kitchen! That girl must spend all her time eatin choc'late drops, for she don't do one mite of housework."

"She ain't too well, I guess," Phoebe said.

"She's gut no business havin mornin sickness at this stage in the game. More like the lazy slut puts it on."

"I ought to go up and see her," Phoebe said. "But there, I been so busy, and she's awful hard to git acquainted with."

"Don't you waste your time. If she cared a hoot about Morgan's folks, she'd treat em better. She—"

She'd go on like this, Phoebe thought, all the forenoon, if something didn't come up to stop her. Phoebe sighed. She glanced, as if electrified, at the clock. "My sakes," she exclaimed. "Them kids'll be late to school." She dusted flour off her hands and made for the backstairs door. "Theo! Wesley! It's eight o'clock!"

"Okay, Ma, keep your shirt on," Wesley called back. "There's lots of time."

"Not if you drive the way you ought to," Phoebe said. "Come *on*, now, Wes. I'm not goin to have you hurryin, the shape that old Ford's in."

Wesley came down the back stairs, buttoning the top buttons of his wool shirt. "I've told you, Ma, the car's okay. Forbes had her down to the garage for two days, and we went all over her, you know that."

"Heb'n sake," said Gram Sarah. "That must've cost you a bill."

Wesley gave her a sideways look and said nothing, but Phoebe, seeing Gram Sarah start to pucker up with irritation, put in quickly, "Felix Beacon paid the bill. It's his Ford, you know. Tell your gra'mother good mornin, Wes, where's your manners?"

"No good ever come to nobody," Gram Sarah stated, "from suckin up to the summer people."

Wesley shrugged. "That's right," he said. "Give em an inch and they'll ga-rind you down for the rest of your life."

"Wes," said Phoebe desperately, "turn around here and let me see if you've gut yourself decent for school."

Wesley gave her a puzzled glance. He always got himself dressed decently for school, his mother knew that. His dark blue pants were immaculately brushed and creased, his shoes shined; he even wore his wool shirt, of black-and-white buffalo plaid, tucked in instead of tails dangling, the way some of the boys did. Wesley had picked up a lot of ideas from his friend, Felix Beacon, who went to a private school in Boston. You could be a hairy ape—go around sloppy and get away with it if it suited you. If it didn't, you'd much better try to be smooth; but not *too* smooth.

Wesley had decided last summer, when he was sixteen, that he was the smooth type, and to a certain extent, he was right. He was long and graceful like his father, and in time would have Sylvanus's great height and breadth of shoulder. His taffy-colored hair had a neat wave that just escaped being curly; combed down flat, it sprang back at once into a sleek blond crest over his tanned forehead. He had Sylvanus to thank, also, for his high, straight nose and pointed chin; but his mouth was not Sylvanus's mouth, nor was it Phoebe's. Anyone who had known Gram Sarah in the days when she was twenty could have told you where Wesley's thin, stubborn upper lip and his full, curving lower one came from.

Shielded behind his big shoulders, Phoebe made believe to

fix his tie, while she shook her head at him in warning. Wesley understood at once that he was to stop making fun of Gram Sarah. He nodded cheerfully.

"Where's Jim and Joe?" he demanded. "Do I have to go all over Robin Hood's barn rounding them up?"

"They went along," Phoebe said. "Said they'd rather walk down today."

The grade school, where Jimmy and Joe went, was in Granite Hook village, but the high school was in Bellport.

"Well, tell Theo to step on it," Wesley said, starting for the door. "I can't wait all day while she moons over her face in the looking glass." As he passed his grandmother, he smiled and said mincingly, "By, Gram Sarah, dear," and closed the door before she could answer him.

Oh, Lord, Phoebe thought. But she might have spared herself the worry, for Theo came tearing down the back stairs, and behind Theo was Jacky, smiling her wide, sweet, meaningless smile.

"*There's* Gram Sarah's baby," said the old lady. Her face lost at once its hatchety look of an ill-tempered fox and seemed to break up all over into a welcoming smile. "Always has a smile for Gram Sarah, don't she, darlin?"

"She smiles like that for anyone," Theo said, and she too made headlong flight out the door.

Gram Sarah rared up, her nostrils flaring, but as usual, there was no one to take it out on but poor Phoebe, who simply gave up and sat down, her elbows on the table, her chin in her hands.

"Socks!" Gram Sarah said. "Bare-legged to her knees, and by the time she comes home, it'll be stormin blue murder and I d'no but hail. Times have changed since I was sixteen, for if I had gone out with no more'n that on, I wouldn't of been able to *fight* the men off, and no more will she."

Jacky went and stood by Gram Sarah's chair and laid her two hands on its arm. Around her small face, delicate as a water flower, her fair silky hair stood out in a fluff. Her eyes had a clear gray depth, their gaze as noncommittal as moonlight. She was eight years old, and she had never spoken.

Gram stopped in mid-spate. "She always has a smile for Gram Sarah, of course she does, don't you, dear?"

When the old lady at last had gone, Phoebe picked up a cup which was standing on the dresser and smashed it on the floor. She stood, her hands on her hips, regarding the shards, a little surprised at herself, but not sorry. Better take it out that way than on Sylvanus and the children. For years she had been trying to keep Gram Sarah and her family out of each other's hair.

That woman, Phoebe told herself, has only got to come into a room to set every livin person in it a-goin. And *she* comes out on top, with colors flyin.

If Phoebe had known the word "catalyst," she would have used it.

WHATEVER Theo had been doing in front of the glass so long, Wesley decided, she hadn't made her face look better. There was a blur of red on her lower lip, as if she had put on lipstick and wiped it off. That was all. She had on her old brown leather jacket, a blue wool sweater and a rumpled wool shirt. Wes gave her an irritated sideways glance as the Ford rattled along the bumpy tar road toward the main highway to town. "Why don't you ever fix yourself up?" he wanted to know.

"Don't give it a second thought," Theo said. "You'll get all worried and sweaty." She was watching the road ahead and she didn't bother to look at him.

"You had time enough," Wes grunted. "What'd you do so long in there after breakfast—besides look at yourself in the glass?"

The spring frost coming out of the road had left some fine wheel-wrenching thank-you-marms, and for a few minutes he was too busy easing the Ford along to know whether Theo answered him or not. He was especially careful of the Ford. It belonged to Felix Beacon. He wanted to be sure nothing happened to it before Felix's arrival in June. It was great of Felix to let him fix it up and use it as if it were his own car.

Felix had written him in March to be on the lookout for a second-hand car that they could use to have fun in during the coming summer.

> "Dad says I can have one, if it doesn't run him over five hundred," Felix wrote. "So you keep your eye peeled, Wes. If you find a good one, let me know and Dad'll send the cash. Dad says just be sure it's okay. After you get it, have the garage overhaul it, and then you use it and work the bugs out of it until I get there in June. Oh, boy, no war, plenty of gas . . ."

Wes couldn't help strutting a little when he showed his father and mother that letter. He used it as an argument to convince them he had a right to drive the car. He felt important and responsible, being trusted by people like Felix and Mr. Beacon. Darn right he knew engines—he ought to, seeing he'd been lobstering with his father since he was big enough to see out over a cheese rind, and there wasn't anything about marine engines Sylvanus didn't know. Wesley had hung around garages, too—Forbes, down at the Central, would always give him a job Saturdays, now. And Mr. Beacon's own car, the big Cad, Wesley couldn't count the times he and Luke, Mr. Beacon's chauffeur, had taken her down and put her back together, smooth as butter. Saved some big garage bills, too.

Wes had known right where to go to find the Ford—Funny-Money Montgomery's Model A, that he'd always treated like an egg. Funny-Money sold her to him for three hundred and fifty. Down at the garage, Forbes let Wesley do most of the work on the overhaul job, though he made it clear at once that it wouldn't make any difference on the size of Mr. Beacon's bill. That was all right with Wesley. He guessed Mr.

Beacon could stand it, and it was, after all, the way Forbes made his living.

Right now, the Model A ran like silk. Wes meant to see to it she stayed that way. The frost-hove culverts bulged up like logs across the road, shedding chunks of last summer's tar; pothole followed pothole where the surface was gone down to basic muck, chowdered up by last winter's tire chains and scooped off by the snowplow. It took careful driving to avoid these and still stay off the shoulder where the mud was a foot deep.

"Good old Scratch Corner," Wes muttered, as, in spite of his efforts, the Ford dropped into a hole with a spring-zinging thump. "Last place to get plowed out in winter, last place to get the road tarred in spring."

"The town'll fix it before the summer people get here, don't worry," Theo said. "Just in time so they won't get tar on the Cadillacs."

"They better," Wes said.

"Or Mr. Beacon will tell them."

"Well, why shouldn't he? He pays a darn sight more taxes than anybody else in town."

"As who doesn't know," said Theo. "And you better be careful how you say 'Scratch Corner.' Everybody knows the Beacons want it called Granite Hook."

"Oh, shut up." Wes glared around at her briefly. "Lay off the Beacons, why don't you?" He stopped the Ford at the intersection with the coast highway, where the fairly new sign did indeed say, GRANITE HOOK, ½ mi., and the older one, pointing at right angles to it, said, BELLPORT. The smooth concrete stretched empty in both directions, shining and darkened a little by the night's damp, and he heaved a sigh of relief as he eased the Ford around the turn.

"If you wouldn't be so standoffish with them," he went on, "you'd have a better time. Get asked places with Jane, the way I do with Felix."

"That's the day I'm just hanging by the neck to see," Theo

said. "Jane and I don't see eye to eye in all things, the way you and Felix do."

"All right, cut off your nose to spite your face, I don't care. But what does it get you? I've got this car to ride around in, and a swell summer job, where I get paid dough just to bat around with Felix."

"And what dough!" Theo murmured. "Five dollars a week, isn't it?"

Wes flushed a little. "You know it's ten this summer," he said shortly.

"If you'll help Mrs. Beacon with her flower gardens, and this and that little odd job, *dear Wesley*."

"Dear Wesley" was what Mrs. Beacon called him on occasion.

"You know darn well I get a lot of other stuff, too," he flamed. "Nice trips and—"

"And you've got on a pair of Felix's cast-off pants this very minute," Theo said. "Wouldn't work with me, chum. Jane and I aren't the same size."

Wes was furious. That crack about the pants was uncalled for. They were perfectly good pants, hardly worn at all, much better than his folks could afford to buy. They felt good on, too, a smooth fit and yet loose and comfortable. He'd taken considerable pride in having a pair of pants cut in the very latest style—the kind boys wore to private school in Boston. He hadn't thought of them as cast-offs at all. Through the years, Felix had sent him a lot of clothes, always good ones. It was like getting a pair of pants from—well, from your brother, when he had extra ones he didn't need. Trust Theo, though, to find some slur about it.

"I'll say she ain't your size!" he burst out. "Jane's no big ox!"

"She *is* fair to middling skinny," Theo said composedly. "And as for riding around in a car, if you call it riding going fifteen miles an hour . . . I wish I had this car. I'd show you some dust. Why don't you step on it? We'll miss Assembly altogether."

"You can't even drive!" Wes spluttered. "And you know I've got to be careful of this car. If it was mine—"

"So it isn't yours," Theo cut in. "When I have a car, it'll be my own and I'll drive it up and down stairs if I want to. And that's the whole business in a nutshell!"

"Well, at least, I got a job." He was casting around in his mind for something to hit back with. "More'n you have."

"Well, I don't know about that. I might have one."

"Such as what?"

"Oh, two or three things."

"Yes, I guess so. Well, you better get busy and hunt one up. You know Pa can't afford to have you loaf on him."

"I might wait on table at Leon's. Leon says I can have a job there."

"At Leon's!" Wes's voice went high, and then for a moment he was struck dumb. A picture came into his mind of himself and Felix and some girl and Jane, going into Leon's for sodas after the movies or a dance; and who would be in there to wait on them—his own sister, right before them all. Such an idea had never occurred to Wes. "He wouldn't want *you*," he said weakly. "Leon—Ma won't let you."

"Oh, I don't know. We can use the money."

She must be kidding. She was saying it to get his goat.

"I take notice you don't make any bones of riding to school in Felix's car," he said, returning to the attack. "You like it better'n the school bus."

"You know Ma makes me ride with you to check up on you so you won't drive too fast." Theo giggled. "Little does she know! Wild Wes, the Thunderbolt!"

"Oh, shut up! What do you know about anything?"

What *did* she know? he thought resentfully. She had no more sense of responsibility than an angleworm, and you might as well try to reason with one. Cuddled down inside his secret self, snug as a bird on a nest, Wes felt a warm glow of loyalty and gratitude to the Beacons—something he couldn't talk about to anyone, but which was there for him to hide behind.

Through summers as far back as he could remember, the Beacons had been mystery and color to him: their cars, their clothes, their manners, the different way they talked. Inhabitants of a far-off, fabulous city, each year from June to September they spun a cocoon of ease and pleasantness and laughter about themselves in the drab little village where Wesley Sewell lived; and lately it almost seemed as if the multicolored silken thread had spread out to include him, too. He had lived for summers, eagerly counting the months between him and the time again of Felix's catboat, Felix's archery set, his Indian and cowboy suits, his tennis on the lawn. Someday he, Wes, would go where they lived and learn to be like them . . . the smiling, confident people who were "better" and "luckier" and "had more things" than a Sewell of Scratch Corner—Granite Hook, that is.

That far-off day might be near, if he worked it just right, Wes told himself. For this June he would be graduating from high school, and what was more natural than that the Beacons, once it was called to their attention, might suggest some job for him in the city?

But Theo couldn't understand that, any more than Gram Sarah could, who called it "sucking up to the summer people."

"I expect I can drive better than you can," Theo was saying, in that icy-clear voice of hers that could be so maddening.

Wesley swung the car into the parking lot back of the Bellport High School building, and parked it carefully before he said anything.

"As far as second-hand stuff goes," he said at last, "I take notice you don't mind using second-hand lipstick. Go wash your face. You look as if you'd sucked somebody's blood."

It was a blind stab that he'd been mulling over, but it turned out to be in the right direction.

Theo turned red and clapped her hand over her mouth. Bell for Assembly was just sounding, but instead of hurrying to

Assembly Hall, she went tearing down the basement steps towards the girls' dressing room. Who'd have thought she'd be squirmy over that lipstick she got from lil ole Emly and hid in the bureau drawer? Why, the whole family knew she had it, and nobody'd have cared a hoot if she'd gone ahead and used some of it, the way the other girls did. Do her good . . . make her look better, anyway. She'd be okay, if she'd fix herself up.

"I'll be darned," he said to himself. "That got her." He climbed the steps to Assembly Hall, feeling better. It happened so seldom.

In the girls' dressing room, Theo scrubbed her mouth until it was so red she couldn't tell whether she'd got the lipstick off or not. She was still sore at Wes for twitting about looking at herself in the mirror. She hadn't known he'd seen her—he must have peeked in the door. For a while, she'd thought she'd got back at him.

Most of the time between breakfast and when she had to leave for school, she'd been in her bedroom looking in the glass. Past her own reflection, she could see the fragile pink-and-whiteness, the golden shiningness, of Jacky, who sat by the window playing with a ribbon—and it hadn't helped any.

"Oh, God, am I pretty?" Theo had said into the mirror. "Oh, God, please, *please*, let me know in some way if I'm pretty."

It was so hard to tell, you were so used to your own face in the glass.

"I know I'm not a knockout, God, or people would tell me I am. They do, the pretty ones. But nobody tells you if you're homely, unless it's somebody like Wes and he'd say so anyway. If I'm homely, God, I want to know."

Emily'd said in horror, "Sakes, honey, you haven't got a *lipstick!*" and had straightway dug one out of a purse and given it to her. "You put some on, see what it'll do."

There was a thing about makeup, though. If you were pretty, you just put it on, it didn't matter. But if you were homely, it stuck out on you like on a crow. Sally Gerrish, that awful blonde senior, came to basketball games and dances with her mouth like a slit in a red apple, and everyone giggled behind her back at how funny she looked.

How could you tell about yourself, when your face in the glass was just your face, to you neither one thing nor the other?

Jacky, by the window, smiled secretly at the secret and mysterious loveliness of the ribbon.

"Oh, you!" Theo said to her. "What do you find to be so happy about? You're pretty, but it doesn't make any difference to you."

Jacky could be happy for hours over some small bright thing like the ribbon. If you took it away from her, she wouldn't mind. She'd find something else right away—the blue sprig pattern in her dress, or the sunlight on the window sill. She never seemed really to *want* anything.

But I do, Theo thought.

Sometimes there seemed to be no end to the things she wanted, without a chance in the world of getting any of them. Wes got things—he'd been studying ever since he was little how to get things out of the Beacons. Or maybe that was unfair to Wes—he really did like and admire them. Worship was a better word. All he did was show it. Still, if Felix Beacon thought getting that Ford for Wes to drive was his own idea, he was mistaken.

If only she could have a car, or a wrist watch, or some new clothes; if something pleasanter or brighter or more interesting could happen than she was sure would happen. If only she knew she was good looking . . .

She had picked up Emily's lipstick and daubed some on her mouth, but it didn't do anything. It just sat there like a blob, and she'd wiped it away. She'd thought she got it all off, but Wes had seen some. He'd come at her so suddenly about it that she hadn't been able to hide how she felt. Now she'd never hear the last of it.

Everybody had gone in to Assembly and the high school

building was silent, which meant that upstairs the Principal was starting morning prayer. She couldn't go up until she was sure she had all the lipstick off; and now she couldn't tell, her mouth was so red from rubbing. She looked into the glass, waiting for the stain to fade.

When she was fourteen, she'd been crazy after lipstick and powder, and had got some, too, putting it on in slathers whenever she was sure Phoebe wouldn't see her.

"You're too young," Phoebe would say, "to go round painted up like a windmill."

Now she was old enough. But one day last winter she'd heard Ida Gates and Pauline Stover talking in the girls' dressing room, about homely girls who only looked homelier when they tried to fix themselves up. They were both pretty—Ida was fat, but Pauline was a knockout. They had lots of dates.

The Bellport girls who'd come up from grade school together had a kind of gang, anyway. They were nice enough to girls from surrounding towns, but sometimes they called them "foreigners." Theo happened, that year, to be the only one from Granite Hook. Not that she didn't have close friends. It was just that girls like Pauline and Ida were intimate in a way the others weren't. Now, talking together, they suddenly noticed Theo, in by the lockers, and they looked at each other and giggled.

Since then, Theo had told herself, she'd show them. She'd stopped using any kind of makeup at all, and had dressed herself with a fine carelessness. Now it was hard to change back again. If you did, everybody would notice it. Besides, she'd wondered about her looks so much that now she wasn't sure what they were.

If your mother could help you, things might be easier to figure out. But Phoebe Sewell had never worn lipstick in her life; her competent strong body was generally clad in a faded neat housedress and apron, and her hair was skewered with bone hairpins into a pug in the back of her neck. A woman was best off as God made her, according to Phoebe's way of thought;

if she were homely, that was hard luck, but nothing to be done about it.

Yet Phoebe was always saying that Theo must be a credit to her folks, meaning, Theo supposed, that she must be smart in school and popular and looked up to. She often wondered just what Phoebe did mean. To be all those things, you had to come out with the foremost ones in all the various rivalries, and Phoebe couldn't have understood to save her life that knowing when to use lipstick had anything to do with it. "Schooling" to Phoebe was a great privilege which she herself had never had; so Theo must get all A's and graduate—and then come home and marry some nice fisherman.

Somehow the program didn't make much sense. Theo doubted, for instance, if Uncle Morgan ever asked Emily what her grades had been in school. "All A's" wouldn't be much use to Emily now, the spot she was in—married for life to Uncle Morgan, even if she did love him. She might as well have quit school in the third grade, the way Gram Sarah had.

Theo didn't want Emily's life, or Phoebe's, or Gram Sarah's. She wouldn't have, even if she'd never found out about any other kind.

When Jane Beacon had worn braces on her teeth, every time she opened her mouth, she'd looked as if she'd taken a bite of wire fence. But last summer the braces were gone. Jane had had pastel-colored sweaters; she had had skirts and slacks to match and white shorts for tennis, and the blond, good-looking summer boys had flocked around the Beacons' tennis court on sunny afternoons.

You might forget about the Beacons, if Wes didn't din, din, din about them or if he weren't always showing off the things he got from Felix. His little radio that he kept in his room and nobody used but him—that had come at Christmas. The tiny airplane engine that would really run, the set of mechanic's tools were, like most of his clothes, Felix's cast-offs. Now Wes had a car to drive.

It seemed to Theo that the desire for a car to drive—any

car not Felix Beacon's—was a vast hungering ache filling her whole body. You couldn't say even to yourself what it was, the white concrete road at night, the wind blowing your hair, the flying through the air inside the gently humming steel.

But I'll get my things with my own money. Not the way Wes does.

She grinned wryly at the idea of ever getting anything from Jane, even if she'd wanted to. From the time they were little, playing together on the shore or among the Beacon flower beds, she and Jane had fought, cats-and-dogs. Jane had always wanted to be the little lady—the bossy, regal, little lady, with the adoring friend. She hadn't appreciated climbing trees or digging for Indian arrowheads in the shell bank, or, Theo remembered with some relish, having her face shoved in the clamflats.

Sylvanus and Phoebe weren't going to like much the idea of Theo's working at Leon's, but they might come around. They knew she had to work somewhere this summer to help out with her fall clothes. You needed a lot of extras, the year you were a senior. She'd maybe have to help out with family expenses, too, if Sylvanus didn't get a good summer's lobstering. Sometimes he did, sometimes he didn't. You couldn't deny it—you looked at your father and you loved him—but you had to admit that he wasn't a very hard worker unless he happened to feel like it. In fact, Phoebe had already suggested that Theo try for a job in the kitchen at one of the summer cottages—it would be so nice, she said, to work for nice people.

With tips, you got a lot of money at Leon's in the summer. It was a combination of ice-cream parlor and restaurant, the best one in Bellport, on the main drag of the town, where the out-of-state cars poured by from June to September. You got a lot of tips there, if you were pretty . . .

Theo stared fiercely at her image in the mirror. Why couldn't you just be yourself, the way you were when you were little, without having to wonder all the time or wish you were different? So many people around were smarter or better looking than you. At home, it was Wes, with all the things. In school, it was a dozen boys and girls, who lived as if within a magic circle, glittering and fortunate. Ida Gates, whose father had money; Pauline Stover, romantic and lovely as a movie star. Gerald Wicks, who was already being watched by professional baseball scouts and who got all A's as well. They had wonderful times—dates and parties. Well, so did she, Theo Sewell, whose face that was there in the glass. But not quite the same.

There must be some one thing that she could be or do—not to stand out conspicuously, of course; only something that she could keep inside herself, warm and secure, never to be taken away.

"Theo Sewell is this or that," or "Theo Sewell has done so and so," it would say, when she needed to know. It would take the place of what she had now, which was questions; which was a feeling like trying to keep abreast in a race up an icy hill, everybody running, and the smart, the pretty, the rich ones out in front.

That was Theo Sewell looking at her. Who and what was she?

*A car drove away from a night club, a beautiful girl at the wheel. "*THEOLINE SEWELL*" the lights over the entrance said, like colored jewels winking off and on. Or maybe a night-club singer would have a name with more punch to it, like Dorothy Shay or Dinah Shore. "*GEORGIA TATE*" the lights spelled out, as the car turned the corner of the city block; and the tall young man with the bronzed face, leaned toward the beautiful girl.*

"Georgia, darling," he said. "You were swell."

The car left the city streets and ran along a vast esplanade by a lake. In the dark water, the star cast a long, dagger-like silver bar, and over it swung a gleaming, golden sphere, that shone serenely in the silent air.

"Georgia," the young man said. "Will you think of me sometimes when you're in Hollywood?"

Upstairs, the bell rang saying Assembly was over. Feet

thundered furiously on the stairs. Theo's face in the mirror, as it always did when she looked too long, seemed strange and pinched—not like hers and a little frightening.

LEAVING Sylvanus's, Gram Sarah went straight back up the road toward home. She was still ruffled up and she'd had to come away without Jacky.

"The dentist!" she spluttered. "Who ever heard of such a thing for a baby?"

Her own children had never seen the *inside* of a dentist until they were old enough to pay their own bills. Unless they had a bad toothache, as Morgan had once. Morgan . . . She came abreast of his house again. There was still no smoke from the chimney. That lazy little— She wasn't up *yet!*

Gram Sarah went straight into the house. She started upstairs, walking with a firm, thudding tread.

Emily was asleep in the front bedroom, visible only as a wisp of yellow hair— "Tow!" Gram Sarah muttered—and a series of lumps under the bedclothes. The pillow beside her bore the print of Morgan's round head. His pajamas were folded neatly on a chair.

"Emly!" Gram Sarah said, and when the girl did not stir, she put both hands on the bar between the foot posters, and shook the bed.

Being mad, she shook harder than she meant to, and the result was one she had not bargained on. This bed had belonged to Morgan's great-grandfather. Generations of Sewells had been conceived and born and had died in it. Through the years its strained joints had weakened, its glue had cracked. Now it vibrated in every part, as in a minor earthquake; its slats clattered out, and it slowly gave up and fell down in the middle of the floor. Gram Sarah stood holding the wooden bar, from which the posters sagged away.

Emily shot up to a sitting position in the middle of the mattress. Her eyes batted wildly without seeing anything. Her mouth opened in a frantic pink O. At first no sound came out of it; then she drew a gasping breath and began to scream.

"My Lord of Heavens!" Gram Sarah said. "I've kilt Morgan's baby. Emly! Git up out of there and le' me see if you're hurt."

But Emily only went on screaming, her eyes shut tight now, her hands fluttering the air in front of her face. In another land than this cold, stony one, this was what you did until somebody came, and so far her addled wits had not perceived anyone else in the room.

Gram Sarah stood the wooden bar against the bureau and laid a bony hand on Emily's shoulder. She started to shake, thought better of it, and tightened her grip instead. "Now, listen, Emly. You ain't hurt if you can holler that loud."

Emily stopped in midscream and began instantly to grieve. Fat tears rolled down her cheeks. Between sobs, she said over and over, "Oh, what has happened?"

Gram Sarah said, "The bed fell down."

The dream had been about a soft spring day, with magnolias in bloom, the wind coming up from the waterfront, sleepy and salt and warm. The young ensigns off the ships walked under the trees. Now and then a big pale pink petal fell on their blue uniforms and on Emily's white dress trimmed with blue for her yellow hair. They were all laughing—and then, suddenly, had come a dreadful crash. Now she was back in Morgan's cold bedroom with his bed fallen down around her and his awful old mother. The dream had had nothing to do with Morgan or his mother and Emily cried.

"For heb'n sake, it ain't nothin but the bed give up under you," said Gram Sarah. "Stop howlin like a little youngone."

Emily said, "I can't help it," and Gram Sarah heard the words as "Ah cain't he'p it." The soft, alien sounds somehow pricked at the back of her neck, started the fur out on her tongue. She took away her hand. "All right," she said. "You blubber it out. I'm goin down and clean up Morgan's dishes. If you start to miscarry, you holler, and I'll call the doctor."

At the door she paused. "You don't feel nothin, do you?"

she asked, with her hand on her stomach. "Nothin down here?"

But Emily, it seemed, was thinking only of herself and not at all about Morgan's baby. Gram Sarah snorted, tramped downstairs and savagely attacked the kitchen.

By the time she had put away the last of the pots and pans and had wrung out the dish towels through several washes of scalding suds, she felt better. The job had been a fine, nasty one—one that you could look at, after it was done, and see where you'd made some progress. She never got half the satisfaction out of cleaning up her own sink, because it was never half that dirty.

Thus when Emily came through the kitchen door, Gram Sarah greeted her amiably. "I guess you ain't got any bleach in the house. I could of gut them dish wipers some shades whiter if I'd had a little bleach."

Emily had not dressed, but had merely put on a rumpled robe of some flowery material. She had slipped her feet into rabbit-skin slippers. Normally, she was a pretty girl and would be so again. Her hair was a yellow fluff that curled with brushing so that she never needed a permanent; her big eyes were blue and innocent. Her flesh had a tender, chubby look, as if she had been able to escape gawky adolescence altogether and to become nineteen without ever having lost her baby softness.

But when the fine silky hair wasn't brushed, it matted and looked woolly. When she cried, her pink-and-white skin mottled in streaks. The baby made her a hopeless lump. She was a sight and knew it. Moreover, the wits had partially come back to her head, and she remembered that somewhere just outside the lovely dream, the bed had been shaken.

"You *shook* the bed down," she announced hollowly.

"Well, I did," Gram Sarah admitted. "I don't wonder you was scairt. I'm surprised at Morgan, lettin that bed go till it was so tittleish. But, there, he's been crazy busy this spring. I hope you wasn't hurt any. The's hot coffee on the stove, and

I'll make you some oatmeal if you want it. The eggs," she added meaningfully, "is all gone."

"You sneaked up into my room and shook the bed down."

"Oh, come. I was only tryin to wake you up when you'd overslep." Gram Sarah glanced at the clean sink, which she intended as a tacit peace offering, and which would have been accepted as such by any other woman she knew.

"You thought I ought to get up *before daylight.*"

"It's nine o'clock," Gram Sarah pointed out. "Oh, don't be such a fool, Emly. Why don't you go and git cleaned up and have some coffee? You look like an Injun devil on a straw-ride."

It was the worst thing she could have said. No lady of Emily's experience had ever been known to look like an Injun devil on a strawride.

"You hateful old woman!" Emily cried. The tears welled up again, spilled over and ran down in big clear drops. "I just wish my grandaddy was here. He'd *whip* you."

Gram Sarah's eyes narrowed. For a brief glimpse, she caught a picture of a skinny old Southern man with a white goat-whisker, coming at her. "Oh, he would, would he? Well, if mine was here, he'd bring out the duckin stool." Her shawl was on the chair back and she put it on, tying the corners under her chin with sharp little jerks. "I've hoed out the sink so's a pig can turn around in it. Morgan'll probly thank me when he gits back. When he lived to home, he was used to clean dishes and his meals on time and his *breakfast gut for him.*" She went out, closing the door behind her with a firm click.

Emily moved aimlessly to the window to peer after her. Well, she did so shake it down, she told herself. I might have been hurt or maimed.

The bleak landscape outside the window made her teeth chatter, just to look at it. Morgan's kitchen faced east, over-looking a rocky meadow that sloped to a fringe of alders along the shore. The alders had put forth some crumpled yellowish blobs that might someday be leaves, though Emily doubted if they'd ever get that far. They seemed just the same as when they started two weeks ago. Here and there in the meadow, patches of pale green grass had begun to come up between the granite boulders and the topknots of weed and last year's timothy. Beyond the alders was the sea, icy gray and remote as a tombstone. Far out on the horizon, a low fogbank lay like a bar of steel.

All winter Morgan had been telling her to wait for spring, she'd feel better when the warm weather came and maybe like the place more. Now he said it was spring. April—and you couldn't go outdoors without the cold clawed right into your bones and twisted them up like corkscrews. She'd just like to show these folks what it was like down home in April, with everything a mass of flowers, and you walked right out in your thin things without any coat. What they had for spring here, the dogs down home wouldn't enjoy for the worst winter they ever spent.

As she watched, something moved in the alders, shaking their thick crooked stems. Emily caught her breath, feeling her stomach crinkle with terror. Only last night Morgan had told her she ought to walk more. Go down across the pasture and walk on the shore, he'd said, it's nice down there. Whatever it was was tan and woolly, threshing around in the bushes. Some kind of a big animal. Suppose she had gone down there today? Suppose she just had and met it face to face!

The alder stems parted and Gram Sarah's cow came out into the open, stepping gingerly across the mud which was deep in the swampy ground along the shore. She was an old cow and her hoofs had grown long from a winter in the barn, giving her a curious flat-footed gait, like a medieval Dutchman in pointed shoes. On one flank was a patch of scaly dried manure. But as she came up the hill, feeling the turf grow springy under her feet and the crisp wind pour along her barn-bound sides, she suddenly tossed her horns and snuffed, then threw her scraggy stern wildly into the air and seesawed across the pasture in a clumping run.

"Oh, my God," breathed Emily. A cow. It was a cow, and Morgan hadn't even bothered to warn her. Well, there it was, the menfolks here just didn't take care of their womenfolks, and she couldn't get used to it, she just couldn't.

Coming here with Morgan in November after the cows had been stabled for winter, Emily had never seen them in the pasture, nor had she associated the fenced-in meadow back of the house with any such horror. Cows were on farms outside city limits, far away from your home, where the back yard was a small tended garden. Emily would have felt much the same if the cow had been a grizzly bear.

Through her misery, she was aware of the smell of coffee and she went to the cupboard for a cup. She realized with some surprise that the dishes were clean.

That was right nice of her, she thought. Only she's done it because it was such a mess, not because she likes me, and Morgan is going to be mad.

The last thing he'd said before they'd gone to sleep last night had been, "For the Lord sake, Emly, be sure not to let Ma or anybody see the kitchen before you get it cleaned up."

Well, it wasn't her fault if her stomach was jumpy yesterday, so she couldn't do her work. People shouldn't snoop around in a body's house, anyway, before she was even awake in the morning.

That was the craziest thing about this place, the way they all bounced out of bed and did their work in icy darkness, as if it would be a crime to wait for daylight. Morgan was nearly always up before four, and he didn't like it if she wasn't. Right now, he put everything on the baby—of course, he kept saying, she'd feel better mornings after the baby came.

He was going to be one surprised boy after the baby came —at four o'clock in the morning, she'd *never* feel better.

The coffee spread out in her taut little stomach, warm and comforting. After a while, she'd go and clean up the rest of the kitchen to match the sink. Down home, if you were going to have a baby, you didn't need to turn your hand over. Everybody came in and helped you with your housework and thought nothing of it. When Cousin Sue was carrying little Joie John, all the relations and neighbors flocked around—brought in jelly and chickens and presents for the baby. Cousin Sue always had somebody to talk to about the funny way she felt. But Morgan's folks here just seemed to be nosy and critical. If the women came in at all, they never had much to say—just sat with their eyes going over her and the things in the house till she thought she'd scream. You'd think, the way they never mentioned it, that having a baby wasn't respectable, or something. Except Theo. Sometimes Emily could talk to Theo, but goodness, she told herself, from the vast adulthood of nineteen, what could you find to say to a sixteen-year-old kid?

Sometimes she almost wondered why she'd married Morgan, of all the nice young men who'd just come schooling around from everywhere while the war was on. Why, she and her sister, Alice May, had had dates every night, and Mama had certainly expected they'd be able to make wonderful choices. Alice May had, of course—she'd married a Major and now she was in Germany, being just *waited on*, if you could judge from her letters. It did seem odd to think of Alice May being better off than she was, when *she'd* always been the prettiest one. But Morgan had looked so lovely in his uniform.

He'd made his far-off home sound so adventurous and romantic—rocky cliffs with the ocean pouring over them, great storms, and the men going out to risk their lives, just like people in the movies. Why, evenings at home, Papa and Mama and sometimes all the relations would sit around spellbound, just listening to Morgan. Papa, who was a bookkeeper for a department store, thought Morgan was wonderful. "What a life that boy's had!" he'd say, kind of wistfully. "You better marry him, Emmy Jane, and get out of the same old rut."

So she had. But she hadn't realized it would be like this. Maybe Morgan had a good time, but all she was doing was waiting around, doing his housework, and looking like an old sack of straw. If anybody had fun around here, anyway, it must be the men.

MORGAN SEWELL had shifted most of his string of a hundred and ten traps into the safest waters he knew of. Some of them had been out of danger anyway, but lately he'd seemed to be getting more lobsters out of the traps in shallow water, so he'd moved a couple of boatloads inshore, taking the risk that the worst spring storms were over. Sylvanus hadn't, he saw, noting, as he jigged around over the various fishing grounds, where most of Syl's buoys were. Doggone it, he wished he had the judgment and the know-how about lobstering that Syl did.

From the rocky bottom off Crack Corn Ledges and Dungeon Island, the tricky tide currents behind Candlemas Head, the spined under-water ridges of the Whirlpool, Morgan hauled up his traps, one by one, stacked them into his boat and dumped them into the Abner Hole. There he was reasonably sure they'd ride out any storm.

He had, he knew, taken more precaution—made more work for himself—than was necessary. Other fishermen with traps near his were hauling as usual, then merely jigging out to set again a few hundred yards farther off the ledges. But Morgan hated to lose gear. In fact, it was said of him that he would rather lose a finger than a trap; and while this might not have been exactly so, it was true that he preferred a day of backbreaking work to taking any more risk than he had to.

He was a little glad, though, that about noon the fog had come in. No one would know until it cleared off just how many traps he'd shifted. By that time, a lot of gear would have been lost, so he'd just be pointed to as somebody smart and lucky. Not that Morgan minded a little kidding. It was just that you had to stop to think up answers when your mind wanted to be busy with more important things.

Now, at early dusk, he was headed home, nosing through the fog to a place where he could hear Granite Hook bell buoy, get a bearing and go on up the channel to the harbor. It was later, by a good deal, than the time he usually got in. Nearly always, he was through by two or three in the afternoon, with his haul sold at the scow, or stored away in his lobster car. But that was on days when he started at four and didn't have to shift traps. Besides, this morning, he'd been late anyhow.

True, he'd taken his boat off the mooring at half-past three, and anyone hearing her roaring down the channel would have said, if they'd remarked it at all, that there was Morgan Sewell headed out to haul an hour ahead of anybody else; but what he'd actually done, once he was out around the Hook, was to keep straight on up the coast to Bellport. When Harry Bates, the best lawyer in Bellport, had come down to open up his office, Morgan had been there waiting for him. As Bates had promised, he'd had the papers ready. They were folded neatly now in Morgan's breast pocket under the dry warmth of his oilskin jacket. All day, whenever he moved his left arm, he could hear them crackle.

They were the deeds to two plots of land, comprising fifteen acres more or less, including Patch's Cove, and especially mentioning shore privilege, once the property of old Mrs. Martha Whiting, but now Morgan Sewell's.

Morgan pulled his gearshift into neutral, let the engine idle a moment, then cut the switch. At once the rushing sound of water stopped as the boat lost way. For a moment the dead silence seemed almost like a vacuum. The fog was thick and woolly; in the small shut-in circle, the sea was a dead, silvery-gray. Big smooth swells humped up astern, at first gray and ghostly, then deep, glass-green as they slid under the keel.

Morgan put both hands on the cheese rind and leaned out to listen. He knew approximately where he was, from the amount of time it had taken to run in from Dungeon Island, where he'd taken a bearing. The shape and spread of the swells told him he was over the wide submerged shelf which shoaled up from deep water to Reefpoint Ledge with Granite Hook just behind it. He should be hearing the bell buoy now, but for hours his ears had been keyed to the hum of his engine, and he couldn't hear a sound.

Morgan felt a slight prickling at the back of his neck under his sou'wester. Of course an engine always flipped over and went at the touch of a starter button. At least, his engine did. It was foolish to get the creeps, even wonder what would happen if it didn't. Shucks, there wasn't any danger, not in a dead calm like this, which would stay calm for hours yet. If he had engine trouble or lost his bearings, he could always anchor and pretty soon, when he didn't show up ashore, someone—probably Sylvanus—would come tearing out and bellow around the channel until they found him.

Sylvanus would have made the entire run in from Dungeon Island with his engine wide open, never thinking about a bearing on the bell buoy at all, until he slowed down for his mooring in Granite Hook Harbor. But Sylvanus had a nose for it; he ran a boat by instinct anyway. He, Morgan, had to *learn* everything and remember it, and, besides, he'd rather be safe than sorry. So when he could, he took a bearing. It upset him now that the bell-buoy bearing wasn't there.

No, it wasn't danger, or being scared, exactly. It was the idea of having to come to a full stop and sit down, empty-handed and helpless, waiting for someone else to take the action. Once or twice in his life he'd been in a spot like that. When he'd had scarlet fever at fifteen and had had to lie around till they were sure it hadn't affected his heart. Most of the time in the Navy, on patrol duty, jogging in an old destroyer up and down the Atlantic Coast. He'd longed after battle duty and what had he got? Patrol, for the whole damned war.

If he thought of those times, which was seldom now, it was with a sort of wave of sick boredom. Work and planning were his life—to get things done and planned ahead, so that no moment of his time would be wasted. The idea of being closed in, even for a short time, with nothing to do, was like an abyss opening up in front of his feet.

Somewhere in the fog, not very far away, the bell buoy clanged once. Good Lord, he thought. There it is, right there. The sound broke the tenseness of his concentration and he was immediately aware that the gray loom, a shade or two darker than the fog off to starboard, was the rounded snout of Granite Hook Head—that it had been there all the time. The reason he hadn't heard the bell buoy, of course, was because the swells were so glassy calm—it was riding them easy, not ringing much. He ought to have thought of that. Sylvanus would have. Syl would have seen the Hook five minutes ago.

But that was pretty good, Morgan told himself. He'd hit the Hook right on the nose. Fog was nearly always able to fool him. What you had to remember was not to stare straight into it, but to look sideways and pick up the darker shade of land out of the corners of your eyes. That he had run blind past Reefpoint Ledge and had missed piling his boat onto it by a scant two hundred feet or so didn't occur to him. He pressed his starter button, and as he had known it would, the engine kicked over smoothly and resumed its deep-throated hum.

He stood relaxed at the wheel, a stocky, long-chinned young man, whose looks seemed to say more than anything else, solid dependability. His reassured mind went back at once to the papers in his pocket. They were going to start a row, he had known that from the beginning. That was why he had gone at the whole thing in such secrecy. Only his mother knew that he was planning to build a herring weir in Patch's Cove. Even she didn't know that he'd bought up the land around the Cove to sew up the weir privilege.

For years, Morgan's cousins, Job Carter and his boys, Warren and Berry—or "second cousins and once removed," as Gram Sarah was always careful to say, seeing they were so disreputable—had flubbed around Patch's Cove in the herring season, with a patched seine and two battered dories. They scared away more herring than they caught, but, nevertheless, made a shaky living out of it. Job had never done anything else. He didn't even have a string of lobster traps. Morgan didn't doubt but what Job considered the Cove his own personal property. Whatever anybody did down there, the old man wasn't going to like it.

During the war, Job had raised the godfather and godmother of a row because some Bellport seiners had sealed off a big school of herring in the Cove by running a long net of herring twine across the mouth of it. Job couldn't work on that scale. His old seine wasn't long enough nor deep enough to cover the Cove entrance. His method was to wait until the herring got in there, and then run his seine around by guess, sometimes getting as few as fifty or a hundred bushels out of a school that might run to ten thousand. It seemed odd that he should grudge the Bellport seiners the bulk of a school, particularly since they were fair about it—said he could dip out for himself as many as he wanted; and the herring were so badly needed for sardines for the soldiers at war.

But Job said what the hell was the war to him—he hadn't declared it. Besides, if them piggy boys took herrin out of the Cove ten thousand bushels to the clip, the time would come when there wasn't any herrin left. As for him and the boys, they took out a hundred bushels or so whenever they needed cash for groceries, which ought to be a-plenty for any man. The seiners could take their pink-crucified net and get out of his territory; or they could suffer the consequences.

Since herring, as well as being essential to the war effort, were selling at a dollar-twenty to a dollar-forty a bushel, the seiners hadn't gone; but they had been harassed in many unpleasant ways—even to the attempted cutting away of their net—and after they disposed of their first school, they hadn't fished the Cove again.

The story, which Morgan had heard when he got home from the Navy, had given him his own ideas about Patch's Cove.

The place was a natural for a pocket weir. The narrow, deep entrance widened out into a lagoonlike inlet of quiet water, not too deep at high tide nor too shallow at ebb. Most people had been quite tickled at the way Job had routed the herring seiners. They'd been on Job's side, as most people always favor the underdog; besides, the herring seiners had been from out of town. Morgan guessed he might have to buck some public opinion at first. But, after all, the majority respected an investment, and the project was one that he'd have to put quite a lot of money in. It wasn't as if he was turning old Job out of his home—the Carters would be welcome to live in the shack at the Cove, where they always had, providing they didn't bother the weir.

At first, Morgan had thought he couldn't buy the weir privilege, because old Mrs. Whiting hadn't wanted to sell. She was ninety now, living in Bellport with her grandson, but the Patch Cove place had been her childhood home.

The old white farmhouse had burned down long ago; sheds and outbuildings had rotted into ruin. The only structure left that kept its original shape was an old vegetable storage house on the bank of the Cove, which some early Whiting had built out of two-by-fours over a deep potato cellar lined with brick. Years ago, Job Carter had turned it into a camp. His boys had been born in it and his wife had died there. Mrs. Whiting, not wanting to use the place for anything, had never bothered the Carters, but that was no reason, Morgan told himself, why Job should consider the Cove his, even by squatter's rights.

Morgan himself was up on the law. As long as the place was worth money and Mrs. Whiting paid the taxes, the rights were hers to dispose of, and, the Lord knew, Job hadn't made any improvements. There had even been some talk that he'd set fire to the old farmhouse one night, because he'd heard that someone planned to rent it and move in there; or maybe just because he wanted to see it burn. Morgan couldn't remember whether people had said he *had*, or only that he *might have*.

All winter, off and on, Morgan had worked on Mrs. Whiting,

and the lawyer, Bates, had worked on her. Then, when she'd finally agreed to sell, Bates had had trouble straightening out the riparian rights. Morgan wanted title to the shore down to the water's edge—no sense leaving loopholes, just in case—and somewhere back along, somebody had forgotten to transfer the shore privilege when he sold the land. The Whitings hadn't ever thought about it—they'd just taken it for granted the shore belonged to them. But not Morgan. Bates had had to take valuable time tracing back land transfers—valuable to Morgan because he was crazy to start driving piling as soon as the ice went out of the Cove.

By April, the weir should have been nearly done, and he'd be late getting it started fishing. But construction wouldn't take long, now that he was really ready to roll. His materials were waiting, he'd taken care of that during the winter and spring. His big net for the pocket was stored in Syl's fish house. Poles, piling, and weir brush for the leaders were cut and stacked over on Barrel Island. He had spent all his spare time for months on the island—had even built a pile driver over there, finishing it up except for the hammer, which he couldn't hang alone.

People thought he was going to build his weir at Barrel Island. Most of them felt he was pretty dumb, wasting his time and money. There was a gut there, where a weir could be built, but it was exposed to the sea, so that one good summer storm could have wiped him out overnight. Well, they'd find out soon enough now, he thought. As soon as the weather settled down, he'd tow his pile driver across and bring his stuff over to the Cove. And now that he owned the place, lock, stock, and barrel, he'd have plenty to say legally, in case Job Carter wanted to make anything of it.

Ahead, Morgan made out the vague outline of a lobster boat hanging motionless on its mooring. He cut his speed as other craft—moored skiffs, dories, power boats—began to show up through the darkening fog. The water in the harbor was bottle-calm. The V of his slowed wake rolled back two sluggish crests of glossy obsidian. Fog drops hung in the air, heavy with the smell of ripe bait, rotten fish offal from under the fish wharf, tar and gasoline.

Be a storm, all right, he thought. Hell, the weather would cut up, just when he got ready to start work.

He hoped Frank Dalzell hadn't closed up the lobster scow for the night and gone home to supper. Morgan sure didn't feel like fudding around his locked-up lobster car in the dark. Usually, though, Frank waited for a late boat, wanting to buy all the lobsters he could; and he had tonight, Morgan saw, as the light in the scow's deck house showed up through the fog when he came near enough to see. He maneuvered alongside, lifted across his big box of lobsters and jumped aboard the scow, carrying his empty gasoline cans.

In the house, Frank Dalzell was making comfortable with old Uncle Wheat Salisbury and his crony, Foley Craddock, over a bottle and a pack of cards. A sooted-up kerosene lantern gave out barely enough light to see by, and the place smelled like a hen house, if the hens had been smoking old pipes and breathing forth fumes of whisky. The three old men barely glanced up at Morgan, as he stuck his head in the door, so intent were they on finishing their hand.

"Gimme four," Foley said. He was a small wrinkled brown man, his face as sharp as a tack under the long-peaked tight cap he wore, and he had his pipe clenched so tight in his toothless mouth that his short chin nearly met the tip of his nose. Teetering on the edge of a backless kitchen chair, his toes barely touching the floor, the tail of his dungaree jacket stuck stiffly out behind, Foley looked like an old woodcock which somebody had shot years ago and tried, not too successfully, to stuff.

Morgan had been brought up to think of Foley Craddock as the town bum. He was harmless, of course, and he minded his own business, but his way of life couldn't fail to be held up as a horrible example by a woman like Gram Sarah to her children. Uncle Wheat was a long ways above him—a sober, retired sea captain. People had been surprised when Uncle Wheat came home for good, that he'd made a pal out of Foley. The story was that they went on some righteous old drunks together. Not that anyone could say outright that they'd ever seen Uncle Wheat drunk.

As a matter of fact, Uncle Wheat and Foley were lifelong rivals, born within an hour of each other, seventy years ago. They'd gone to school and grown up together; only, Uncle Wheat, as a young man had gone away to sea. When he'd come home to Granite Hook for good, at sixty-five, he couldn't bear to loaf. He'd been a thrifty man, so he bought himself a nice boat and went lobstering.

Foley had stayed in Granite Hook and gone fishing all his life. Fat year or lean, he never saved a cent. His boat was an old demasted Friendship sloop, with a two-cylinder, two-cycle kicker and a cuddy forward, where he lived alone with his cat named Whirligig. He hated women—said a good cat was twice the company, half the fuss and bother; if you got sick of a cat you could chuck it overboard. Not that he'd ever chucked Whirligig overboard, or ever would. Since Foley never repaired gear nor cleaned up his boat until he had to, he was often in trouble with leaks or breakdowns; his whole outfit smelled something horrible. He got drunk when he felt like it, and his shiftlessness was a byword.

When Uncle Wheat came home, he was worried about Foley and told him so to his face. Foley merely said that going skipper of all them vessels hadn't done Wheat a mite of good. He'd come home so big feeling that you had to hire a horse and team and drive hard before you could get near enough to holler to him.

The two of them always went lobstering in company. They couldn't keep up with the young fellows, though neither would admit it, but they could keep up with each other. They started out together mornings—how early depended on what time Wheat could get Foley stirring—and set their traps alongside. More often than not, Foley would have engine trouble and either come trailing home alone after dark, or Wheat would have to tow him in.

Uncle Wheat had had a lifetime of keeping things shipshape. His own boat was spick-and-span, the engine shining, the woodwork scrubbed white after each day's work, the brass polished down to the last screw on the bow cleat. When Foley broke down, Wheat would ride him hard; but it couldn't be said that Foley didn't have ways of getting his own back. Wheat might have God Almighty's boat and gear, but Foley caught more lobsters. They could haul trap for trap all day long, and in the end Foley would be highline. He'd had a lifetime of lobstering, and he was a natural-born fisherman.

One jab about that could send Wheat into a roaring temper; there were one or two other things, too. Foley figured that, in general, they stayed just about even.

Morgan stepped inside the deck house reluctantly, holding the door half-open. He didn't like the smell of old men, he thought, nor the stink of second-hand whisky. "I'd like to sell and get home," he said, "if you ain't too busy, Frank."

"In a minute, in a minute," Frank said waspishly. "I've waited long enough for you."

Foley scrabbled up the cards Frank had dealt him, said, "Hah!" triumphantly and thrust a handful of matches into the middle of the table.

Uncle Wheat glared at him. "What you want to be a thunderin fool for?" he demanded. "You saw how many I drawed. Or can't ya count up to one?"

"I can count," Foley said. "The's fourteen of them matches. That one-eyed pair you gut there ain't goin to do you a mite of good, Wheat."

Uncle Wheat started and was unable to keep from casting a quick glance at his cards. The pair of Jacks he held over his sevens were indeed one-eyed, but there was no way Foley could have known it. Wheat had known better than to give him a chance to peek. He was just a good guesser bluffing again. Hadn't he drawn four cards?

Still you had to look out for Foley. Uncle Wheat sat rumbling indecisively inside his massive chest.

"Shut that christless door!" he bellowed suddenly. "Don't you know no better'n to let that dumned fog in here, night like this?" His voice was not what it had been in the days of the coasting vessels. The magnificent, deep-throated bawl sometimes carried a wheezy note on foggy nights, but it still had authority.

Morgan closed the door. "Look, Frank," he began. "I—"

"Okay, keep your shirt on." Frank spread his fat fingers in the air and flapped his arms as a signal to shut up. He'd laid down his own hand the minute he'd seen the fourteen matches Foley'd put out. Frank wasn't going to risk losing a dollar and forty cents or more. He wasn't going to miss seeing Foley and Uncle Wheat come together head on, either.

"Well, you ain't gut nothin," Uncle Wheat said at last. He laboriously counted out fourteen matches, wetting his stiff old thumb on his lower lip.

"Your blood's dried up, Wheat," Foley said. "You ain't the man you was. Ten years ago—one year ago—you would of raised me."

Uncle Wheat's whiskers shook. He observed sourly, "If you're in a hurry, Foley, go som'ers with the kids and play slapjack. Give a man a chance t' finish countin." He added six matches to his fourteen.

Foley gleefully put out ten more, at which Uncle Wheat stared as if they were snakes.

"That's *raisin* me again," he said accusingly.

Foley picked up the bottle and took a hearty pull. "You gut the kind of money says you wun't knuckle under? What I hold here in my hand'll knock the tossles off of a lousy little one-eyed pair."

Morgan shifted from one foot to the other. He still had a lot to do tonight—had his evening all planned out. And here he was held up while these old jackasses gabbled over a poker game. "Damn it, Frank," he exploded. "I can always put my haul in my car."

Frank sighed, hoisting his ponderous body to his feet. He was a fat man, moving only with difficulty; he made much of this infirmity now, as he got slowly and lingeringly away from the table. "No need, no need, Morgan. I'm comin."

Uncle Wheat, closing his mouth with a snap that dented his pipestem, had pushed all his remaining matches into the middle of the table. "That's all I got," he howled. "Le's see you cover em, or haul out a the game."

"I'll call ya," Foley said swiftly. Without counting out any more matches, he laid his hand face up on the table. He had held the Queen of Clubs and had drawn four small clubs to go with her.

Uncle Wheat was stunned. For a moment he glared at Foley's cards, then he gathered up his breath and let go. "Why, you blarsted, thievin son of a shoremongerin lighthouse keeper!" he roared. "You led me on t' think you was bluffin. I ought to take you t' pieces and feed you to the gulls. By God, I believe I will!"

He began to heave up and down in his chair, making tearing motions with his hands. Frank got between him and Foley. Frank's face was red from holding back laughter; once he slapped his thigh, big as a keg, with a resounding whack.

"Have a drink, Wheat," he wheezed. "H-have a drink. It's the last you'll git for a long time after you pay Foley."

"Oh, for God's sake," Morgan said.

Uncle Wheat turned on him a pair of bloodshot eyes. "What the roarin old red-eyed blazes ails *you?* D'you hev t' come in here, freezin everybody t' death and bellyachin around, and bust up a peaceable card game? I told your father twenty years ago that if I was him I'd put the hosswhip to you, learn you some manners. By God, I see he didn't. Go on, Frank, buy his lobsters and git him off the scow, fore he itches a hole in her!"

Morgan turned and went out through the door of the house.

Frank paddled hastily after him, moving quite light-footedly now, weighed out his lobsters by lantern light and figured out the balance due him. Occasionally he shook massively and gave forth the croaking "Hack, hack, hack," which passed, with Frank, for laughter.

"Want your gas cans filled?" he asked, as Morgan stood tucking the bills in his wallet.

"Haven't got time tonight," Morgan said shortly. He'd pick up some gas somewhere else, later on.

"Up to you," Frank said. "Storm tomorrow, I guess."

"Looks like it."

"You won't be able t' git near Barrel Island for days, let alone drive a weir out there," Frank said, with a certain amount of relish in his voice.

Morgan swung himself down onto the platform of his boat. "Who said anything about building a weir over Barrel Island way?"

"Why," Frank said, taken aback. "Why . . . everybody, Morg. Phil kind of run of an idea you wanted him to work over there."

Phil was Frank's oldest boy, whom Morgan had already spoken to about helping him build the weir.

"I'm buildin it in Patch's Cove," Morgan said. "I've never had any plans for one at Barrel Island."

He wished it had been lighter, so he could have seen Frank's face. Even the dim, flabby square he could make out looked astonished.

"Patch's Cove!" Frank said. "Job and the boys'll hev your heart's blood. They'll run ya out a there, won't they? They have everybody else."

"Not unless they want to see the state cops down," Morgan said. "I own the Cove now."

"You own it!"

"Ayeh. Land around it and shore privileges. Got the deeds today. Look, tell Phil we'll start work, as soon as the weather clears, will you, Frank?"

"Oh, sure. Sure. I'll be darned." His face hung above Morgan like a dim moon.

Morgan knew he was dying to get back into the deck house and tell Uncle Wheat and Foley the news. Frank was a terrible gossip. Tell him something and it would be all over town in five minutes. Working on the scow the way he did, he saw about everybody in the course of an afternoon. He'd start with the first boat that got in from hauling, and maybe tell a story twenty times before he went home to supper.

Morgan grinned as his boat slid smoothly into the fog toward his mooring. It wouldn't be long now before Job found out. Besides, Foley Craddock and Job were lifelong friends.

When Frank went back into the deck house, Foley and Uncle Wheat were amiably figuring up how much Foley owed Uncle Wheat, with the amount of the poker debt taken out. Foley had won four dollars and twenty cents, but it still wasn't enough to cover a loan he'd got out of Wheat sometime in the winter.

"What d' ya know," Frank said. "Morgan just told me he ain't buildin his weir on Barrel Island. He's goin t' build it down to Patch's Cove."

Foley said, "Haw!"

Uncle Wheat grinned. "How long's he think it'll stay there?"

"I d'no," Frank said. "He mentioned the state cops."

"He'll need em," Foley said.

ALL through the early hours of darkness the fog hung pit-black and spongy, a second atmosphere not of air, but of air turned to water. No ripple stirred in the glassy running out of the tide. The boats in the harbor dropped twelve feet between six o'clock and midnight as the water sucked away beneath them; but they lay without movement, parallel to the silent flow.

Sometime after eleven, the oily circling current in the Whirlpool, a thousand yards off the seaward side of Granite

Hook Head, slowed down and stopped. Devil's aprons and ribbands of kelp floated upright and motionless. A small starfish, sensing slack tide, let go the life-or-death clutch of his legs and inched upward on the rock.

In the shoal water by Candlemas Island, one of Foley Craddock's lobster traps lay on a rock three fathoms down. The warp hung from a glass toggle and a wooden buoy which floated motionless side by side. Two short lobsters and a sculpin were inside the trap and a bait pocket of mush which had once been herring.

A mile to sea, Crack Corn Ledges, the peak of an underwater mountain, lay ramp after ugly black ramp a foot above the tide. Up one of them in the watery darkness, a crab the size of a quarter marched, leaving a slight trail of phosphorescent flakes. Thousands of cuckoo-shells sucking to the rocks made a soft hissing like light rain. But the sea itself made no more sound than if it had been water along the wall of a cistern.

Somewhere to the east, lost in ink-black night and muffled in a terrible privacy, the vast suction which for six hours had set away from the land, had worn itself out.

At twelve o'clock, an air current drifted in over the land. It was nothing that could have been called a breeze. But suddenly, into the stagnant atmosphere was thrust a wild and savage ocean smell, made up of salt and iodine and seaweed, and something else that said cold, said indescribable lonely space. Its passage did not so much as shake a drop from the folded alder-buds; but over the water and along the fiercely indented shapes of the land, the fog began to move.

Six miles to sea, off Dungeon Island, a school of herring which had surfaced and was swimming northward, suddenly sank, a million vanishing phosphorescent arrows. The crab on Crack Corn let himself down by strings of seaweed from shelf to shelf, to a deep hole under the wall of granite.

A ripple washed over the shoals, sliding along the ledges

with a scarcely perceptible murmur of water. The lobster buoy and the glass toggle ticked together, drifted a few inches apart. A puff of wind wrinkled the harbor; the moored boats, all together, swung in a slow arc heading southeast. In one of them an empty gas can, lying on its side, set up a slow, melancholy clanking. The fog was gone, leaving a black sky, over which tumbled a vast procession of clouds.

Out to sea, the tide had changed and was coming in.

THEOLINE SEWELL and Ida Gates slid onto two high stools in front of Leon Gitchell's soda fountain. They were out of breath, having run at top speed from the high school grounds—partly because it was pouring rain, but mostly because it was only three-fifteen and they wished to be seen on the street as briefly as possible.

From behind the counter, Leon eyed their yellow slickers which were streaming water all over his clean floor. "How come you're here early?" he asked morosely. "I figgered I had fifteen minutes."

"We sneaked out on the last quarter of study hall," Ida said. She was a chunky girl with taut round cheeks and a pouty, baby mouth. Her fair hair stood up in moist ringlets all over her head.

"What's old Laughin Water goin t' have to say about that?" said Leon. "Laughing Water" was the principal of the high school, so called because his not unusual name happened to be Laffin.

"He won't know it," said Ida. "Unless you tell him."

"Well, I'm liable to tell him," Leon said. "Every day at half-past-three when all you hoodlums get out of school, hell breaks loose in here and I figger half-past-three is early enough. Why couldn't you of dreened them oilskins off a little, out under the awnin? Place'll look like a pigpen."

Ida giggled. "You won't tell him," she said. "Put some newspapers down, why don't you?" She was too absorbed in going over the Kinds-of-Ice-Cream list, posted over the counter, to give Leon the snappy comeback he expected.

"Sheet iron might do some good, but not newspapers," said Leon. "Well, what'll it be? Pie and cake?"

Leon's grouch act was put on every day for the high school kids and they liked it. He was aware that it was one reason why he got so much of their trade and the drugstores so little. Half the time he was merely saying exactly what he thought, but they wouldn't have believed that. They just went on thinking his bark was worse than his bite, which was all right with him. Today, too, he was talking for the benefit of two drivers who had come through on an oil truck and were picking up a late lunch in a booth at the back of the restaurant.

"I'll have a chocolate malted," Theo said. If she saved twenty cents out of her remaining lunch money, she'd have just enough to make up the cost of a three-cornered picture scarf at Whitcomb's.

"That's fodder for you, after a day's work," Leon said, jerking his head to the drivers. He picked up a container and began putting together the malted. "No sanwich to go with it?"

"We-ell . . ." If she were going to make sure of a job here, she'd better keep on the good side of Leon. "Make it a piece of coconut cake." The scarf would have to wait.

Ida sat up straight, her eyes shining. She had decided What She Was Going To Have. "I'll take a banana split, Leon, cherry ice cream. Everything double except the banana."

"My God," Leon said. "You kids'll rot your stomach out, all that sweet stuff. I get the heartburn just thinkin about it. Besides, a double banana'll set you back seventy cents, Ida."

"I don't have to worry about that," Ida said smartly. "Why should you?"

"Put the sarse to me, would you?" Leon said. "Go on and git your double banana at the drugstore."

Ida giggled again. Leon was already putting together the banana split. Now that her order was settled on, she had become aware of the two drivers in the booth. She unbuttoned her slicker, spreading it far back on her shoulders, dug in a pocket for a lipstick, and proceeded to do her mouth in the fountain mirror.

"Why don't you wait till after you eat?" Leon said irritably. "I spend half my time diggin that cussid red stuff off'n my tumblers." He set their food in front of them and stood back, an expression of deep disgust on his round pleasant face.

That Ida was a cute little trick and she knew darn well the two drivers were watching her. She'd better watch her step—one of them was Howard Thurlow, who wouldn't need a second invitation. Leon would sure like to see Jack Gates, Ida's father, walk in through the door right now. Jack kept a tight rein on Ida when it came to men. Not that it did much good.

As for Leon, if it came to a choice, he preferred Syl Sewell's girl, Theo. She was nice and quiet and standoffish. Fix her up some, and she'd look all right, too. She just wasn't the type to get away with wearing any old rag, the way some kids could. Leon had just the type blue uniform dress with white apron that she'd look swell in. Get Polly Gerrish, his other waitress, to show her how to touch a little lipstick on, not too much, and she'd be a knockout—just the kind of girl who'd appeal to the conservative old ladies from the summer estates when they came in to afternoon tea. To a lot of other people, too.

"How about it, Theo?" he asked suddenly. "You decided to work for me this summer?"

Ida stopped eating briefly and regarded Theo with a surprised stare. So this was why she'd wanted to slip out before last study period was over.

"Why, I don't know," Theo said. She'd been wondering how to bring the matter up. "I'd have to be sure it was definite, Leon, before I brought it up with Ma and Pa."

"It's definite," Leon said. "Fifteen a week and tips. It's a good job. I pay high, because I like to git good people. It ain't as if I run a joint here. I don't have to hunt to fill my jobs, either."

"I guess you won't, Leon," Ida said eagerly, her mouth full

of banana and whipped cream. "Not at that pay. Why, I'll take it myself. I'd *love* to work here this summer."

She glanced up, caught the eye of one of the drivers and saw that he winked at her. For a moment she had a vision of herself as the gracious waitress, feeding all the tourists, hungry and male, and of course good looking.

Why, the big pig! Theo thought. She'd asked Ida to come over here with her, because Ida was one of the few who dared to skip out on study hall, now that Mr. Laffin had laid down the law about it. Ida would risk anything for an opportunity to eat; besides, her father owned the Bellport Marine Store and nothing much would happen to her. Ida wouldn't offer any competition, either; she didn't have to work summers and had never been known to. Some of the girls would give their eye-teeth to work for Leon. He had a rough side to his tongue, but he was a prince to work for—always saw that you got as much money as was coming and a little more, if he could manage it. But here sat Ida, with her mouth full of whipped cream and plenty of spending money to buy more, trying to grab the job right out from under Theo's nose.

"No, you don't, Ida," Theo said. "I want it myself."

Ida dimpled demurely. "I guess if I want it, you'll give it to me, won't you, Leon?"

"Why, no, Ida," Leon said. "I wouldn't."

"Why not?" Ida said, startled.

"Your Pa'd skin me alive. Besides, I've got to have somebody won't eat up all the stock on me."

One of the men, the very one who had winked at her, laughed. All at once Ida decided she was going to have that job if she killed somebody for it. At first, she hadn't cared, but now things were different. If she didn't like the job, she could throw it up later. "I should think you'd want somebody whose people you *know*, Leon," she observed icily, "instead of you-don't-know-who from Scratch Corner."

She was so completely unprepared for Theo's reaction that when the open hand smacked against her nose she had a spoonful of banana split halfway to her mouth. Her mouth stayed open and the succulent mess plopped off the spoon onto the front of her dress. The slap had been harder than Theo intended. Quite a lot of long-bottled-up resentment had gone into it.

"Wow!" said Leon. Inside himself he burst into a guffaw, but he kept his face straight and even scowled a little. "Okay," he said. "That's enough. If it's like that, I d'no's I want either one of you. Beat it now. Far as that goes, Ida, I went to school with Sylvanus Sewell."

Ida slid down off the stool and made for the door. "You'll hear about this," she stormed, "from *my father!* And you didn't get the job either, Theo Sewell, and I'm glad of it." She marched out.

Theo was stunned by what she'd done. It had happened so quickly that she hadn't had time to stop herself. That temper—if she could only hang on to it . . . She sat speechless and overcome. If just Leon had been here, it would have been bad enough, but to do such a thing in public, before two strange men . . . And she'd lost the job into the bargain.

"Finish your cake," Leon said. "No use to have t' scrape it out."

"I don't want it."

Leon suddenly gave a strangled sound and she looked up. He was laughing, wiping away the tears with one hand and patting the top of his bald head with the other.

If he thought it was funny—

The truck drivers got to their feet and came down to the counter to pay for their meal. One of them settled his check and went out. The other, the one who had winked at Ida, straddled the stool next to Theo and leaned his elbows on the counter top.

"Who would your friend be, Leon?" he began engagingly.

"Beat it, Howard," Leon said irritably.

"Oh, come, Leon. I've got a wildcat I want skun."

"Well, you go skin it," Leon said.

"Okay," Howard said with a grin. He pulled on his peaked driver's cap over some very smoothly waved dark red hair. "See ya next time through." He went out the door whistling.

"Just has to be a skirt," Leon muttered under his breath. "That's all." He turned back to Theo who was still sitting, transfixed with misery, in front of the half-eaten piece of cake.

"Le's see. School closes second week in June, don't it?" he asked.

"The first week."

"How soon after that could you go to work?"

"Oh, Leon—"

"You come and start in around the tenth. I got a bundle of new blue uniforms you can take along home, see if your ma can fit you into them."

"I thought you didn't want me."

"Oh, I only said that for Ida's benefit. Oh, my God!" Leon went off again. "That little nitwit! The look on her face!"

"WELL, I don't think much of it," Phoebe said. "Your father won't either." She was bustling around getting supper, her hands making the familiar motions, but her mind completely free to deal with a family problem. After so many years, housework was automatic to Phoebe. She did not remember that once she had hated it. "Tom, Dick and Harry and all their relations go through that ice cream parlor in the summer."

"Ice cream isn't all Leon sells, either," Wesley said from the sitting room. He was stretched out on the couch with a book, waiting to be fed, with his ears wide open.

Theo had brought up the matter of working at Leon's to her mother in private, when Phoebe was combing her hair in the bedroom before supper. Phoebe didn't ever consider anything in the family private, though. She was still having it over.

"Leon sells beer and gin." Jimmy put his oar in. "Out the back door, if you go round there."

The kids were hungry, with the terrible appetites of ten and eleven, and they had been hanging around the table, waiting to see if they could swipe a slice of ham off the plate when Phoebe's back was turned.

Phoebe was quite aware of this. She was just waiting for one of them to make a move. She didn't mind having them around underfoot while she was getting supper—stepping over kids was one of the automatic motions of housework—but she did draw the line at having them glom into things before the meal was ready.

"And when Warren and Berry Carter get drunk, Leon's is where they get it," Joe put in.

"For *heb'n* sake!" Phoebe rounded on them. "You kids hush up that kind a talk this minute! Where you ever hear it, is more'n I know, and all the other trash you ain't supposed to know nothin about."

"Down to the shore they said so," Jimmy said, rolling his eyes sideways at his mother to see how much further he could go.

"Hank Haskell says—" began Joe.

"Listen to em," Theo said. "Aunt Jimmy and Grammy Joe, the two worst gossips in town. Oh, Ma, if anyone could just *once* discuss their private affairs without Wes and the kids sticking their noses in up to the ankles—"

"Ole gin mill Theo," said Joe. "Wants to go work in a gin parlor."

"That's enough!" Phoebe said. "You heard me, Joe. Theo isn't going to work in a gin mill. We're just talking about it and—"

"For heaven's sake, Ma! We are *not* talking about a gin mill!" Theo tried hard to keep the exasperation out of her voice. "Leon's is a restaurant. The high school kids go there. *Mrs. Beacon* and that crowd go there!"

"Not at night," Wes's voice came in from the sitting room.

"You'd be likely to know what goes on at Leon's at night," Theo called back at him.

"I know what I hear. And that's plenty. Puh-lenty."

"What *do* you hear, Wes?" Phoebe turned toward the door, and Jimmy, thinking she had for once relaxed, darted his hand out to the ham plate. Phoebe pounced like a hawk. She caught the hand and whacked its knuckles, not too hard, on the table.

Jimmy puckered up and began to bawl at the top of his lungs.

"There, young man!" Phoebe said, above the uproar. "You git away from that table, and *you, too, Joe.*"

Joe, who had been hanging in the offing, ducked under the table.

"Oh, my soul, there's your father now. Put the chairs round, Joe. Jimmy, you stop bawlin and help him. Theo, you turn out the water. My heavens, I can't do everything alone." Phoebe went into high, getting the supper on the table.

Wes, frustrated in his chance to tell what he had heard, appeared in the sitting-room door. "Well, Ma, you know, they *do* say around town that Leon sells booze."

"Who says so?" Sylvanus, who had been bumping around in the entry taking off his boots and oilskins, came through the door. "Don't you let me hear you repeat that anywhere, Wes."

Sylvanus's broad red face was streaming with rain and there was about him a faint redolence, not unpleasant, of damp oilcloth and tar and bait shed. He had been down working on traps all day in his fish house, seeing there wasn't an earthly thing a man could do outdoors in the storm; or he had been doing what all the men of the community called "working on traps," which was merely to be sociable in the fish house, and once in a while, to paint buoys or repair trap heads. He made at once for the wash basin, ladled into it a generous dollop of hot water and proceeded to scrub his hands and face.

"I only know what I hear," Wes repeated, his voice sulky.

"Well, who'd you hear it from?" Sylvanus said thickly through the towel.

"Why, everybody—"

"Well, everybody's a big liar," Sylvanus said cheerfully. " 'Everybody' most always is."

"Must be something, if there's talk," Wes said.

"There ain't. Lord sake, Wes, I've known Leon for years. He never sold a drop of booze in his life. Anyway, if he did, he'd lose his summer cottage trade. Mrs. Beacon and all the rest of them good ladies wouldn't drink their tea in a booze parlor. You been out today, Phoebe? This is some storm."

"My goodness, no!" Phoebe said. "I see how hard it was rainin, I sent the kids to the store. Supper's ready when you are, Syl."

"Well, you ought a walked out the road, just to see the sight," Sylvanus said. "The Hook's buried up—big rollers comin right slap in over the top of it. I ain't seen a spring storm like this for years."

"Ah, there'll be some traps lost tonight," Joe said in a sepulchral voice. He had been for some weeks driving everybody crazy with his imitation of a news commentator, perfected by listening to the radio. He was pretty good at it now, and Sylvanus grinned.

"Darn right, Gabe," he said, sitting down and thrusting his long legs under the table. "This keeps up, they'll be piled in windrows. Matter of fact, some was piled up last night and today."

"You think you'll lose many, Syl?" Phoebe asked.

"M-m, no more'n usual, I guess. It'll be tough all round, though, if this keeps up. Where *is* everybody?" he went on, glancing around the table at the two empty places. "Jim, what ails you?"

Jimmy had crawled in behind the stove, where he was sulking.

"He got his knuckles thumped for swiping ham off the plate," Phoebe said. "And he better come quick if he wants some now. There ain't hardly enough to go around." She winked at Sylvanus, noting a slight stir behind the stove. "Jacky's up to her gra'mother's."

Sylvanus grinned. "You lost," he said.

Phoebe bridled. "I always do, as well you know," she said. "I most always say peace at any price, but I do'know's it's worth Jacky's having a spell with her stomach."

"She might've brought her home before dark," Sylvanus said. "Save me a trip up there tonight."

"Oh, she's hopin we'll let Jacky stay all night, of course. I spose the poor old soul gets lonesome, but—"

"Ma? Lonesome? No, she just thinks it ain't healthy for Jacky to live with her folks. Well, after supper I'll go up and blast her loose. Kind of like to hear Ma hold forth on Morgan's latest, anyway."

"Don't you dare go up there and plague your mother!" Phoebe flared. "If you do, I'll kill you, Syl."

"I see Job today down to the shore," Sylvanus said. "He wouldn't speak to me. Don't know why. Nothin to do with me."

"Don't you *dare* git into it, Syl."

He raised his fine eyebrows at her. "Why would I git into it?"

"Morgan'll come runnin to you, see 'f he don't, the minute there's the least trouble."

Sylvanus grinned. "That ain't his idea of it," he said. "Did Ma take Jacky's raincape this mornin?"

"Yes, she did. Why, I don't know, except it was rainin. She usually don't bother with anything, long's she gits Jacky."

"Maybe I better take along an extry sweater." Sylvanus was always restless when Jacky was out of the house. She was, actually, the only one of his children he felt comfortable with. The others he loved, of course, but they weren't good company. They were grasshoppers jumping around the edge of Sylvanus's inner calm. He couldn't poke his head inside the door at home but some one of them was after him for something—permission to do this or that, or, mostly, it was money. Money and things.

Sometimes Sylvanus was shocked, seeing how deep the itch went with them—like a disease, a walking typhoid of wants. But Jacky didn't have any more wants than a kitten. In some ways, she was a good deal like one, lovable and undemanding. Even if you didn't know what was going on inside her head, you at least could be sure it wasn't some plan or project that you'd have to tend to, or iron out, or pay for.

Sylvanus thought he knew where it was he parted company with his kids, especially with Wes and Theo. They all thought he ought to work harder, bring more money home. He didn't doubt it was mostly because they were kids. Things would jiggle down into proportion for them, when they got older and found out that nobody could have everything. For himself, he felt he did all right. A man took care of his family, saw they weren't in need. Sometimes he worked extra to provide a few luxuries and some good times. But beyond that, he didn't feel it necessary to go.

Sylvanus loved his work. From boyhood, the varied process of making a living out of the sea had carried excitement and fascination for him. Even now, after years of it—he was forty-two—he never got tired of the details of fishing, perhaps because on any two successive days they were never the same. The weather changed, or something came up—engine trouble, or you lost gear; or you caught something unusual with a trap or a trawl, like the time he'd got a thirty-five-pound Atlantic salmon on a hake trawl off Dungeon Island Head. It was all satisfying. Going down to the shore in the early morning through the heavy wet grass, launching the punt and rowing off aboard the boat in the still clear water. Seeing the sun come up out of the ocean, a million miles off—the way it looked on different days, like a gold plate or a button, or a fried egg that had busted in the pan. Smoking home through weather—fog, or a westerly, or a northeast snowstorm, with the winter cracking on, and knowing that unless something unforeseeable happened, you had the skill to take you in.

Sylvanus knew he had more than usual skill at his job. Deep inside himself, it was a satisfaction to know that he could have fished circles around most men, if he'd been willing to drive. Right there was where he'd always disagreed with his mother and Morgan, who *were* drivers. He liked to work slowly, getting the flavor; which you couldn't do if you tore at things just for the sake of the money there was in it.

There were times, of course, when money *was* the only thing in the world. Hard times, when you didn't have enough to buy groceries or to pay the doctor if the kids were sick. Sylvanus had seen plenty of them, when fish were scarce and prices low. He'd humped himself then, all right; sometimes it had been touch and go, but Phoebe and the kids had never gone hungry.

They'd had as much, too, as most Granite Hook families. The house he and Phoebe had pinched and saved for after they got married wasn't anything grand, but it was warm and comfortable. Phoebe hadn't had a lot of frills to furnish it with. She hadn't wanted them. She was the only woman Sylvanus ever saw who wasn't always needling her husband for new stuff she didn't need to dress up a house. Phoebe liked things clean and simple. He'd known her to swap with a neighbor a Christmas gift of a set of frilled lace curtains for some plain pairs that didn't cost near so much, and feel that she'd got the best of the trade.

A long time ago, when Gram Sarah had been going through one of her spells of sounding off about his shiftlessness, Sylvanus had heard Phoebe say something he'd never forgotten. He'd come unaware into the woodshed and had heard through the open door the last part of his mother's speech. It had made his hair curl. He knew he wasn't what you could call shiftless; still, he hadn't been married very long and a thing like that wasn't exactly what a man liked to hear said to his wife. There'd been a little silence, and then Phoebe'd said, clear as a bell, "Well, Ma, I never married expectin to git rich. *Syl himself is more important than the money he makes.*"

It summed up in short words the way he and Phoebe felt about each other. If he lived his life at his own pace and took time once in a while to get the taste of it, why, Phoebe did that often enough herself to understand how things were with him. He wished the kids could realize that such things had a place in the world alongside of getting as rich as a fool; but you couldn't blame them when they looked around and saw the summer people's cars and yachts and speedboats on all sides of them, and had it dinned into them by the movies and the radio. Well, maybe they'd get over it sometime. Maybe everybody'd get over it, if they could find in the world what he and Phoebe had.

He couldn't admit, even to himself, that Jacky, the lacking one, was the best-loved of all his kids. He merely said he felt lost when she was out of the house. As soon as he finished his supper, he'd go straight up and fetch her home, rain or no rain.

"If 't wasn't that Gram'll probly put her to bed with a bag of candy," Phoebe said, "I'd say leave her up there tonight. It's stormin awful."

"Oh, Jacky and me, we'll enjoy the rain," Sylvanus said.

"C'n I go?" Joe spoke huskily through a mouthful.

Sylvanus sighed. "You'll git soakin," he said. "Oh, all right, if you ain't choked to death over them big mouthfuls by then." He went on, realizing he'd been a little short. "If we hurry, we might be in time t' stroll down and see the rollers comin in over the Hook. Well, look who's here!"

Jimmy, partly because of the proposed walk to the Hook, but mostly because he'd heard with misgivings about Joe's big mouthfuls, had come out from behind the stove. He knew Joe, and there *hadn't* seemed to be a great deal of ham. He slid into his chair, looking as if he were doing everyone a favor, and shoved his plate at his father to be filled.

"Jimmy," Phoebe said. "You pick up your plate and pass it nice. You hear me?"

Jimmy picked up the plate. His father, after all, had saved him a big slice of ham.

Joe slowed down at once. He'd had his eye on that piece.

Theo had been sitting silently, wondering how soon Wes or Phoebe would bring up the subject of Leon's. She hadn't been able to eat much, she'd been thinking so hard how she could manage to talk to her father alone, but she knew just from the look in Wes's eye that she wasn't going to.

"Go on, ask him," Wes said at last. "You know he isn't going to let you."

"What's that?" Sylvanus said. He might've known they couldn't get through a meal without something coming up.

"Leon's offered Theo a job," Phoebe cut in. "Wes doesn't think that restaurant's a fit place for a girl."

"Fit?" Sylvanus said. "Why, Leon's a good man, Phoebe. What *is* this, Wes? What was all that, anyway, about Leon sellin booze?"

"Wes's afraid some of his swell friends'll see me in there waiting on table," Theo said angrily. "He don't want the Beacons to know that anybody in the Sewell family has to earn a living."

"Oh, nuts," Wes said, but he turned brick red.

Sylvanus stared at him. "That's a bad yarn to git started about a man, Wes. Might ruin his business. You put your finger on any special one's said Leon sells booze?"

"Alton Curtis said the Carters bought all their booze off of Leon," Joe piped up.

Sylvanus looked amused, then grim. "Alton said that, did he? When?"

Joe looked uncomfortable. "Oh, the other day."

"If you heard him say it, you must know when it was."

"Can't remember."

"You look here. That story's one I know ain't so. If you can't remember when you heard it, I'm goin to tan you, Joe."

Joe rolled his eyes at his father, then looked scared. "Wes

gi'me and Jim ten cents to say Alton said down round the shore the Carters bought their booze at Leon's," he said.

"Well, for God's sake, Wes." Sylvanus fixed Wes with a cold eye. "What's the idea?"

"Oh, Pa, make him stay out of it," Theo cried. "He's lied his head off to Ma about Leon, and it's only because he's afraid Jane Beacon'll know his sister's a waitress."

"What's wrong with waitin on table? It's honest work and good pay," Sylvanus said.

"Well, it's not what you'd call a high-class job, is it?" Wes said.

"I guess you've come to a place where you feel any kind a work but wet-nursin Felix Beacon hauls ya down in the world, that it?"

"Oh, hell!" Wesley flung himself up from the table. "If a fellow only tries to be somebody around here, he hasn't got a prayer!"

"That's enough a swearin. Family holds you back, eh?"

Wes said nothing.

"By God, Wes, I ought a knock you down. I'm a good mind ever I had to eat, to make you go lobsterin with me this summer, so's you'll know how it feels to git your hands into a little honest bait again."

"No, Syl," Phoebe said. "I don't think Wes meant it that way."

"You know darn well what he meant. You've heard enough of it this winter, ain't you? Beacon this and Beacon that! Plans to spend his own summer tarryhootin around in white flannel pants, so he figgers his sister can't work, because she won't be a credit to him. That beats all! I gether your feelins carried you away, Wes, but if I hear any more of this talk about Leon, I'll take my belt to you as quick as I would to Joe. You talked it around anywheres else but home?"

"No." Wesley turned on his heel and stalked into the sitting room. They heard the stairway door shut behind him with a dignified click.

"My Lord, Phoebe, what ails that kid? Couldn't he even of banged the door a little?"

"Those are his Felix Beacon manners," Theo said.

"Shush, Theo. He'll outgrow it, Syl," Phoebe said.

"Criney, I hope so. Before I'm clean wore out tryin to live up to him."

"But, Syl—*I'm* worried about letting Theo go to work in a restaurant. I don't know's it's a good thing, so young."

In the beginning, Sylvanus would have agreed with her. But he was more outraged than he cared to say by the way Wes had acted. If there was anything Sylvanus hated, it was a snob. Now he'd made up his mind Wes wasn't going to get away with it. If Theo had the spunk to try Leon's this summer, he was going to see she had a chance.

"How'll you git back and forth to work?" he asked.

"The bus. I'll be home nine-thirty, all except two nights. Then Leon has to have someone stay till eleven, on account of the other waitress has a night off."

"Nights!" Phoebe said, horrified. "I never thought of that."

"Hold on, Phoebe," Sylvanus said. "Leon'll look out for her. I'll go see him."

"We'll talk it over, Syl."

"But I promised to tell Leon tomorrow!" Theo's eyes were beginning to shine. She looked from her father to her mother and back again.

"Well, all right," Phoebe said reluctantly. "I guess you can try it. But the least little thing, Theo, and home you come at a gallop."

"Well, come on, kids," Sylvanus said, getting up from the table. "Shove on your oilcoats, and le's go git Jacky."

He thought, walking soberly through the early dusk, while Jim and Joe raced through the puddles ahead of him, it sure did beat him, what went on in a kid's mind. Wes was seventeen, almost a man. Hell, he *was* a man. When Sylvanus had been seventeen, he'd had a boat and gear of his own and had been earning his own living for three years. If Wes was going to grow up to be underhanded, Sylvanus meant to take steps, though he wondered what on earth any steps he could take would be.

ON the afternoon of the fourth day, the storm blew itself out. The wind stopped in the middle of a gust, as if all at once it had got tired; the sky lightened and in the west appeared a patch of milky cloud, mottled with baby blue. It seemed in almost a matter of minutes the sun was out and the clouds low down on the eastern horizon. For a while they lay, a narrowing strip that changed from blue-gray to silver, and then to pearl, as they slid out of sight in the distance. On the sea, big rollers still tumbled, but the arrogance was gone out of them. Crack Corn Ledges were a full acre of foam, boiling white against blue, but the breeze across them was soft and warm, smelling of wet leaves and loam from the land.

The storm had left the earth as sodden as an old mop. Mud squelched underfoot, gave way suddenly and overran rubbers. Hardhack Brook was out of its banks and lay in a series of crazy lakes in a dozen fields. The shore line was littered with wreckage—seaweed torn from the sea bottom, starfish and shells, mashed into a vast tangle with lobster buoys, warp and traps, and a hundred varieties of flotsam. On the end of the Hook, a twenty-foot section of fish wharf, broken away from somewhere down the coast, washed up and down in the breakers, its big timbers grinding to fur on the bare rock with a noise like thunder.

The village came out into the golden weather. Windows were thrown open. Little boys, where they could get out of sight of their mothers, took off shoes and stockings and ran wildly through puddles of icy water. It looked as if the storm in its ramping had found somewhere the first warm and pleasant afternoon of spring and in departing had dropped it down carelessly over the land.

Emily Sewell came out of her house and went fearfully down the pasture lane to the shore. She had made up her mind that after the storm she was going walking, come what would. She just couldn't bear to stay in the house any longer. Morgan had hooted at her for being afraid of cows; but he'd told her that if she stayed in the lane, which was fenced on both sides, she couldn't possibly meet any. Nonetheless, she wasn't taking any chances. It didn't look like a strong fence. She almost ran down the lane, especially where the bushes closed in, being careful not to stumble, of course, on account of the baby. On the shore, where Morgan had convinced her that cows couldn't come, because they'd break their legs, she found a sheltered niche, high on a sloping ledge, and sat down in it to get her breath.

The sea was running up the rocks in fine style. As far as the eye could see, big humpbacked waves were parading in, blue and smooth until they hit the shoals, then curving green and silver, just before they crashed. The sun was strong and warm, the air full of smells. . . . You'd always heard the sea smelled so wonderful, Emily thought. But it didn't. There was a kind of salt smell, all mixed up with another, strong one, that was like an open-air privy.

After a while, Emily took off her heavy coat and folded it on the rock to sit on. It was a lot nicer down there, looked at close to, than she'd thought it would be. Anyone might even enjoy sitting here in the warm, knowing the leaves were at last coming out in those bushes over there, if only she could sit still and not be worried. She was feeling better today, not sick to her stomach at all, though she didn't believe she'd ever get used to the queer, jumpy sensation she got when the baby moved. Things might be ever so much better, only she just didn't know what to make of Morgan.

When they'd first been married, before they'd come here to his home, he'd been so different. Anything she'd wanted, he would do—would come on the run at her first hint. He'd been so good-looking, too, in his spick-and-span Navy uniform, with his hair clipped short across the back of his pink neck. One of the things she'd liked when she first fell in love with him was running her hand along the back of his neck, feeling it silky one way and prickly the other. When he'd had his shore leaves, they'd gone everywhere—to dances and movies and on little picnics out in the country; and all her friends had thought he was such a jolly boy, always laughing and full of fun.

Now, when he came home at night, he ate supper in his same old clothes that he'd worn out fishing all day—the pants, that is, he seldom bothered to put on a jacket at the table. Not that she wasn't used to work clothes on menfolks, but Morgan's did always have that horrid smell of lobster bait, he said it was. It wouldn't have taken him a minute to put on different pants and a clean shirt. His hair always seemed to be shaggy over his collar, too. He said he couldn't take time off to go have it cut. He'd wanted her to trim it for him, and she had, but it didn't look the same as a barber's haircut. He didn't seem to care.

He didn't care, either, whether he ever went anywhere. Of course, there weren't many places to go here; but there was a movie over in Bellport and dances around different places on Friday nights. Not that she cared about dancing now, she looked too funny—but nobody would see you if you went and sat in a movie. Morgan, though, said he was too tired to go out nights. He'd sit down after supper with his account books, and then he'd either lie on the couch and go to sleep, or he'd go off upstairs to bed at half-past-eight. When she'd suggested that he sleep later mornings, so he wouldn't be so tired at night, he'd looked at her as if she were crazy.

Oh, he wasn't mean to her or anything, and he waited on her and got his own meals when she felt sick. But if she felt all right, he seemed to think now that it was her place to wait on *him*. He'd just purely forgotten all the nice little things he used to do. Worst of all, he didn't seem to remember that she liked company. When she'd lived at home, the house was always full, people running in and out, something going on every minute. Now she was by herself almost every day. She could scarcely wait for him to get home at night and then, when he did come, he didn't have three words to say.

Thinking about down home, Emily felt the tears start in the corners of her eyes. She cried a lot lately, and today she'd said she wouldn't. But the tears wouldn't stay back. After a while, she let them roll down. Maybe he'd let her go home for a visit, she thought; but oh, he wouldn't, he was so funny about money now . . .

She was wiping away the last of the tears, feeling a little better, when she heard a slight shuffling noise behind and below her among the piled ledges. She froze with horror. Had the cows got down here, after all? Morgan had told her there wasn't a thing . . . She turned around.

Two apparently disembodied heads stood at the end of the ledge, which sloped down to a dropoff from where she was, as motionless as if somebody had cut them off and set them there on their necks. One had a dried brown monkey face under a peaked cap, on the other, a yellow sou'wester was pushed far back over beady black eyes and an immense curly white beard.

Emily gasped, "Oh!" and the heads were instantly withdrawn.

From the ledge below, a voice said, "The's a woman up there."

Another voice said, "Who in hell is it?"

The things were human then. Maybe she needn't be quite so scared. Still there was no way off the ledge except to walk right down by them. On the other side of her was the sea.

There was a slight silence, during which the owner of the first voice must have peeked up over the ledge again, for he said, "It's Morgan Sewell's wife—that Southern woman."

"Well, what's she doin?"

"She's a-settin on a rock."

I never heard anything so impolite, thought Emily. Peeking at people and discussing them.

As a matter of fact, Foley and Uncle Wheat thought they were lowering their voices. Uncle Wheat's was about half its usual volume, and Foley had conversed with him so long that he didn't realize he'd got into the habit of speaking loud, too. If you had asked them, they would have said they were whispering.

"She see us?"

"Sure, she see us. She's scairt to death. It's that wool carpet you wear on your face, Wheat."

"Scairt?" Uncle Wheat said indignantly. "I never scairt a woman in my life!" He stuck his head up over the ledge again and bellowed, "Excuse me!"

"Oh," Emily said again, faintly. She knew who he was now—Morgan had pointed him out to her as Gram Sarah's next-door neighbor. He lived with his daughter, Mat Dawes. She didn't know the other one. But no need to be afraid of them, they were only a couple of old men.

She got up and walked down the slope of the ledge. "I was just going home," she said distantly.

"Didn't mean to bother ya," Uncle Wheat said. "Foley 'n me was passin by, like, walkin the shore line to see what's washed ashore. We didn't know the' was anybody up there."

"That's *quite* all right." Emily paused in the middle of the ledge. How had she got up here? It seemed a good deal steeper, looking down. Where the two old men stood, it was almost as high as their heads and cut off straight down. Oh, yes—just beyond them were the two steep steps up which she had come.

"Come on, Wheat," Foley said. He jerked his head impatiently. "Come on!"

But as Emily passed him, Uncle Wheat saw that she had been crying and he was staggered. She *had* been scared! She was pretty, too. For a moment he was speechless with contrition, then he came charging around the ledge.

"Why, us two big lunks!" he roared. "Standin there gawpin

at a lady! Somebody ought to of kicked us in the— Somebody ought to of kicked us. But when we stuck our heads up, there, we was as took aback as you was. For a minute, I thought it was a mermaid."

Foley uttered a sound which was halfway between a strangle and a blat. "Well, I'm goin, Wheat," he announced.

"You wait a minute, Foley, an stop your blartin." He smiled up at Emily. "Foley, he ain't got no use whatever for the wimmenfolks," he said confidentially. "That's kind of steep there, Mis' Sewell. You step over here, I'll help you down." Gallantly, he held out his hand.

Emily had been admired too often in her time not to recognize admiration when she saw it. It was balm to her spirit. She hesitated, then smiled back. "It is steep here, isn't it?" she said. "I was just wondering how I got up here." She took hold of his hand and stepped heavily down the rock.

The hand was hard and dry and warm, a little like an old stick that had been lying in the sun, but it felt strong and oddly comforting. Besides, that had been a nice thing to say, that about the mermaid.

"Thank you, Captain Salisbury," she said.

Uncle Wheat beamed like a whiskery sun. "By darn," he said. "I never had no idea you knowed who I was."

"Oh, yes," Emily said. "Even if we haven't met yet. Morgan told me. But I don't know your friend."

"Him? Oh, that's Foley Craddock."

Foley gave Wheat a distant stare. "*Mister* Foley Craddock," he said.

"Howdy do," Emily said. "I know you're some of my neighbors, but I haven't been out around much since I came."

Uncle Wheat said heartily, "Well, I should just guess not!" and then, seeing her blush, passed it over quickly. "When I see you was cryin, I could of fell right over. Been scairt myself, though, 'f I'd looked round onexpected into that lookin mug of Foley's."

"Oh, no," Emily said brightly. "It wasn't Mr. Craddock. I

was looking at the ocean. It was so beautiful, I had to shed a tear or two."

"Ei?" Uncle Wheat glanced around in bewilderment at the water. "Oh. Well, 'tis a modrit high sea, ain't it?"

"I was going to take a walk," Emily went on. "But I'm not used to cliffs like these."

"Cliffs? Oh, the ledges. Well, it's smooth down along the beach. The's a nice path, too, along the shore."

Emily smiled at him. "I'd love to know the way along there."

She was feeling better again and this was more sociable than she'd been in months. Captain Salisbury was as nice as he could be. Mr. Craddock didn't seem to like her much, but that was only because he was shy of women. He was marching along the rocks in front of her, his back upright and stiff. It was a challenge not to be liked by a man, even an old one, and Emily's eyes began to brighten. She noticed now that he was carrying a big bucket, half full of assorted objects.

"Oo," she said, peering. "What funny things, Mr. Craddock. What are they?"

Foley did not turn around. "The's severeal objects in there," he said. "Which one was it you was intrusted in?"

"Why, that one." She indicated a swirled shell, pointing, so that he had to look to see which one she meant.

"That," Foley said remotely, "is a cuckoo."

"Oh. For goodness' sake!" She gave a little puzzled laugh. "I just know you gentlemen will think I'm dumb! I don't know my way around here at all, everything is so different. Down where I come from, I always heard a cuckoo was a bird."

"Well, it ain't," said Foley. "That's a cuckoo, right there."

Uncle Wheat, puffing along behind, let out a wheezy bawl.

"Foley! Don't be so goddam dumb! How d'you know but what it ain't a bird, down where she lives? You ain't never been south a Vinal Haven."

"Oh, my!" Emily exclaimed. "I don't know the least thing in the world about it, Mr. Craddock, but I do seem to remember a poetry piece in my seventh grade reader that went 'The cuckoo tunes his merry note, Tu whit, Tu whoo.' Why, there, Mr. Craddock, I've just thought. I reckon you must mean cockle!"

Foley did not slacken his pace nor turn his head.

"Foley," Uncle Wheat bellowed, "she had it in her *reader*."

"I don't care where she had it. A cuckoo's a cuckoo. I never heard him tune no note except to say squeak when he sucks onto a rock. 'Tu whit, Tu whoo,' for God's sake!"

Emily laughed again. "It does sound foolish," she admitted, "when you put it that way."

Foley snorted. His pace had carried him on ahead of them and he clambered down a rock face and was lost to view.

"No more manners'n a gander," Uncle Wheat spluttered. "Now, you don't want t' mind Foley. He ain't himself when the's a woman around."

"I don't mind him at all," Emily said. "I think he's *sweet*."

"Ei?" Uncle Wheat digested this in silence as they climbed down onto the beach. "Who? Foley?"

Foley was already halfway along the beach, putting distance as fast as possible between himself and them.

"What does he use the cuckoo for?" Emily asked.

"Darn fool biles and eats em," Uncle Wheat said. "Don't see how he can stomach it. Me, I'd just as soon eat a goddam angleworm. Or a snail."

"Oh, snails," Emily said. "I've eaten them. You get them at a French restaurant."

"You've et *snails?*" Uncle Wheat said. "Oh, no. You can't of et snails."

"Oh, yes. They're good. Are cuckoos like them? I reckon I might like cuckoos, too."

"My Lord!" Uncle Wheat stumped along for a minute in silence. "Them French," he said. "They'll eat anything. We hed a French cook once, board a the vessel, tried t' git me t' eat frogs. I said I would, if he'd drink some brook water and brouse. Turned out, it warn't a bargain."

"What on earth is 'brook water and brouse'?"

"Hot water and . . . er . . . molasses," Uncle Wheat said hastily. "Look, there's a cuckoo right there Foley missed."

Emily pounced and picked it up from the sand. "I'd like to try it. I'm going to take it home and boil it. What else does he find? Could we find some more?"

"I guess so." Uncle Wheat followed her out along the beach. "You wun't want more'n one," he said.

It seemed there were many things on the beach worth finding. They piled up a sizable heap of cuckoos—or Emily did, Uncle Wheat wouldn't touch them—along with three big stranded sea crabs which still showed faint signs of life; and Uncle Wheat, burrowing under the seaweed, found four or five lobster buoys with length after length of tangled warp.

Emily forgot she was a sober married woman now, going, in a few months, to have a baby. She galloped awkwardly from pile to pile of driftwood, pouncing on her finds with squeals of delight. She never would have thought a beach could be such fun.

Some things about her certainly surprised Uncle Wheat, but, he thought, she was a nice, pretty girl. Of course, any of the womenfolks around here, in her condition, wouldn't have hung around the beach with him and Foley. But, by darn, he thought it was nice, and by darn, if he could see any harm in it. If he knew that work machine of a Morgan, she probably hadn't been having much fun—not the kind of fun, anyway, that a young girl was entitled to. By darn, he liked to see a boy work, but not the way Morgan did—as if he only had ten minutes, and five of that to finish his life in.

Well, she was having as good a time now as a little kid, and Uncle Wheat didn't know but so was he. There she was, climbing up that bank like a ten-year-old, after something she'd spotted up there. Her cheeks had got pink and her hair was fluffed out with the damp air.

When Foley came back, having underrun his end of the beach, Uncle Wheat was resting, his back against a comfortably slanting boulder. He had heaped driftwood sticks together and had a fine fire going. Emily was out of sight somewhere up the bank. Foley had watched her go up there. She hadn't come back, so he was pretty sure she'd gone home. But he was still wary. "She gone?" he asked, peering.

"Where you been?" Uncle Wheat greeted him. "I thought you was never going t' git back here with that bucket. I found three crabs. Hustle up and put some water in it and stick it on to heat. I'm starvin to death."

"Oh, Mr. Craddock," Emily called.

"Why'n hell don't she go home?" Foley said. "Well, I'm headed there, right now."

"Ain't you goin t' eat? Hell, Foley, we always eat. I gut a whole box a buttered saltines here. You know, she told me she bet she'd like cuckoos," Uncle Wheat went on, hoping to soften Foley's mood.

Foley set the bucket down. A glint came into his eye. "Did, did she? Well, damn if I don't bile some and give em to her."

"My God, Foley! Them cussid things ain't fit fodder—make her sick's a dog."

Foley merely grinned. He dumped his bucket and carried it down the beach, where he rinsed it carefully and half filled it with sea water. Then he brought it back and set it on the fire.

Uncle Wheat looked worried. But a cuckoo couldn't be much worse'n a snail, he thought. If ever she'd et a snail, which of course she hadn't.

Emily called again cheerfully from the top of the bank. "Isn't Mr. Craddock back yet?"

"Ei?" Foley grunted.

"I've found a buoy with your name on it and some rope, only it's up in a bush and I can't get it down."

"That so?" So far, Foley hadn't found any of his own buoys. He'd begun to think he'd got off lucky. He scrambled up the bank, finding it a little steep for his spindly legs, and came out on top beside her.

The buoy was caught in a scrawny alder which had taken a

beating in the storm—the sea had evidently broken clean up over the bank at this point. Foley bent the alder over and hauled the buoy out. The warp was caught on something on the other side of the bush, and walking around there, he saw it was his trap.

"I'll be darned," Foley said, in his absorption forgetting Emily belonged to the hated tribe. "Trap 'n all's on it. Must've been some roller, hove that way up here. That was one I set out by Candlemas Island."

"Where's Candlemas Island, Mr. Craddock?"

Foley pointed. "Second island, way off there. T' other one's Lurvey's."

"You mean the sea was strong enough to carry that heavy thing all that distance?"

"Sure was. It never walked."

The top laths of the trap were smashed in, but the bows holding the heads were intact, and in the trap were two lobsters and a sculpin.

"Big rollers picked it up, washed it in, must of, right over the tops of the rocks without hittin much," he marveled. "See, it ain't smashed bad, considerin."

"Oo!" Emily said. "What's that funny thing?"

Suddenly he observed she was right at his shoulder. He recoiled. "That's a sculpin. You have him in your reader, buildin a nest?"

Emily giggled. "I don't remember him," she said.

Foley coiled up what remained of the warp and tucked it for safe-keeping inside the trap with the buoy. Then he gingerly picked out the lobsters and without another word, went back down the bank.

The water was boiling and into it Uncle Wheat had chucked his three sea crabs. "Where'd you git them?" he demanded. "Them's short lobsters, Foley."

"Make all the better eatin," Foley grunted.

"They alive? If they ain't alive, they ain't fit to cook."

"They ain't too dead." Foley chucked the lobsters into the bucket. On top of all, he poured a generous pile of cuckoos.

Uncle Wheat made a retching noise.

"Go ahead and puke," Foley said. "All I care." He put a rock the size of his head on top of the brew to hold it down, and then stretched out, his hat over his face.

Emily said wistfully, "Well, if you gentlemen're going to eat, I reckon I better run along home. I've had a lovely time."

"Go home before the fodder's done?" Uncle Wheat protested. "Why, the's plenty for all. You stay'n have a mug-up with us."

Foley grinned, without moving his cap off his face. "Like to have you stay 'n try the cockles," he said politely.

"Oh, thank you!" She plumped down at once beside the fire. "I do love a picnic. I was hoping you'd invite me. We always had a lot of picnics down home. My whole family and all our friends."

"Picnic country, down south, I guess," Uncle Wheat said.

"Oh, yes! It's lovely. All flowers and the spring comes early. Not cold, like here." She hesitated. "I don't mean it isn't nice here, of course. It's just— Well, I—"

"I know what you mean," Uncle Wheat boomed. "Darn climate here ain't fit for an Esquimau. Colder'n hell, up to July, and then it starts to be fall. You ain't used to it. Don't seem like home."

"Oh, no, it doesn't at all. And down home, we had so many friends. Here, I'm not very well acquainted, I reckon."

"Kind of lonesome, is it?"

"You mustn't think I don't like the people here, and of course Morgan's lovely to me, but—"

"Well, now I'll tell ya," Uncle Wheat said. "When I was on the vessel, I used t' git round a lot a places. I was to Baltomore, once," he said. "Baltomore, Maryland."

"My goodness. You were a long way from home."

"Yes, sir, I was."

"I was to Bangor, once," Foley muttered, under his cap.

Uncle Wheat went on. "And you know, I couldn't git acquainted there."

"You couldn't?"

"No, sir, I couldn't. If I was to of died and rotted on a post in the middle of the town, I wouldn't a knowed a soul, nor would they a knowed me."

"Like me, here," said Emily.

"But after I was there a month—I gut held up on repairs to the vessel and waiting for a cargo—after I was there a month, I had all the friends I could stick."

"I've been here almost *six* months."

"You ain't had the advantage," Uncle Wheat said. "Now, me, I warn't goin to have a baby—excuse me. What I mean is, I was out 'n around a lot. You pick up and go callin on some of the wimmenfolks around, whether you know em or not."

"Oh, I couldn't . . . wouldn't they mind?"

"They'd like it. That's what they're waitin for. Folks round here is always slow to git acquainted, that's all it is. Take the wimmen, the's all kinds, a course, some's worth knowin, like anywhere, some ain't."

"Who of em is?" said Foley morosely.

Uncle Wheat grinned and jerked his head. "He's crazy as a hoot owl. All you got to know is how they tick."

"Sometimes I think I'll never know how they tick," she said dolefully. "Morgan's folks . . . Phoebe. She's come calling, but she doesn't talk, and I can't think of one thing to say to her."

"You wait till you get acquainted with her. Phoebe's one of the nicest wimmen I ever saw, only she don't lep right into the gabblin, the first time she sees ya."

"It takes so long—"

"Well, yistiddy, you didn't know me and Foley, did ya?"

"Why, that's right, I didn't!"

"You come see my girl, Mat," Uncle Wheat said. "That's Mat Dawes, over to my house. She'll talk your livin ear off. I'll tell her you're a-comin."

"I will," she cried. "Oh, that's ever so nice of you, Captain Salisbury. I'll come soon."

"You do," he said. "Foley, ain't the fodder done?"

Foley grunted and got up. Using his cap for a pot holder, he emptied the hot salt water out on the sand, dumped the rock, and without a word set the steaming bucket down beside Emily.

Uncle Wheat looked distressed. He said nothing, however, but reached into the pocket of his jacket and brought up a flat box of saltines.

"Nothin like buttered crackers t' go with cuckoos," Foley said, smacking.

"Now you have some crabs," Uncle Wheat said. "Them cuckoos ain't fit."

"Why, of course I'm going to try them," she said. She picked one up and dropped it, flapping her fingers. "Oo! They're hot! How d'you get at them?"

"Here," Foley said. Holding one of the steaming shells in his horny fingers, he speared out its coiled, unpleasantly mottled inhabitant with the small blade of his jackknife, and held it out to Emily. It looked a little like a snail, she saw, and she put it on a cracker and ate it. For a moment, a faint look of astonishment crossed her face. Then she said, "Why! That's odd tasting, fishy, but isn't it nice! Could I have another?"

Uncle Wheat, who had closed his eyes, popped them open and stared. Then he said, "Haw!" and slapped his leg.

Foley looked dazed. A slight, foolish grin appeared on his face. He handed her the knife. "You use this, Mis Sewell," he said. "I'll use a splinter."

WHEN Morgan came home to supper at five-thirty, he was surprised and concerned to find Emily not there. It wasn't like her—always before, she'd met him at the door with an air of having waited for hours.

That's funny, he thought. He set his dinner bucket on the sink drainboard, and tramped through the sitting room to call up the stairs. No, she wasn't upstairs lying down. She wasn't in the shed. The oil burner in the kitchen range was turned down, the way he'd showed her to fix it if she went out anywhere. Morgan turned it up and set the teakettle forward on the stove. Might as well start things going a little, before he looked around. He was in a hurry and hungry; after all, she'd probably just gone out walking and hadn't got back, it was such a nice day. She'd said this morning she might try going down on the shore as soon as the weather cleared off. If anything really serious was wrong—if she was sick or had to go to the doctor, somebody would have come after him down to the Cove. It wasn't as if the whole village didn't know where he'd been all afternoon.

As soon as it had stopped raining, he'd rounded up Phil Dalzell and Alton Curtis, the two fellows he'd hired to help him build weir, and they'd all gone down to Patch's Cove. What he'd wanted to do was to take the boat and dories over to Barrel Island for a load of weir stuff; but the sea was still too rough. You could have landed all right on the loo'ard side of the island; getting off again with a couple of loaded dories would have been something else again. This west wind was knocking the sea down fast, though.

Patch's Cove was sheltered, and they'd been able to pile up some rocks, which, later on, he could use to brace against the leader poles, in shallow water. They might have handled more, if Phil and Alton hadn't felt they had to talk with everybody who came by. Morgan hadn't said anything today; he sure was going to put a stop to that, though, if it kept on. He wasn't paying them a dollar and twenty cents an hour to beat their gums.

The Cove was about a quarter of a mile down the shore from the village—just about a good walk—and quite a few people, including some womenfolks, had walked that way today. They'd let on they were stretching their legs in the good weather after the storm. What it was, they were hanging around to see if there was going to be any kind of a flap between him and the Carters.

They might have saved themselves the trouble. The Carters hadn't even come over from their shack on the other side of the Cove. All the afternoon, Morgan could see them—Warren and Berry moving around doing something to an old punt—calking her, looked like; and the old man, his father's cousin, stretched out on a sunny boulder, apparently asleep. It bothered Morgan. They must know, by now, what he was doing—everybody else did—and Morgan had expected Job to come boiling right over, the first day he set to work on the weir.

Morgan even had what he was going to say all planned out. He was going to show his deeds and say pleasantly that as long as Job and the boys weren't any trouble to him, they could live on his land. Otherwise, they'd have to move somewhere else.

Not doing anything at all wasn't like Job. He was usually raring and cussing around at the slightest provocation. But maybe having to move out of the Cove was what Job had foreseen.

Well, it was all right with Morgan. He was the last one to want trouble.

Where in thunder could Emily be? If he had to wait around for her or go hunt her up, it would sure put a crimp in his plans. There was a section of fish wharf pounding around on Granite Hook Head, knocked loose from somewhere in the storm. Before dark, he meant to go and tow it in.

From what he could tell through his glasses, it was a pretty good section of wharf, not too big for one man in a boat to tow, if he could get a line on it and it wasn't grounded too hard on the rocks. He'd been planning to build a wharf with a fish house on it over in the Cove, to have for a landing place and to store his nets and gear in, winters. It looked as though here was the start of it, if only he could get it before someone else did. On the high water slack, the sea ought to have gone down enough so he could go in close to the Hook in his boat. It might be taking a chance, but by morning, everybody in town would be off there after that wharf.

Morgan fretted, going from one window to another. The teakettle boiled and he made tea, thinking that there was one thing he wouldn't have to wait for her to do when she got home. He was just setting the tea on the back of the stove to brew when he heard her coming, talking away to somebody ten to a dozen.

That's funny, he thought. I didn't know she knew anybody here that well.

He flung open the door and saw her, flanked by Foley and Uncle Wheat, coming up the walk.

"Oh, Morgan," she called out. "I was just hoping and praying you hadn't got home. You *are* early, aren't you, dear?"

"I was home at five-thirty. It's six now."

"It is!" she wailed. "Oh, your poor supper, I'm so sorry. But I've had the loveliest time, wait till I tell you." Her cheeks glowed and her eyes looked brighter than they had in months. She went flitting past him into the house without noticing his mood. "Mr. Craddock," her voice came back, accompanied by a furious rattling of tins, "you set that pail right down while I get a pan. Morgan, Mr. Craddock's given us some cuckoos, and I'm going to fix a sauce and give you some for supper."

"Cuckoos!" Morgan said, staring at Foley's pail. "Good God!"

Foley merely stared back at him, dead pan, without saying anything.

What *is* this? Morgan thought. Cuckoos weren't poison, but you wouldn't think of eating them, any more than you would a skate or a dogfish. He'd heard it said that Foley'd tried all three—didn't care what he lived on, just so it filled him up. But to offer a nice woman a mess of them for supper—anybody but Emily'd have known better than to accept them, too.

After all, Foley was a crony of Job Carter's. He could be expressing his opinion of the Patch's Cove business.

Emily appeared from the kitchen with a big agate iron kettle. "Oh, don't you like them, Morgan? Captain Salisbury doesn't either, but they're just like snails, dear, except for a little odd, sea-foody taste. You remember the time we had the snails with that lovely sauce at the French restaurant, down home? Well, I know how to make the sauce."

Morgan caught the shadow of a grin on Uncle Wheat's face. So that old devil was in on it, too!

"Now, this kettle's too big, Mr. Craddock," Emily said, "but it's all I could find. I don't want you to rob yourself."

Foley, without comment, emptied into the kettle his entire supply of cuckoos.

"Oh, you won't have any left! Just a few'll be enough for us, won't it, Morgan?"

"That's all right. I can git plenty more," Foley said.

"Well, thank you a thousand times," Emily gurgled. "Oh, Morgan, we've been beachcombing and had such fun. Won't you gentlemen come in to supper, anyhow?"

Foley, without taking his noncommittal stare off Morgan, said no, he guessed he'd have to step along home, feed his cat.

Uncle Wheat merely said, "No, thanks. Good night, Mis Sewell. Evenin, Morgan," in a dignified voice and walked off down the path.

"Why, Morgan," Emily said. "You weren't a bit nice."

"Gentlemen!" Morgan burst out. "*Captain* Salisbury! *Mr.* Craddock! Where in God's name you been?"

"Down on the beach, dear. I told you. Where you said to go. We had a fire and cooked a lot of things, and I don't know if I can eat a mouthful, but I would like to try some with that sauce. I've—"

"Have you been on a *picnic* with those two old rips?" he asked in an icy voice.

"Why, yes. Why not?"

"They're soused half the time and neither one of them talks fit for a woman to hear, that's all. Foley's the worst old bum in town."

"They weren't drunk. They were every inch a gentleman."

"My God! You've got funny ideas of a gentleman."

"Why, Morgan! Down home, we went around with all kinds of people. Some of the Navy boys used to drink and swear, sometimes. You did yourself."

"That was different. That was in the Navy. This is at home."

She turned on him like a flash, tears of anger in her eyes.

"Well, that was *my* home, I'd just like you to remember, Morgan Sewell. My folks put up with a lot from you boys. I don't know why you're fussing, anyway. All I did was spend the afternoon with two perfectly nice old men, and make your supper late."

"Nice! That Foley ain't even human. You hang around on the beach with tripe like that, you'll get yourself talked about."

"I'm sure that's the first time I ever heard that these folks around here could talk," she blazed at him. "Maybe they talk *about* people, they certainly don't talk *to* them. Well, I'm just done sitting around the house, Morgan Sewell, waiting for you to come home and eat. If I find somebody to be friendly, I'm going to talk to them, that's all!"

"You ain't bent over backwards to be friendly, yourself," Morgan said. "At least, that's what Marm says."

"I suppose you call what she does being friendly. Shaking people's beds down and snooping around their kitchen and calling them pigs!"

"She was only helping you out. The place did look like a pigpen, the day she cleaned it up."

"Oh!" For an instant, she was speechless with rage. "You know perfectly well I was sick."

"Oh, thunder, Emly! Call it off, will you? I've got to get back to the shore. I can't chew the rag all night. Cook me some supper, will you?"

"You can just cook your own cuckoos, Morgan Sewell!"

"Oh, for the love of God!" Morgan had forgotten the cuckoos. He gave the kettle on the step a boot, sending it bottom-up out across the grass.

Emily burst into tears. She turned and went into the kitchen, and in a minute he heard her feet go pounding up the stairs.

He hesitated, thinking, Gee, I ought to go make it up. After all, she hadn't known about Uncle Wheat and Foley, or about cuckoos, either. Maybe he'd been a little harsh, and getting mad like that couldn't be very good for her. But some of the things she'd said had hit him on sensitive places. She was the only one around here who knew that he'd let go and had some fun while he'd been in the Navy. Away from home, like that, he'd figured a man was entitled to. She hadn't any reason, though, to make out he'd been a souse, because all he'd done was take a drink now and then, when the other fellows were drinking. He didn't even like the stuff. Hell, let her get over it by herself. He'd make up later on, when he had time and after he got some supper. He jammed his cap over his ears and stalked out of the house, headed for his mother's.

Gram Sarah had finished her supper and cleared it away, but she had plenty and she was delighted to warm it up again for Morgan. When she heard he was in a hurry, she set before him in jig time a noble repast of fried potatoes, baked beans and apple pie.

"Emly sick again?" she asked, sitting down to talk to him while he ate.

"No," he said briefly.

Hah! Gram Sarah thought. They've had a fight. "Jumpy," she said aloud. "She'll feel better after the baby comes."

"Lord, I hope so."

Ordinarily he would have made excuses for Emily, but tonight, she saw with pleasure, he didn't.

"Seems as though she could manage to be on her feet a little more, with you workin so hard," Gram Sarah said.

"She is on her feet. She's been down on the beach to way past suppertime."

"On the *beach!* The shape she's in!"

"Well, I suggested her takin a walk this mornin. She hasn't been out of the house since God knows when. But I never supposed she'd make a day of it." Between bites, he recounted the picnic, while she listened with a face of indignation that made him feel much better.

"Why, them two old hellions!" she exclaimed. "I hope to the Lord nobody saw her, Morgan."

"Oh, they probably did. Be all over town tomorrow."

"Well, I hope you told that girl a thing or two."

Morgan was feeling himself again. Having his supper had helped, and by now he was beginning to wish, a little uncomfortably, that he hadn't told his mother quite so much. If he knew her, she was quite capable of lighting into Emily about it.

"Oh, well, of course she didn't know," he said, pushing back his chair.

"That ain't no excuse. And them cuckoos, Morgan! You wait till I see that Foley."

"Well . . . look, Ma."

"You needn't smooth me down. Maybe you'll take a slur like that, but I wun't."

Oh, heck, of course she'd talk it around. She'd light right into Emily and she'd light into Foley, and then the fat would be in the fire. Right now, what Morgan wanted was as little trouble as possible with anyone. It was hard to realize, sometimes, that his mother was so old, getting a little childish. He racked his brain to think of something that would get her off on another track.

"Look, Ma," he said. "I'd rather you didn't mention this, specially to Emily. She's already kind of upset about it, and you know it don't do her and the baby any good. I'd kind of like to get her calmed down, get rid of a few notions. Lord knows, she's got plenty now—why, the latest is, she wants to go to the hospital."

"To the hospital!" Gram Sarah said, shocked. "She sick?"

"To have the baby." Morgan, actually, didn't think it a bad idea—as a matter of fact, he'd told Emily so, and she was planning, when the time came, to go over to the Bellport Hospital. But if he'd wanted to sidetrack Gram Sarah, he couldn't have done better.

"Don't you have nuthin t' do with hospitals, Morgan! All they do is kill ya and charge ya a bill. A woman's better off to home, where she can git good care."

"Oh, I don't know," Morgan said, to nail it down. "I could afford it, if it would make her feel better."

"You tell her no! A woman . . . it ain't decent, all them doctors a-lookin . . ."

"I've got to hustle, Ma," Morgan broke in. "Wish I could stay—I will another night. Thanks for the meal." He picked up his cap and was gone through the door before she had half finished what she had in mind to say, which, Gram Sarah thought, wasn't a bit like Morgan. He always stayed at least until she got through talking. He must be in an awful rush about something.

As soon as he was out of sight down the road, she took her spyglass out on the doorstep and focused it on his boat, out in the harbor. Sure enough, there he came, rowing out in his punt. In an awful hurry, too, just shoving the punt through the water. She watched him get aboard, start his engine and cast off. The boat headed down the harbor, then sheared across toward the end of the Hook and ran in close to shore.

"Now, what's he foolin around over there for?" she fretted. "He knows better'n to git in so close to them breakers."

The spyglass, sweeping along the foam-covered shore line of the Hook, picked up the section of wharf floating in the surf. As she looked, a breaker boiled up and broke across it, burying it in spray.

"Oh, my Lord!" Gram Sarah didn't wait to fold up the glass and hang it on its hook. She left it on the doorstep, grabbed her shawl, and hot-footed it down the road to get Sylvanus.

THE surf was still pretty high on the Hook, Morgan saw, as he drew in close to the ledges. But high tide had floated the wharf free of the rocks; it was plunging up and down, just behind the place where the big green ones curled over and smashed in a boiling welter that ran high up the shore. The west wind, blowing across the Hook, was pushing the wharf off; the breakers, running up from the southeast, were trying to push it on again. If only the wind were a little stronger—but now, after sunset, it was more likely to go down.

The backwash from the surf sucked out under the boat and a comber that seemed larger than the others gathered up just behind him. For a moment, it towered, humpbacked and green, looking as big as a house. Then the boat slid smoothly up and over it and shot down to smooth water on the other side. But Morgan heard it hiss as it went by—he saw the green crest start a foamy curl just beyond the stern of the boat.

Holy smoke! he thought. I guess I'm in a little too close. That one almost broke over me.

He opened his throttle and jigged off, just in case. There was an underwater ledge that stuck up along here somewhere; he was pretty sure he knew where it was—he wasn't anywhere near it. One thing seemed certain, he wasn't going to be able to get near enough to that wharf to get a chain on it.

He'd brought what he hoped was the right rig—about forty feet of light mooring chain, with a big hook wired to one end of it. The other end he had fastened to the boat by hooking two links over the stern cleat and taking a couple of turns. The chain had been part of his father's gear. He hadn't any idea what the old man had used it for, but it had been lying around in the fish house for years. Maybe it would be some use at last, if he could get close enough to that wharf to catch the hook over something.

That last breaker had been the biggest of the lot, he saw, as he waited from a safer vantage point and watched them roll in. None of the others seemed anywhere near its size. The sea was going down. Maybe if he waited until another big one broke, then ran in as close as he dared and gave the chain a heave—still, it was quite a chance to take, and the hook probably wouldn't catch on anything. There was a jagged timber, though, which had started off, probably broken when the wharf tore away. If he could throw the chain over the end of it and take up the slack, the hook might, just possibly, get wedged in the crack.

The next wave broke—it still wasn't as big as the first one —and following it came four, five, six, seven peewees, which were hardly more than washes up the rocks. One of them didn't break at all. Then came another sizable one.

The wharf seemed to be drifting inshore. Or was it? He couldn't tell. Anyway, if he wanted it, he'd have to do something. It would be dark pretty soon. And he did want it.

Morgan felt the sweat break out along his shoulder blades. He set his teeth and went in over the backwash of a small breaker, running wide open. He got within ten feet of the wharf, jammed his wheel hard over, and, as the boat swung, let go the chain in a mighty heave out over the stern. Then he jumped back to the wheel.

The hook arced out, fell with a splash on the other side of the wharf.

That sure was a good heave, he thought, with satisfaction.

Watching the chain pull along the wharf toward the timber, he almost forgot the boat was running at full speed. He yanked the throttle back just in time and crunched into reverse. Even so, the jerk as the chain fetched up banged him up against the coop with a thump that fairly knocked the wind out of him. The hook had caught all right. He couldn't tell how securely, but the chain was wedged tight under the jagged timber.

Morgan eased the throttle ahead, feeling the engine start to labor. It was a tough tow for a boat this size. Nothing at first seemed to move. Then he saw that the ungainly mass of timbers was slowly gathering way. It moved about ten feet before it fetched up on something with a grinding crash and heeled over in the water.

He went cold all over. That was a ledge! That was the ledge he'd been wondering about, and he'd been right in over it. His boat didn't draw so much water as the wharf did, that was all. It was God's living wonder he hadn't plunked her and ripped the bottom right out of her.

He gave the engine all it could take, but the wharf didn't budge. He had towed it hard and fast, onto the ledge, and the tide, by now, if it hadn't already started to ebb, would start pretty soon. He'd have to cast loose. Have to give up and lose his chain, too.

Chagrin washed over Morgan in a hot wave. If he'd only remembered just where the ledge was, he could have towed the wharf out by it at an angle. He punched at the throttle, but it was up to the last notch, and the engine was already giving forth a powerful smell of hot oil and metal. He'd burn out a bearing if he didn't quit. Furiously, he eased her off and left the wheel to go back and cast off the chain.

A big breaker nudged the boat sideways, its momentum starting to boost her along on its crest. Morgan got back to the wheel just in time.

Getting loose was going to be a job. A chain wasn't a rope that you could cut with a slash of a knife. He hadn't thought, when he'd hooked those links over his stern cleat, that he might have to cast off in a hurry. He gauged his time between breakers, and managed to get back to the stern.

He found he couldn't cast off the chain. The links were wedged hard against the metal of the cleat.

He ran back to the wheel, straightened the boat up again, and got a hammer. The hammer wouldn't start the links. An ax wouldn't have started them.

Morgan began surging the boat against the chain, letting her drop back for as much slack as he dared, then slamming the throttle wide open. He hoped to break a link, or to jerk the stern cleat out of its screws; but nothing happened except that each time the boat fetched up, it was as if somebody had hit her with a sledge hammer.

He'd have to get out of here pretty soon, because the tide was going down. It wouldn't be long before ledges thrust out of water, nearer and nearer. Riding those combers, too, wasn't the same hung up to a chain as riding them free and easy. The boat's stern was hung down, now; every time a big comber rolled in, she shipped a barrel or so of green water.

It was this predicament Sylvanus found him in when he came roaring at full speed around the end of Granite Hook Head.

From a distance, Sylvanus was yelling, "Cast off, you damn fool! Cast off!" But he stopped as soon as he got close enough to realize about the chain. He maneuvered alongside in the tossing water and hove Morgan a tow rope. "Get up forward and make fast, quick!"

"I can't leave the wheel," Morgan roared back.

"Never mind your christly wheel! If you make fast quick enough, I can straighten her out."

Morgan did as he was told. Presently Syl's big boat was comfortingly at the end of a long towline, holding Morgan's boat head on to the seas.

Sylvanus did no fruitless pulling and hauling. He surged ahead on the towrope once, till he satisfied himself that the combined strength of his boat and Morgan's was only enough to rock the wharf a little on the ledge. Then he merely kept the rope taut until a comber the size of a house rolled in, while Morgan fumed and yelled at him to pull. When the comber humped up under the boats, Sylvanus yelled, "Okay, now. Give her all she's got!"

The engines thundered, the boats strained. Tons of water

washed up on the ledge and the wharf heeled over. With a grinding scrape it slid free.

Together the two boats towed the salvage into Granite Hook Harbor. All the way in, Sylvanus did not look around once from his wheel.

All right, Morgan gritted. It was dumb. But I've got the wharf.

He was icy all over from sweating, but the panic had gone out of him. It was going to be a darned handy wharf.

Inside the harbor, Sylvanus slowed down and dropped back alongside. "Where to?" he asked briefly.

"I'm going to put her into Patch's Cove," Morgan said. "I can handle her from here on. Thanks just the same, Syl."

Sylvanus looked at him quizzically. "Oh, I'm hooked on, might as well help finish it up."

"No need to. I've bothered you enough." Morgan was starting in to worry over whether Sylvanus meant to claim part of the wharf. According to salvage, he could, of course. Sylvanus needed a wharf. He had no shore privilege at all—had to borrow some every time he wanted to put his traps on the bank. It would be a tremendous help to Sylvanus to own part of a wharf with Morgan in the Cove. Glancing up, Morgan saw that Sylvanus had guessed exactly what he was thinking. "Well, cast off, will ya?" he said shortly.

Sylvanus burst into a roar of laughter. "You cast *me* off," he said. "It's my rope."

PART THREE

July

AT lunchtime, Leon's was filled with tourists who wanted to eat and get gone in a hurry. From twelve to two, Theo and Polly Gerrish, Leon's other waitress, were kept on the jump, trying to keep abreast of the orders. Leon himself cooked the short orders on a grill behind the fountain, occasionally, when he got jammed up, bawling for Henry, the chef's assistant, to come out and help him. If the chef could spare Henry, he came, but more often than not, big Biff Sweeney himself, his broad red face running sweat and crowned by his white chef's cap, would thrust out through the swing door and bawl back, "Henry's busy!"

This was a fine touch of local color for the customers and also helped convince them that everything possible was being done for their satisfaction.

At first, Leon's had been like a madhouse to Theo. For a week she never got anything right and sometimes it seemed as if she never would. Her feet ached, her back ached; her arms felt as if they'd drop out of her shoulders. The first time Biff yelled at her, she almost jumped out of her skin and burst into tears. Biff was astounded, and spent the afternoon muttering indignantly to himself.

"Don't pay no attention to him," said Polly. "Chefs is all alike, a beller with a man around it."

Quite soon, Theo found out that Biff's sandpapery yawp didn't mean a thing, except maybe he wanted a teaspoon.

Polly Gerrish was forty, weighed two hundred and was as deft as a bird. She had a steady job at Leon's every summer; in winters, she worked at a similar place in Boston, where she was known. Her folks lived in Bellport. She was pleased, she said, to come and visit from June to fall, but she wasn't like the town—if she died through the winter, she didn't believe she was liable to come to in the spring.

Waiting on table was Polly's profession. She liked it.

"I done good at it," she told Theo, on the first day they met as colleagues. They were putting on their neat blue uniforms in the dressing room at Leon's. "Never wanted to do nothin else, not even to git married. I seen a good many men in my time, and by and large, they're poor things. That bow ain't tied right, honey. Here, turn around."

Her pudgy fingers moved smartly among the crisp lawn strings of Theo's apron. "There. That's fine. You look like a bluebird. Need a little touch of lipstick, though . . . Oh, hey, not too much. Take off about two-thirds. Some girls can stand slathers, but you ain't the type. Not with them red cheeks."

As for new waitresses, Polly said, she'd broke in a million of them. All Theo had to do was to watch her and holler if she got in a jam.

A dozen times during that first hollow panic-stricken week, Theo thanked the Lord for Polly. Even though June wasn't a busy time at Leon's—the tourist season didn't get really under way until July—Polly did two-thirds of the work, sometimes taking over some of Theo's booths when she got behind.

"Now, that's all right, honey," she would say. "You'll jiggle down." Polly never minded how much work she did. Finishing her own, she would like as not go out to the kitchen and help Henry with the dishes.

But by July, Theo was doing her share, the panic gone. As her muscles toughened, she learned to carry loaded trays, as Polly said, "as if your arms was on swivels." She no longer mixed her orders, or, if she did, she knew how, now, to apologize for the mistake without going numb with embarrassment.

Of course, it took second sight, Polly said, to know when to kid a customer, when to let him kid you, and when not to open your frozen-faced yip. But that was something you learned in time. Theo wouldn't need to concentrate on that part of it, seeing she wasn't liable to make waiting on table her lifetime career.

Theo agreed with her. She'd never be as good as Polly was, but she didn't want to be. She'd work the summer out, she told herself, gritting her teeth, because she couldn't let Leon down, and because she wasn't going to take the kidding she'd get at home if she quit. But never again—if she could find any other way to earn money in the summer.

It wasn't the work itself. Polly and Leon were fun to be with; old Biff wasn't bad when you knew him, and Henry was a vague, friendly soul. It was the customers. It was what happened to quite ordinary, pleasant people, when they stepped into a restaurant and sat down to be waited on by a waitress.

Polly said, "Oh, pooh! You don't want to let that bother you. Most people ain't nobody when they're to home, and eatin in a restaurant is the only chance they get to throw their weight around. It's only human nature."

Theo snorted. "Well, it doesn't look human to me. If everything's so lovely in Massachusetts, why don't they stay there?"

She had just waited on a quietly dressed, middle-aged couple who looked nice—as if they went to church on Sundays. They had complained about everything, telling each other how much better the restaurants were back home in Attleboro. They had made it plain that they were leaving no tip here because the food was bad and the service worse.

Polly chuckled. "They was only tryin to make you think they was somebody rich and famous, used to feedin on the fat of the land in the very best of places. Why, back home in Attleboro, he probly works in the A & P and she don't git a chance to eat out once in a year, on her birthday, if that. They've took a week's vacation where nobody knows em, and they're suckin it dry. I've known five million of *them*."

"Why should they care what I think?"

"They have to care," Polly said. "One way you look at it, it's kind of sad."

"Sad? It's a howl, if you ask me."

Polly looked at her thoughtfully. "Someday you'll likely git that idea," she said. She shrugged. "Now, it ain't them kind of people, it's them fat men in shorts and floppy hats that gives me the bellyache."

At two-thirty, except for a later-comer or so, the noon rush was over. Then the place had to be cleaned up for the next crowd, which would appear promptly at four—the ladies from the big summer "cottages" in and near Bellport, who brought daughters and guests for afternoon tea.

Years ago, when Leon's had been a modest ice cream parlor, run by his father, the mothers and grandmothers of the present ladies had started making rendezvous there, because Leon's father knew how to make superlative homemade ice cream.

Bellport was less of a booming tourist resort then; the ladies were the wives and daughters of conservative well-to-do families, whose big summer estates lined the waterfront. Now, Leon had branched out to catch the transient trade; but the present ladies saw no reason to change an institution which their mothers had established; not so long as Leon made a special effort to cater to them.

Every day in summer, at three-thirty, Henry set up four neat folding screens across the rear third of the restaurant and opened the big double back door that looked out on Leon's vegetable garden. Leon's friends kidded him about his vegetable garden being put to such a use. Why didn't he plant flowers, they said, the way other tearooms did? Leon's reply was that he'd always planted vegetables back there; he wasn't going to waste the land. If the ladies wanted to look at flowers, they could go somewhere else. But Leon knew his ladies.

Piloted by their neat chauffeurs, or driving their own impeccable roadsters, the ladies alighted at Leon's front door at four. They slipped between the discreet screens, sat down at his doily-freckled tables—they didn't care for the booths—and looked at his vegetable garden.

It was a fine garden. Leon always had two yards of manure dumped there every fall and plowed in with a ton of rockweed and some bushels of rotten herring. The maroon and green of the beet leaves glistened in the sun with the cream and green of the swiss chard; the young cabbage leaves had a fine smoky bloom. Glossy bean leaves were a frontispiece to the shining curves of the corn. Later in the season, Leon's famous lettuce, which now was crinkled scroll, would be great heavy bosses sprawled on the black earth. His peas already were waist high, showing succulent dangling pods.

The ladies looked on this abundance with approval far more lasting than they would have looked on roses and portulacas. It was not alone the good food, though that was a consideration, and the green potential, previewed here, would appear in its fulfillment on their tables, sold by Leon to their housekeepers all summer long. But it also gave them a glimpse into Leon's private life, the intimate work of his hands, and offered tangible evidence of the deep solidarity and worth of common people. Here, over the tea and the ice cream—for though Leon served Frojoy to the tourists, he still made up his father's recipe, to be frozen by Henry in the back room each day, for his ladies—here they could be reminded that, no matter what the papers said, the foundations of society couldn't be too shaky, when ordinary working people were busy with wholesome creations like Leon's garden.

The afternoon tea hour was Leon's, presided over by him in a white coat, with Theo to help. Polly was too professionally branded for this gathering, so she stayed inside and took over incidental customers at the fountain. The ladies preferred a wholesome local girl—somebody they had watched grow up summers, or whose mother, perhaps, had worked in their kitchens. It kept things simple and homely, which was the keynote of afternoon tea at Leon's.

Theo knew now that this was one reason why Leon had offered her her job at such good pay, when he could have had a choice of any number of older, more experienced girls. Mrs. Beacon was something of a social leader among the ladies. Others of them, too, had cottages around Granite Hook.

The Beacons had arrived to open their cottage in mid-June, as soon as they comfortably could after Jane's and Felix's schools were done. Wesley, of course, had seen them at once, since his job began on the day of their arrival. He was seldom at home now when Theo was, but Phoebe had passed his glowing reports along.

Mr. Beacon had a brand-new dark green Lincoln this year. Mrs. Beacon had taken the Cadillac for hers. They had a Filipino houseboy, whose name was Gino, whom Felix and Jane, and, of course, Wes, called "Gizmo." Jane had grown much prettier; Felix was two inches taller. He had been crazy about the Ford, but now he was talking speedboat. It was just possible that his father might get him one, and, if he did, Wes was to run it, teaching Felix how.

"They seem to think an awful lot of Wesley," Phoebe said, with a certain amount of pride. "Seems as if they'd trust him with anything."

"Seems as if," Theo answered. She kept her face politely blank, listening to her mother, but inside she felt shriveled up with disgust. So Wes was talking motor boat now.

Her own first sight of any of the Beacons this year, had been at Leon's when Mrs. Beacon and Jane came in for tea. She had been standing beside Leon at the tea urn, watching the ladies as they came, greeting each other, past the screens. A good deal of greeting went on, because it was early in the season.

They were the same formidable ladies who had never seemed to change for as far back as she could remember—neither their large, calm faces nor the kind of clothes they wore. Leon said that if Gabriel should blow his horn in the summertime, the Bellport ladies would all attend Judgment Day in long white flannel skirts, flat white shoes, droopy coat sweaters and Leghorn hats with organdy scarves around the crowns.

Leon was very respectful to the ladies, but he said the most outrageous things out of the corner of his mouth, when it looked as if what he was doing was giving Theo directions about the tea.

"There comes Ma Westerly," he would murmur, indicating a plate of sandwiches. "Where in hell d'you suppose she gut that hat? I swear, she's hed the same one for eighteen years. Don't spill nothin on it. She'd never find another one of those, and she rather come out start-nekkid in her skin than come out without that hat."

Round, bald and dignified, Leon would bow formally to Mrs. Westerly.

At first, Theo had trouble keeping her face straight, but if she so much as started a giggle, Leon would turn on a scowl ferocious enough to chill her blood. After a while, she was able to nod gravely, while she moved the plate of sandwiches one inch to the right or left, as the case might be.

When Mrs. Beacon and Jane came in, she saw with relief that they hadn't noticed her—or if they had, they didn't show it. They sat down at a table with a stalwart old lady and a girl who looked to be a little older than Jane. But when Theo took around the tea, Mrs. Beacon smiled and nodded.

"Why, it's Theoline Sewell," she said, as if she had just that moment noticed it. "My goodness, you've grown up overnight, just the way Jane has. How are you, Theoline? Wesley tells me your mother and father are well."

"Oh, yes, they're all right, thank you, Mrs. Beacon."

Jane smiled remotely and said, "Hello."

Theo said, "Hello," and went back for the ice cream. Jane might be prettier than she'd been last year—who wouldn't be, with those clothes?—but she still had a long nose. It wasn't many summers ago, Theo remembered, that she'd pushed that nose into the clamflats.

Serving the next table, Theo heard the old lady sitting with Mrs. Beacon say in a voice like a fog horn, "Who's that girl, Agnes? I don't seem to place her." But through the clatter of talk and dishes, she could make out only a part of Mrs. Beacon's reply.

". . . brother helps us out with odd jobs. He keeps Felix occupied, too, for which I'm grateful."

At least, Theo thought savagely, the Attleboro tourists just talked about the food and the service. Poor old Wes! Maybe after all, he did pay a little something for what he got. How he'd feel if he knew Mrs. Beacon said that, when he figured he was a chum and not a chore boy! Mrs. Beacon, though, had tried to keep her voice down.

The other lady had no such scruples. "Well, she's a very pretty girl," she boomed. "What's her mother thinking of? Much too young to be working in a restaurant."

Theo went on mechanically setting the ice-cream dishes down, going back to the serving table for more tea cakes. It was an odd way to have an answer to prayer come, but if God had meant to fix things so she'd be sure she got an honest, detached opinion, He couldn't have done better. A hare lip or club feet would have got much the same type of interest—as if the old lady had seen them on a statue.

Nonetheless, down somewhere in the region of Theo's stomach, a small round spot of bliss began to glow and shine like a warm sun, across which was written the words, "a very pretty girl." Theo thought, I'd like to go kiss the old horror, right in the middle of her ugly puss.

DINNER hour—from six to nine—and just afterward when the early movie let out, were the best times at Leon's. Then everybody came in—people who had worked during the day, but to whom evening was playtime; the high school crowd, jamming around the fountain. There were plenty of tourists, too, but somehow their strangeness didn't seem so daunting, blended with familiar faces and voices that bawled jovially, "Hey, Theo, bring me a spoon, will you?" Or, "Hey, Theo, what's the matter with the service in this joint? No napkins."

Working at Leon's would have been a horrible bore if it hadn't been for the nights. Nights, there, were like being in another world. Things drab by day took on a shine and mystery. Especially on Saturday nights, which were gala in town.

Theo had had to do some fast footwork to convince Phoebe that she ought to be allowed to work evenings. Old people were so funny about nights—you'd think the minute dark came on, wild animals began ravening around the streets. But things calmed down after Sylvanus went to see Leon. Leon had promised on his soul, that four evenings a week, he'd personally see that she got on the nine-thirty bus. The other two—she had one day off—he'd have to keep her till eleven. On those nights, either Polly or Henry or Biff would be having time off, and Leon couldn't manage with too small a staff. "She'll be okay,"

Leon told Sylvanus. The bus went past his restaurant almost to Sylvanus's door in Granite Hook, and Chandler Warren, the driver, they all knew well. "She's a smart kid, Syl, takes care of herself good."

Sylvanus thought so himself. She was young, maybe, but a kid had to learn her way around sometime. Personally, he thought Phoebe was being old-fashioned about it, and he told her so. After a while, Phoebe had come around.

The second Saturday in July had been one of the fine clear days of summer weather. "Money weather," Leon called it, when entire populations are on the move, or so it seems in a tourist town. Bellport hotels and cabins were jammed, with a vast overflow brimming out into any private dwelling that had rooms to let. All day, Leon's had been busy without a breathing spell. Even afternoon tea hour lacked its usual serenity, for beyond the screens, the crowd made summer holiday, and Polly and Henry went crazy trying to cope with it.

One brash young couple, not finding an available table, thrust blithely between the screens, arguing in aggrieved tones that there were empty tables in there, they saw them. But they withdrew, silenced, on seeing the groups of tranquil ladies, who had not glanced up from their tea.

At dusk, a big burnt-orange moon rose out of the sea to the east, and set sail grandly over Bellport harbor. From Leon's plate-glass windows, the waterfront roofs at the foot of the street were black angles against a great mat of quicksilver. The neon signs made a fine colored pattern on the concrete, woven over by the endless procession of cars—cars of all shapes and descriptions, from the long, wickedly shining, out-of-state sedans to Funny-Money Montgomery's latest second-hand Chevvy. Behind the strolling crowds, the shop windows were squares of gold. Boys and girls in couples and groups moved up and down the sidewalks; people from the villages around Bellport went by, stiff in their best clothes and loaded down with paper bags and bundles from the A & P. Strangers in bright holiday clothes were everywhere; and Leon's was jammed, booth and table, with people standing six deep at the fountain.

From the small side window of the kitchen which overlooked the street, Polly glanced at the moon with a snort of disgust. "That ties it up," she said. "That's just what we needed!"

"What is?" Biff hauled a caldron of clams off the stove and dumped it in the sink, his upper half disappearing briefly in a cloud of steam. "If we gut anything on God's green earth we need, I'd give somethin to know what 't is."

"The moon, you big dope." Polly ran her eye expertly over the tray Henry had loaded, slung it to her shoulder and disappeared through the swing door into the restaurant.

"What's wrong betwixt her'n the moon?" Biff asked Theo and Henry. Abstract problems deeply concerned Biff, particularly those having to do with man and the universe.

"Oh, I don't know." Theo was trying to concentrate on what side dishes she'd written down for six shore dinners, and hardly heard what he said.

For all Henry was so vague, he was very intelligent about mixed-up side dishes. He was loading the last of them when Polly came back with her empty tray.

"If you 'n I was a-settin somewheres, bathed in moonlight," Biff said, "I bet ya you wouldn't have no fight with the moon, Polly."

"Oh, shut up," Polly said. "Three more lobsters, and the lady would like a small one. She says big lobsters is tough. If I was anywhere bathed in anything, beautiful, it would be with my feet in a tub of hot water."

"Don't like the moon," Biff said, tonging three bright red lobsters onto platters. "That ain't natural in a good-lookin woman."

"Baloney. If it was raining some a them pilgrims might go home, but with a moon like this, they'll be on the gallop all night. We'll be lucky if we git out a here before daylight. Right now, my feet ache clear up to the back a my neck."

"I, myself," said Biff, "am standin in two ponds a sweat; if my shoes was bigger, I'd have t' swim for it. There's your lobsters, and tell the lady she can go plumb to Canada, where little ones ain't illegal."

"I'll do that," Polly grinned. "Theo, there's a hero in your second booth's clankin on his glass with his fork. You want I should spill a salad over him for you?"

"No," Theo said, a little breathless from her loaded tray. "He's next, after these."

She wasn't as fast as Polly—few were—but she'd prided herself that all day during the rush, she'd kept up with her orders. When she pulled up alongside booth two, her knees were still shaking a little from the weight of the last tray, but she was caught up. "I'm sorry to keep you waiting," she said automatically repeating the formula. "We're terribly rushed tonight."

"I'll be darned," said the customer. "If it isn't the wildcat. So you got the job after all."

It was, she saw, the young truck driver called Howard, who had been in Leon's the day she'd socked Ida on the nose. Only now he had on a neat dark blue uniform and a snowy yachting cap lay on the seat beside him.

"How's your girl friend?" he asked, grinning at her. "She speaking to you yet?"

"Oh, my, no!" Theo said. "I don't think she'll ever speak to me again." She poised her pencil over her pad, but he seemed in no hurry to give his order. He merely sat looking at her, his eyes merry and intimate, over the menu.

"Aren't you going to order? The way you were whanging your tumbler, I thought you were in a hurry."

"I just wanted somebody to come. Now you're here, let's talk."

"I can't. Please order."

"Okay. Cheeseburger and coffee. Bring one for you and sit down and have it with me."

She thought Leon eyed her rather sharply as she gave him

the order at the fountain. She wanted to tell him that it hadn't been her fault she'd stopped to talk with a customer, but she hadn't time. Howard Whoever-he-was was nice looking, with all that curly dark-red hair and sunburn and his bright impudent eyes. But he knows it and he's fresh. He's going to get his cheeseburger set down thump, and that's all.

But when she took his order back to him, she set it down quite carefully.

"You don't appear to remember me at all well," he said plaintively. "Howard Thurlow, the handsome truck driver?"

"But I never even met you. And you're not a truck driver now."

"I never am, summertimes," he said. "I sail Mr. Grover's ketch, *Wanderlust*."

Yes, and you're proud of it, she thought. Like Wes. She couldn't help saying, "And they call you captain, and everything."

He burst out laughing. "Oh, that's only the summer people. Me, I never rated anything but buck private. Show you my scar, sometime."

"Don't be foolish." She turned to go.

"Wait. Have a ride with me later on, when you quit work?"

"No. Thanks just the same."

"Okay." A little to her surprise, he seemed to lose interest at once, and started in on his cheeseburger.

Well, she thought, I have to catch the bus anyway, and it's going to be late when I get home. It would be fun, though, to go to Leon's again on a summer night, not to wait on people but just to have a good time yourself, with somebody who looked like Howard.

The people who had had the shore dinners were looking around impatiently for their dessert. By the time they were pacified, and the dirty dishes taken to the kitchen, booth two was empty.

It was nearly ten o'clock when she came out into the street. There were still a few minutes to wait till bus time, and she leaned against the cool metal frame of Leon's big front window, taking deep breaths of the night air. It seemed so sweet she could almost taste it, after the stifling restaurant smells. Over Bellport harbor, the moon was riding high, the water a cold blaze of shifting silver from point to spruce-black point. Down along Land's End Drive, where the summer estates were, she could see the big gray-shingled roofs, wet with dew and softly glimmering in the moonlight. She was so tired, she thought, she'd never get up tomorrow.

A car slid slowly along the street and rolled to a stop in front of Leon's. It was a new Plymouth sedan, she saw at once, with white sidewall tires and a shine in the moonlight like something out of a fairy tale. Was there anything in the world more like something out of a fairy tale than the shine of a new car in the moonlight?

The driver leaned over and opened the door next the curb. "Would you like a ride home, I wonder?" he said. "I was going over Granite Hook way."

For a moment she was startled because her heart gave such a leap. How could it do that, when she had seen Howard only twice and talked to him once?

But it wasn't Howard, she saw, as the neon sign across the street flashed light on his face. It was a friend of Leon's—at least, she supposed he was Leon's friend, she had seen him several times talking with Leon at the fountain. He was a little man with a bald head and his name was Roger Drummey.

ROGER DRUMMEY hadn't been going to Granite Hook; or, at least, he hadn't thought of it until he had seen Theo. Then it occurred to him that he might as well go that way as any, since all he was doing was riding around in his car, and the youngster was probably tired and would welcome a ride home. Besides, he himself would welcome someone to talk to—if she turned out to be someone he could talk to.

Two hours ago, his wife had sent him into town from the overnight cabins after a case of cigarettes. In the rush, today, she'd sold nearly all her stock, and it looked as though she were going to be able to sell a lot more. Ordinarily, Roger would have gone right back with the cigarettes; but he had been working at his desk all day, and suddenly it had seemed he couldn't stand being inside four walls any longer. Evelyn, his wife, would be annoyed because her stock had got low; she would be furious with him because he had gone off riding. She hated to have him out at night in the car, knowing he was likely to pick up chance acquaintances or even strangers and take them where they were going for the sake of their company.

"Hitchhikers!" she would say. "Pickups!" They'd knock a man on the head for two cents, steal his car and his money. Especially a puny man, who anybody could see would be flap-handed at defending himself. She made no bones of saying just how capable she thought he might be in a fist fight.

Roger and his wife ran the Green Hill Overnight Cabins, on the state highway, a few miles north of Bellport. Or rather, she did. Roger had little to do with them. Mrs. Drummey hired a man for the heavy work, and an Italian girl for the house-keeping around the cabins. She herself did the renting, handled the bookkeeping and the money. Occasionally, if it happened to be necessary, she even threw out drunks.

Being brawny and six feet tall, Evelyn Drummey was far more capable of heavy work than Roger was. He had always been small-boned and delicate. When he was a child, his mother had several times despaired of raising him; throughout his life, his health had kept him from any kind of active existence. As a young man, he had tried to fit himself for college teaching, and for a time had been an instructor at the state university. He had enjoyed teaching and had been successful at it; some instinctive sympathy in him seemed to reach out to touch groping and unformed minds, and his classes were popular and full. But after several bouts of illness, he had to give up his job. With rest, his health had grown slowly better, for a time. Now, at forty-seven, he was a slight little man with a frail body, not half the size of his tremendous and overpowering wife.

Roger had been married to Evelyn for twenty-two years. He had never loved her; he had married her largely because his mother insisted—after the first weeks as an invalid at home, he had given up going against his mother. The strain of argument made him ill and the illness always made him yield. A sick man had little enough integrity anyway; he found he could keep his only by turning his real life inward and presenting a smooth surface of pliability. His mother was worried about his future. She didn't see how he could possibly ever again earn his living; she herself was not well and her small income would cease with her death. A hard-headed business woman like Evelyn would be just the wife for a bookish boy, inclined to be antisocial—as Roger was, after his illness. Such a wife, too, old Mrs. Drummey felt—and said—might knock out of him the preposterous ideas he had about being a poet.

Well, she had been right. Evelyn had done that.

Still, Roger felt he had no right to complain. His marriage, even though not his own idea, had been a bargain, entered into with his eyes open. He had never been able to square it with his conscience, but at the time he hadn't seen what else he could do.

As an invalid, lying for weeks in his mother's house, he had tried to work out some philosophy that would enable him to live his life as it must be lived as a dependent, his career gone. At first it had seemed impossible—everywhere he looked, a blind alley.

Then, slowly and painfully, he evolved a kind of philosophy of compensation. It was difficult and, he told himself, hypocritical; for he had always prided himself on a crystal-clear honesty in his relationships with people—perhaps this was one reason why he had got on so well with the young. But a man whose frail body and appearance made him something less than other men must find his protection as best he could. And unless he built some kind of a fortress of inner self-sufficiency, this life would be the end of him.

Evelyn wanted him; she had money. Even then, with what her father, a hotel man, had left her, she was starting on her plans for the hostelry that would someday be the Green Hill Cabins. She was generous with money; and in her curious, ugly fashion, Roger knew she loved him.

Very well. He would take from her his living and the leisure he needed to live the contemplative life he loved. Insofar as he was able, he would return payment by going through the ordeal of being her husband. She wanted to dominate and domineer; he was used to that. He hoped the payment would be in full. He had no way of knowing. It seemed, in many ways, a cruel and odious thing to do to a woman.

He found, very shortly, that the bargain was not one-sided. She had toward him a fierce, almost pathological sense of possession, and in her attempts to dispose of his daily life she was ruthless. To meet her continual, carping invasion of his spirit, Roger had set about building his fortress.

As a young man, he read a great deal and went fishing. He liked nothing better than to take his car and an armload of books and drive north to one of the lakes to spend the day lying in the sun. Evelyn had no objection to fishing, and he did, generally, catch something to bring home. But actually, he was laying out for himself courses of study in literature, continuing college work, which he finished with the bright leaves of the lake shore rustling over his head while his colored dobber floated in the clear, still water.

Outdoor life agreed with him. As he grew stronger, he came to feel an almost mystic relationship with the region of lakes and forests, the ocean shore lines and the windy islands off the coast, set with their green and secret trees. He discovered that he was an instinctive naturalist and, after a while, began to keep notes on birds and flowers, which, through the years, he classified and filed, hoping someday to turn them into a book.

Tucked away in the back of his mind, he had kept for years the conviction that someday, after a lifetime steeped in the masterpieces of other men, he would be able to rise above his frustrations and create his own. Writing poetry, after a year or so of marriage, had become futile and even distasteful to him. He didn't blame Evelyn—she was as she was, and there had been no law forcing him to marry her. But you paid for everything. He was aware at times of a deep inner homesickness for a plane of the mind which he had known as a young man trying to write poems, a place still and solitary where he had been able to listen and set down some part of what he heard. He had not, since then, penetrated to it, and now he was not sure he ever would. For, without warning, his world, so carefully created out of self-sufficiency, began to go awry.

Just when the change had taken place he couldn't say, but suddenly he was lonely. While he had worked and studied to build his hollow place of peace, the flavor of everything had subtly drained away. All at once, after a lifetime of solitude, he wanted to talk to people.

Perhaps it was because his life, up to now, had been a storing away, he told himself in bewilderment; he was full of impressions and ideas that he needed to communicate. Now might be the time to start his writing. He tried it. The words that had come so easily from his pen at twenty seemed to flow stiffly and stuffily at forty-seven. He got out his youthful poems and found them mawkish and young. Roger decided that he had not been, and might never be, a poet.

He took to dropping in on friends, even some to whom he hadn't paid attention in years, so that they had become acquaintances; and he found that a frightening thing had happened. Beyond the commonplace phrases of everyday, he hadn't any talk. The mine of ideas lay untouched at the back of his consciousness; but the tunnels to it were clogged. He had got in, and he couldn't get back out again. Roger Drummey, who had thought himself a man of many words, suddenly found himself a man of none. At least, he couldn't write; and he couldn't talk to any of the people he knew.

It occurred to Roger that the doctor to whom he went for his periodical checkups had been noncommittal—too noncommittal—about the last one. Perhaps health was what was wrong—that bogy had always stood at his shoulder. If it were, Roger preferred not to know. He felt a sick, choking disgust, thinking of himself as bedridden in the house, without solitude and without respite. It was not to be borne; and, after a time, quietly, he put such affairs as he had in order.

He tried riding around nights in the car, picking up acquaintances—or strangers—for company; which was what Evelyn wanted to put a stop to. Roger had never openly gone against her; a part of his tacit pact with himself had been that she should have her way, so long as he didn't lose too much of his soul. But it was useless to try to communicate to her the urgency behind his night travels. When, silently, he began to slip away, as he had done tonight, she turned ugly in an unexpected way. She thought he must be running after another woman, and Evelyn, jealous, was a devil.

Nevertheless, he couldn't help it. On moonlight nights like this, his loneliness was worst. The sky, midnight blue with a scattering of stars, seemed so deep, and the moonlight on the water so cold. The lush green of this countryside, growing out of rock, had always seemed to him a special subtlety; he had loved it. Now it seemed bleak, impersonal—an icy core of granite written over with a hopeless, undecipherable squiggle of leaves. A man was small, huddled within himself; a bug on a rock in the midst of a waste of waters.

He had seen Theo Sewell several times at Leon's—she was the pleasant youngster who waited on tables there. Leon had mentioned where she lived. Maybe a kid like that, innocent and without too much sophistication, would be somebody he could talk to. At least, he could remember a time when he had talked easily to the young, to his own pleasure and, he hoped, to theirs. But the car was halfway to Granite Hook before Roger said a word, and then what he said was, "Nice night."

"Yes, it is," Theo answered. "A swell night."

He thought, as he had often, in the days at the university, What lovely voices some young girls have, when they aren't being shrill and strident.

"You've got a nice car," she observed, after a few moments.

"Pretty good one," Roger said absently. "I enjoy riding around." He stopped, waited for words to take shape in his mind, and, when they didn't, managed to say, "Moonlight nights."

He certainly was a silent man, Theo thought, didn't seem to want to talk at all. Well, it was a lot nicer going home in a new Plymouth than on the bumpy old bus, and anyway, you never expected older people to have very much to say. "Moonlight nights are just the time for riding," she said. "The moon makes the concrete look white, doesn't it?"

Roger said,

"White in the moon the long road lies,
That leads me from my love."

He had been thinking of how the students had flocked to his poetry course, and her remark had reminded him of *A Shropshire Lad*. But he caught himself up with a sort of croak. "Quoting poetry," he said. "Foolish habit in a way."

"It sounded nice. The part about the moon was nice."

It had been, too. He had a deep, quiet sort of voice that gave the words a sound like music and made you want to say them over again to yourself, the way you wanted to hum a tune you'd heard and liked.

White in the moon. The long road. Only that made you think of driving—the whispering engine and the softly singing tires; the hair flying and the hands on the wheel that felt as if it were alive. Oh, if only I had a car like this one!

"It's a horrible bore to most people," Roger said.

"What is?"

"Poetry." She sensed, in the dim light reflected through the wind screen, that he had glanced around at her. "Doesn't it bore you?"

"We . . . ll. They make you learn it in school."

"Mm. That's usually a sad introduction. Spoils your life, at the time, doesn't it?"

"Mm-hm, it does."

"What kind of stuff do they make you learn?"

"Awful. One time, a great long glop of *The Vision of Sir Launfal.*"

"Oh, my heavens!" Roger said.

"Wasn't it? And I had to get up and say it in front of the class." She giggled. "I broke all to pieces over the part where Sir Launfal made morn through the gladsome gate."

Roger burst out laughing. What a nice youngster this was, he thought, suddenly aware, with a sense of astonishment, of how long it had been since he had laughed like that. "So now you don't like any poetry?" he said, as soon as he could speak.

"Not much. I liked that little piece you said a few minutes ago. It made me think of driving. Cars."

"Cars?" he asked. "Oh, yes, of course. The white road under the moon." His voice changed a little. "It made me think of loneliness. And that, I suppose, is the difference between us."

She thought, a little startled, He does say odd things. But she liked him, she decided. For one reason, he talked to her as if she were a human being who interested him, not the way most older people did, as if she weren't anything at all. He was maybe unhappy or upset about something to talk like that. She wasn't sure just how to answer him.

"I'd never be lonesome," she said at last, "if I had a car like this."

"A car?" Roger said. "What on earth difference would a car make?"

His tone made her still more unsure, and she laughed a little.

"All the difference in the world. You could drive and drive over all the roads. It'd be such fun you'd never be lonesome."

"That's right." For a moment, Roger felt disappointment flood over him. She was car-crazy, of course, like most of the kids her age. She couldn't think about anything else. You might as well try to talk to an unborn egg. Then he pulled himself up. How on earth could you blame the youngsters? The first word a baby learned to say, nowadays, was "mama," the second one was "car."

"Why are you lonesome, Mr. Drummey?" she asked suddenly.

The question was so unexpected and so simple that he gave it a simple answer and thought, even as he spoke, that he sounded like a schoolboy. "I can't talk to people," he said.

But it was a communication she seemed to understand. "Why, neither can I, quite often."

"You can't?"

"I can't, if I don't know the people. You can talk to people you know, can't you?"

"No," he said. "For a long time, I haven't been able to talk to anyone. I can't think of the words. They don't come."

A part of his mind said to him, I'm being mawkish and simple-minded. But it had been a relief, he realized, to be able to express his trouble in any words at all.

"Maybe if you thought of the thing you wanted to say, instead of the words," she said soberly. "That's what I do, sometimes. What would be something you wanted to say— I mean, what would it be about?"

"Why, I . . . why, the moonlight," Roger said. "I started to tell you, back there, that the moon made me lonesome . . . because it makes me feel so small." He felt like something long buried that had started to come out from underground; but he floundered on with it. "A man's a small thing, anyway, and you take a night like this, when the sky's so deep blue— Did you ever feel when you look into the sky as if you were looking down instead of up? I read that somewhere—'*What terrible abyss might open up before your feet.*'" He came to a dead stop. "I suppose that sounds crazy."

"No. It doesn't. It gives me cold chills."

It did, too. The sky no longer a safe canopy, blue with curling clouds, but a vast depth, a precipice . . .

"I've never thought of it, and it's scary. Oh, Mr. Drummey, you've gone right past the Granite Hook turn. It's back there."

"I'm sorry," he said. "I was woolgathering. Look," he went on, not wanting to let her get away so soon, "wouldn't you like to drive the car? Take her down the highway a ways?"

"Oh, could I? I mustn't, it's so late. Ma'd die."

"I'll take you home now, of course. What am I thinking of?" Roger said. "We'll turn at the first crossroad."

The first crossroad was high on a hill, overlooking the countryside and the sea. From it in daylight, the coast highway could be seen for miles, rolling its languorous curves to the south, by night pricked out by car lights, fast traveling and gay. The moon stood high over a vast eastern sea of cold fire. Full in the moon path, six miles out, Dungeon Island lay, black and secret as man's essential loneliness.

Roger caught his breath as he pulled the car into the turnaround. "What lovely country this is," he said, almost under his breath. "Heartbreaking, but lovely."

He was aware of a slight shiver beside him. "I don't think so," Theo said. "Oh, the moon's pretty and all, but everything's so dull and drab."

"Dull?" Roger said wonderingly. "Drab? But don't you know it's full of marvels?"

"No, I don't. Not when you think of Florida or California or . . . or the Sahara Desert, or far-away places like that. As soon as I can, I'm going away from here."

He nodded. "It's natural, I guess, to want to see other places than the one you know. But people are the same anywhere, wonderful and tragic, and places—" He stopped, sensing her impatience. They had to find out for themselves. No one could tell them, and that was right, too.

Old people! she was thinking. They're so settled and dull. What did he find wonderful about Bellport and Granite Hook?

"Have you ever been on Dungeon Island?" he asked, indicating it out across the water with a little sweep of his hand.

"Why, no. I didn't suppose anything ever went there but gulls."

"I don't suppose they do, now."

"Have you ever been there?"

"Oh, yes. It's one of the few islands hereabouts where petrels nest. I used to go there a night each spring to hear the petrels come home."

"Petrels?"

"Mother Carey's chickens—Carey chicks."

"Oh, yes. At night?" Mr. Drummey must be pretty brave. There was nothing on Dungeon Island but a few stunted trees, piles of driftwood, and the steep-walled granite ledges from which the island took its name. Gulls and other seabirds nested there, and sometimes gunners or hunters after seabirds' eggs landed, but always by daylight.

"Yes," Roger said. "I used to get one of the lobster boats to land me there and pick me up the next day. It wasn't bad, with a pup-tent and blankets."

"Weren't you lonesome?"

He was silent a moment. "Oddly enough, then, I wasn't. I'd fix my tent on the ledges and lie there with my head out the flap. In the middle of the night, I'd hear the petrels come home. They seemed to be coming from far away, as of course they were. You'd hear a rustle of wings and a twittering sound in the darkness, maybe to let their mates on the nests know they were coming."

"Couldn't you see them?"

"No. I never saw them. I suppose," he went on reflectively,

"it's one of the wonders of the world, the way the Carey chicks find their way home through hundreds of miles of night and fog. I used to think so, anyway, when I'd lie there with the dark so thick I couldn't see my hand."

Theo drew a long breath. She was suddenly aware that goose bumps had come out on her arms. It did seem wonderful. For a moment, listening to the deep voice, she had sensed the dark space and the sea and the small birds flying.

Roger slipped the car into gear and turned back along the highway. "I mustn't bore you," he said, in a quite different tone. "I must take you home."

"Oh, no. You weren't," she protested.

"I'm afraid I was. Getting long-winded over proving a point." He laughed apologetically. "For a moment, it seemed important that you shouldn't think everything so dull."

"Well, I'm like you, sometimes," she said in a little burst. "I can't think of words."

"You liked it, about the Carey chicks?" he asked.

"Yes. I did."

Roger stopped the car and got out. "Don't you want to drive the car down to the Hook?" he asked. "I expect you'd like that, too, wouldn't you?"

For an instant, she couldn't believe it. Then, wordlessly, she slid over under the wheel. Her entire driving experience consisted of the few times, last spring, she'd driven the jalopy belonging to Billy Dodd, a rather pimply sophomore, whom she'd sometimes gone out with. Mr. Drummey's car, of course, was different. You had to *feel* how it went. At first, she was shaky and nervous. Then the softly meshing machinery seemed to move with a rhythm that was the rhythm of her body; the wheel seemed to grow into and become a part of her hand.

In a silence born of pure bliss she drove the car back along the highway, turned down the Granite Hook road and brought it to a stop at her father's front door.

"Oh, *thank you*, Mr. Drummey," she said, her eyes like stars. "I don't know how to thank you."

"Nor I you," said Roger Drummey promptly. "Maybe you'll let me ride you home another night, and," he finished, smiling at her, "we can talk some more."

MORGAN'S weir was done and fishing. That is, it was ready to fish, but in the three weeks since he had finished it, it had caught only a few driblets of herring. Five bushels, two, one, on scattering nights; the most he'd ever found in it at any time was ten.

Ten bushels wasn't to be sneezed at, with herring at eighty-five cents a bushel. Still, it was funny he hadn't caught more. On the night he got his ten, Gordon Wescott, a few miles up the coast, had caught seven hundred. Morgan chafed and fretted. He'd been so sure about the fishing in Patch's Cove, and had lived so long, sleeping and waking, with the idea of a weir there, that he couldn't even consider that his gamble might not be a sure thing.

Dropping in to Sylvanus's fish house one afternoon to borrow a handful of trap nails, Morgan stopped long enough to ask Syl what he thought. After all, there were few people who knew more about the habits of various kinds of fish than Syl did.

"Hell," Sylvanus said. "How long you been weirin? Three weeks. I've known a new weir to fish for three years and not ketch nothin but silver hake and monkfish." He was lacing some heads into a batch of traps, and he stopped his leisurely motion to look soberly at Morgan. "Set down," he invited. "You ain't goin nowhere in a hurry, are you?"

To his surprise, Morgan did sit down, or at least, halfway. He leaned against the workbench.

"Ever you try any of this Nylon for trap heads?" Sylvanus asked. Always willing to stop work for any reason, he reached in his pocket for his pipe, indicating with his other hand the ball of heading twine on the bench. It was beautiful stuff, shimmering, blue-green, looking more like some kind of expensive tapestry cord than anything else, and Morgan recoiled from it.

"My God, Syl! That's seven dollars a ball!"

"Know it," Syl said. "Terrible, ain't it? Everything's high out of all reason now. I figger that Nylon'll outlast anything else five to one. Be cheaper, in the long run."

But Morgan couldn't get past the idea of the price. Seven dollars, his mind said, and stopped right there. "So they say," he said. "I don't think it's ever been proved."

Sylvanus grinned. "Only one way to prove it," he said. "Thought I'd give it a try." Contentedly, he rasped tobacco against the horny palm of his hand. "The preservative you dip it in turns it that blue color," he went on. "Pretty, ain't it?"

"Phil Dalzell was havin over that same business about a new weir's not doin much fishin, the first season or so," Morgan said, his face setting in lines of worry. "Anything in that, Syl?"

"Could be. Herrin's a mystery. Nobody knows what they'll do."

"Phil said a weir, even in a place where they've run for years, might make things different enough to scare em away."

"Don't think it's ever been proved," Sylvanus said.

"Oh, all right. But could you git your mind off of ribbin me long enough to tell me what you think?"

"I ain't ribbin ya." Sylvanus glanced at him in mild surprise.

"Okay," Morgan said. "Skip it."

Never, as long as he lived, he thought, would he be able to talk to Sylvanus without getting mad. Syl could have helped him a lot. If I could sit down and chew the rag with him for a couple of hours, I might in the end git out of him what I want to know. But hell, that's the only way. Even if I had the time, I couldn't. In his frustration, he said aloud, "God damn it!" and started for the door.

Sylvanus said, just as he reached it, "I d'no's I'd worry about that part of it, yet, if I was you."

Morgan swung around. "Why not? There's always been

herrin in Patch's Cove, when herrin's runnin. And they're runnin now."

"Must be a reason, then, wouldn't you say?"

"Gordon Wescott caught seven hundred. I ought to—"

"A new weir or a net won't scare a school a fish half so quick as a couple a hefty rocks chunked into the water at just the right time," Sylvanus said. "How's Emly?"

Morgan's eyes narrowed. "You mean Job Carter? He ain't peeped since he found out I bought the land. Job knows when he's licked, Syl."

"Job never in his life knew when he was licked. How *is* Emly? She must be close to time."

"Oh, for the Lord sake, you know she is."

"If you wasn't home a night or so, you'd want t'git somebody to stay with her."

"I don't plan to— Oh." Morgan stopped. "You think I might stop down around the shore, nights on the high water, see if Job's botherin the weir. I did do that at first, Syl. He didn't do anything, so I gave it up."

Sylvanus looked amused. "That's just what Job figgered you'd do."

"I don't believe it's him. I let word get around I'd have the state cops down, if I had any trouble."

"Job's had two-three hurls with the law. It warn't him come out on the bottom."

"Just the same, I don't think he wants to monkey with it. Short lobsters and haulin other people's traps and gunnin out of season—it wouldn't take much of a cop to find something to shove him for."

"Kind of hate to see him git sent up," Sylvanus said thoughtfully. "Old bugger's a damn nuisance, but the's quite a lot *to* him, in a way. Ain't scared of nothin, never knows when he's beat. Never did."

"Heck, Syl, you can't sit around and let him destroy your property—not if you're like me and haven't got time."

"H'm," Sylvanus said. "Up to you. You asked me what I thought."

"Oh, hell! I'll watch some more nights then."

"Phoebe'd stay with Emly."

"No sense botherin Phoebe. I'll ask Ma."

"They'll tear each other's lights out. Ma's on a regular string about Emly's goin to the hospital, these days."

"I know it. What can you do?"

Sylvanus grinned. "Listen, I guess," he said. "If you want to watch tonight, I'll watch with you. High tide's at two."

I spose he don't think I know when high tide is, Morgan thought irritably. The hours when the tide served, it seemed to him lately, were burned into his brain in figures of fire. "I'll handle it," he said aloud.

"Three to one's slim odds."

"That's all right. I don't aim to get in any fist fights."

"That's what you think," Sylvanus said, but he said it to Morgan's retreating back and wasn't sure whether he heard it.

Darn fool, Sylvanus thought. He'd be quite a man if he only had good judgment. Nerve enough to handle an army, but no sense at all. Ma sure spoilt the hell out of him, letting on to him and everybody else he was so smart.

It wasn't often, Sylvanus told himself, knocking out his pipe and going back to his trap heads, that he bothered to criticize anybody. But one of these days when Morgan monkeyed with a buzzsaw, without figuring out ahead of time where it was going to land him, he was going to get himself killed deader than a crab. That wharf business—Sylvanus couldn't help grinning, thinking how comical it turned out. He didn't believe for a minute, though, that Morgan realized to this day just how close he came to having a bad accident. Sylvanus could probably have hauled him out of the water; but if they hadn't been able, by the skin of a hair, to tow that wharf loose, Morgan's boat would have filled and sunk. Just towing the wharf loose had been a fluke, too. It happened that a big enough comber rolled in before the tide got too low.

Underestimating Job Carter was just like Morgan. Job had never given up in his life and he could outwait Judgment Day. Morgan might think he was the only one who ever had the idea of building a weir in Patch's Cove. As a matter of fact, he was the only one of a number who hadn't given it up as a poor investment, knowing Job Carter and his boys.

Morgan, having made up his mind to watch down by the weir that night, laid his plans. He didn't believe he'd have any trouble, even if he was alone. He meant to take down his shotgun—not loaded, of course; but just the sight of a gun with a purposeful eye behind it, ought to scare off a tribe like the Carters. Old Job might have plenty of nerve, but the boys weren't outstanding. Both Warren and Berry had wriggled out of going to war, first because they could claim that, as fishermen, they were in essential war work, and then, when the draft had caught up with them, it turned out they both had the same kind of defect in one ear that the old man had. Morgan guessed they'd heard about the way returned veterans knew how to handle guns. He even doubted if he saw them at all. In spite of Syl's advice, Morgan was convinced that Job had given up all claim to the Cove. If he'd been going to do anything, he'd have shown up before now.

Morgan wasn't sure just how he could get the shotgun out of the house without Emily's seeing him. He didn't want to scare her, and he didn't want her mentioning to Gram Sarah that he had walked away from the house carrying the gun. So when she was in the sitting room he took it down from the antlers over the door and set it out in the shed. When he left for the Cove, after dark, he could line it up along his bootleg until he got far enough away from the house. He didn't tell Emily he was going to watch out on the Carters, it might worry her. He just said he'd be late—had some work down at the fish house that wouldn't wait.

Emily didn't want Gram Sarah to come and stay with her. She said she'd rather stay alone until he got back. She'd felt a little nervous, maybe, that afternoon, but all right again by suppertime. Nothing would happen; and it was true that if Sylvanus hadn't mentioned having someone stay, Morgan wouldn't have given it a thought. But if Syl thought there was some danger in leaving Emily alone now, why, probably there was.

Gram Sarah was delighted to come. It wasn't often Morgan asked her to do something for Emly.

Some time after he had gone, she came hurrying along the road in the luminous summer darkness, carrying her night supplies—her nightgown wrapped in a newspaper in one hand and an old-fashioned chamber pot in the other. Morgan had an upstairs bathroom, and while Gram Sarah had nothing against bathrooms—she was, as a matter of fact, very proud of Morgan's—still, she couldn't feel at home in one and besides she couldn't see herself traipsing all the way into another room whenever she had to go, which sometimes in the night was often. Emly, of course, wouldn't have a pot in the house; if she had, she wouldn't have the sense to offer it. So Gram Sarah meant to have her own at hand, right under the edge of the bed.

She hadn't expected to meet anyone on the short walk over to Morgan's. Anyway, it was dark, and the only reason she'd wrapped up her nightdress was because she was afraid it might get damp from the dew. So she was horrified when she went by Mat Dawes's house to meet Uncle Wheat, face to face, out leaning on Mat's picket fence enjoying the fresh night air.

He said, "Evenin, Sarah"; and perhaps if she hadn't pattered right by him with her head in the air, he wouldn't have said any more. But Gram Sarah had had a down on Wheat ever since the picnic, and since she'd found out that Emly had made a friend of him and Mat. Why, Emly hung out half her time, now, over to Mat's house. No good would come of it. Gram didn't even wish Uncle Wheat good evening.

If there was one faculty that was left to Uncle Wheat unimpaired, it was his eyesight, trained for fifty years at sea to pick out objects in darkness and starlight. He said ruminatively, "Pond lilies, ain't it?" and was pleased to see a further ramrod-stiffening of her back and a quickening of her gait. He couldn't actually see the pond lily design tonight, but there had been times when the pot had taken the air on Gram Sarah's back step. Chances were it was the same one. He chuckled as soon as she was out of earshot in the darkness.

Gram Sarah came into Morgan's, fuming. This was the kind of old rip her son's wife had made a bosom friend of, him and his disreputable offspring. Before the evening was out, she meant to speak her mind about it.

But she was disappointed. She spoke her mind all evening about Mat Dawes and Uncle Wheat, leaving out neither Wheat's drinking nor Mat's separating from her husband and living with another man when she wasn't divorced. Gram Sarah waited for Emly to say something back.

But tonight there didn't seem to be much fight in Emly.

Morgan spent three hours alternately prowling the shores of the Cove, his shotgun in the crook of his arm, and sitting hidden in the warm darkness inside his fish house. The fish house was his new one, built on the foundation of the salvaged wharf. It was done except for the tar paper on the outside. He could sit and overlook the weir through a window.

But during the hours he watched, nothing moved—not a breeze among the alder leaves, not a ripple on the water. He had a hard job after twelve o'clock to keep from going to sleep. Once he did drop off and came to himself with a jerk, wondering if he'd heard a noise; but when he listened, there was nothing.

Syl's crazy, he told himself. I might just as well be home to bed.

He went outside to wake himself up and walked the few steps down to the end of the wharf. It was the dark of the moon, tonight, but the starlight was bright. He could make out the framework of the weir, the black rails a foot or so out of water, the blacker drapery of the net hanging below them.

Must be darn near high tide, he thought.

The far shore of the Cove was narrowed down to a bar by the flood. The water was high up on the shore near him, almost up to the top of the low bank. It was a dusky silver color, reflecting an occasional star. A still night on the dark of the moon was just the kind of a night for the big schools of herring to run. As he stood on the wharf wondering what he'd better do—stay or give up and go home, a soft little breeze puffed out of the west at his back, and rippled across the water.

Southwest, he thought, automatically. It'll get stronger by daylight. Well, might as well go home. Or no, maybe not. Ma was with Emily. It wouldn't be much longer till daylight, and time to tend the weir. He might as well catch a little sleep on the workbench inside the fish house. Save himself the walk back through the woods.

Just as he turned to go back through the fish house door, he heard a heavy muffled splash, as if somebody out by the entrance to the Cove had rolled a boulder, or something, into the water.

Morgan whirled. As he listened, tensely straining, the sound came again.

Somebody, by God, *was* throwing rocks into the water to scare away the fish! It wasn't the weir they were bothering around, it was the entrance to the Cove where the herring came in. He'd wasted his time, watching over here by the weir. He ought to have thought about the damage that could be done at the Cove entrance, which wasn't fifty yards from Job Carter's shack.

A sudden vision of the hundreds of dollars he was losing this very minute, if those rocks had landed in the middle of a school of fish, went agonizingly through Morgan's mind. He jumped into his punt and fairly made her sing through the water to the other side of the Cove. As he beached the punt by the entrance and climbed out, old Job Carter walked right up to the muzzle of his shotgun and twisted it out of his hands.

Sylvanus, coming down the path through the field back of Job's shack, heard the sounds of battle beginning down on the beach. There was a rattle of frantic rubber-booted feet on beach rocks, the thuds of fists on flesh; and somebody let out a loud "Wahoo!"

That's Job, Sylvanus said to himself. He broke into a run. Morgan had walked right into it, as usual. In a way, he, Sylvanus, was to blame. He'd planned to be here himself—had stayed late down in his fish house, so as to be ready to come over when it was time. The thing was, he'd caught what he supposed was going to be a catnap, on a pile of old rope.

The path, beaten hard by the comings and goings of the Carters, was clear to his eyes, a wandering white stripe in the darkness across the field. Somewhere along here, he remembered, used to be the ruins of an old shed—he ought to be able to pick up a piece of two-by-four or something there, to use for a club. When Job and the boys started a fight, a club was the only way to stop them. If anything would, which Sylvanus doubted. To get Morgan down here on a dark night alone was just what they'd been waiting for. They'd beat the living daylights out of him.

Sylvanus saw the jumbled ruins of the shed loom up in the dark a little off to one side. Stopping, he lighted a match to see by. The flare revealed plenty of rotten two-by-four; it also lighted up a tangled thicket of dry grass that hadn't been cleared away for years. Beyond it, the field that had been Marm Whiting's mowing land sloped down for fifty yards or so to Job's shack and the beach. It, too, hadn't been cut for years. Sylvanus knew, having seen it by daylight, that in some places the old fog and dead bushes were knee high.

He said, "H'm," dropped his match into the thickest mat of grass he could see, and went away from there on the long lope.

Behind him the brush went up like a minor explosion. Before he reached the beach, running as silently as a shadow, he could hear the dry timbers of the shed beginning to crackle.

The mêlée on the shore, which he could make out only as a dark, clotted swirl of arms and legs, suddenly broke apart, disclosing three upright figures and one prostrate one. One of the boys—Sylvanus judged it might be Berry—let out a strangled screech. "Jeezis, Pa! Somethin's caught afire up in the field!"

Old Job said, "N-nah! Now, what barstid's done that?" and went tearing past Sylvanus on the dead run.

Sylvanus stood in the shadow of a ledge to let him go by, the boys close on his heels. He heard the rocks rattle as they scrabbled up the bank, then the lessening thud of their boots as they ran along the path.

Morgan was just beginning to roll his head a little, trying to get to his feet. Sylvanus got the bailing scoop out of the punt and scooped cold salt water onto his head until he gasped and sat up.

"Holy smoke!" he said hoarsely. "What'd you do—set their house afire?"

"Well, no, not exactly," Sylvanus said. "You feel like gettin yourself into the punt? Not that they won't be busy for a while, but no use hanging around, is the'?"

Morgan groaned and heaved himself over the gunnel onto the stern seat of the punt. Sylvanus took the oars and pulled out into the placid waters of the Cove.

"I caught em chunkin rocks, like you said." Morgan dipped his handkerchief over the side, wrung it out and tried to stanch the blood dripping from his nose. "I had my gun, but they—"

"You had your *gun?* What in hell's name for? You might've plugged somebody. Where is it?"

"Must be there on the beach somewhere. I—it wasn't loaded."

"Wasn't loaded?" Sylvanus sounded weary. He turned the

punt around and pulled back to shore. Then he got out and hunted around the beach, using up a whole series of matches before he finally found the gun thrown down behind a boulder. "No use losin a good shotgun," he said, bringing it back and leaning it in the bow. "Serve you right if you had, though. I don't see the idea of a gun, anyhow, but an unloaded one was pure damfoolishness."

Morgan's cuts were stinging from the salt water. His throat felt as if he had a hot coal in it where Job had choked him. "Oh, jaw at me sometime when I can talk back, will ya?" he said irritably.

"All right," Sylvanus said.

"Oh, you're always so goddam *right!*"

Sylvanus said nothing. He merely rowed the rest of the way across the Cove, held the punt for Morgan to get out, and steadied him up the rungs of the short ladder on the wharf.

"Boy!" he said, glancing around. "Good fire."

The old Whiting field was ablaze from end to end. The calm water of the Cove burnt red from reflected flame. They could see the frantic silhouettes of the Carters, flailing with spruce limbs and flinging buckets of water to keep the fire away from the shack.

"One of em's gut a darn sore eye," Morgan said thoughtfully. "I gut my thumb into it. You think they'll git that out before it burns the house, Syl?"

"Maybe. Maybe not."

"Think we ought to go over and help em?"

"Well, le's see." Sylvanus rubbed his chin. "The path'll keep it from spreadin back to the woods, with the wind this way. Look's to me like Job's started a backfire around the house there. No, I wouldn't say so, Morg. Do that old field good to burn over, git some of the cultch out of it."

"WHAT'S the matter?" Gram Sarah said. "Don't you feel good?"

Emily said, "I'm cold."

She had pulled a rocking chair up close to the kitchen stove. For a while she had crocheted, but now she just sat there like a dummy.

"I don't see how you can be. You've gut a fire there hot enough to cook a minister and you're right on top of it. I'm bout roasted myself."

"I'm sorry. I reckon I wasn't thinking. I'll put on the light in the living room. Maybe you'd like to sit in there." She started to get up, then thought better of it and sat back in the rocking chair, her eyes looking very blue and dark in her white face. "Oh, dear, what time do you think Morgan will be home?"

Gram Sarah had opened her mouth to say she certainly was not going to set alone in the *setting room* and not be sociable. But she changed her mind. "Morgan won't be home before daylight," she said, looking at Emily sharply. "You wasn't expectin him before then, was you?"

"Oh!" Emily's face puckered and tears formed in the corners of her eyes. "Not all *night!* He didn't say he'd be gone all night!"

"What'd you think he gut me to come over'n stay for?"

"Why, I thought— He doesn't like to leave me alone at all now . . . and I didn't suppose he'd want you to have to go home so late."

"Wouldn't be no sense to go watch on the Carters unless he was there at high water. They wouldn't do nothin round the weir till then. That ain't till two o'clock." Which any of the womenfolks brought up around here would know, and some folks might take the pains to learn, she said to herself.

Emily stopped crying. "Is that where he is? He might have told me. I thought he'd be home around twelve."

"No call t' git mad about it. He just didn't want to worry ya."

"Well, I'm worried, whatever he wanted. I thought I could wait for him, but I can't. My baby's starting."

"Oh, fiddle," Gram Sarah snorted. "No first baby ever comes quick. All you've gut to do, anyway, is to go to bed while I call the doctor."

"You know I'm going to Bellport to the hospital," Emily stated. "Morgan told you. My bag's all packed. You'll have to go find somebody to drive me."

Gram Sarah's mouth clicked shut. "The ain't no God's livin need of it. It'll just cost Morgan a big bill. It's all cussid foolishness—"

"I know," Emily said. "You always had yours at home. Please go get hold of somebody with a car."

"You ain't even had any pains yet."

"I've had them since just after Morgan left."

"They ain't comin reg'lar?"

"Yes, they are. Every fifteen minutes." They weren't actually. She felt so panicky she hadn't dared to time them, thinking surely she'd be able to hold out till Morgan got home. In the afternoon, she'd had some intermittent cramps and she'd felt funny; but during the short time Morgan had been home, when she'd been hustling around getting his supper, the cramps had gone away. She'd thought it was just indigestion or something. After supper, they'd come back, getting worse all evening. She knew she should have mentioned them before; but, oh, dear, she *didn't* want Gram Sarah mixing in. To be alone with Gram Sarah at a time like this was awful beyond everything she'd ever dreamed.

To say every fifteen minutes, Emily realized at once, had been a mistake in timing. Gram Sarah had started as if stung; then she fairly bleated with triumph.

"You ain't in no shape t' ride t' Bellport, then! You git to bed. I'll git Dr. Gerrish." She started for the door, pulling her shawl around her head and grumbling, "I'll ketch my death this late at night. Why you couldn't have said before . . ."

Emily had visions of Dr. Gerrish. He was seventy-five if he was a day, and he had the shakes. Most people, nowadays, called in some one of the Bellport doctors anyway. But Gram

Sarah'd for years had Dr. Gerrish and she was always going to. Emily realized suddenly that she felt dreadful. Something seemed to blow up inside her head.

"Oh, you horrid interfering old *woman!*" she cried. She brushed past Gram Sarah, pushing her out of the way so that the old lady sat down in a heap on a kitchen chair and came near teetering off onto the floor. In the shed, Emily caught up her raincoat from its hook—it was the only thing she could get hold of quickly—and flung it over her shoulders. She ran down the steps, hearing the shrill notes of rage piping from the kitchen.

"You've pushed me down! You've kilt me! Oh, oh, oh!"

It wasn't far over to Mat's, but Emily ran every step of the way, as if devils were on her heels. Mat and Uncle Wheat were having some tea in the kitchen before they went to bed. Emily burst in on them sobbing and gasping for breath, and it was a minute before they could find out what was the matter. With a few quick questions Mat gleaned the facts about the labor pains. Then she put her arms around Emily and let her cry into the blue apron bib on Mat's birdlike bosom.

"Now, you listen, dear," Mat said reassuringly. "From the way it acts, it's probly nuthin but a plain stomach ache." She didn't think it was, but no use telling Emily that, the poor youngone was scared silly, as it was. "We won't take no chances on it, don't you worry. Somebody better go git Morgan. Pa, who's got a car that's liable to be up, this time a night?"

"Oh, there isn't time to go get Morgan!" Emily's tears broke out afresh. "He's down around the Cove somewhere. Please, let's just go to the hospital."

"That's right," Uncle Wheat said. "No knowin what part of the Cove Morgan'd be. Young Wes's car's out in front of Sylvanus's, or was before dark. No trouble t' git Syl up, if he's gone to bed."

"Where's your things, dear?" Mat asked Emily. "You got a suitcase ready?"

"Yes. It's in the hall by the stairs. *She's* over there, though."

"Who? Gram Sarah?" Uncle Wheat grinned. "Mat, you run down get Syl. I'll get the suitcase."

"Oh, no. She's awful mad. I'd rather go without it."

Uncle Wheat put on his hat and marched out.

"He'll git it," Mat said. "Now, you lay there, dear, on the couch. Don't git up. I'll be back sooner'n you can spit."

Emily lay on Mat's oilcloth-covered sofa, with a crocheted afghan across her legs. Already she was comforted and she thought she felt better. It was nice in Mat's kitchen with a fire going in the white enameled stove and the clock ticking on the shelf. She liked Mat's kitchen. It was done in what Mat called "modren," everything white and a blue linoleum on the floor. Emily had spent a good deal of time here during the past weeks; for since she had taken Uncle Wheat at his word and called, she and Mat had become fast friends. Mat's house was always peaceful; she and Uncle Wheat thought the world of each other. Oh, they made believe put on a battle royal, every once in a while about something they disagreed on—like the oilcloth sofa she was lying on now. Mat wanted it out of her "modren" kitchen, she said; it was a false note. But the sofa was Uncle Wheat's. He liked to lie on it after supper awhile before he went to bed. He said she could get rid of him sooner than that sofa. And, actually, Mat would have cut off a finger, rather than do anything drastic about it.

Emily closed her eyes, feeling taken care of. Then, suddenly, she had a real pain—a doubling-up one that tied her whole body into knots, and made the others she'd had seem like nothing.

Uncle Wheat made pretty fair time getting over to Morgan's. His knees held up good, he told himself proudly, as he went up the back steps. Sometimes they shook when he hurried. He had his hand on the doorknob, when the door flew open in his face and Gram Sarah stood there.

She was took aback to see him, Uncle Wheat realized. She must have expected it was Emily, come crawlin back. Also, she hadn't forgotten about the meeting with him earlier in the evenin. She said, "What d' *you* want, you drunken old lout?"

Uncle Wheat had planned to ask her nicely for Emily's suitcase, but he changed his mind. She probably wouldn't give it to him, anyway. He didn't see how he could get by her, with her standing full in the doorway; so he made claws of his hands and crinkled his fingers. Every one of his stiff old finger joints cracked right in her face. He bawled out, "Look out for me! I'm comin a-rapin and a-murderin!" He hoped she'd think, by darn, that for once he *was* drunk.

She did. She bounced back clear across the kitchen to the sink cupboard. She looked up over the door for Morgan's gun, and then, seeing it was gone, opened up a drawer and began fumbling in it for a butcher knife.

Getting her away from the door was enough for Uncle Wheat. He flipped spryly through the kitchen, across the sitting room and into the hall, where he found the suitcase and let himself out the front door with it. By the time she had followed him in there with the butcher knife, he was down the steps and away into the darkness. He heard her screech something after him, but not to make out what it was. He was still chuckling when he came back into Mat's kitchen, but at the sight of Emily, he stopped. He said, "Oh, dear, dear, dear," in a gentle voice, and went over and let her hang onto his hands.

Mat wasn't far behind him. She'd had farther to go, but she could run like a whippet, and she'd only had to run one way. She hadn't found Sylvanus at home. Wes had left the car there, but he himself had gone off on a camping trip to one of the islands with some summer boys. Phoebe had gone to bed. The only one up was Theo, who had got home late from her job and was having a lunch in the kitchen. When she'd answered Mat's questions and heard what the trouble was, she said, "I can drive. Come on."

Mat said, "You better call your Ma, Theo."

"What for? She can't drive a car. Besides she sleeps like a rock. It'd take me fifteen minutes to wake her up." Not heeding Mat's protests, Theo went flying out to the car and climbed in. "If only Wes has left the keys—"

Darn a fool kid, Mat thought. This wasn't any junket to take a kid on. "Why don't you just let me take the car?" she suggested.

"Oh, no! I want to go. I'd love to go!"

What does she think it is, a party? Mat thought. She couldn't argue all night—she didn't suppose they were in too desperate a hurry, but no telling. The important thing, of course, was getting the car. She certainly couldn't think where they'd find another, this time of night. And seeing the menfolks were all gone, there really wasn't anybody else but Theo. Oh, well, if she couldn't drive, Mat could take over. She climbed in beside Theo. "You don't think you better let me drive?" she asked doubtfully.

"Oh, no," Theo said blithely.

Wes had left the keys. She backed the Ford out of the driveway, turned up the tar toward Mat's house. She felt a pleasurable excitement in the lateness of the night and in being called on in an emergency. It was going to take her a minute to catch onto the way Felix's car drove—certainly was an old rattletrap compared to Mr. Drummey's, which she'd driven several times lately. She'd show Mat, though. No one ever wanted to let you do any of the important things.

Often she'd dreamed of herself as the bright-haired heroine, hurtling over pitch-black roads at the wheel of a fast car—she, the only one who could save the city, carry the message or the serum or the secret information. Now she was a Red Cross nurse, driving through the night to the hospital. She had on a snowy uniform with a white cap and a dark blue cape. Too bad it was such a nice night. A blizzard would have been better.

At Mat's house, she turned the car around while Mat went

in. Through the kitchen door, she heard Mat say, "Oh, my Lord, Pa! What'd be best to do—call Dr. Gerrish?"

Uncle Wheat said, "She says no—she's scairt t' death to have him. And what's he good for, once you get him? Besides, time we get him rousted out, we could be in Bellport."

"Just the same," Mat said, her voice going high, "I wish Morgan or some of her folks was here to say."

"Syl's out there, ain't he?"

"Syl wasn't home. Theo come."

"*Theo!* For God's sake, Mat!"

"She was all there was to home, Pa. I think we better call a doctor—let her have it here."

Emily's voice, strained and high, said, "No, Mat, please. I've got to go to the hospital. I can stand it, if you hurry."

"We'll git you there," Uncle Wheat said. "Mat! Git that big cushion off'n the couch for her to sit on, take the bumps. Come on. *Don't stand there!*"

Theo saw, with a little clutch at her heart, that Emily was all doubled over as they helped her into the car. The Red Cross nurse vanished somewhere into oblivion, and Theo Sewell's hands felt clammy on the wheel.

For all Wes's bragging, Felix's Ford didn't seem to be much of a car. It coughed and missed, going up the hill to the highway; once or twice it almost stalled. Felix had been driving a lot since June, though, and Felix was hard on a car. Theo suddenly realized that the engine wasn't behaving well at all.

A cold feeling started somewhere down in the middle of her back and came slowly up to the roots of her hair. Suppose the boys hadn't left enough gas! She hadn't thought of that, or to mention it to Mat. Wes was always moaning that Felix spent his allowance for other things, so they never had enough gas to go all the places they could have gone. Suppose the car ran out, and Emily's baby were born here on the highway? What could they do? The engine certainly was making a funny whuffling noise.

They weren't halfway to Bellport when Emily began to scream.

Mat said, "My God. Theo, you'll have to step on it."

Theo jammed down on the gas, but the engine only missed and slowed down.

"Oh, for heaven's sake, stop and let me drive," Mat said sharply.

"It's the car," Theo gasped. "It won't go any faster. Something's the matter with it."

"Shut up, Mat," Uncle Wheat said. "You're needed right here in the back seat. Do the best you kin," he added in a calm voice. "Everything's all right, back here."

Everything wasn't, Theo knew.

In her imagination, the times of driving a powerful car on noble missions had been times of exaltation and high purpose. The exploding guns, the dark pursuing figures, the menacing terrors in the road ahead, had always been dangers escaped—by a hair's breadth, it might be, but escaped. In your dream, you knew they were never going to get you.

But this danger was here and now; it might happen the minute after next. If the old car stalled, Emily might die. The baby might die. A muffled, dreadful something had started to go on in the back seat. Screams, more like coughs; a floundering, like something that had been run over.

"Look, Theo," Mat said. She had the jitters and for the life of her she couldn't keep still. "When we git there, Pa and I won't be able to leave Emily. You park as close to the entrance as you can git. Then you fly in as fast as God'll let your legs go, and git them doctors out. Don't stop for nuthin."

Theo croaked something in reply. The car seemed to be doing a little better now; the engine was picking up. Maybe it had had a plugged gasline. But, she realized, they were going down hill now—the long uphill into Bellport was still to come.

Uncle Wheat took in a breath to tell Mat to keep her trap shut—the kid was doing all right, and she was scairt enough as it was—then he let it out in a puff. Feelin the way she was, Mat had better be let to talk or she'd have the laughin hollers, and then the scouse *would* be all over the galley stove.

Theo saw the lights of Bellport begin to glow up over the rise ahead, and felt the engine labor as they started up the hill. The car seemed to slow down to a crawl.

"Theo!" Mat said. "It ain't no use now to ease over the bumps. We've got to git there!"

Theo didn't answer. She was feeling with her foot for the exact spot where the accelerator held the engine and didn't make it cough and miss. She found it; and the car, wheezing like a teakettle, made the top of the hill. Then they were rolling along Main Street. Theo automatically slowed for a red light.

"Don't stop—ne'mind any cussid lights," Mat said.

Theo went straight through the light. A more experienced driver might have hit the big, night-traveling produce truck that was turning in from a cross street; but instead of slowing down, Theo bulled right on through. The all-night cop at the corner of Orchard and Main, let out a strangled squawk, and the driver of the truck slammed on his brakes with a stream of startled oaths.

The cop blew his whistle and started to run after the Ford.

Uncle Wheat rolled down a window and stuck out his head. "The's a woman hevin a baby," he trumpeted. "Don't you know nothin, you scouse-scrapin son of a hooer?"

The blast stopped the cop dead in his tracks. The car went on up the interminable length of Orchard Street. It turned at last into the white gates of the Bellport Hospital.

The nurse at the desk turned a calm, questioning face as Theo burst through the revolving door into the hushed quiet of the reception lobby. She nodded briefly, as the gasping sentences began. "Has she made her arrangements here?" she started to say. "What name, please?"

"Oh, hurry. Do hurry. She's having it—she's having it in the car."

The nurse grabbed for a phone. The hospital went into action. They had had people cut things fine before; not always so fine as this. Emily was having it in the car; she barely made it to the delivery room.

There was no point in sticking around, Uncle Wheat said. The doctors had taken over—best thing to do was go back to Granite Hook, hunt up Morgan. Mat had tried to telephone with no success. She called Dalzell's number, seeing he was a fairly near neighbor to Morgan and would step over with the message.

"They've all gone to bed and died," she said disgustedly, coming back from the phone booth down the corridor.

"Oh, Morgan ain't to home yit," Uncle Wheat said. "The cussid fool. Tarry-hootin round on his big affairs, when he'd ought a ben to home tendin to things."

He forgot to keep his voice down, and the reception nurse, behind her glass window, looked up at him with acid disapproval. She had a rather stern, unfriendly face anyway, and Mat, who had a wholesome respect for most kinds of authority, pulled at Uncle Wheat's sleeve. "Sh, Pa."

But Uncle Wheat was getting his reaction. Maybe Mat and them felt better now that everything was over, but he didn't. He felt awful.

"Don't deserve a nice wife and baby," he bawled. "Come dagnabbed near losing both of em, if you ask me. God damn a Sewell!"

His voice blasted like a thunderclap down the corridors, with their blank walls and bare, polished linoleum. Two nurses, standing at the far end of the lobby, whirled around and started toward him. The reception nurse came flying out of her coop. They arrived, one behind the other, and one of them said, "Stop this racket at once."

"Ei?" Uncle Wheat said, astonished. "What's the matter with *you?*"

"This is a hospital. You ought to be ashamed."

"What of?" Anything he hated, it was one of them four-eyed women always pickin at a man, and this was one if he ever saw one. "Excuse me," he said, with great dignity. "You tend to your business, mam, I'll tend to mine." He closed his mouth with a snap and stalked along the lobby to the door. "Him and that Sarah's enough to kill the devil." He pushed through the revolving door, went down the steps and got into the car, banging the door resoundingly. He was still grumbling on, when Mat and Theo caught up with him.

"Pa, they're her *relations*," Mat said, with a sideways glance at Theo. "You mustn't—"

"I don't care if they're her blood mother," Uncle Wheat snapped. "And what's *she* doin, comin on a hoot like this? It warn't no sight for a pure young girl to see, in front of all them men. Well, *git in!*" he roared. "What you waitin for?"

"I better drive," Mat said in a subdued voice. "You go round on the other side."

"Okay. I'm pretty tired anyway." Theo had been wondering how on earth she could get into the car and drive it home. It wasn't like this that the daydreams ended—not in this almost unbearable sense of ugliness and shame. She wanted to creep away deep inside herself and forget that tonight had ever happened.

Uncle Wheat heard her, and as always, when he'd overspoken himself, compunction flowed over him like a wave. "Well, you done all right," he spluttered. "If you're tired, you gut a right to be."

Theo sat huddled in the corner of the seat while Mat sent the car puffling along the highway. She couldn't get out of her mind the picture of Emily as the orderlies carried her into the hospital. Thinking of babies, you always saw them pink and white, lying in a bassinet. But not any more.

Somewhere in the back of her mind she had known, as everyone did, that it hurt to have a baby. But when you imagined it was you, the pain was always ennobled. You, the sufferer, bore it with fortitude and in silence. You came through it, as you came through all pain, tempered and fine. Your face, of course, showed what you had been through, but in a quiet, beautiful way; you didn't show it by cries and moans, or threshing your arms and legs around.

But Emily had. Emily had been like a hurt animal. It was true she was what Gram Sarah called a "screamer"; but you knew, looking at her, that this wasn't anything she could help.

You made your dreams, you'd always thought, out of the real things. And the real things, when at last you came to them, would be of the same shining stuff, only lovelier—the excitement intensified, the pleasure more lasting.

It's *like* that, she cried to herself. I'll never believe it won't be like that for me!

She shut her eyes tight and tried to think of other things—of Georgia Tate, the night-club singer who had gone to Hollywood, seeing the talisman of a great golden sphere floating on before her in a starlit sky. But Georgia Tate and the Red Cross nurse had gone down the same trackless road together.

Mat was talking ten to a dozen, as if tonight's occurrence were all in her day's work. ". . . Southern women's maybe different, got warmer blood or something, but I never knew of a first baby comin on so quick or with less fuss'n bother. Must a ben what they call a natural birth. . . . Pa, where'd we be most likely to find Morgan?"

But nobody was destined to find Morgan that night, at least in Felix's Ford. Three miles out of Granite Hook, the engine sighed and died. They walked the rest of the way into the village. And that was why it was nearly daylight before Morgan found out he had a son.

He had the blackest kind of an eye and his shirt was half torn off his back, but it took Sylvanus and Uncle Wheat together to persuade him to go back to the house and change before he lit out for the hospital.

PART FOUR

August

MR. GROVER'S ketch, *Wanderlust,* on which Howard Thurlow worked, had been for a cruise along the coast. Since Mr. Grover liked to explore harbors and islands—"gunk-holing," he called it—anchoring at night in some solitary cove, the three members of his crew hadn't seen the lights of town for a week. As soon as Howard came ashore, he dressed up in his best blue uniform, the one he couldn't wear on the boat, to go uptown.

Howard wasn't the skipper of the ketch, as he had implied to Theo, but only a member of her crew. He didn't figure it was a lie to say he sailed her; he did help to. Aboard, he wore a natty sailor's blouse with bell-bottom pants. He had had the uniform tailored for shore wear because he liked the cut of it and the white peaked officer's cap, with the small gold-braid cord, was more becoming to him than a gob's pancake.

Howard had come to Bellport a year ago, from Atlantic City, one of the original crew hired to sail Mr. Grover's new ketch north to his summer home. Mr. Grover had kept him on through the summer, and then in the fall, had offered to pay him a nominal salary through the winter, if he'd show up to sail again the following June. It was all gravy to Howard. The life on the ketch was fine—no very hard work sailing a sixty-five-foot ketch in the summertime, keeping her shipshape, and being polite to the boss and his company. He enjoyed handing the ladies aboard, making them comfortable in wicker chairs with cushions. Since he had an air about him and was very presentable, the ladies liked him. Mr. Grover saw he didn't lose anything by it.

Howard liked Bellport as well as any of the places he had drifted around in. At twenty-three, Howard had seen a lot of places. He had been born on a truck farm in the New Jersey flatlands. He supposed he still had an older brother, swarming with kids, on the truck farm. He didn't know or care. He hadn't been home since he was fifteen.

His brother had brought him up—if you could call it that. When Howard was ten, the family produce truck had met a sedan head-on on a four-lane highway—the sedan having blown a tire and crashed over into the wrong lane—and his father and mother had died under the load of tomatoes and beans. Howard, when the cops dug him out, was still alive. He spent three months in a hospital with his splintered bones—the legs and pelvis healed all right, but one of his arms had to have quite a good deal of muscle surgery that took a long time.

When he got home, still wabbly on his pins, his brother Fowler and his wife had taken over the farm. Fowler resented the hospital bills which had used up all of the old man's money. He and his wife made a chore-boy out of Howard, working him from dawn to dark in summers, and after school and week-ends during other seasons; until one morning they got up to find the early chores undone and Howard gone. Since they wanted the truck farm, and legally it would be part Howard's when he came of age, they didn't bother to notify the police that he was missing. So far as Howard was concerned, they could have the farm and welcome. He never wanted to see it—or them—again.

He had gone on the roads, hoboing it for a couple of years, getting as far south as Delaware, where he spent some time with the oyster boats, clawing up oysters out of Chesapeake Bay. Boats and fishing appealed to him. There was something he liked about the relaxed life on a boat, maybe because it was so different from a farm. He hitchhiked back north at the end of the season, to Hoboken, with some vague idea of getting on a liner or a freighter; but such jobs were hard to find and the pay was poor. So he did odd jobs around the piers, finally getting into the longshoremen's union.

He was twenty when the war picked him up and set him down in a number of places, where for two years he saw enough hard work and blood and dying to sicken him on all three for the rest of his life. In the Battle of the Bulge, a bullet tore the ligaments of his patched-up arm. He found himself out of the Army for good on veteran's pension for partial disablement until he was ready to work again.

Such possessions as Howard had were in Hoboken; he figured that was his home. He went back there, couldn't find much reason for sticking around. The old longshoreman's job, for a while, was out of the question. Most of his cronies were gone.

He drifted down to Atlantic City to be near boats and the ocean. It seemed a good enough place at least to take a room in a rooming house. He found an occasional light job along the waterfront, at the hotels. Mostly, he spent his time fishing from the sands with a pole.

There he struck up an acquaintance with a boat builder who owned a boatyard near the city and came down to the beach week-ends to rest and fish. Sunday after Sunday, they talked fishing and boats, and the builder, whose yard had been working on picket boats, occasionally invited Howard over to see how the job was done.

The builder was proud of his yard. In the past he had specialized on pleasure craft and would again. He showed Howard the blueprints for the "Sweetest little ketch that ever sailed out of the port." When war orders slacked off, he laid the keel for *Wanderlust*.

With *Wanderlust*, so far as Howard was concerned, it was love at first sight. He hung around while she was building, even helped a little at light jobs, like painting and polishing brass. Mr. Grover and his wife happened to come aboard one day while he was there. They were on the best of terms with their builder, as well they might be. Any friend of his was welcome on the boat; besides, Howard was an interesting and attractive young chap in his own right. They watched him going over her fore and aft, unable to keep his hands off the bright brass, the gleaming wood, the beautiful appointments of the wheel.

The Grovers were shy a hand out of the three crew members they needed to sail their new ketch up the coast. On the builder's say-so, and what Howard could tell them, they hired him, but not so much for his experience as because Mrs. Grover liked his looks. Except for his one season oystering, Howard's seamanship had grown out of longing and what he'd gleaned from lending library travel books, though he didn't say so.

Mr. Grover, who owned factories, had hired a great many men in his time. He felt that looks were a poor basis on which to take on a hand. He made it clear that the job might end as soon as the ketch was berthed in Bellport. But on the way north, Mrs. Grover found out that Howard was a returned veteran with a bad arm, which explained why he wasn't so lively on the ropes as might be expected. She dropped a word to Johnny Fleming, the ketch's skipper, knowing Johnny had a soft spot for veterans. It had seemed to her that Johnny was being a little hard on Howard. By the time they reached Bellport, the job was secure. Now, it looked as though Howard could have it for the rest of his life if he wanted it that long—or, at least, as long as Mrs. Grover stayed interested in yachting.

And, he told himself, he did want it. Never, so long as he had a say about it, was he going to take on anything that involved responsibility or hard work. He'd had enough.

Since he was on short pay winters without much to do, he'd got a job that first fall, driving an oil company's truck between Bellport and Ferriston, the county seat near by. He took a room in Bellport near the waterfront, so he could watch boats go in and out of the harbor and be handy to Mike's poolroom. He blew his winter's pay as fast as he made it.

Toward spring, he wished he'd saved some. He didn't care for horsing a darned ark of a truck through snowbanks, and while he supposed he could have the job again in the fall when he was through sailing, he had a better idea. With a little money ahead to tide him over, he could go south winters, get a boating job somewhere on the Florida coast and come back when Mr. Grover wanted him again in June. Maybe he could find a regular winter job down there. The idea grew on Howard. That would be a fine year-round life—north summers and south winters, like a plutocrat; all boating and lying around in the sun. Now he'd have to save something out of his summer's pay, a hard thing to do. In summer, there were a lot more things going on.

The blue uniform looked pretty swell, he decided, standing in front of the mirror in his room. It was fresh from the cleaner's—he always sent it out to be cleaned and pressed just before he left on a cruise, so it would be immaculate when he got back for his time ashore. He wore a pale blue shirt with it and a plain navy tie. The blend of blues was fine with his dark red hair and deep bronze tan. Showed off the color of his eyes, too, which was green. He'd never seen but one other person with eyes that exact shade. She was a barmaid at Wally's Bar and Grill in Hoboken, but he'd only taken her out twice before he'd decided that green eyes was the only thing they had in common.

He planned to eat the lobster dinner at Leon's, then find a girl somewhere and take in a dance. Johnny Fleming had said he wasn't going to use his car—he hadn't seemed too keen about lending it, but he'd come around. Since it was Friday night, there'd be a pick of dances in the surrounding towns; on any night, he told himself, there was a pick of girls. They'd be mostly dated up by now, but it wouldn't be the first time a girl had broken a date to go out with him. If the first one wouldn't, the second or third one would. He wasn't worried.

At Leon's, Howard sat down in the only empty booth, which happened to be one of Polly's. He liked Polly. She was a darned nice old war horse, who spoke his language.

"Hi-ya, babe," he said, as she came to a halt beside his booth, "how's about the dance tonight?"

"Oh, my smartin eyes," Polly said, taking in his splendor. "Me? Any number of girls would fall flat on their faces."

"On their backs, you mean," Howard said, grinning.

"That'll be all that kind of talk," Polly said icily, eyeing him. "What you want to eat?"

"Okay, okay," Howard said hastily. "Don't get mad, sweetheart, you'll break my heart. You too sore to bring me the shore dinner?"

"I'll bring it," Polly said, "and haul it down over your head."

Waiting for his food, Howard glanced leisurely around the room. He liked to eat at Leon's. It was a nice place, served the best food he'd ever eaten at a restaurant. He liked Leon, too. The old boy was over behind the fountain with the sweat running down his bald head, frying hamburgers like crazy. Howard lifted a hand to him when Leon turned around, but Leon didn't seem to see it. He must coin the money with this place. Everybody came here.

And, by golly, there was that kid waitress who'd turned him down for a date the last time he was in here. He'd thought she looked quite interesting, and he'd forgotten all about her. He lifted a hand to her and she smiled, a tense, hurried little smile in reply. She was very busy.

Maybe there was his date for tonight, Howard thought, watching her speculatively. She looked like a sober little thing; probably his first approach had been all wrong. Kind of young, might bore the pants off him. But sometimes the youngest ones were the nicest. Anyway, he liked the look of her. Besides, she'd turned him down for a date.

"Hello," he said, as she passed his table with a tray of dishes.

"Hello," Theo said. She went on through the swinging door to the kitchen.

Eating slowly through the courses of the shore dinner, Howard watched his chance to speak to her again. It took quite a while to get just the right combination of circumstances—he wasn't going to hurry things this time. He was having his dessert before Theo had a temporary breathing spell while Polly was out of sight in the kitchen. Seeing her glance at him, he made motions as if something were wrong on his table, and crooked his finger. She came over at once.

"Did you need something more?" she asked.

"Yes," Howard said, with his best polite smile. "I need to apologize."

"Oh!" She looked puzzled. "What on earth for?"

"Well, I was fresh the last time I was in here. I got to thinking about it. I'm sorry."

Theo was pleased. Besides, Howard's best smile was a very nice smile indeed. "Oh, that's all right," she said. "I was busy that night. Tired, too. I guess I wasn't very nice, either."

"I was thinking," he went on. "Friday night being dance night and all, you wouldn't care to hunt one up, after you get through work here, tonight, would you?"

"Oh," she said. "I'd like to."

Duck soup, he thought. He could see by her face that she wanted to go.

"I guess I can't, though. It's an early night, but they expect me home at nine-thirty."

"Couldn't we just go, and you let on you had to work tonight?"

She did want to. Maybe she could get away with that. And if she didn't, she thought, rebellion starting up within her, at least she'd have had the good time. It would be worth a jawing. All summer, it seemed, hadn't been anything but bewilderment and hard work. "I'm afraid I wouldn't be very dressed up," she said. She had, she thought thankfully, worn a new light summer dress to work that morning.

"Nuts, we won't go any swell places where you'd need anything flossy," Howard said. "I'll meet you outside when you get through. For the Lord's sake, what ails Leon? He's glaring a hole right through us."

Theo jumped. She turned around to a neighboring table and got a salt shaker, which she set down in front of Howard. Some people down the room were ready for dessert, she saw, and she hurried down to get their orders. Leon didn't like her to talk too long to customers—maybe he'd just think Howard was asking her for some salt. But as she passed the fountain, Leon beckoned her over.

"What in hell," he demanded, eyeing her, "did that feller want with *salt* on his ice cream?"

Pale green and white, yellow and blue, the summer dresses flashed across the floor of the Dream Hill Dance Pavilion. Five hundred feet hissed on the polished wax. In the breathless air, most of the men had shed their jackets and danced in light colored shirts and slacks. Only the orchestra sweated in tuxedos, playing the wild and searching tunes, their instruments a blare of brassy glitter against the blue screen behind their box. "I want, I want, I want . . ." the music said. It was twelve o'clock and no fairy godmother, however gay the dresses.

The windows of the pavilion were open, but no breeze stirred through them; only if you leaned close to the screen, you could smell the soft, sweet air of the summer night. Theo sat near one of them at a small side table where Howard had left her ten minutes ago. He'd said he'd be right back, but now he was dancing with someone on the other side of the hall—someone bright haired and tall in a green dress, whose face she couldn't see because it was against his shoulder.

It seemed odd. When you went out with a boy, he didn't usually leave you for someone else, unless he was sure you had a partner. But maybe things were different where Howard came from. *He* certainly was different from anyone she knew.

So far, they had had a lovely time. Riding over to the pavilion—it was on a hill in the woods overlooking the sea, ten miles from Bellport—Howard had been as gay as could be, talking and laughing, telling her about himself. She'd been so interested she'd just let him talk, without saying much herself, thinking enviously that it must be wonderful to have been so many places and done so many things when you were only twenty-three. At the pavilion, up to now, they'd danced every dance. He was a wonderful dancer who liked to do intricate and unpredictable things with his feet. Often she couldn't follow him. He seemed, as the time went on, not to talk nearly so much.

She wondered if he were getting tired. She wasn't. She felt as if she could go on forever, feet sliding on the smooth floor, music thumping through her body. So, when halfway through a dance, she stumbled quite badly and he hadn't said anything, she'd asked him if maybe he didn't want to sit down. He'd said, "God, yes."

But he hadn't been tired at all, she thought, watching him across the hall with that bright head against his shoulder.

He'd bought himself a highball and her a lemonade—she'd wanted a highball, too, but it was going to be bad enough when she got home, without Phoebe smelling liquor on her breath. His highball sat now, half-finished, across the table, as if he planned to come right back and drink it.

She sipped her lemonade, looking around cheerfully and brightly, so no one would think she minded being left alone. Of course he'd be right back—probably had just run across some girl he knew.

Howard hadn't, but all evening he'd been watching the girl in the green dress. She was a honey, she was a pip, and could she pick up her feet and set them down! She was built like a race horse, long and graceful, with a dark, oval, secret-looking face. Some summer girl, she must be—he hadn't seen her around before. He made up his mind he was going to dance with her.

He was having a nice enough time with Theo—but she was a cute young kid and that was all. It had been fun talking to her at first. She listened so big-eyed and impressed with all he said. But after a while, he'd kind of run out of talk, and she didn't give anything back. If you didn't talk, she just sat and looked at you. That was fine, as far as it went. Nobody, least of all him, wanted a talking machine, but after all, he liked a girl to put *something* out on the air. The main trouble, though, was she didn't dance anything extra, and Howard liked them extra.

The dame in the green dress was extra all right, in more ways than one. Howard danced not one, but two more dances with her.

There was no clock in the pavilion and Theo didn't know what time it was, but she seemed to have been sitting alone forever. Two or three times, a man or a boy had come past, looking at her tentatively, and she had looked away. One of them had even asked her to dance, but she said no, she was waiting for her partner who'd be right back. She thought it would look so funny to Howard if he came back and found her gone. Besides, she felt so miserable she didn't even know if she could dance.

He was still dancing with the girl in the green dress. They were floating around the floor, as if hypnotized, two long, graceful people, lovely to watch, even while you curdled inside with longing, wishing you could look and be like them. At the end of each dance, she thought surely he'd escort the girl to a seat and come back to the table, but he hadn't. Each time, they stood laughing with each other until the music began again, then slid effortlessly into their languorous waking dream. If he didn't come soon, she certainly was going to dance with someone else or go find the ladies' dressing room. Anything to stop sitting here alone and having people wonder.

A voice said, "Why, look who's here!" and she glanced up a little wildly, thinking at first it was nobody she knew. Then she saw it was Roger Drummey.

She felt she already knew Mr. Drummey pretty well. Three times he had waited for her outside Leon's, after work, and each time he had let her drive his car. Once he had let her drive it a long way down the coast highway—she'd been late getting home that night, too, and Phoebe had jawed, saying that one or two more tricks like that, and she'd have to stop working at Leon's.

Oh, dear, Theo thought, I do wish I knew what time it is.

All the time, Mr. Drummey had sat beside her in the car and talked—oh, how he talked. About anything and everything under the sun. Usually she was so absorbed in driving that she didn't hear half he said nor remember much of it, except sometimes he quoted poetry and that was nice.

One night he'd said softly:

"Rose of all roses, rose of all the world,"

and she'd looked around, startled, to see what he'd meant, but his eyes had been fixed on the white concrete road ahead of the car, and his face had a faraway, locked-up expression.

Now he sat down in Howard's vacant chair and beamed at

her across the table. "Here I find you," he said. "The one civilized thing in this barbaric place."

"Hello." She was glad to see him.

"How do you happen to be here?" he said, as if it were the last place on earth he'd ever expect to find her.

"Oh, I came with . . . with a boy," Theo said. "He's gone out for just a minute."

"Good! I hope he stays for a long time . . . gives me a chance to say hello and get back my grip on my staggering senses."

"Don't you like it here?"

"I find it appropriate," he said. "Look at that orchestra! Attendants on the altar of a heathen god. Hautboys blow. Tootle-ootle-oot. Alarms and excursions. Enter the head of John the Baptist on a platter, or is it an atom bomb? You tell me."

Theo giggled. Sometimes she couldn't make out whether Mr. Drummey meant half he said, or even if he knew what he were saying. "Why did you come, if you don't like dances?"

"Left to myself, I wouldn't. Evelyn dragged me. Evelyn—that's my wife—hates it as bad as I do, but she thinks it's the thing successful and civilized people ought to do." He leaned across the table and said in a half-whisper, "I'm a terrible dancer. You ought to see us dancing. I look like a beetle on a sunflower stalk."

She couldn't help laughing, though it was an outrageous thing to say.

"Do you dance, my unicorn?" said Mr. Drummey. "Will you dance with me?"

"Yes, I'd like to," she said.

"Why did you call me a unicorn?" she asked, as they circled slowly about the hall. The orchestra was playing a waltz, and it was surprising, but Mr. Drummey danced as well as Howard—he wasn't half so hard to keep step with either, and you didn't have to worry about his doing unexpected things. She felt as light as a feather and knew she was dancing well. "I thought a unicorn was a fabulous monster," she went on. "Is that a nice thing to call anyone?"

"Very nice indeed," said Mr. Drummey. "Take that word 'fabulous.' Something rich and rare and seldom seen. 'Monster' we'll skip, because a unicorn isn't one. A unicorn's a lovely animal. There's a story about a man who saw a unicorn—his wife couldn't see it, even though it was there, so he had her carted off to an insane asylum. But I couldn't do that," Mr. Drummey said, executing a smooth reverse turn on his light little feet. "I couldn't do that to Evelyn."

When he took her back to the table, Theo felt better. He sat down at the table opposite her and shamelessly mopped his face while he beckoned to a waiter. "Not so young as I used to be," he grinned at her. "But, my! I enjoyed that dance. I never enjoyed a dance so much as that when I was young."

"Oh, you must have. You're such a liar, Mr. Drummey."

"Liar?" he repeated, looking hurt. "Oh, never. Not to you. To you, I tell the unashamed truth . . . to all others, the lies. Waiter, bring us— What will you have? I want a Scotch highball."

"I'll have—" Theo stopped. "I had a lemonade before," she said glumly.

"Two Scotch highballs," Mr. Drummey said to the waiter, "and take away these shards." He waited until the waiter had gone, taking the empty lemonade glass and Howard's stale drink.

"Your troubles," Roger went on, "may as well come doubly as alone. You bear them anyway, no matter how many. There are those at home who'll take exception to the smell of liquor on you, is that it?"

"I'll say it is," Theo said.

"One highball won't hurt you, and if you must learn to drink, as children seem to in these piping times, remember the magic formula: For times of despair: One highball, solace. Two, double solace. Three, a burden to the body. Four, a burden to the spirit. Five, despair again. And there you've made the circle. Five, God willing, you creatures of bright morning shall never know." He raised the glass which the waiter set down before him. "To innocence," he said. "To innocence and ancient evil."

He made the highball sound so desperate and exciting—she touched glasses with him and tasted hers, and looked across to find him watching her with a smile.

"Nasty?"

"Oh, no. I like it very much," she said hastily, and took a big drink to show she did. She could hardly help from making a face.

"Well," he said. "Drink it then, and wait for the piper at the gates of dawn." The smile left his face. "But soft, what light through yonder casement breaks?" he said under his breath.

A very tall, raw-boned woman in a yellowy-orange dress with spangles, was striding up the hall.

"Not with a bang but a whimper," Mr. Drummey said. He got up and bowed to the woman as she stopped beside the table. "Did you enjoy your dance, dear?" he asked politely. "Evelyn, this is Miss Theoline Sewell. Miss Sewell, Mrs. Drummey."

Mrs. Drummey acknowledged the introduction with a brief, coldly glittering stare. "I wondered where you'd got to," she said. "If you're not going to dance with me, Roger, we'd better go home."

"But you were dancing with Joe Cambrini," Mr. Drummey said. "A more forthright dancer than I but, let it be said, not a better one. Shall we dance now?"

Mrs. Drummey jerked her head indicating yes.

He did not look at her, but tilted his glass and drank the rest of his highball. "Good-by, Miss Sewell," he said, bowing. "A pleasure to have known you." He trailed off after his wife's stalwart back.

They did look odd dancing together but not in the least like a beetle and a sunflower. Mrs. Drummey was the odd-looking one. She was a horrid person. But for all Mr. Drummey was small, he had a great deal of dignity.

When Howard finally came back to the table he was a little sore that he was stuck with one girl and had to take her home, when he might have had a better time with somebody he liked better. If he took Theo home in a hurry, he could get back before the dance was over. It was time a young kid was home, anyway.

Josephine Brown was the girl's name—Jo, she said to call her. She was on a vacation from her job in Kansas City, staying at one of the Bellport hotels, and she had a car of her own.

Theo greeted Howard with a bright smile. "If you hadn't come soon, I was going to have another highball," she said.

"Holy smoke," he said, staring at her glass. "Well, how about it—you rested yet?"

Why, he'd thought *she* was tired. He'd been waiting till he was sure she was rested.

"Oh, yes," she said. "I could go on dancing all night."

"Well," he said doubtfully. "Holy smoke, I forgot about the time. Didn't you tell me you had to be home early?" He pulled out his watch. "My gosh, it's ten to one. Your Ma will tear my head off. I was going to say, let's dance, but we better go, hadn't we?"

"I expect we had," Theo said regretfully. He was right, of course, only she had wanted to dance at least once more with him. Pauline Stover and Gerald Wicks and some of the other high school crowd had just come in, too. If they could have seen her dancing with Howard . . . Well, anyway, they'd see her leave with him, and think she'd *been* dancing with him. "Even this early, it won't be your head Ma'll tear off," she told him.

They left the pavilion and went down the rustic steps on the hillside to the parking ground. A small, salt breeze was beginning to come in from over the sea, cold from the east and heavy with damp and fog. Howard put the car over the road at a fast clip.

Let's see, he figured. About thirty-six miles, altogether. I can get back easy by one-thirty. The dance wasn't over until three, and Jo'd promised to wait for him. Whether she would or not was another matter. You never could tell with those kind of dames.

"Too bad to have to go so early," he said to the silent figure beside him. "Evenin's still a pup."

"I know. I'm afraid I've spoilt your good time."

"Oh, heck, no." No sense ruining the kid's evening. "It's my bedtime, too. Working man, you know. I already done enough for three men, today, out on the ketch. Maybe next time, we can rig it to stay later, huh, honey?"

Theo's heart leaped. He hadn't had a bad time at all, and he was going to take her again! "Oh, I'd *love* to go again," she said warmly.

"H'm," Howard said. "Sometime we will."

But he wasn't setting a time for a regular date, and he didn't sound very interested. There must be some way to interest him. "You like it around here?" she ventured, after a silence.

"Oh, sure. Good place, in the summertime."

If he'd only talk, the way he had on the way to the dance.

"But not winters?" she prompted.

"Heck, no. Too cold."

"You won't stay here, I guess, next winter."

"Don't plan to." Howard wanted to concentrate on his driving. Johnny Fleming's old car wasn't much of a bus, and he wanted to go as fast as he could, and still return her to Johnny all in one piece.

He's going awfully fast, Theo thought. But it was swell, sailing along like that. Or would be, if she didn't feel that the evening was going dead on its feet.

"Where will you go?"

"Go? Oh, you mean next winter? South, I guess."

"On Mr. Grover's boat?"

"No. He lays her up in Bellport winters." What was this, Howard thought, a catechism?

He wasn't going to talk or anything. He was just getting her home as fast as he could. She *did* like him. If only she could think of something to say.

"I've always wanted to go south," she said chattily. "I don't know how I ever could, though, unless I had a job down there. Have you got a job down there?"

"Not yet."

"What will you do?"

"Oh, whatever turns up."

"Sailing a boat, the same as you do here?"

"Maybe. Or try running a fishing cruiser for a sporting camp. There's lots of jobs in Florida."

"Sporting camp! Why, for goodness' sake!" She didn't know what ailed her, the words just came out for want of something to say.

Howard moved his shoulders impatiently. "What's wrong with a sporting camp?"

Oh, dear, that was just plain dumb, and now she'd made him mad. She cast about in her mind. "Why, nothing, of course. It's just . . . that is . . . Why, I've got an uncle who runs a sporting camp somewhere in Florida," she lied desperately. "I was just surprised, that was all, to hear that's what you wanted to do . . . go to one, I mean . . . it seems like a coincidence."

She was aware, suddenly, that the car had slowed down.

"Sure does, doesn't it?" Howard said heartily. "Where's he located?"

If she'd wanted to interest him, she certainly had succeeded. He was giving her all his attention and the car was bumping along at a near-normal speed.

"Why . . . why, I hardly know," was all she could think of to say.

Howard grunted. "Oh, well, skip it." She must be afraid he'd go try the old boy for a job, he thought resentfully.

"The thing is," Theo said. She gave a little bleat intended for a laugh, and even as she did so, thought how false it sounded. "The thing is, he's been gone so many years, we hardly ever think of him any more. He was a . . . sort of a black sheep in the family," she improvised hastily.

"I'll be damned. How'd you know he's got a sporting camp?"

"Oh . . . some friend of Pa's, I forget just who, spent a winter down south a few years ago—somebody Pa knew over to Ferriston. Joe Knowles, it was, he died last winter." That, at least, was true. Joe Knowles *had* died last winter. "When he came back from down south he said he'd seen Uncle . . . Uncle Oscar. Said he had a big sporting camp on one of the islands—keys, I mean."

It was going more smoothly now, unreeling like the pictures in a movie, or in one of the adventures she imagined for herself.

"This man, Joe Knowles, I mean, said it was a regular hotel, built out of big white blocks, like . . . like those buildings down there are, you know, and a lot of rich men went there to go fishing."

"What d'you know about that!" Howard said. This was something like. It might be the contact in Florida he was looking for. If he went to this girl's uncle, said he was a friend of his niece's, up north . . . "What's your uncle's name?"

"Oscar. Oscar C. Sewell. He's my father's brother."

"Did Joe Knowles say whether he ran fishing cruisers?"

"Oh, yes. He has seven or eight, maybe more by this time. The . . . Joe Knowles said he was making money hand over fist." Theo went on, drawing freely for atmosphere from some stories about sport fishing in Florida, which she'd read in *The Saturday Evening Post*. By the time she was through, both she and Howard had a definite picture in mind of Uncle

Oscar Sewell's sporting camp in the Florida keys, and they were both entranced with it.

But at the same time, Theo was a little scared. Suppose he mentioned it to someone around Bellport who knew her folks? Most anybody would know Sylvanus Sewell didn't have any brother but Morgan. Suppose the story got back to Sylvanus and Phoebe? Suppose Howard found out she was lying?

"Your father'd remember where it was, wouldn't he?" Howard was saying.

"Look," she said earnestly. "I wouldn't even dare mention it to Pa. I've talked about a lot of things I'm not supposed to, Howard—I don't know how I could have, except you brought up sporting camps, and . . . I was so surprised. You see, Uncle Oscar did something awful around here—I don't even know what it was, but it was so awful he had to get out, and we never talk about him. We . . . we never speak his name, on account of the police might . . . might find out where he is. If my folks found out I'd talked, I'd get into awful trouble at home, Howard. You won't mention to anyone I told you, please, Howard, will you?"

It might have sounded false to Howard if he hadn't already been so beguiled. Already, in his mind's eye, he was seeing a picture of himself, in his blue uniform, driving Uncle Oscar's cruisers into the spray of the Gulf Stream. "Oh, sure not. Don't worry. Won't say a word."

The first thing, he thought, was to get on more than speaking terms with her. Then she'd be more interested in finding out just where Oscar Sewell was; maybe she'd even write to him about Howard.

He turned the car into the leafy darkness of the Granite Hook road, slid off the tar to a flat spot under a big tree and cut the engine.

"You and me haven't had a chance to get acquainted, baby," he murmured, sliding over. "Tip your puss up here."

He put an expert hand around her shoulders, with the other tilted her head back and kissed her on the mouth. Holding her so, he felt the initial startled jerk of her body grow quiet and the surprised tentative response from her lips.

"That's the girl," he said softly.

Darn, she was a nice kid!

"You're a sweet baby," he said. "With sugar and cream." He kissed her again, and after a little, she had to push him away. That was all right, too.

"I better take you home," he said. "You're getting in my blood."

She could, too, he thought, without very much trouble, if he wanted to get tangled up, which he didn't.

He started the car and coasted smoothly down the hill to Granite Hook. "Go out tomorrow night, baby?" he asked.

"Oh, dear, I can't, tomorrow's my late night to work."

"Sunday?"

"Maybe Sunday, if Ma'll let me."

"I'll see you at the restaurant. We'll go again soon, don't worry." He could still, he thought, make it back to the dance in time to go home with Jo Brown

"Oh, yes!" Theo was breathless and frightened by what had started to go on inside her—something smoky with bewilderment, yet shot through with streaks of almost unbearable brightness.

ROGER DRUMMEY trained his field glasses on the top of the spruce tree and waited. The spruce was an old "wolf" tree, on which four or five big lower branches had gone wild and grown into trunks, spreading out from a tremendous crotch. The main trunk, a little taller than the others, was some fifty feet from its spiny green tip to the ground.

Roger's glasses were good ones. He could make out the neat design of the upper twigs, carrying their load of brown cones with the slight smears of pitch dried out by the sun. But no glasses could have penetrated the green secrecy about four feet from the top of the tree, into which he most urgently desired to see.

Ten minutes ago, his quick eye had caught a small, tawny flash vanishing behind those twigs. Except for the moment when he sat down on the ground and braced his elbows against his knees to rest his wrists, he had had the glasses focused on that spot ever since, but he hadn't seen the bird reappear. It might have got away unnoticed, of course. The thick growth was noncommittal, and motionless except for the stirrings of a slight breeze.

As he watched, a tiny mite of a bird slipped out from somewhere behind the twigs and tilted obligingly in the full focus of his glasses. It even turned around so that he saw it front and rear, and showed off its red poll.

I'll be darned, Roger said to himself. A slight grin appeared on his face. If that were a Cape May warbler, it was the first one he'd ever seen; and if it weren't a Cape May, it was his twin brother. He watched the bird until it flew, getting a fine uninterrupted view of its size and markings. Then he put down the glasses, flipped through his pocket field manual and found the picture.

Yup, that was the fellow, all right.

He jotted down his notes with a fine feeling of satisfaction and stretched out on the grass, his eyes on the feathery waving treetops. He'd give a good deal to be able to climb that spruce. So far as he knew, only one authenticated nest of the Cape May warbler had ever been found in the United States. Not that he had any scientific reason for thinking there might be a nest behind those twigs—doubtless it was empty now, anyway, the fledglings flown. But he did have a kind of hunch. Something, maybe, about the way the bird had acted, as if it were at home. If there were a nest there, and it could be identified, it would be rare. Darned rare. Something, maybe, for a museum.

How long had it been, he thought suddenly, since he'd

even contemplated climbing a tree? He must be getting better. Certainly, the nightmare in his spirit was easing—at least, in the past weeks he hadn't felt quite so much like a ghost in the world of the living. God knew why, unless it was because he had found he could speak again like a human being, as he had on several occasions with the little Sewell girl. He was more grateful to her than she knew. Of course she didn't listen to him always—who could expect her to, when her devoted head was bowed in worship over the smooth plastic wheel of his car? But it hadn't mattered deeply. She'd helped him to break an evil web; and when she did respond it was with sensitiveness and a quick humor that delighted him.

He sensed, rather than heard, a slight sound not far away and, turning his head, saw that Evelyn had come out of the trees at the edge of the clearing. Good Lord, she must have followed him down here from the house, an hour ago. She must have been standing there quite a while, watching him. That was something new. She hated the woods.

"What is it?" he said, getting to his feet. "Is something wrong, Evelyn?"

"It's suppertime," she said, in her heavy, flat voice.

"Yes. I know." He began gathering up his paraphernalia, glancing at his wrist watch. "I planned to be back by six," he said, unable to keep the impatience out of his voice.

"I'm sure you did," she said. "I just thought I'd come on down and see if what interested you so much in these woods might not interest me, too."

"I doubt it," Roger said briefly.

"Well, I wasn't so sure."

The latent sarcasm in her voice enlightened him. She hadn't been herself since the night at Dream Hill, when she'd seen him having a harmless highball with Theo. It was preposterous, of course; she must know that the last thing in the world he would think of would be to come off down here in the woods to meet anybody. But she'd obviously brooded herself into a state of mind about it.

"If you've been watching me," he said, "I'm quite sure you know now what interests me here."

Evelyn stared curiously from him to the spruce. "What's up the tree?" she asked.

"A bird. Possibly a nest. Quite a rare one."

Her eyes narrowed. "I'll have Dominick come down and get it for you."

He sensed her triumph at his slight gasp of consternation.

Dominick, her handy man, was a good shot—at least, he prided himself on being able to blow crows to pieces with a shotgun.

"No," Roger said carefully. "It's not worth the trouble."

She turned on her heel and started back through the woods to the house. Something awkward about her walk puzzled him, until he saw that, instead of the spike heels she always wore, she had borrowed a pair of Dominick's old sneakers for this expedition, and was finding them extremely uncomfortable. It might be poetic justice, he thought, if the backs of her legs were as lame, tomorrow, as they doubtless would be. Her dress and hat were the kind she usually wore, in flowers and bright colors. The combination was an odd one, with Dominick's sneakers.

Roger had always disliked Evelyn's clothes, without the consolation of feeling he had a right to say very much about them. She dressed her big body violently, as she did everything with violence—in reds and yellows and purples, as if she wanted to thrust its ugliness in defiance before the world's eyes. At times, Roger had thought her clothes pathetic and the courage that wore them admirable. This afternoon, seeing them invade his woods, he hated them.

She stalked along, saying nothing more until they were coming into the yard at the back of the house. Then she said, "There's Dominick now."

"Listen, Evelyn. If I want a bird for my collection, I'm quite capable of shooting it myself."

"If you don't get sentimental," she said contemptuously.

"But what's your collection going to amount to, if you let the rare ones get away? Dominick can kill it, if you haven't got the guts to."

Ordinarily, his better judgment would have kept him silent; because if Evelyn were let alone in her rages, after a time she got over them. But the picture in his mind of Dominick shooting around through the spruces with his gun set Roger to raging, too.

"Look here," he said. "You keep out of my affairs, Evelyn. As I keep out of yours. I don't want that bird killed. I'd rather shoot—" In his fury, he almost said "you," but changed it in time to "Dominick," and saw at once that she was quite aware of the change.

"I've no intention of keeping out of your *affairs*," she said between her teeth.

Roger hauled himself up with a jolt. Reasonless, pathological jealousy was what was behind this. She couldn't help it, any more than she could have helped a disease. Damn it, it might be fiendish at times, but he ought to keep a tighter check on himself. After all, she had in her lifetime done a great deal for him. Why let yourself get mad at something that was as unreasoning and uncontrollable as a tempest?

"I'm not carrying on with anyone, Evelyn," he said soberly. "You must know that. Please don't be idiotic."

She said nothing. At supper, she ate silently through the entire meal without glancing up from her plate, chewing her food with short little chops of her jaws.

I can't stand this, Roger thought. My God, no man could. He pushed his chair away from the table.

"Where are you going?" she said harshly.

"I thought I might drive down to the drugstore after some Players."

"Common Luckies or Camels won't do, I suppose."

"No," he said politely.

"I don't think you're going out tonight."

"Of course I am," he said, looking at her curiously. "If I wish to, Evelyn."

She got up and stood in front of the hanging mirror to comb her hair, with short, grating strokes that tore through the tangles, as if she were currying an animal. Only, Roger thought, no animal would stand for it. He turned to go out the door.

Behind his back, Evelyn laughed. "You hear this?" she said. She jingled something in her pocket with a sharp, brittle sound. "That's your car keys. They're in Evelyn's pocket. Evelyn's got to be over to the Cabins until late, and she's taking no chances, Roger, honey."

Roger stopped short. "Really," he said disgustedly.

" 'Really,' " she mimicked. "You thought you had it all set, didn't you? Well, you haven't."

He regarded her for an instant silently and turned back toward the door.

"Well, what are you going to do about it?" She came after him, peering determinedly as he crossed the hall.

"What would you do in my place?" Roger asked. "Walk?"

"No, you don't!" Evelyn said. Her hand shot out and caught him by the front of the shirt.

"Stop it, Evelyn!" Roger said evenly.

He tried to pull away but the twist she gave him almost lifted him off his feet.

She contemplated him for an instant with a kind of grim amusement, then drew him to her, holding one arm around him in a powerful embrace. "Little Roger," she said in a cooing voice. "Doesn't want to kiss Evelyn before she goes to work?" When he did not move, she put the other hand under his chin like a vise and turned his face up to hers.

Roger stood quietly while she kissed him, feeling her big hand like a stone pressing against the small of his back. She would make two of him, and right now she wouldn't mind a chance to hurt him.

She kissed him again, this time with passion. "Evelyn'll

be home late," she said. "But she'll be home. You be here, honey, see?"

"If this goes on," he said, not moving, "you'll make it impossible for me to live with you at all."

He was unprepared for the look of sickly unhappiness that came into her face. Then she pushed him violently away from her and went past him out the door. He heard her solid footsteps go thudding down the walk. After a moment, he heard them come thudding back again. She opened the door and put in her head.

"I hope you know where you'll go," she shouted at him. "You'd only starve to death if you left me."

She slammed the door, and this time, was gone for good.

Roger let go his breath wearily. What could you do? There seemed to be so very little. Scenes with her had been bad, before, but never so bad as this. She was, of course, more deeply unhappy than he was and in worse cause, because she had no resources that he had ever been able to discover, with which she could meet her inner dissonance. Something in his behavior to her lately had brought this about. What was it? He thought back, but could recall nothing. He had, in fact, leaned over backwards since the night at Dream Hill to reassure her, reminding himself of his life's bargain, and thinking, surely she couldn't believe seriously that he was involved with a schoolgirl or anyone else. He didn't think, now, that she actually did. It was only a more violent version of the emotional game she had always played to attract his attention.

Later, he would have to think out what to do. Now he couldn't reason to any purpose. He was still shaking a little, with revulsion. He went into the living room to his chair by the window and sat for a long time looking out into the dusk.

Had someone been gossiping to Evelyn about Theo Sewell? But who . . . and why? He had seen the child two—possibly three—times, looking forward with a kind of mild anticipation to taking her home from work, letting her drive the car. The poor kid never got a chance to handle a good car, and she was car-crazy. But she was something else, too, Roger had to admit. That first night, he had felt as if everybody else in the world were substantial flesh and blood, through which he passed without leaving a trace; as if he shouted in a streetful of people who heard everybody's voice but his own. Remembering his pleasure after that first drive, he had done it again, quite soon. In the meantime, he had spent some time planning up things to say.

The same transformation had taken place on each of the scented summer nights; driving back home, he had felt within himself the flood of an incredulous warmth and sense of release. He was back in the world again, a human being who had a friend to talk to. Not to bring forth ideas that would shake the world—he had none; but to communicate the simple, everyday utterances of a man's spirit.

Had the small measure of happiness made such a change in him that Evelyn noticed? And if she had noticed, why should such a thing threaten the whole structure of her security? For it was threatened, Roger had no doubts about that. He realized suddenly, thinking back over his life with her, that there was no escaping the conclusion—Evelyn had always been happiest at times when he was ill or unhappy. It must be she wanted him thus; that she felt herself of more value to him when he was less than a normal man.

Roger shuddered a little. He had not known much of spiritual relationships when he entered upon his bargain. For how could two people, bound together upon such a foundation, do anything but destroy each other?

He got up out of the chair and went out to the kitchen. The car had duplicate keys, of course—Evelyn knew that as well as he did. They were kept on the shelf by the clock, and they were there still. Either she had meant to leave one set, or she had forgotten it. How fathom the illogicalities of a mind like that?

If he had been able he would have stayed at home. But

he couldn't bear any longer to be in the rooms that reeked of her—not a physical smell, of course, unless you could say that a personality had a tangible quality your nose could detect. He backed the car out of the garage and sent it rolling down the concrete toward Bellport. He would get his cigarettes at the drugstore; then he would drive around for a while before he went back home. Perhaps, by then, he'd be able to think constructively; think of something he could do.

An ancient, battered car was standing in front of Leon's. Roger didn't notice it, except he had to park behind it while he got out. He came back, tore open the new pack of Players and lit one. Bellport's Main Street was pleasant tonight with its colored lights. Beyond the stores, the elm trees, meeting overhead, made a warm brown tunnel, where people strolled in groups of two and three. A bunch of young fellows on the corner by the drugstore joshed and laughed with each other. It must be near closing time at Leon's. Should he wait and offer to drive Theo home? Probably better not; but how much invasion of his spirit should a man suffer before his spirit went out of him and did not return?

No, Roger didn't notice the battered car until, suddenly, Theo came bursting out of Leon's. Then a tall young fellow came away from the group at the corner and met her, catching her by the hand. Howard Thurlow, Roger saw, craning up to peer out through the windshield. A boy off one of the yachts, whom he knew by name.

Theo was delighted to see Howard. They climbed into the old car and drove away.

Well, of course a youngster would have a boy friend, he might have counted on that, but—Roger was suddenly astounded at the violence of his feelings.

He sat where he was, watching the red taillight, like a diminishing evil eye, draw away down the street. The elm trees cast a darkness, but he could see the red bead for a long way, until it went over the slope in the highway and was gone. With it, the anger died out of him, and through the tumult replacing it, he realized what, through the incredibly few weeks of the slow-paced summer, had been happening to him.

I should have known, he thought, horrified. I was a fool not to have known. Evelyn . . . was this what she had sensed? It must be.

His appalled mind ducked and dodged away from it, trying to reason against the thunder of his unaccustomed blood.

She is a schoolgirl, he told himself. And I am a ridiculous little man, with a formidable and frightful wife.

But even though the picture was clear before his eyes, the indestructible beauty stood within him like a flower.

WESLEY was worried. Felix Beacon had a friend visiting him from his school, Kenneth Murray, and things weren't going at all well.

The week before Kenneth's arrival, Felix had spent singing his praises. "Everybody thinks he'll be the champion swimmer of the school next year—wait till you see his overhand crawl. He's a wonderful tennis player, too. Boy, what a serve!"

Christmas vacation, Felix had visited Ken's father's place on Long Island, where they had sailed Ken's dinghy with the "frostbites." Felix was impatient with Wes, because Wes said the only kind of "frostbites" he'd ever heard of were the kind you rubbed snow on. He started to explain with patience and in great detail how you were supposed to sail a dinghy—which seemed odd to Wes, since he'd taught Felix how to sail a skiff with a sprit-sail when they were kids. Yet, for all that, Wes had looked forward to Kenneth's arrival. Anybody Felix liked that much must be a heck of a good guy.

Now that Kenneth was here, everything seemed to be out of focus. Wes couldn't put his finger on what the trouble was. But his opinion didn't seem to carry the weight it had before; the things he could do that Felix couldn't didn't seem, somehow, to be very important.

Felix had never been a strong boy. His build was all right—he was as big as Wes, though now that he had started to get tall, he was inclined to be skinny. But he had never seemed to have much staying power and he had always been a duffer at machinery or sailing—most things Wes had taught him had to be taught afresh at the beginning of each summer. It wasn't that Felix didn't try. He tried terribly hard and he yearned with a passion to be outstanding in all kinds of athletics. But his muscles didn't co-ordinate right. He'd always said, himself, he was the dub of the world.

It was understood, of course, that Wes would never crow or rub anything in, even though he could circle Felix in most of the things they did. As a matter of fact, Wes never considered Felix fair competition at all. Felix couldn't help it if he wasn't strong. He was like a younger brother, somebody to be taken care of—built of finer stuff, maybe, his abilities elsewhere than in athletic stunts.

But after Kenneth came, things began to be different. Thinking back, Wes wondered if this summer hadn't started out to be different, anyway.

Take the Ford. He'd expected, when Felix arrived in June, to do most of the driving for him, because Felix had never been any good at driving a car. But Felix wanted to do it himself; and what was more, he didn't want to take any advice. As a consequence, he'd raised heck with the engine. He slammed the car over any kind of an old rough back road he took a notion to; never cared whether he had oil enough or water. The day he'd decided to see what would happen if he put her into second going forty, he'd practically stripped the gears.

"Who cares?" he'd said, when Wes pointed out that, starting from a dead stop, he couldn't change gears anyway without clashing them. "An old Ford—that's what she's for, to bat around in."

Now the Ford sat, scarcely ever touched, in Wes's back yard. The last trip she'd made was to take Emily to the Bellport Hospital. Wes fairly turned cold when he thought of that. If he'd only been home, he'd have borrowed a car. It was enough to scare you to death, thinking what might have happened.

Felix had given the Ford outright to Wes. He didn't want to use his pocket money for the repairs she'd need; besides, he was all taken up now with the new mahogany Chris-Craft his father had bought him. Wes supposed glumly that someday he might get enough ahead himself to fix up the car, but he didn't quite see how.

The first few times they'd taken the speedboat out, Luke, the Beacons' chauffeur, had gone along, until Wes caught on to the engine. After that, he and Felix had gone alone. Felix learned how to start and stop her, advance and retard the throttle, and steer. Wes was horrified to find that Felix was inclined to treat the speedboat much as he had treated the Ford—wanted all the time to try stunts in her, forgetting all about the machinery. Wes didn't believe it was on purpose—Felix just didn't have it in him to handle engines carefully or with skill. But there was a way to do stunts without wrecking engines, if you bothered to learn it.

The day after Kenneth Murray arrived, they had all three gone swimming in Patch's Cove. On the way down, Kenneth had challenged Wes and Felix to a race.

"Not me," Felix said hastily. "I know when I'm outclassed. Wes'll take you on."

Wes was proud of his swimming. He had been in and out of the water ever since he could walk, and while he didn't suppose he was anything remarkable, he knew he was as good as anybody around Bellport. He'd raced summer boys before.

He said, offhandedly, "Sure," and wondered why Felix looked amused.

Wes liked Kenneth. Ken was a dark-haired, tall boy, with the kind of skin the sun turns to a clear gold-brown. He might be a little thick through the shoulders, but except for that he had a swell build. In bathing trunks, he looked like a million dollars. He had a quiet way about him, too, of always knowing where he was and what he was going to do next—the kind of boy who, in school, presides at meetings. In Wes's own school, Gerald Wicks, the ball player, was like that; only Jerry'd never see the day when he'd look as smooth and self-possessed as Ken did.

At the beach, Wes casually waded into the water, but Ken took a long, clean, running dive, vanishing with scarcely a splash. He came up twenty feet or so away, gasping.

Wes said, "Didn't you tell the guy it was cold, Felix?"

Felix, who was still standing barely ankle deep, said, "He knows it. He's been swimming everywhere."

"Feels good," Ken called. "Where'll we race to?"

"Out to the end of the weir and back?" Wes suggested.

"Okay, Felix can umpire, in case it's a close finish."

They started with a running dive from the beach, but before Wes was halfway to the turning point, he knew he was beaten. He realized with a sudden twist of envy that never except in movie newsreels, had he seen anybody swim the way Ken could. Ken used an effortless, overhand stroke that sent him through the water as cleanly as a fish. He was back on the beach beside Felix when Wes had covered a little more than half the return trip. Wes landed panting like a puffer; Ken, it seemed, wasn't even blown.

Even so, Wes wouldn't have minded. It was no disgrace to be beaten by a better man. But coming up the beach, he caught a grin on Felix's face, and wondered, suddenly, if the two of them hadn't put up a job on him. He was sure of it when Felix said, "Ken says that isn't a crawl stroke you use —it's a kind of an outsize dog paddle."

It rankled, especially since Wes had been trying, for summers back, to teach Felix a stroke the Bellport boys called the "Australian crawl."

Wes said, in a voice he tried to make casual, "Boy, it sure isn't the same kind of crawl his is. That was the best swimming I ever saw, Ken."

"It isn't a crawl at all," Felix said. "Is it, Ken?"

Ken grinned. "Well," he said, "it's no slouch of a stroke, Wes. But the crawl goes like this." He demonstrated. "Yours goes like this. See?"

Wes nodded. "Could be." He'd meant to be merely noncommittal, but Felix took it he was arguing.

"Ken knows what he's talking about," he said sharply. "He's had the best swimming instructors in the world."

"I don't doubt that."

"Well, what are you talking about, then? He didn't even have to stretch to beat you. Show him your racing stroke, Ken."

And Ken did, and it was something.

A few days later, Felix said to him on the pier one morning, "Look, Wes. Ken wants to sail. D'you suppose we could fix up the catboat?"

What with the Ford and the speedboat, the catboat hadn't even been in the water that summer. She needed calking and paint and to soak her seams some before she'd be fit to use. Ordinarily, Felix and Wes would have turned to and given her a working-over together—would have had a swell time doing it, too. But, today, Felix and Ken merely helped Wes slide the cat out of the boathouse onto the pier. Then they went off somewhere. After a while, Wes heard the Chris-Craft engine start up from her mooring off Mr. Beacon's pier.

Ken, Wes knew by now, could run the speedboat as well as he could. Ken was used to any kind of a boat; he'd been pretty sharp too about picking up the navigation marks of Bellport harbor and adjacent waters. So Wes guessed they didn't really need him; but it was a swell day for going out in the Chris-Craft—blue sky and water and just enough of a breeze to make a smart chop outside the point. Gloomily, he watched the big double white crests that marked the V of the speedboat's wake go out of sight, behind the point, before he turned back into the boathouse for the calking tools.

He was lying on his back under the catboat's cradle, tunking a piece of oakum into a weakened seam, when he saw Mrs. Beacon's white sport shoes and her ankles, all he could see of her, come briskly along the asphalt ramp that led to the pier. Since it didn't seem respectful to be peeking out from under a boat like that, Wes hastily turned away his eyes.

She didn't have the same scruples about looking at his legs, though. She stopped alongside them where they stuck out from under the catboat.

"Why, Wesley," she said. "Is that you?"

Wes dropped his tools and scrambled out. "Yes'm. You looking for me, Mrs. Beacon?"

"No," she said. "I was going down on the pier to sit in the sun. I thought you'd all gone out in the boat. Didn't I hear it start up a while ago?"

"Yes'm. But Felix wanted the cat fixed up for Ken, so I—"

"The scamps!" A little frown of worry appeared between Mrs. Beacon's eyes. "Felix knows I don't allow him out in boats without you. I'll have a word to say when they get back."

"Oh, they're all right, honest they are, Mrs. Beacon. Ken's as good as I am with a boat—maybe better. He's got all kinds of boats of his own down on Long Island."

Wes had a pretty good idea of how Felix would feel if his mother jawed him about taking Ken out without Wes. "Er . . . I wouldn't have let them go out, Mrs. Beacon, if it wouldn't be okay."

She smiled at him. "I'm sure you wouldn't. You're such a comfort, Wesley." She sat down in the lee of the boathouse, where the clean planks of the pier were warm and baked brown by the sun. "Boating on Long Island Sound isn't quite the same as it is here, though. Sam says—Mr. Beacon says—the winds and tides are altogether different. I hope Ken knows about that."

"He does, all right. We've been out enough, so's I could teach him the harbor marks. Of course, Felix knows his way around out there, too."

"Felix!" Mrs. Beacon said. "He doesn't know his way around in the bathtub."

Wes couldn't help grinning. He guessed between them he and Mrs. Beacon had Felix pretty well sized up. His self-assurance was coming back. He was needed, all right, even if Felix was beginning to act as if he wasn't.

"Do go on working, Wesley," Mrs. Beacon said. "Will I bother you if I sit here for a while?"

"Oh, gosh, no!" Wes beamed. He reached under the boat for his tools. No reason why he couldn't do this side of the cat first—work on the keel seams later.

"I've hardly had a chance to talk to you all summer." She opened her knitting bag. "You and Felix have been so busy."

"We have been kind of on the go."

"Felix is always on the go these days. I suppose it's something to do with growing up. Is that the way it feels to grow up, Wesley, wanting to be on the go all the time?"

"Oh, gosh, I guess so, Mrs. Beacon. I like to, too."

She nodded. "It worries me sometimes. There must be something to interest a boy besides fast boats and cars and speed, speed, speed. Something quieter—more constructive. Do you think he'll outgrow that, Wesley?"

"Gee, Mrs. Beacon, I dunno . . ." It seemed to Wesley that nothing could ever take the place of boats or cars, no matter how old you grew. He started to say so, then changed his mind. He'd better say something more like what she expected him to. "Oh, sure, it's just a phase you go through. I'm getting over it, myself."

He was rewarded by her smile of approval. "I thought you were. Now you're out of high school, you'll have to be thinking about a job, won't you?"

Wes's heart started to thump with excitement. What was she thinking? Maybe she was going to suggest something . . . He stopped work and stared at her expectantly, but when she looked up her eyes had gone blank and her mouth was calm and careful. She said, "Wesley, what really did happen to Felix's Ford?"

The quick change of subject was hard on Wes. Hard to take his mind off some kind of dazzling career in the city, backed up by the Beacons. "Well," he said dubiously. "Of course it was a second-hand car to begin with."

"Yes," she said. "You were to find one that was in fairly good condition, I know."

Heck! He realized suddenly she had put him in a spot. He couldn't very well tell on Felix—say outright that slapdash driving was what ailed the Ford. Still, he couldn't very well let Mrs. Beacon think he hadn't done the kind of a job she'd learned to expect from him.

"His father and I thought it was going to keep him busy all summer," Mrs. Beacon went on. "The first thing we knew, the Ford was finished—Luke said it was beyond repair—and Felix was talking speedboat."

"It was a pretty good car," Wes said. He'd had some time to think. "To begin with, Funny-Money Montgomery owned it, and he takes good care of a car. Forbes, down at the Central Garage, overhauled it."

There, now if Mr. Beacon wanted to check up on him, all he had to do was ask Forbes. Wes felt better.

Mrs. Beacon nodded. She didn't say that Sam, her husband, had already had a talk with Forbes—not that she didn't trust Wesley, of course. "I was just wondering what had happened," she said. "If there'd been an accident or something that wrecked it."

"Oh, no," Wes protested hastily.

"You know, Wesley, if there had been, it would be all right to tell me." She laid down her knitting and regarded him with the confidential look that he had come to know well.

Wes turned red.

"Just between you and me, Wesley, Felix's father and I are a little worried about him. He seems so restless. We try to give him what he wants, but nothing ever satisfies him for long. We thought, with the Ford this summer, and you to drive it, he might settle down a little."

"Well, the way it was," Wes said, "Felix wanted to do the driving."

"I see." She nodded, apparently expecting him to say more.

"He . . . isn't a good driver."

"I know. But is that all?"

"Seemed like he wanted to ruin it," he blurted. There. It was out.

"I thought so," Mrs. Beacon said. "When he was little, if he wanted nicer playthings, he'd wreck the ones he had. We'd hoped he was over that."

"I know," Wes said eagerly. Cripes, he'd have to say something to help things out. She was plenty stirred up, and if she ever let Felix know he'd told about the Ford . . . "I've noticed he is over it a lot, Mrs. Beacon. Gosh, I know he is. He's a lot carefuller of the Chris-Craft than he's ever been of anything else."

But she didn't brighten up any. "You think so?"

"Sure, he is. You ought to go with him once, and see how he handles her. Just like an egg." If she did go out, he could prime Felix, so he'd know what she was going for.

"You're such a lamb, dear Wesley. I'm sure, if he is changing, you're partially responsible."

The praise was balm to Wesley's soul. He took a deep breath, and in his relief, poked a piece of oakum clean through one of the seams of the catboat. But his joy was short-lived. Mrs. Beacon's next remark sent it scattering like mist. She sure was a one to change the subject quick.

"I notice Theoline's working at Leon's," she said.

He mumbled, "She's just doing it for a stunt, to buy her fall clothes."

"It's enterprising of her. A job like that for the summer would do Jane no end of good, if she only thought so."

"Jane?"

"Surely. Why not? Take her mind off herself. The only

reason I mentioned it, Wesley, was because I hoped it wasn't permanent—Theoline's surely going back to school in the fall?"

If she weren't, Mrs. Beacon wanted to know, because she needed a housemaid, in the city, this fall, and she'd been considering Theo—if, of course, the girl was leaving school.

"Oh, sure," Wes said. "It's just for the summer."

Mrs. Beacon sighed. "That's fine. Does she know what she wants to do when she's finally through school?"

"Going to be a nurse. All settled." He'd never heard Theo mention nursing, but it was as good a profession for her as any, and he had to say something to bring the discussion around to his own career, now they'd got on the subject again. "I wish I knew what I was going to do, as well as she does."

"Nursing's a fine job for a girl. Very hard, though. I hope she knows that." Mrs. Beacon's eyes were blank and careful again. She began to gather up her knitting and poke it back into the bag.

"I guess I could stay here and go lobstering," Wes said desperately.

"Oh, my, no, you mustn't do that. Such a waste! My goodness, I'll speak to Sam, Wesley. Maybe he can think of something." She went up the pier, her white shoes flashing in the shadow of the boathouse.

Well, it was a step in the right direction, Wes thought glumly. But it wasn't much.

THEO saw Felix Beacon's crowd sitting in one of her booths when she came back from a trip to the kitchen with a loaded tray. She craned her neck to see if Wes was with them—he was, sitting jammed into a corner of the booth. There was Felix and Jane, a strange summer boy and girl, and Wes. They were all dressed up—probably had just come from the early movie, and were headed somewhere for the Friday night dance.

Wes had on a dark navy jacket, a soft shirt, and, she didn't doubt, ice-cream pants out of sight under the table. The wave was just beginning to come back into his hair, where he had slicked it down with water. He would have looked swell, if he hadn't looked so mad. The others were laughing and talking, but Wes sat with his mouth puckered up, as if he'd just bitten into something sour.

Okay for you, Theo said to herself. You're sore because they've come in here. Well, boy, this is how the other half makes a living.

Jane had been into Leon's plenty of times this summer, but so far, Wes and Felix hadn't. Theo didn't doubt that Wes'd had something to do with that, because all the young summer crowd hung out at Leon's after the movies.

Wes needn't think she cared a hoot. After this summer's experience, she would have waited on the President of the United States, the King of England and all their wives and relations and never turned a hair. Besides, she had something more pleasant to think about tonight than Wes and his eternal Beacons. Over in one of Polly's booths, leisurely eating his hamburger, sat Howard, and every time she looked that way she could see his bright head. Later on, Howard was going to drive her home.

She went over and stood by the Beacons, her pad and pencil ready. Jane looked blank, as usual, but Felix glanced up and grinned. "Hi-ya, Theo, old gal."

"Hi-ya, Felix. What'll it be?"

"Haven't laid eyes on you all summer," Felix said. "Mother said you were busy, though, working in here like crazy."

Theo said, her eyes dancing at Wes, "Why, haven't you been in? No night life?"

"Too much," Felix said airily. "Grace, this is Wes's sister, Theo Sewell. Theo, Grace Westerly, Ken Murray. Cary Grant, over there, I guess you know." He grinned, glancing at Wes, and Theo caught the glint of malice in his eyes. Why, Felix knew perfectly well how Wes was feeling! He'd introduced her on purpose. She'd been surprised that he had, and now she knew why. She felt a sudden pang, seeing Wes's sickly attempt at a smile. Oh, poor old Wes! He feels awful. For a moment, she contemplated hauling off and letting Felix have one right in the middle of his silly, turned-up nose. Instead she said, "Orders, please?"

"Yes," Jane said. "Theo's probably got a million people sitting around here eating up their serviettes."

"Napkins, to me," Theo said.

She was suddenly aware that the dark-haired boy, Ken Murray, was looking at her with considerable appreciation. She took their orders and left, feeling better.

It wasn't entirely coming into Leon's that ailed Wes tonight. He'd got over some of that, as soon as he found out what Mrs. Beacon thought about it—as soon as she'd said, so casually, that a job like that might not hurt Jane. Wes's trouble, tonight, was an accumulation of things. Ken and Felix had been having a righteous good time for the past week without him; at least, whenever Felix's mother or father didn't insist that Wes go along. Mrs. Beacon still hadn't said a word about the job for the future. Wes was nervous about that. And to cap the climax, tonight Ken and Felix had girls, while he had none. Felix hadn't mentioned his asking one probably, Wes thought, because it would crowd the Cadillac, since Luke was going along to drive them to Dream Hill.

Since the back seat only held four comfortably, Wes had volunteered to ride up front with Luke, and nobody had objected. Now he felt like the fifth wheel. His nerves were jangled, and all at once he couldn't to save his life go on acting in a way he didn't feel. He could see Felix was sore—insisting on coming in here to Leon's and practically going out of his way to arrange things so Wes wouldn't have any girl. But there it was, and the heck with it.

Actually, Felix was furious. His father and mother both had bawled him out about wrecking the Ford, using as a basis the information Mrs. Beacon had gleaned from Wes. Ordinarily, Wes would have covered up for Felix, but this time he hadn't. Felix thought he knew why. Wes was still sore about having his leg pulled about his swimming. At the time, it had been only a joke; Felix couldn't deny, though, that he'd got a good deal of pleasure out of seeing Wes taken down a peg, Wes was always so smart. He hadn't thought Wes would get back at him in such an underhand way.

The episode had set Felix to thinking. Times in the past his parents had seemed to know more than they should have about his personal doings. He'd never suspected Wes of tattling, but all of a sudden Felix realized, it would explain a lot of things. For a long time, he'd been fed up with the way his father and mother always insisted he take Wes along on his expeditions. Maybe that was the reason—so they could keep a check on him. The more Felix thought about it, the more convinced he became. If that was what Wes had been up to, then Felix was through with him. He'd never trust him again.

Ken Murray said to Wes, across the table, "Why don't we take your sister to the dance with us, if she can get off tonight?"

Ken was a perceptive youth—he had more than a vague idea of what Wes's position was at the Beacons', and he felt sorry for him. It was a rotten spot to be in, split on the fence that way between Felix and his parents. Besides, Ken was stuck for the evening with Jane, who he thought was awful and who couldn't stand him.

"I don't think Leon'd let her off," Wes said sullenly, perfectly aware that Theo was always through early on Friday nights. He grunted with amazement as he received a sharp little kick on the shin, and looked up to see Jane glaring at him.

Unless he was mistaken, Jane was indicating that she wanted Theo to be taken along to the dance for Ken; and that meant, he thought, his spirits soaring upward, that Jane wanted to get shut of Ken and go to the dance with *him*. A slow grin appeared on Wes's face. "Hey," he said, as if suddenly remembering. "Of course, it's Friday night. She gets through early. Why don't you ask her?"

Theo was astonished. "Oh, I'm sorry, I can't," she said, thinking of her date with Howard. If you could call it a date, just driving home.

Chances to see Howard alone for very long were hard to get now. At first, they'd gone out together some evenings, and for a Sunday afternoon. Then Phoebe, getting jittery over a young man she'd never seen before and whose folks she didn't know, had sent Sylvanus over to talk with Leon. Theo didn't know what Leon had told him about Howard, but the result was that Phoebe had cracked down. No more dates with him, or tooting off to dances. Otherwise, working at Leon's was finished, and that was that.

"I've promised to come straight home from work," Theo said, explaining.

"Ma wouldn't care, if you went with us," Wes said.

She regarded him with some surprise. It wasn't like him to be so cordial, regarding a party with the Beacons.

"Call her up," Ken said.

"No phone at our house. Besides, you people are all dressed up." Theo was impatient, wanting to be about her work so she could get through.

"Let's drive her home," Ken said. "She could tell her mother and change—wouldn't hold us up long."

"I don't think—" Theo began. An idea came fizzing into her head and her eyes brightened. "Where would we go? Dream Hill?"

Felix nodded. If Ken wanted Theo to go, she was going, that was all.

"All right," Theo said. "I'll hustle."

The first chance she got, she whisked into the back room and scribbled a note to Howard, telling him about the dance.

". . . if you'd like to, you could be at Dream Hill too and we could get some time together."

Since Sylvanus had been over, Leon was keeping a sharper eye out than ever, whenever Howard was in the restaurant. Darn him, Theo thought, why can't he mind his business? She had to wait till Leon's back was turned and then slip the note onto Howard's napkin as she hurried by his booth. She watched him read it, grin at her, and nod. Shortly after, he paid his check and left the restaurant.

Howard didn't mind at all going over to Dream Hill to the dance—as a matter of fact, he'd planned to go anyway, with Jo Brown, as soon as he'd taken Theo home. He went out and called up Jo, asked her if she'd mind driving over in her own car. She didn't—she understood he had to beau Theo around some, until he found out some more details about his winter job. At least, she said she did. If she lifted her eyebrow a little about it, why, that was all. She didn't make any fuss. Howard didn't believe her feelings were involved with him any more than his were with her. Which was fine, he told himself, that was just what he wanted. No entanglements.

Still, when he got to thinking about it, he didn't know but it'd be a feather in his cap to make Jo fall for him. She was footloose and on the prowl; hard as nails in a way. Might be . . . Oh, well. The summer wasn't over yet.

Howard drove over alone to Dream Hill in Johnny's car. When he got there, Jo had arrived, but Theo hadn't. He danced a couple of dances with Jo; and thought he could have gone on doing that all evening. But when Theo's crowd arrived, he saw Theo was paired off with that good-looking, black-headed summer kid. They seemed to be having a swell time together, too, laughing and talking. Jo didn't lack for partners; so Howard made his way through the crowd toward Theo, but before he got there, she and the black-headed kid were out on the floor dancing.

Why, the son of a gun, Howard told himself, watching them. He's trying to make time with her.

He watched his chance, and when they swung by, he went over and cut in.

Ken Murray was getting sorer by the minute. He could have been having a swell time dancing with Wes's sister. The music was good and the floor better. Theo was just the right size to dance with him—taller than most girls, which was what he liked. They danced well together, too, and she was fun to talk to—bright as a new pin.

But every time, just as he was getting into the swing of some good tune he liked, this tall, red-headed boat captain or something kept cutting in. Cutting in was a custom of course, at school dances, but Ken didn't think it was at these countryside pavilions. At least, nobody else seemed to be doing it. As the evening wore on and he got madder, he began cutting in himself, right back again.

Howard said, his lips close to Theo's ear, "The Prince of Wales is getting his little back up at me. Next time he cuts in, I'm going to let him have you for a couple of dances. But the second intermission after this one, you steer him over to the fountain. We'll put another wheel on his wagon."

"You won't get into a fight, will you?" Theo was having a wonderful time, but she felt a little panicky. The last time Howard had cut in, Ken had all but squared off at him.

"Me?" Howard grinned. "Fight a punk like that? All you do is introduce me to him. Okay?"

"Well, I'm not sure." Suppose they did fight? It would be awful, of course, but you couldn't help thinking it would be exciting. Something like that would happen often, in real life, to a person like Georgia Tate, the singer.

Ken approached with a face like a thundercloud and Howard gave in with a grin and a shrug of resignation. After a while, Theo saw him dancing with the girl who, the first night at Dream Hill, had had on a green dress. Only, tonight, she wore magenta. She and Howard seemed to be having a hilarious joke about something.

Ken saw him, too, with a sigh of relief. The fellow'd gone for good, he hoped. Anyway, he'd found somebody else. Ken finished the dance in peace and danced the next one. But at the fountain, where they'd stopped for a drink because Theo said she was thirsty, he found himself ranged up alongside the red-haired guy who was standing there deep in conversation with his dancing partner.

Howard glanced up and said casually, "Hi," and then as if it were an afterthought, "Oh, Theo, this is Jo Brown. Jo, Theo Sewell."

Miss Brown smiled and shook hands. She smiled and shook hands with Ken, when Theo introduced him. She had a husky humorous kind of voice, which sometimes broke in the middle of a sentence, making ordinary remarks sound interesting and funny. Somehow, when they got seated on four stools at the fountain, Miss Brown was between Ken and Theo, with Howard on Theo's other hand.

It was casually done; even Ken couldn't have said just how it came about; but when they were finishing their drinks, Miss Brown said to Theo, "You won't mind if I dance one dance with your boy friend? He thinks he knows how to do the Charleston." She laughed. Her laugh was deep-throated, too, like her voice. "He thinks he can show *me*. I was *born* when the Charleston was the style!"

Ken wondered just when he had asked her to dance. They'd been talking about the Charleston, but—

Howard cocked his head to one side, watching them go back together to the dance floor. Miss Brown seemed quite purposeful. Ken followed, more slowly, on behind.

"Never knew what hit him," Howard chuckled. "Well, baby, now we've given Junior his bottle, let's go."

Theo was dubious—it didn't seem like a very nice thing to do to Ken. She'd liked him a lot. She'd wondered, dancing with him, how it was possible to have such a good time with somebody else, when Howard was in the offing. But as Howard caught her hand and they slid unobtrusively out the side door of the pavilion, she forgot about anybody else.

Howard had had a grand time as long as there was competition. But as he and Theo were climbing into Johnny Fleming's car, he suddenly felt a little flat. No use talking, the kid sure seemed like pale goods alongside of Jo. Jo was a darned good sport, too—she'd fallen right in with the plan to annex Ken. Howard wondered all at once why she'd been so ready. Maybe she liked his looks. You never could tell, with Jo.

Oh, well, he'd get back there pretty soon and bust that up. Meanwhile, he'd take Theo to some nice quiet place and sit for a while, prod her up a little about locating Uncle Oscar. It was time he found out something definite about Uncle Oscar. He'd made some discreet inquiries around Bellport, but people just looked blank and said they'd never heard Sylvanus Sewell had a brother Oscar. It convinced Howard that they all were covering up for the Sewells—it was just the way these close-mouthed folks around here would act, if there was a reason. Howard drove back on the coast highway, and parked the car by a sand beach near the old road that went out on the Hook.

At the end of the first dance, Ken felt uneasy. He didn't see Theo anywhere on the floor, though, and Miss Brown was having a wonderful time. So was he. At the end of the second dance, he still didn't see Theo, but by then he didn't care.

Just before the dance broke up at three, Ken told Felix he wouldn't be riding home with him—he'd made some friends who were going to take him back to Granite Hook. Wes and Felix took it for granted, when Theo didn't show up, that she'd gone with Ken. Since, by the time Wes got home, Theo was there and in bed, nobody knew the difference and no embarrassing questions were asked.

Theo wasn't asleep when Wes came in. She didn't believe she'd go to sleep all night, she told herself, thinking in a kind of waking dream of Howard. She was in love with him and he with her. He must be. No one could kiss you like that unless he were in love. Or think about the difficulties you'd have at home and take you there earlier than he wanted to. She would have stayed, she thought, if it hadn't been for Howard. She would have stayed with him all night.

On the bureau was the letter she'd written as soon as she had got home. It was stamped and sealed, and addressed to The Chamber of Commerce, West Palm Beach, Florida. It read:

Dear Sirs:

I understand my Uncle, Mr. Oscar C. Sewell, runs a sporting camp somewhere in the vicinity of your city. If you know where, or can locate him, would you ask him to write me?

Theoline Sewell.

She didn't know what else she could do about Uncle Oscar. Howard seemed so interested in him, in an amiable, but quite persistent way, and she had to do something. It had been his suggestion that the Chamber of Commerce in some of those Florida cities might know something. At least, he said, they could look in the phone directory. They might not even answer her, but if they did, saying, of course, that there wasn't any Oscar C. Sewell around, at least the letter would be something to show Howard.

One thing she knew, she couldn't bear to have Howard find out how she'd lied. Having Uncle Oscar was the only thing that kept her from being the drab, uninteresting Theo Sewell who had to hurry home each night from a day's work in a restaurant, and had never been farther away from Granite Hook than Ferriston.

It said in the books, in the magazines, in the movies, that the world was full of strange and wonderful adventures, happening all the time to everybody. Not to you, nor the people you knew, unless you pulled yourself out from under the dullness that covered you like a bushel basket put over a plant to keep it from the sun.

Someday, if she and Howard went on together, he would have to know, but that was in times to come, when he'd be so much in love that nothing else would matter; and by then, maybe, Uncle Oscar, who after all was nothing but a phantom, could be gone away or dead.

Now, when she was drifting off to sleep, Uncle Oscar seemed quite real—a Sylvanus in fine clothes like Mr. Beacon's, who had made money and lived in a colored castle by the sea. In front of his house, a white sand beach stretched away to infinity, blown over by the warm smell of great exotic flowers. Now you had pushed over the bushel basket of dullness, leaving it overturned on a soil outcropped with granite, and you were soaring away inside a golden sphere of dreams.

OUTSIDE in the starlight, Granite Hook village lay tilted toward the sea, casting faint shadows on its hill of stone. Day was beginning somewhere very far off, as yet no more than a thin whitening behind the sky. Weathered boulders in yards and pastures looked gray and papery, the texture of old hornets' nests. Between them, the heads of midsummer grass sprawled heavily under the load of dew.

Gram Sarah's two-hundred-year-old lilac bush was a black dome against the immaculate white of her house. First settlers had planted the bush; it had stood full grown on the lip of an old foundation when her grandfather had built his house there, before she was born. Once it had been cut down. Ernest, her husband, had wanted to see out the sitting-room windows and he had whacked off the stems two feet above the ground. But that had been forty years ago. Now, inside the bush, the lopped-off trunks held up a jungle of new growth. They were six inches through, rough and twisted, charred by age as if by fire. Underground, their tough old roots nosed deep beneath the foundation stones.

A white-throated sparrow lived in the bush. The light breeze coming up with the morning flapped a wet leaf against him. Wakened, he started his pure silvery pipe, struck a sour note in the middle of it, and stopped. His song was out of season, spring long gone; the air was damp and cold and it was not yet morning.

The sound was enough to waken Gram Sarah from her light sleep, which, nowadays, was little more than a doze. An hour ago, she had been lying awake, waiting for some sign of morning. In her vegetable garden, the young beets were ready to can. She had a lot of them this year; enough to put up for herself and for Morgan's and Sylvanus's families, was what she'd planned on. The beets were just right now. They ought to be pulled in early dew before the sun had time to wilt the crispness out.

"Birds singin," she told herself. "Time t' git up."

But as she got out of bed, something inside her seemed to let go a little, as if a mainspring had slipped, slackened, and then gone on smoothly working as before.

Puzzled, she glanced down at her legs, of which she could see scarcely more than a forked outline in the dim light. They felt all right now—maybe a little cold and heavy.

"H'mp!" she said. "Had a little turn, I guess."

Just like a cussid human bein, rarin to go in the middle of the night and at daylight lazy as a mahone soldier.

"Well. It ain't the first time in my life I felt tired in the mornin. Somethin I et."

She'd better not stop to see about a fire and breakfast, if she wanted them beets before the sun got on them.

Outside, she was surprised to see that the stars were still out, though beginning to grow pale in a white sky. Over in the east, a bar of yellow lay low down on the horizon.

"Earlier'n I thought. Never mind. I'll be that much ahead of myself all day."

In the garden, the beets stood in orderly rows, the green

bleached out of their leaves by the colorless light, the maroon of their stems darkened to black. Gram Sarah knelt on the ground and put her hand into the ice-cold, drenched nest of leaves. She felt a fine tug of satisfaction inside herself as the root broke and came loose with a little tearing sound.

The beets were just right, as she'd known they'd be, none bigger than a baby's fist, some a little smaller. They had grown smooth, too, not a blemish on them. She held one up to see it better against the yellow bar of sunrise in the east. Behind it, the sea was a deep slate color to the horizon and the white sky put out its stars one by one.

In Morgan's house, sleeping beside him in the four-poster bed, Emily stirred and raised herself drowsily on one elbow to look over at her son. She wakened automatically now, sometimes before feeding time, just in case. But young Jasper James Sewell slept peacefully in his crib, perceptible only as a small oval mound under the blankets and a slight fragrance of milk and cleanliness in the room.

"Jamie," she called him, and sometimes, "Why, Jasper James!" Never "Jarsper," as Gram Sarah did, setting Emily's teeth on edge, nor "Jarp," which was Morgan's nickname for him.

She had Jamie now, Emily thought, lying down again. "Jamie and I," she said aloud softly, and went to sleep again.

Morgan slept as he always did in the early morning, exhausted and unmoving, as if his unconscious being clutched desperately at the last few precious moments of rest. In half an hour now, his alarm clock would ring and he would stumble out of bed, yearning for sleep, even while he thrust himself into his stiff, chilly work clothes and went downstairs to make his breakfast in the kitchen.

In a minute, something was saying to him, in a minute, the alarm will go off like a gunshot, so get what sleep is left to you and get it hard.

He lay like a coiled spring, his mouth slightly open and stretched as if he had been running.

All along the coast, in sheltered coves and inlets, dawn spread the water with saffron. On the surface nothing moved more than a splash of a kingfisher's wing. But to the shallow underwaters, the night's flood had brought cold arrowy life, which now with the ebb was hurrying secretly back into the sea.

Somewhere in deep water, days ago, mysterious forces had set in motion a great migration of the herring. Vast phalanxes swam north, blackening the water, and after them went masses of feeding fish—sharks and porpoises, dogfish, schools of sea pollock and mackerel. Nearer to shore, seals ducked in for the kill, and overhead, in daytime, flew a convocation of swooping gulls. For when the herring move, the life of the sea moves with them.

Off Dungeon Island, a great shoal had divided from the main horde and turned in toward the coast. For five nights, the school had kept to deep water, edging in a little closer to the shore line each night, following who knew what instinct, or feed, or exact serving of the tide. Now, at three o'clock in the morning, they filled a hundred tidal basins along the coast almost to the roots of the drowned marsh grass.

Ebb tide had started when Berry Carter, who had spent the night, wrapped in a ragged bed quilt, by the entrance to the Cove, woke up. He had gone to sleep accidentally, while he waited for high tide. On quiet nights, when the tide served right for herring, one of the Carters was always hidden under a slanting ledge just above high water mark, where, even if Morgan did come along, he'd have trouble finding anyone.

Last night had been Warren's turn, but Warren had had a cold. Berry'd watched two nights now, and he was sick of the whole thing. For days, he and Warren had been trying to persuade the old man to give up pestering Morgan. It was cold out on those ledges at night. A man could catch his death lying under that damp rock, and Warren pretty nigh had. They needed their sleep. At first it had been a game, keeping herring out of the Cove, but now it was a darned nuisance.

Lately, Warren and Berry had had to quit growling, because when they did, the old man just about went off the hooks. He'd been losing a lot of sleep himself, too, and when he was like that it was worth your life to monkey with him.

He'd made his brags, Job said, that Morgan wouldn't seine a doryload of fish this season, and by God, he meant it. Of course he had other tricks in his diddy-bag besides chunking rocks into the water, but why go to any more trouble than you had to? What did the boys think he had them live seals for, penned up in the salt pond over on Barrel Island—meat? Did they want the job of sackin them seals over and turnin em loose in the Cove, say Morgan did get a haul? Job'd been all summer ketchin them seals; it was hard work going over there every so often to feed em. Didn't that give the boys some idea of the trouble he was willin to go to? Or that barrel of coal oil—he'd paid good money for it, and they could use it next winter. Did they want to have to dump that out into the Cove?

But, by God, he would dump it, and any other kind of a stinkin mess he could think of that would kill fish, if the boys let a school of herrin git by. They could either help him watch nights, or he'd take a club and clunk the livin daylights out a them. They could take their pick.

So last night, Berry'd taken Warren's turn, while Warren nursed his cold, and along about midnight, he'd rolled up in the quilt. Next thing he knew, it was nigh daylight and the tide had started to ebb.

Berry chunked rocks for a little while, just so he could say he had, but all he could think of was a fire in the stove at home and some hot coffee. As soon as he was really sure the tide was ebbing, he set out across the ledges on a dead run.

The few rocks he had thrown had landed right in the front section of a school of herring which had gone into the Cove in the night, and had started to come out on the turn of the tide. Terrified, the herring turned back and began an endless, frantic circling.

At daylight, a seagull which also had spent the night huddled on a ledge by the Cove entrance, took off into the air and set up an excited skreeling. In five minutes, a thousand gulls from night roosts near by—from the end of the Hook, from Candlemas Island, from Dungeon Island, six miles away—had heard the grapevine message and were in the air heading for shore.

Their racket over the Cove waked up old Job, who crawled stiffly out of his bunk in the shack and looked out the window.

To some, the big white birds soaring and darting over the pale yellow water would have been a fine sight; but old Job began to curse steadily into his whiskers. He hauled on his pants and, still cursing, went down to the water's edge and launched his punt.

To Morgan, it was the finest sight he could remember having seen. When his alarm clock went off and waked him, he glanced out the bedroom window. Past the patch of woods that lay between the village and the Cove, the sky was alive with wings; and sleep left Morgan like dry sand before a wind.

On Foley Craddock's boat in the harbor, his cat Whirligig waked at dawn. She slid lankly through the narrow crack of the cuddy hatch which Foley had left open for her and landed with a slight thump on the platform, drenched with the night's dew. Her feet, as she crossed the platform, left delicate black prints on the wet boards.

Waiting for Foley to get up and feed her, Whirligig settled herself in her spot behind the stump of the Friendship's sawed-off bowsprit. She washed daintily her mackerel-striped sides, as morning came. Then, neat and clean, she sat and looked overboard at the harbor pollock who lived under the boat.

Watching their dark streaks in the shimmering water, she switched her tail and made a soft yickering noise in her throat. The light from the sunrise caught her eyes, turning them into pools of emerald fire.

In the cuddy, Foley got leisurely out of bed. He'd been awake since daylight, when the lobster boats had started up in the harbor and gone out past his mooring. Foley always waited until all the boats except Wheat's were gone, before he made his breakfast. Some of the boys thought it was pretty funny to go roaring past wide open, so that the wave from their boat's wake sent the Friendship wildly thrashing up and down. If he had any kettles on the cuddy stove, they were sure to jounce off onto the floor. Once he had lost a whole pot of beans that way, pot and all.

When he got his fire going and the coffee on, Foley came out on deck. He took a clam out of a covered roller on the platform, cracked its shell and baited a light line, which he tossed casually over the side. A pollock grabbed it on the way down, and Foley hauled him in, slatting him off the hook. Almost before he struck the platform, Whirligig was down off the bow.

Foley liked to watch Whirligig handle a pollock. They were a pretty smart fish when they came out of the water, flipping all over the boat. But Whirligig had dealt with a good many of them—she lived on them—and she knew just how. She watched her chance until the fish hesitated an instant in its frantic flapping, then she dove in and bit him once, hard, on the back of the neck. Purring, she folded her tail around her feet and settled down to a meal.

Foley caught four more pollock, which he dressed and took below to fry on the cuddy stove. He sat down on his rumpled bunk to eat, his mug of coffee handy between his feet on the floor.

Most people didn't like harbor pollock, he reflected, chewing heartily, with a hard store roll in one hand and a fried fish in the other. "Turd" pollock, they called them. Well, the more fools them. You had to cook them the same day they were caught, that was all. Take one and roll him in corn meal and fry him before the last flip was out of him and you couldn't ask for anything better.

A man was well off living on a boat. Nobody around to bother him and a whole food supply swimming around under the keel. If he got sick of pollock, he could fish on bottom and catch flounders. The flats were full of mussels and clams. When he felt like eating lobsters, he could boil up some. Or he could drop a line overboard when he was outside and yarn him up a cod or a haddock. Right now, the mackerel season was coming on. What was better than a fat mackerel, soaked all night in a bucket of sea water to get the blood out of him, rolled in flour and fried in pork scraps?

Foley smacked his lips. When Wheat came along, this morning, he'd have to see if Wheat wouldn't give up hauling for today and go mackereling. He washed down the last of his breakfast with a cup of coffee and went out on deck to look for some signs of Wheat. The sun had come up warm. It was going to be too nice a day to fool around working. Wheat was late, which probably meant his legs had got stiff overnight.

He settled down in comfort with his back against a bait tub, stretched his skinny legs into the sun. Whirligig, her belly round as a ball, stepped onto his lap, turned around twice and lay down.

Someone on shore launched a punt, shoving her down the beach with a rush. Foley could hear the pebbles grate and grind under her bottom.

Hell of a way to launch a punt, he thought lazily. Couple a years, she won't hev a whole bottom board left.

It was Morgan Sewell, going somewhere on the hop, as usual. He watched Morgan scrabble onto the thwart and start rowing off to his boat as if, off on the water somewhere, he had caught sight of a cent that was getting away from him.

There was one of the piggy boys, right there, who worked his arms off to the hips, so's he could put money in the bank to set there until he died.

Foley put out a hand and rubbed Whirligig's silky scruff until she purred. "Ei, pretty girl," he said. "You and me's gut a fine round bellyful, ain't we? What we need now's a nap."

When Uncle Wheat came chugging along, half an hour later, Foley and Whirligig were both dead to the world.

Uncle Wheat's legs had indeed been stiff this morning. When he'd first woke up, they hadn't had any more bend to them than a couple of crowbars. It had taken him almost an hour to get limbered up enough to crawl out of bed, and they still didn't feel steady under him.

He wasn't in any too good a temper anyway, and the sight of Foley snoozing in the sun made him mad. Foley was doing it a-purpose, of course, rubbing it in that Wheat was late and he himself all wore out with waiting so long. When he didn't move as the boat bumped alongside, Uncle Wheat was sure of it. With a grunt, he leaned over the washboard, scooped up a pint of cold sea water in a bucket and tossed it up in the air, so that it showered down all over Foley.

Whirligig shot straight up, spitting, and landed on the platform with every hair standing on end. Foley, too, bounced to his feet and stared wildly about. The cat exploding in his face had scared him more than the shock of the cold water. When he realized what had happened, his face puckered up with rage. Nobody ever treated Whirligig so she acted like that. He glared at Wheat, and at last he said in a strangled voice, "You goddamned old crow!"

"Godsake, Foley," Wheat said loudly. He was a little ashamed of himself. When he'd hove the water, he hadn't noticed Whirligig on Foley's lap, or he wouldn't have done it. Foley thought the world and all of that cat. "You ain't makin out a little water's hurt nothin aboard there, are ya?"

"You le'me once git my hands on you!"

No use, now, trying to pass it off as a joke. Besides, Wheat was on too short a string himself, this morning, to offer much peace. "Well, why don't ya clean up aboard there once in a while?" he demanded irritably. "Pu! That's the only fishhawk's nest I ever see that would float."

"It ain't none a your business," Foley said, "if I don't wash my bait with soap and rag, the way you do. What you need aboard a *you*, there, is one a them white monkey caps and a mess a summer people. I d'no why you bother with lobsterin."

He turned and went down the hatch after Whirligig. Uncle Wheat, standing open-mouthed and astounded at the enormity of the insult, could hear him scrabbling around down there and calling, "Kitty, kitty, kitty."

Uncle Wheat opened up his engine and stood away down the harbor. Maybe the old skunk did catch more lobsters than he did, but it was below the belt to twit about it. The more he thought about it, the madder he got. If Foley had come out, he would have gone right over alongside of him and told him what he thought.

But Foley didn't come out. Uncle Wheat kept a weather eye open for him all day, while he hauled his traps, and when he came past Candlemas Island at four o'clock, he saw Foley lying at anchor in under the lee, throwing out mackerel chum. As Uncle Wheat went by, Foley, noncommittally, held up an eighteen-inch mackerel.

Uncle Wheat didn't even turn his head. The old son-of-a-gun, he thought bitterly. It had been an unwritten agreement between them for years that they'd go mackereling together the first time in the season. Whoever caught the first mackerel, the other one had to pay him a dollar. Now, Foley had stolen a march on him.

All right. If he thinks more of a cat than he thinks of his friends, Uncle Wheat said to himself, by God, he can come to *me*, if he wants to make it up.

It was another insult—bad enough, but not comparable to

the first one. After all, you didn't tell a topnotch lobster catcher that all he and his boat were fit for was to sail summer people.

MORGAN, when Foley had seen him launching his punt that morning, had been hurrying to catch up with Sylvanus. By the time he had got down to the shore and found out that not only his weir, but the entire waters of the Cove outside it, were swarming with herring, Sylvanus had gone out to his traps.

Morgan stopped in the village long enough to call up a couple of sardine factories down the coast. They could take any amount of herring, they said, start dipping this afternoon. Their sardine boats were all out and would have to be got in touch with by ship-to-shore phone—that is, if he had enough fish to make it worth while calling them in. How many did he think he had?

Morgan said, "If things break right, ten thousand bushels." He hung up on the fellow's startled gasp. Well, it sure looked like that many; if only he could dope out some way to seal off the entrance to the Cove. The fish penned up in the weir were all right—they could be held for a week, if he had to; but the ones loose in the Cove were another matter.

It was a living wonder so many had stayed in there, anyway. The way to escape was wide open, and there was no reason why they shouldn't have gone out when the tide started to ebb—unless something, seals, maybe, had scared them. They could go out anytime, of course. So far, they hadn't. The school was in there, circling around and around. Sylvanus would know how to help him, maybe suggest where he could borrow a net long enough to seal the mouth of the Cove. To save his life, Morgan couldn't think of anyone who had one. It was a contingency he hadn't thought of, his mind had been so full of just the weir.

He found Sylvanus placidly starting to haul traps off the

inner shore of the Hook. Morgan roared up in the boat, crunching his gears as he tried to reverse in time to stop alongside Syl; but he'd been traveling wide open and he overshot by about thirty feet. As he backed up, he saw Syl's deadpan expression, which, without moving a muscle of his face, said as plainly as a yell, "That's a hell of a way to treat a good engine."

"Syl, I've got a haul," Morgan said.

Syl said, "Big one?"

"The weir's full and so's the Cove. I figger must be ten thousand bushels in there."

Sylvanus whistled. "I thought a few must a gut past Job when I see the gulls this mornin. Why ain't you ashore tending to them? Old Job's probably in there right now, eatin em one by one."

"Syl, who's got a net I could borrow? I've got to have a net to seal off the mouth of the Cove."

Sylvanus said, "H'm." He took a turn around the winch head of his hoisting gear with the warp he held in his hand and started to bring up his trap. The wet rope snaked, smooth as silk, around the polished bronze drum.

Morgan fidgeted. Either Syl was thinking things out, or there wasn't any way to save the haul. He waited a minute, then burst out, "Look, Syl, I ain't got all day."

There wasn't anything in the lobster trap except a few five-fingers and some crabs, which Syl threw out. He put in a fresh bait pocket, jogged ahead fifty feet or so to straighten out the warp, then let the trap slosh back overside. Morgan, red-faced with anger and frustration, watched him go. Syl might show a little feeling, seeing a man have to let a fortune slide through his fingers.

But Syl, having reset the trap, was coming back. "You can't borry a net all of a heap. Best way to get herrin twine is to get some from a sardine factory. They keep it on hand for just such cases as this. But to save that haul, you'd have to put it across right now. Them fish's liable t' go out anytime. You can't hold em."

"Damn it, Syl. There must be some way—"

"There ain't. Not unless you'd had the twine on hand. Why didn't ya, if you thought you was going into it this big?"

"I didn't think— Besides, they cost five hundred dollars."

"Nearer a thousand, the net you'd need. You'd have t' have fifty fathom of herrin twine, eight fathoms deep to seal up the Cove. Hell, Morgan, you can't do nuthin about it."

"How about making some kind of a racket at the Cove entrance—splash or something? Turn the school back if they start to come out?"

"Not much use in it. Might try."

"I could phone the sardine factory to send over a net when the boats come."

"You already called the boats? Holy God, Morgan!"

"Well, I thought—"

"You'll hev t' think faster, if you git a passel a sardine boats over here, and no fish. Well, come on. See what we can do."

It was quite a sight to see Sylvanus go into action, Morgan thought, tailing him up the channel. Syl's boat would travel—it wasn't often you saw him run her wide open.

The old son, Morgan said to himself. He was dying all the time to get a hand into saving that haul.

Morgan didn't doubt for a moment that Sylvanus would save it.

Sylvanus, himself, however, knew how few the chances were that anything would stop the school from coming out, once it started. He'd had some idea of running his engine outside the Cove entrance, jogging up and down across it in his boat—the propeller, under water, would make quite a touse. But as they came into the channel off the Cove, he saw his first conclusion had been right. The water was black with herring, streaking for sea.

"Well, there you are," Sylvanus said. "No use cryin over spilt milk."

Morgan was leaning, stiff-armed, on his cheese rind, staring overboard. His face was congested and red. His eyes bugged out a little, and a line of sweat had come out on his upper lip. He was seeing thousands of dollars slip away into the water.

"No use bein so tore out over somethin you nor no man could help," Sylvanus said. The sight of Morgan's face made him uncomfortable. It was like seeing him naked. At the same time, Sylvanus couldn't help being sorry for him. "If you'd planned for it—had a net here to hold em—and then lost em, you'd have a right to feel bad."

But nothing, it seemed, was making any difference to Morgan.

"Look," Sylvanus said impatiently. "You've probly gut quite a haul in the weir, much as any man could expect. Le's go have a look."

He started up his engine and steered through the narrow entrance into the Cove. After a while, Morgan followed him. Sylvanus had laid his boat alongside the weir and was tied up to a piling. He was leaning, relaxed, against his cheese rind. His face was as expressionless as a stick of wood.

Morgan stared at the weir. "I ain't takin this," he said hoarsely.

"No," Syl said. "I wouldn't, myself. You sure you let that drop net down, Morg? You was pretty excited."

"Of course I did. I—" Suddenly Morgan realized he couldn't remember whether he had or not. "I remember going up on the rails and lookin in," he finished weakly.

The drop net was the weighted, rectangular net that could be let down to block the mouth of the weir. It was neatly rolled up and tied in its place. The weir was empty; in the whole, deserted water of the Cove, there wasn't a herring.

"You ain't sure?" Sylvanus said.

"Damn it, Syl, I—" Morgan came across Syl's boat and climbed up on the rails. The rails were parallel poles, nailed for hand and foothold to the pilings around the entire weir, and Morgan swarmed along them like a monkey. "I thought so," he said triumphantly, feeling of the drop net. "It's wet, Syl. I knew I couldn't have been that dumb. Of course I let it down. By the Judas—" He clambered back aboard his boat and started the engine.

"Where you goin?"

"I'm goin to get the law started after the Carters."

"Hold on a minute."

"Now, look, Syl—"

"What proof you got?"

Morgan stopped his engine. He stood looking at the weir, his face set in lines of bitterness and frustration. "Then, by God," he said hoarsely, "I *am* goin over there with a gun."

Sylvanus leaned out over his washboard, staring speculatively at the water. He could see herring sign, all right. There was red feed all through the water. "You know what I'd do, if I was you, Morg?"

"Go kiss Job, probly," Morgan said.

Sylvanus let it pass. "First thing, you hustle to a phone, tell the sardine factories your fish gut away, not to send the boats. When you call Kedge Harbor factory, ask Bean Billings over there if he can spare fifty fathom of herrin twine."

"What's the use of that, now?"

"Well, I d'no. Maybe none." Sylvanus was still staring at the water. He even spat into it casually.

"Looks to me as if I'd wasted enough of Billings's time," Morgan said. He was weak from reaction. What he felt like was giving up and crawling away out of sight somewhere.

"Nobody knows to count on what herrin'll do," Sylvanus said. "Maybe the creepin tar's been scairt out of em, so's they'll take out for Europe. Maybe they'll be back in here tonight. I'd say, chances are they will."

"They will!" Morgan stared at him, galvanized. "How'd you know, Syl?"

"I don't *know*. If 't was me, I'd have some twine here." He raised his eyebrows in the quizzical gesture Morgan knew well. "Don't bother, if it's against your judgment."

"Oh, sure, I'll get the twine, but—"

"I was talkin with Charley Getchell a few days ago," Sylvanus went on, almost absently. "Goes on one a the Bellport seiners. Spoke me, outside. Said they'd had their eye on a big school a herrin for three days off Dungeon Island, been soundin em nights. Said each night they come a little closer inshore. Charley's been watchin Candlemas Cove like a hawk. He was figgerin that some night part of that school'd be in there."

Sylvanus glanced over at Morgan. "I don't doubt this is the school. I've known em hang around one place three-four nights, if the tide's high at night and it's calm, on the dark of the moon. Charley's out of luck—they come here instead of Candlemas, can't depend on the cussid things. Can't depend on their comin back here tonight."

"But you think they might?"

"I think they're liable to."

It was a long speech for Syl to make, and it convinced Morgan. The sullenness left his face. Animation came back into it. "I'll go phone and get the twine," he said. "Will you stick around tonight and help me out, Syl?"

Sylvanus nodded. "See ya around two o'clock," he said. He cast off, started his engine and went out through the channel to finish hauling his traps.

Billings, at the Kedge Harbor factory, was pretty sore with Morgan over having called in his boats for nothing. They wouldn't, of course, lose a great deal of time, since Billings could get in touch with them at once by ship-to-shore phone; but they would lose some. Billings said with some force that he had herring twine Morgan could use; Morgan would have to come and get it, though, and he'd better stay out of Billings's way if he didn't want his ears torn off. That afternoon Morgan went to Kedge Harbor and got the twine.

The herring twine was a big net, three hundred feet long and forty wide, with lead weights along one side to hold it on bottom when it was set, and floats on the other to keep it upright in the water. Stretched across the Cove, each end fastened to boulders or trees on shore, it would effectually seal the entrance.

The factory people helped Morgan put it aboard his boat. They kidded him some about his ten thousand bushels and he was glad to get away from there. He took the twine back to the Cove and left it in his boat, which was tied up to a piling at the weir.

Halfway through his supper, he thought suddenly what if Job got afoul of the twine? He left his dessert uneaten, over Emily's protests, and tore back down to the Cove. On the way, he stopped to cut a maple sapling and lopped off about three feet of the butt of it. If Job or his brood showed up, they were going to get a clunk of green maple right between the eyes.

But they didn't show up. Morgan stayed aboard his boat, catching a nap on a pile of lifebelts up in the bow, until Sylvanus came down at half-past one.

Sylvanus came leisurely down through the trees, following the path that Morgan's impatient feet had worn there through the summer. He made so little noise rowing out from the shore that Morgan didn't know he was anywhere around until he stepped aboard the boat.

"Nice twine," Sylvanus said, running his hand over the pile of net.

"What now? Go out and set it?" Morgan asked.

Sylvanus was over his talkative mood of the morning. "Ought t' learn a business before you go into it in a big way," he said shortly.

"Well, for chrissake, I'm tryin to, ain't I?" Morgan snapped. "If you wasn't so close-mouthed, nine-tenths of the time, might help me out some."

Sylvanus made no answer. "Get her into the dory," he said, laying hold of the net. "Need the punt, too—tow her on behind."

They rowed the dory, with the net aboard, over to the entrance of the Cove and rigged one end of it to a heavy projecting boulder. It was awkward working by flashlight. Sylvanus didn't give many directions. Morgan had a feeling his own fingers were all thumbs. Toward the last of it he gave up—held the flashlight for Syl and let him tie the knots.

"Okay," Sylvanus said, giving a haul on the lines to settle them around the boulder. "That'll hold—unless somebody cuts her." He reached over and took the flashlight from Morgan. "Now, we'll just step up and make sure nobody does." He went out of sight up the bank, silently as a cat.

"All right," Morgan heard him say. "Come outa that. You ain't goin t' like it a mite, if I reach in there after ya."

Morgan went up the bank in a rush. He was just in time to see Sylvanus collar Warren Carter, who was crawling out from under a ledge. Sylvanus held the flashlight on him with one big fist and grabbed him with the other; and Warren, who was a pindling young man of twenty-five or so, hung limply, blinking.

"You tell your pa," Sylvanus said, "that I've knowed about that cave since I was a kid and played in it. You tell him, if there's any more of this foolishness, I'm comin over there personal and clean him up." There was a note in Syl's voice that Morgan couldn't recollect having heard before, and Warren turned white with terror. Syl gave him a shake. "You hear?"

Warren croaked something that ended in a hollow cough.

"Git home and tend to that cold," Sylvanus said. "I'm goin to be here all night, and I'll have the haslet out of anybody shows up on these rocks."

He let Warren go and Warren fled, scrambling over the rocks like a scared rabbit.

"Damn him," Morgan said furiously. "I'd a beat the daylights out of him."

"Don't doubt you would." Sylvanus went back down the bank. "How bout you rowin the punt, while I do a little soundin?"

Sounding was what the seiners did, when they wanted to find out about a school of herring. Someone let down a light lead sinker on the end of a piece of thread. If there were herring in the water, you could feel them brush against the thread. Sylvanus was going to make sure, before he went to the trouble of setting the net.

Morgan rowed the punt silently out in the middle of the Cove. He sat impatiently waiting while Sylvanus dangled a sinker over the side. "Well, don't you feel anything?" he said at last.

"Go over a little nearer the mouth. Don't splash, Morg."

"Well, ain't there anything?"

Sylvanus made no reply, and Morgan shut his mouth with a snap.

The punt drifted silently without a ripple. The tide running soundless and unseen in through the mouth of the Cove carried her with it so that she turned in the slow eddies; once she grounded lightly on the shore and Morgan shoved her back into the deep water with his oars, swearing under his breath. For hours, it seemed to him, they hadn't moved. Sitting still—if there was anything he couldn't stand—

Sylvanus gave a low chuckle and he almost jumped out of his skin.

"Take it easy," Sylvanus said. "No time t' upset the punt. Here. Feel." He handed over the end of the thread.

At first, Morgan couldn't feel anything. Then he realized he was holding the thread against the gunnel of the punt. He moved his hand to let it hang free. It seemed to come alive in his fingers. He peered over the side of the punt, but the silvery-black, imperturbable surface was as still as metal. Only the thin thread, leading up from its sinker, deep down, quivered along its length with a light, continuous vibration.

"They're down there!" he said, in an excited whisper.

"Ayeh." Sylvanus reached over and took the thread. He sat holding it a minute between his horny thumb and forefinger before he hauled it in. "H'm," he said. "Pull ashore now."

Ashore, to Morgan's astonishment, instead of starting in at

once to set the net, he pulled out his pipe and sat down on a rock for a smoke.

"Well, come on," Morgan said. "What you waitin for?"

"You're a hell of an impatient feller. Them fish's liable to be runnin in here till pret' nigh slack tide. Might's well git all we can."

He sat smoking silently, the faint glow from his pipe occasionally bright enough to light up his face. When he had finished, he knocked the pipe against a rock, put his foot on the dottle to make sure the spark was out, and went down and climbed aboard the dory.

Working swiftly and without comment, they rowed the dory across the mouth of the Cove, paying out the net on the way. Even on the high-water slack, with no tide to complicate matters, it was a tough job. The net, heavy and stiff, had to be payed out with care; the dory, deep in the water, rowed like a barge-load of stone. But at last they got across to the opposite shore, made the end of the net fast to a leaning tree and tightened the lines. The mouth of the Cove was sealed tighter than a drum.

Morning was lightening in the east—a fine, clear dawn.

Morgan dropped down, tuckered out, on a flat ledge, and heaved a great sigh of relief. A look of exultation was beginning to replace the strained anxiety in his face. "Wow!" he said. "What a haul! But, by God, there she is."

"Ayeh. I don't doubt you got you a haul." Sylvanus was glad himself the job was done. "You better go up to the house, have some breakfast. Bring me back some coffee."

"You're as tuckered out as I am."

Sylvanus didn't believe he was, but he merely said, "Ayeh. I'll rest here while you go git the coffee. I'll row ya acrost here in the dory and you can take the punt."

Morgan made no further objection. Some breakfast would go darn good. He tried, rowing across the Cove to the wharf, to peer down into the water, see what kind of a haul he'd got, but it was still too dark. Daylight was coming fast, though. By the time he got back, the sun would be up. He moored the punt to the end of the wharf, swarmed up the short ladder, and set out through the woods on a run.

Sylvanus sat down on a comfortably sloping boulder and pulled out his pipe. He felt a deep sense of satisfaction, seeing the net floats, glossy and dark with wet, emerge across the entrance to the Cove as daylight came. It had been a handy job, even with Morgan bolluping around to gum things up.

It was too bad, in a way, Sylvanus thought, puffing contentedly, that a man couldn't handle a job like that alone, keep his mind on it instead of having to answer questions. If he'd been alone, for instance, he'd have sat there in the punt a while longer hanging on to that thread. No need of it, of course. Maybe it was just because he liked the feel of the thread in his fingers, the ghostly movement of it that told you what you wanted to know. Water at night, like that, was a secret—what went on in it none of any human being's business, in a way.

The gray light whitened on the water. Looking across the Cove, Sylvanus suddenly noticed that the spar-mooring, on which Job usually kept his old double-ender power boat, was empty. The boat wasn't anywhere in the Cove either.

That's funny, Sylvanus puzzled. Wonder where the old man's gone. Apparently he'd left Warren to guard the Cove, while he and probably Berry—had gone off last night somewhere. Maybe he'd had engine trouble and was broke down, his kicker wasn't anything to write home about. Well, he'd be all right, anchored anywhere in this calm weather. Some of the lobster boats would probably spot him and tow him in. You'd hear ducks quack, too, when Job got back to the Cove and found that net there, so he couldn't get in to his mooring.

In some ways, Sylvanus thought, he didn't blame Job entirely in the row with Morgan. Of course, law and property rights were all on Morgan's side. No man was going to put up with that kind of depredations when he had a small fortune at stake, least of all Morgan. Job would probably end up in jail, if he kept on. And that was a thing Sylvanus would hate to see. The boys, Warren and Berry, were no-account, as pliable as a couple of licorice sticks, with a little chewing down. But there was a good deal to Job. He wouldn't break and he wouldn't bend. Sylvanus had always liked him.

Sylvanus glanced thoughtfully around the Cove, letting a pale blue cloud float peacefully upward from his pipe. The Cove lay gleaming in the sunrise, its surface faintly stirred. Woodland grew down to its edges—dark green, stiff spruce trees, light green birch and alders, making a muzzy reflection in the water. It was a fine, quiet place; worth fighting for, especially when a man considered it his home and his livelihood. And Sylvanus didn't doubt that old Job's stubborn mind was all mixed up with ideas about squatter's rights and what belonged to him because he'd had it and used it most of his life.

It wouldn't hurt Morgan to offer to share a little with the old man, let him have a chance to seine out the few fish he needed to keep him going. Job probably wouldn't accept the offer—he'd chuck it right back in Morgan's face. But it'd make you feel a little better about it.

That wasn't Morgan, though. Thinking back, Sylvanus couldn't remember a time when Morgan had ever offered to share anything with anybody. He was a good, decent, honest guy—he'd die rather than touch anything that didn't belong to him, and within the limitations of his judgment, he was a worker. But when it came to things he considered his own, he leeched onto them . . . worked like a crazy man and put away every penny; he thought not twice, but twenty-five times before he ever parted with any of it. And the way he went at things, with his you-be-damned chin out, was enough to make any man mad, sometimes. It wasn't very surprising that old Job was out to gum him up.

Sylvanus heard the asthmatic kicker in Job's boat a few minutes before he saw the boat itself. He got up unobtrusively and stepped out of sight behind a ledge.

The double-ender came chugging in around the point and up the Cove's entrance to the net, where she stopped. Job stuck his old crane's neck out past the sprayhood and stared at the net as if it were a sea serpent.

"By God, Berry," he said. "Look what that barstid's done, now. Must have fish in there, all right. Wouldn't have, if I hedn't hed t' spend all night tarryhootin round over on Barrel Island. You wait till I git my hands on Warren."

"Nuthin Warren could help, probly," Berry said sullenly.

"Keepin a man away from his home," Job said. "I c'd hev the law on him."

"Boom 'er right in over, Pa, net'n all," Berry said.

"You a fool? Clean the propeller right off'n the boat. Besides, Morg never done that alone. I don't want no truck with that Sylvanus."

Sylvanus, behind the ledge, grinned slightly.

"No," Job said. "Might's well put over the kedge, leave the boat out here. All we gut t' do is row these fellers over in the punt, let em go inside the net."

Sylvanus watched them while they broke out an anchor and rope, and moored the boat. Presently they hauled their punt alongside and unloaded into it three squirming, wriggling sacks, tied up at the top, which looked as if they were pretty hard to handle. He was completely mystified. What in the devil have they dreamed up now? he asked himself. Looks like pigs, but it can't be.

He went down the shore to the dory, pushed off quietly and sculled along the inside of the net. Berry, sitting in the stern of the punt, saw him first.

"There, Pa!" he burst out. "I told ya. If once in your God-forsaken life you'd listen t' me—"

"Shut up, Berry!" Job said. He turned on Sylvanus a beaming smile, made all the more pleasant by the benevolence of his white whiskers and his guileless blue eyes. "H'yar, Sylvanus. Ain't seen you since the night you tried t' burn my house down."

"That's right," Sylvanus said, with a grin. "What you got in the bags, Job? Pigs?"

"Nope. Lambs, Sylvanus. Lambs. We was keepin it kind of quiet, seein they come from that flock of Higginses he keeps over on Barrel Island, the idea being they ain't our lambs. All in the fambly, ain't it, Sylvanus? Don't believe you'll set the law on us."

"Last thing I'd do," Sylvanus said, eyeing him. He leaned and peered. His eye caught a movement of Job's scrawny hand on the oar and he hauled back hastily. "Kind of big lambs, Job."

Job giggled. "Well, sheep, then. Sheep, if ya like that better. Lambs last March. What dif'rence it make?"

Sylvanus burst out laughing. His puzzled eye had at last made out the outlines in the bulging lumps of the sacks.

"You beat all, Job," he gasped, as soon as he could speak. "You deserve to git away with it, by God, you do. Ain't another man in the world would've thought of that."

"Ain't but very few could've caught em, either," Job said.

"You know, there ain't. Is that where you been all night?"

"Well, I've hed em a spell. In the salt pond. Hed quite a touse, seinin them out a there, was all."

"Seined em, eh?" Sylvanus said admiringly. "I've got to hand it to ya, Job. Well, cut em loose and let em go. Seals don't do herrin no good, turned loose in a bottled-up cove."

"I'll be damned if I do," Job said. "Them seals is pets. I spent two months tamin em, and here I am bringin em home t' enjoy. Here you hold me up when I'm mindin my own business and tell me t' cut em loose. I c'd have the law on you."

"Yes. But I don't b'lieve you will, seein it's all in the family. Come on, Job. Do you cut em loose, or do I?"

"To hell with ya," Job said.

Sylvanus reached a big hand across the net and grabbed the gunnel of the punt. "Cut em loose," he said. "Or over you go. Take it easy with the oars, Job, or over you go anyway."

"Cut em loose, Pa, for Godsake," Berry said.

Braced in the big, heavy weir dory, Sylvanus quite easily could have upset the light punt, and neither of them thought he was bluffing.

Old Job didn't bat an eye. "You'll hev t' pay me for em," he said in an aggrieved tone. When Sylvanus made no reply, he pulled out a battered jackknife and cut the strings on the sacks, scooping the seals, one after the other, overboard, where they vanished like black lightning.

"Little mite standoffish for pets, ain't they?" Sylvanus said, releasing the gunnel of the punt.

"So'd you be, if you'd been cooped up in a bag for two hours," Job said sourly.

"I don't doubt. Well, Job, what you goin t' do? Keep on with works like this, till Morgan gits you a jail term?"

"He ain't caught me doin nothin," Job said.

"No. But I have."

Job grinned. "You wouldn't send no man t' jail, Sylvanus."

"I'd be more likely to lick the tar out of him," said Sylvanus. "My soul, think what you're doin, man. You know Morgan. No spite war's worth a spell in jail."

He realized, seeing Job start to grow red around the eyes, that the old man had heard only the first sentence of what he'd tried to say.

Job said, spluttering, "Take more'n you t' lick me, Sylvanus. I hed more beef the day I was born 'n you gut right now."

"Don't doubt it. But, Job, have some sense. I don't say you ain't gut a lot on your side. But Morgan's paid good money down for the Cove. Legally, it's his now. The law's against you and so'll everybody be if you make a man lose a lot of money."

It wasn't any use, he saw regretfully. He'd only reminded the old man of his grievance, made him really mad, now.

"All right," Sylvanus said. He twisted his oar in the net, held it under water a little, so Job could row the punt across it. "Only I'd take it easy, if I was you."

Job rowed into the Cove and pulled away for his beach without another word. But fifty feet or so away from Sylvanus, he suddenly shipped his oars and began slapping the blade of one of them with loud smacking noises on the water. Sylvanus saw the surface heave and roil as terrified herring crushed over each other, trying to get out of the way. You could smother a lot of fish, scaring them like that, when they were in a confined place.

Sylvanus sighed. Stubborn old devil, he said to himself. I might have known it.

He turned the dory around and pushed out after Job.

Seeing him coming, Job put for another part of the Cove, making the punt fairly bubble through the water. At a safe distance, he began slapping with the oar again.

In the big dory, it was useless to try to catch him, and Sylvanus didn't. He leaned on his oars and shouted, "So you can lick me, can ya, you old bluffer? Come on ashore and try."

Job hesitated. He stopped slapping with the oar and turned toward Sylvanus a face of blind fury.

"Nothin but a damned old brag," Sylvanus said. "Huh! I always knew it." He turned the dory and began to pull leisurely over toward Job's beach.

Even though Job was quite a way behind him, the punt reached the beach before the dory did. She hit the beach rocks with a crunch, coming out of water half the length of her bow. Job jumped out, took an oar and handed one to Berry.

Sylvanus had oars of his own. He used one to fend the wildly flailing blows until his feet were off the slippery rocks at the water's edge; then he watched his chance and gave Berry a sound poke in the pit of the stomach. Berry doubled up and sat down, temporarily out of commission.

Job, taking advantage of the diversion, tried to serve Sylvanus the same way, but Sylvanus grabbed the oar and jerked it out of his hands. As the old man dived at him with a yell, he sidestepped and got a firm hold on Job's belt and collar.

"Quit it, now," he said, shaking him. "I'll only have t' hurt ya."

It was a good deal like trying to hold a spitting cat, Sylvanus thought, stiffening his arms and waiting for Job to wear himself out a little. When he did, Sylvanus boosted the old man up the beach and into the shack, trying hard not to be too rough with him.

The workmanlike construction of old Mrs. Whiting's potato cellar had kept it from rot through the years. It was built up from solid rock under the shack and lined with brick. No man could get out of it, unless someone opened the two-inch plank door, which could be barred from the outside with a substantial flat strip of iron. Any man who had played as a boy around the Cove knew about the Whiting potato cellar. Sylvanus did, at any rate. Without a word, he hustled Job down into it, and left him there howling threats of murder and sudden death through the barred door.

He didn't wait to hear what Warren, raising a sleepy and astonished face from one of the bunks, had to say. He went back outside to round up Berry. Berry, however, was no problem. He was still sitting doubled up on the beach, crying over his aching stomach.

"Come on," Sylvanus said, scooping him up by the collar. "I gut just the place for you fellers, till you cool off."

He fixed the iron bar in place across the cellar door, driving in a rusty ten-penny nail above it, so it couldn't be jerked out of place. Then he went up the cellar steps into the kitchen, and confronted Warren.

"That cellar's no place for a man with a cold's bad's you've gut, Warren," he said, "or you'd be down there, too. They're stayin down there till Morgan gits his fish out today. If you let em out, or show outdoors yourself, I'll tend to you."

Warren shrank back into the bunk. "I wun't," he said earnestly.

"See you don't. If they git out I'll know who done it." He started for the door. "You can tell your pa I tied you up, if you want to." Glancing over his shoulder at Warren, he saw his threats had taken sound effect. Warren wouldn't do anything.

He sure did hate to do a thing like that to Job, Sylvanus thought, rowing over to the wharf to wait for Morgan. They'd be all right in there for a while—the cellar was ventilated, but it was probably cold and damp, wouldn't do an old man's bones any good if he had to stay there long. But the injury to his self-esteem was worse. Job had laid out for years that he was the toughest fighter on the coast. He wouldn't stop to figure out, either, that Sylvanus had probably saved him a jail sentence by locking him up for a few hours. He'd be in there right now, deciding how many of Sylvanus's lobster buoys he was going to cut off to pay for the loss of his dignity.

As the water deepened away from the shore of the Cove, Sylvanus caught his breath, seeing the magnitude of the school of herring. Nowhere, as he rowed, could he see bottom. The water was black with frantic, darting shapes. Sometimes, where they fled in terror at the quiet dip of his oars, the fish seemed to force each other in layers almost above the surface of the water.

Holy smoke, Sylvanus said to himself. He did a little rough calculation. It looked as though Morgan had his ten thousand bushels, all right, and maybe more.

He was tying up the dory at the wharf, when Morgan, carrying a tin lunch bucket, came down through the woods.

"Hi," Morgan greeted him. Breakfast had chirked him up considerably. "Guess you can use some grub."

"Ayeh," Sylvanus said. He sat down, opened up the bucket and broke out the thermos of coffee.

"Any idea how many we caught?" Morgan asked.

"Row out and look at em," Sylvanus said briefly, his mouth full. He watched speculatively, as Morgan climbed into the punt and started rowing around the Cove.

Morgan went all the way around, pausing at intervals to stare overside into the water. He took his time about it. When he got back, Sylvanus was screwing the cap onto the thermos bottle and closing up the lunch box.

Morgan's face was flushed. His eyes were as bright as beads. It was obvious that he had been doing some thinking.

Sylvanus got to his feet. "Guess you can make out without me, from now on," he said.

"Well, I—" Morgan looked off over the water. "I'll need somebody to help seine. The sardine boats are on the way over now, so I'll have to hire . . ." Something in Sylvanus's face stopped him. "Heck, I'll pay ya goin wages," he finished, in a forced voice.

Syl had that wooden expression—Morgan couldn't figure out what he was thinking.

"Twenty dollars?" he hazarded.

"Better make it twenty-five, hadn't ya?" Sylvanus said, his eyebrow quirking. "Lost my day's haul."

"Sure. Twenty-five's okay."

"H'm," Sylvanus said. "No, I guess you'll have t' hire somebody else."

Morgan's eyes narrowed. "I spose you think I ought to give ya a cut on the haul," he began angrily.

"That warn't exactly in my mind," Sylvanus said. He looked Morgan up and down. "Most people would, I think."

"Well, I don't see that. Oh, I'll make it right with ya for your haul and some extra, but— After all, Syl, you ain't— I own—"

"Skip it," Sylvanus said, "before you blow a cylinder head. You could hire Alton and Phil for ten dollars apiece, and the two a them would make one of me. You'd save five bucks that way." Sylvanus went down the wharf ladder into the punt, untied her and rowed out into the Cove toward Job's beach.

Goddamn me for a fool, he told himself. I don't want his money, but darned if I don't wash my hands of his troubles.

Warren lifted a scared face as Sylvanus came into the shack, and then drove his stuffed-up nose into his pillow.

Sylvanus went down the cellar stairs. He hauled out the ten-penny nail which secured the iron bar, took down the bar itself and let the door swing open. "Here I am, Job," he said.

Old Job came out swinging. Sylvanus let him land a couple of wild haymakers on his cheek and jaw, then he quietly folded up and slumped limply to the floor. Through his half-closed eyes, he saw Job half-squatting over him, hands on his knees peering down.

"Biggest man on the coast," he cackled, "'n n'jazzus, I knocked him out in two cracks. You see me, Berry?"

Sylvanus stirred slightly and uttered a hollow groan. "Lord God, Job," he said, waggling his jaw with his fingers. "What a wallop you pack, behind there! I feel's if I'd been kicked by a horse."

Job chortled. In his glee, he fairly danced up and down. "Told ya I c'd lick ya. Didn' I?"

"Ayeh. Never b'lieved ya, though. Do now." Sylvanus climbed stiffly to his feet.

"Godsake, boy," Job said. "I hurt ya, didn' I? Come upstairs an hev some coffee. Berry! Git up there, you tarnation fool, and put the coffee on!"

Sticking a bony palm under Sylvanus's elbow, he helped him up the stairs.

All day, the big sardine boats loaded herring at Patch's Cove. Morgan hired Phil Dalzell and Alton Curtis to help him. They ran a seine out from the big net, drove part of the school into it, and the boats dipped four thousand bushels that day. But it seemed as though no fish at all had been taken out of the swarming water, which still curdled black with herring.

It came home to Morgan, when he got his money for the day's load, at ninety cents a bushel, what a stake he still had in the water. He took no more chances. He called the state police.

That night, a heavy fog blew in from the south. The darkness around the Cove was thick as fur. When old Job, using it for cover, sneaked along the rocks and started to cut away the net, two state troopers caught him in the act and arrested him.

THE fellows who hung around Mike's Poolroom liked to kid Roger Drummey. He so obviously didn't know the answers. Or what he did know were screwball—half the time nobody could tell what he was talking about. Except that he shot a pretty good game of pool, he was a funny one to hang around a place like Mike's—acted more like a minister or a college professor than a common ordinary human being. Some of them, who knew him, explained that in his younger days, he had been a teacher.

The fellows at Mike's were quite a cosmopolitan mixture, made up of local boys who worked in garages, stores or hotels, and city chauffeurs, houseboys and gardeners from the summer estates. Most of the local boys knew Roger; nearly everybody who had been in town longer than a week knew who he was. He was Evelyn's husband; and Evelyn was "The Old Drum," who ran the overnight cabins where you could take a girl and no questions asked—provided you paid five dollars down and didn't make a racket.

There were all sorts of stories—funny ones, of course—about the little guy and Evelyn. Some of the boys felt that these stories were all the funnier because, it was well known, Evelyn started them herself. She would pass the time of day quite sociably with anybody who wanted to stop by at the office, up at the Cabins, and almost always, if you jogged her up a little about it, she'd start in on Roger. Some felt that it was pretty raw to have over a guy's private life in a place like Mike's, especially when it was his wife who'd started the stories going; but the kidding wasn't at all ill-tempered. Most of it was behind Roger's back anyway, and what was said to his face he always took in good part, as no more than any other man at Mike's had to take, when occasion arose. The spirit of it was far different from that of sparrows who sometimes tear to pieces the member of the flock that has the white feather in his tail. Most of the boys liked Roger.

Roger had not been back to Leon's. After a few days, he had seen Theo, one evening, again with Howard Thurlow. They were walking along arm in arm under the street lamps, and Theo was as oblivious of Roger as of any other stranger she passed by. Nights, when he could get away from home without too much unpleasantness, Roger drove around the countryside in his car. He went over back roads, unlighted and unfrequented, except for the occasional parked cars of lovers; and when the dark roads and the woods and the cold wheeling of the stars became unbearable, he dropped in at Mike's on the waterfront and played pool.

He had given up most of his daytime ramblings through the woods, too; not that he felt, now, that Evelyn's suspicions were important. A few days after she had spied on him in the spruce grove in the pasture, he had gone back there, to find that she had had Dominick cut the "wolf" tree down. There had been a nest of some kind in it; but the ponderous fall of the tree—or something—had torn it unrecognizably. Roger hardly glanced at the tiny handful of debris. Such things no longer seemed to matter deeply.

He had withdrawn again from the world, so that, at Mike's, the occasional raucous kidding bothered him not at all. He even found himself answering it in an absent sort of way; not as a man would speak in reality, but with a reflex, as a knee jerks when the nerve is tapped. He played pool the same way, finding that, not caring whether he made his shots, he played it rather well.

Tonight the tables were crowded, with a number waiting their turns to play, and, as Roger finished his game, he thought he might as well make way for someone else. But as he laid down his cue and turned to make his way to the door, he saw that Theo's redheaded friend was sitting at the bar. Not knowing exactly why he did it, Roger went over and sat down on the stool beside him.

Mike, seeing Roger, raised his eyebrow. "Look who's here," he said. "Your ol' lady 'lowin you hard liquor now, Roger? What'll you have?"

"Scotch," Roger said.

"Something like," grunted Mike. "Most a these cheapskates drink beer—an don't pay for that." He reached to the shelf for a half-filled bottle.

"I'll have a fresh bottle, please, Mike, and leave it down," Roger said.

"A binge, eh?" said the man on the other side of Roger, who clerked daytimes in a local hardware store. "Evelyn spank."

Roger said, "What?"

The clerk grinned. The other night, Evelyn had told a gang of the fellows up at the Cabins how she made the little guy toe the line. He was about to say more, but Mike leaned out over the bar and swept away his empty glass.

"Shut up, Fred," he said. "Time you went home." He dumped the glass into the hot-water tank under the counter. "He's plastered," he said.

Roger nodded. He was aware that Evelyn was taking her crude revenge on him. It didn't matter.

The clerk leaned closer. "Hey, I got a riddle. Why is the toilet like the grave?" he asked the assembled company.

Someone said, "That's got whiskers on it."

"The grave?" Roger said absently. "It's a fine and private place." He picked up his jigger of Scotch and drank it straight. "And none, I think, do there embrace." He glanced at the clerk. "That's not the answer," he said politely.

The clerk let go with a guffaw. "Heck, no. The answer is, 'When you gotta go, you gotta go.' See it? 'When you gotta go, you gotta go.' "

"Oh," Roger said.

The clerk glanced at him uncertainly.

"Oh, go wan home, Fred," Mike said. "You make my elbow ache. Have another drink, Roger."

"Thank you, I will."

The first jigger had tasted raw in his throat, but the third had hardly any taste at all. Somebody, it seemed, had merely dimmed the lights a little, so that the room seemed darker, washing the color out of even the bright bottles on the shelves before Mike's mirror on the wall.

"I've heard," Roger said to nobody at all, "that dogs see everything in a monotone. A kind of dirty gray."

Mike was busy at the other end of the bar; the hardware clerk had turned away. On the other side, Howard was deep in conversation with somebody.

"All on one level," Roger said, his hand clinking the bottle gently against the jigger glass. "As if color-blind."

His own words, as they had a way of doing lately, echoed in his ears, unreal and far away. "*As if color-blind.*"

Beside him, Howard's pleasant voice cut in, destroying the faint sound. ". . . don't know what you're talking about," Roger heard him say, to someone along the bar. "I had her up at one of The Old Drum's cabins the other night and was she . . ."

Roger didn't hear what she was, because the fellow on the other side of Howard roared with laughter.

Roger sat with his hand frozen on the bottle, while something in his chest seemed to curdle, then, slowly, turn to stone.

The girl Howard was talking about was Miss Josephine Brown of Kansas City, whom he had met often lately; but Roger had no way of knowing that.

Mike, coming back along the bar, said, "Hell, Roge, you're drinkin it too fast. Let up a little, why don't ya?"

"What?" Roger said. "Oh. Perhaps I am." He had filled the jigger too full; a small stream was running along the bar toward Howard's neat, blue-clad sleeve. Mike, grumbling, mopped it up with his bar cloth, and Howard, glancing around, said, "My God. That's a waste of good liquor."

Roger set the bottle down on the bar. For a moment his fingers remained tightened around the neck of it, then came carefully away. "Have the rest of it, by all means," he said. He turned to Mike. "What do I owe you?" He didn't wait for Mike to say, but laid a ten-dollar bill on the bar and went out.

Howard looked amused. "Gee, sure," he said. "I couldn't turn it down." He picked up Roger's full jigger and drank it, reached for the bottle, sliding it neatly out from under Mike's hand. "Generous little dope, ain't he?"

Roger went along the sidewalk in front of Mike's and climbed into his car. He wasn't drunk; at least he didn't seem to have any signs of it. He didn't feel dizzy and his hands were steady on the wheel. His own words kept echoing in his head—*"What do I owe you? What do I owe you?"* But that was nothing new.

"What do I owe you?"

"Thou owest me a million; thy love is worth a million."

He thought grimly, The schoolboy's mind, meeting its emergencies with a quotation. Association of words, playing the old trick in a head full of the ragtag and bobtail of reading. No one, of course, owed him anything.

He had been a schoolboy when he had married Evelyn . . . or she had married him. He had been going to be a poet, his head full of fine words then. And Evelyn had been tenacious and unbreakable, a cage of green timber full of knots. With his help, she had kept him from any true experience of the world, as untouched as a fetus in a bottle, a fly in amber. So that now, inside a weakened and aging body, he was a schoolboy still, a boy of nineteen with his first dramatics. And his first love.

Ah, there it was again.

Roger Drummey, riding along the dark highway toward his

home, made a slight, acknowledging bow to his mind, which with unfailing accuracy always presented the right quotation: *"Deliver me, O God, from the body of this death."*

IN the small back room off the restaurant was a rolltop desk, where, half-buried in piles of receipted bills, advertising throwaways and old newspapers, Leon kept a battered typewriter. He called the room his office, but he was seldom in it, and any of the help who wanted to use the machine was welcome to, provided he didn't try to clear up any of Leon's mess. Leon said the desk might look confused to most people, but he knew where everything was; when a man ran most of his business inside his head, he had to have his paper-work handy. Everybody used the typewriter, off and on, especially Henry, who had a girl in Ferriston to whom he wrote every day, sitting down and punching out his words of tenderness with a stubby forefinger. Henry liked his love letters neat.

He had looked into the office three times today, getting grumpier and grumpier as he realized the typewriter was going to be in use all through the slack time, as it had been yesterday. Theo sat in Leon's creaky swivel chair in front of the desk. She had sat there yesterday, in the hour between afternoon tea and dinner, when the help had time for a rest period; but the neat rectangle of paper in the typewriter was as blank now as it had been then.

It had seemed so easy to plan out a plausible letter when she was alone in her bedroom in the dark before she went to sleep. The phrases came, smooth and convincing; she had written the whole thing in her mind without a pause, even down to the name, signed in a free, flowing handwriting. *Lovingly, Your Uncle Oscar.* Or perhaps, *Affectionately* would be better, seeing Uncle Oscar was what he was.

But putting things down on paper was different. So far,

Uncle Oscar had been words spoken and gone; once you were through talking, nothing of him remained. He had been a game, played for fun, growing more and more fascinating as his shining details took shape. Now she had to make him something more. She was scared and she wished she didn't have to.

It was more frightening to think what would happen if she didn't. She had waited long enough to be sure, feeling the empty unbearable certainty grow.

After the answer came to her letter to West Palm Beach, Howard had said, "Mm. Might try Miami," and she had; but to the second letter she hadn't yet had an answer. Howard had kept asking, and at last, one night, he'd said, "Oh, well, skip it, babe. What do we care about him anyway?" He'd kissed her good night, the same as usual. And she hadn't seen him since.

No one could make believe love anybody. That is, *he* couldn't. Not to say all those things. It happened in the movies, of course, but the girl always had some way of knowing. You couldn't feel the way you did just seeing him come through the restaurant door or walk along the length of a block away unless he loved you, too. No. It was something else. It was all tied up with Uncle Oscar. The thing was, Howard hadn't money enough to get married on. He'd hoped Uncle Oscar being so rich would give him a job. Now that she couldn't find Uncle Oscar, Howard had decided to give her up. He'd be feeling bad about it, in despair. She couldn't bear it, knowing she felt that way, too.

If it *were* Uncle Oscar, she could fix that. She could make Howard believe for a while in that sweetly curving Southern beach, with the white buildings and the palms, and the big boats sailing the blue and the spray of the Gulf Stream. He'd have to believe it long enough to marry her; and when they were married, who cared how hard they'd have to work? She didn't. After all, Howard would have her. He'd thank her in the end, when it came out; because all she was doing was taking matters into capable hands, as a woman should, to show him that money and a job didn't count when people had each other and their happiness.

But Uncle Oscar, when she tried to put down on paper the letter he would actually be supposed to write, suddenly stopped being a pleasant ghost and became a bogy. Something out of darkness.

She typed in tentatively, *West Palm Beach, Florida,* and the date, and *My Dear Neice,* and stopped in horror, realizing that she couldn't remember whether "niece" were spelled "ei" or "ie." Somewhere, back in ages gone by, the teacher in English class in school had made everybody learn a rhyme:

> *Put "i" after "e"*
> *Except after "c"*
> *Exceptions to this rule are:*
> *Something . . . something . . . "neigh-bor" . . .*

No, it was no use. She couldn't remember how it went. It didn't seem that "niece" had been one of the exceptions. But you couldn't tell. One thing, Uncle Oscar would never misspell a word like that. It might give the whole thing away, let Howard know it was a fake.

She sat staring at "*Neice,*" which seemed to change from wrong to right and then back to wrong again, and suddenly something inside her grew very cold.

Fake. *Fake.* It had been there all the time, outside her mind, knocking as if on a closed door. For that was all everything boiled down to in the end. A fake.

Henry stuck his head in at the office door again and stared at her, thrusting out his underlip in a pout. "That must be some love letter," he said crossly, "t' take all this time."

"Oh, go away," she said irritably, and was sorry, seeing how Henry's big Adam's apple started to work and how red he turned. Poor Henry, he wanted to write his love letter. She wished it were a love letter to Howard that she were writing.

But the thing that had knocked its way into her mind wouldn't go away.

What will happen, it said, *if you fool a man into marrying you? Will he ever think anything of you when he finds out?*

Yes, he will. If he loves you to begin with.

But does he?

Oh, he must! He couldn't make believe a thing like that and have it seem so true!

You, yourself, are making believe something and having it seem true.

But if I don't, he'll go away. He's already gone . . .

Then, does he love you?

She sat looking bleakly at the typewriter, and saw opening out ahead of her the future with Howard gone away. A future bereft of soft summer nights, bereft of magic. School opening, the bare desks, the colored warmth of autumn on dusty walls. Ida Gates giggling. Winter, and the ice growing around the black rocks at Granite Hook, driving iron into the land. Spring . . .

Oh, Howard. *Howard.* I can't bear that spring will come and I won't have you.

The door in her mind closed with a sharp little click. She took the sheet of paper out of the typewriter, put in a fresh one and started typing.

She was still typing, bent over the machine in absorption, when Henry looked in for the last time. "Leon says you better come out and git goin," he said sourly. "If you think you could tear yourself away."

She finished up the long letter she had written, tore it out of the machine with a rush. The only letter she had ever had in her life from Florida was in her pocket. She took it out of its envelope and tore it into small shreds, dropping them into Leon's wastepaper basket. The envelope had the Chamber of Commerce's return address in one corner. She tore it off, folded the letter she'd just written and put it in the envelope. Now it just looked like a letter from anyone, opened carelessly, but the postmark was there. When she got out of work tonight, she'd get it to Howard somehow. If he didn't come in . . .

Work started badly out in the restaurant. Things weren't busy, because the weather was a fog and a drizzle and not many people were on the move.

It was a good thing they weren't. Theo didn't feel like working anyway, and Henry, being good and mad at her, was unco-operative. She couldn't be sure it was his fault that the orders kept getting mixed. She knew it wasn't hers. After a couple of bad mistakes, she snapped at him.

"Henry, can't you be careful? That last course was all wrong."

Henry, it seemed, was just waiting. "It wouldn't of ben," he said, "if your mind was on your work instid of on writin love letters."

Theo turned red. Polly was listening and so was Biff, turning his red wattles away from his bubbling kettles so he could hear better.

"You mind your own business, you nosy little twirp!" Theo said. The hot anger seemed to rush up from deep inside, and it felt good.

If there was one thing Henry couldn't stand, it was a slur on his size, which wasn't small, but wasn't above average, either. On account of Theo, he'd had to skip writing to his girl for two days—he didn't want her to know he wrote such a poor hand. He leaped into the fray with pleasure.

"If it's that redheaded feller you're a-writin to," Henry said, "you needn't bother. I seen him over to Ferriston last night with a blonde. I seen him two-three times lately with the same blonde."

Polly said, "Henry, shut your trap!" She saw the look on Theo's face and came over from the other side of the room with a rush. "If I was as ig'nerant as you are, you slab-sided clam digger," she said to Henry, "I'd go tunnel me a hole and live in it, not hang around where I could show off what I was.

You git busy with them orders, or I'll wrap that steam table round your neck so hard you'll think you was a fritter!"

Leon said from the door, "What the rampin ole red-eyed blazes is goin on in here?"

Henry babbled, "Well, I never . . . I warn't . . . I *did* see him with a blonde."

"I don't care if you saw Harry S. Coolidge with a purple-haired mermaid. You git movin! People hollerin, and not a waitress on the floor . . . What's the matter, Theo? Henry, who did you see with a blonde?"

"Howard Thurlow," Henry said sheepishly.

"What's it to anyone here who you saw *him* with? Tomorrow night, you'll see him with a different one. Theo ain't foolin around with no poison like that, she's gut too much sense. Come on, now, the whole lot of ya, le's see some action."

Theo shook off Polly's arm which lay protectingly around her shoulders. "I don't feel well, Leon," she said. "Could you spare me if I went home?"

"Have t' spare ya, if you're sick."

"I . . . I'll be back in the morning . . ."

"Don't give it a second thought," Leon said. He went on gruffly, "You want I should walk out to the bus with ya?"

"No, I—"

"Well, better hustle. You gut just time t' ketch the five-thirty bus." He stood looking after her as she ran into the dressing room.

Theo caught up her coat and ran out the side entrance. At the bus stop, the bus was waiting in the thin rain, but she didn't get on it. She ran by to the corner, went through a couple of back yards, and came out on the long street that led down to the waterfront. At the end of it, back of the wharves, was Howard's rooming house. She knew where it was—he'd pointed it out to her one night when they'd been riding around. His boat was in, she knew that, too, because a little while ago Johnny Fleming had come into the restaurant.

Howard was lying on his bed in shirt and stocking feet and

an old pair of dungarees. He got up to answer Theo's knock and stood looking at her in amazed irritation.

"What you doing in here?" he asked.

"I had to see you," she said. "I had a letter from my uncle —you know, the one in Florida. I thought you . . ."

"Well, couldn't you have mailed it? Gee whiz, I mean—well, you hadn't ought to come to a man's room like this." He grinned suddenly. "You found the old boy after all. Well, come in."

He shut the door behind her, slipped his arms around her shoulders and kissed her hard on the mouth. "You're wet like a starfish," he said. "Must be raining out."

The feel of his arms was like coming home to a safe place after a bleak and hungry time, and Theo clung to him.

"Oh, Howard."

"What's the matter, you dope?" He gave her a little shake. "Has the old boy gone broke? Or hasn't he got a place at all, or what?"

"Oh, he has, Howard." She felt in her pocket for her handkerchief, wiped her eyes, and before she thought, gave her nose a resounding blow. Oh, dear, she thought.

Howard, however, hadn't noticed. "Let's see the letter," he said, holding out his hand. She gave it to him.

"He's got a great big place, Howard, with boats and all, and he wants us to come and work for him."

Howard stared at her. "Us?" he said blankly.

It had been a mistake, of course, but she recovered quickly. "See what he says, there—he wants a girl to wait on tables and a man to run a cabin cruiser. A couple, he says—do I know where he could find a young couple. I guess it was me thought of the 'us,' Howard."

"I guess it must've been," Howard said. He sat down on the bed, holding the open letter in his hand. "I'll be darned. Does, doesn't he? Sounds like a nice old feller, too. Two-fifty a month and all found. Wow!"

He turned the envelope over in his hand, glanced at the postmark.

Theo's heart gave a lurch. For a moment, everything turned cold and sick and ugly. He doesn't believe it, she thought.

But Howard only said, "Letter's been a heck of a time on the way, hasn't it? The West Palm Beach feller must've located him right after he wrote you." He fixed in his mind the name, Congo Key. Near West Palm Beach, he thought, and handed the letter back to her.

A warning had sounded somewhere deep inside him, but it hadn't been suspicion. The idea that the letter wasn't all it seemed to be had never entered his head. The thing was, and Howard knew it well, this kid wanted him to marry her.

If Howard had thought of it first, he might have. He liked her, he couldn't deny, and if a man wanted to settle down, she'd make a nice little wife on the slow side. But, he suddenly thought, he was being chased. He'd been chased before, and not one of them had ever got a hook into him. Not one of them was going to . . . *He* was going to be the one.

When he got ready, he could slide down to Congo Key and see old man Sewell and tell him he knew his niece. Maybe he'd get a job. In the meantime, he had a few more weeks here with Mr. Grover. Just about right to finish things off proper with Jo Brown and take himself off, alone, to Congo Key. Jo was all he needed while he was here. She was no young kid, either. Get yourself involved with a young kid, no knowing what kind of entanglements you'd run into with her relatives. Some of these fishermen around here, say her father, looked as if they'd have a darned heavy fist. Better end this up, right here and now. But looking up to do it, the blow poised, Howard met Theo's eyes.

Gee, the poor kid, he thought complacently. It'd be tough. I can let her down easy, not all-of-a-thump.

"It'll take a lot of thinking over," he said, shaking his head.

He couldn't meet the eyes for long. He looked away as if

he were, actually, thinking things over. "We'd need so much stuff," he said, and it sounded lame even to him.

Theo caught at the sound of the "we." Her eyes shone.

"What do we need we couldn't get? If we wanted to?"

"Well, look. I wouldn't think of going down there blind without some way to get out in case things went wrong. I wouldn't go down there, even alone, without a car."

"A car?" she said slowly. "Couldn't we go on the train?"

"Whose got the money for train tickets?"

"I might have," she said. She wished now she'd counted up what she had left in the shoebox at home. There'd have been more out of summer's earnings, but she'd been helping Phoebe with the expenses, and Phoebe'd borrowed some, too. "How much does it take, Howard?"

"I couldn't say offhand. A lot. But I wouldn't go anyway without a car. Too easy to get stuck."

"Oh."

"You better hop it," Howard said. "My old landlady, here, she's got a mind like a sink. We'll think it over, kid, keep your shirt on." He got up and shepherded her toward the door. "All these things got to be thought out. If we had a car, we could drive down, get married on the way—" He stopped, noting in something of a panic the flare of joy that came into her face. "But we haven't got a car," he finished hastily.

Wasn't he going to kiss her good-by? she thought. But at the door, he did.

"Maybe," she said, putting her hand over his on the doorknob, "maybe Uncle Oscar'd send us the money for a car."

Howard chuckled. "Can't you see him doing it?"

No. She couldn't. You could count on Uncle Oscar for almost anything you could mention except something you had to put your hands on like money or a car.

"I told Leon I was going home, Howard," she said hopefully. "No one expects me there till nine o'clock."

For a split second, Howard hesitated. God, he'd like to. She was a sweet kid and she'd be wonderful. But what would it get him afterwards? A fishy fist square in the teeth, and after that the least he could expect was a shotgun wedding.

"Beats the deuce," he said, and the regret was as sincere as it sounded. "I told the boss I'd come back aboard the boat this evening. He's got some . . . some sails. You trot along. I'll see you soon."

GRAM SARAH could have killed the cow. She would have, too, she told herself, if once she could have got her hands on the critter. Three times she'd hunted her out of the alders and headed her for home, and each time the cow had gone galloping past the bars as if she'd never seen such things, eyes rolling and stern to the sky. She was an old cow and a gentle one, but tonight she was "on time." Wildfire poured in her thickened veins too heady for a stable on a summer night. Now she stood on a tussock, shaking her horns, ready to take off again if Gram Sarah so much as made a move.

"You contry old fool," Gram Sarah said balefully. "You're too tough t' beef, but you'd make mincemeat. An don't think you wun't, if you don't git in there an stop your cussid actions."

It warn't no use to blame the cow. The fault was in the times, with everything gone to pot—menfolks too lazy to keep stock, so's the'd be a bull handy to tend to a poor critter when she come to the call of her natural ways. No, they couldn't be bothered to milk or cut hay. They'd rather pay to have a quart of dishwater a day delivered to their doorsteps in a bottle that no knowin what dirty old men had had their hands on, and that you could see bottom in a fathom of, for all the cream the was in it.

Times she could remember all the fields were green as serpints' backs, with the cows pastured on them and the good dung bringin up the grass. Now, nobody bothered to cut so much as a sprill of hay. It laid in the fields year after year, until the old fog got so thick it soured the land and all come up to gitchell birch and alders.

That cow hadn't freshened for three years and time she did, poor thing. But what could you do when there wasn't a bungie within twenty miles, and Sylvanus and Morgan, when she asked them who'd be likely to have one, acted like they'd never heard a such a thing?

Gram Sarah took a deep breath and found she could get it all the way down. She'd been so winded she'd had to breathe as fast and shaller as a kitten. She tried again and let the second breath out in a cracked, long-drawn call: "Co-o-o, boss! Co-o-o-o, bossy, bossy, bossy!"

The call had a wild and melancholy sound, as if some old seabird, flying over, had let go his night cry among the darkening trees. The cow slatted her head against it, but she had been called so before. Perhaps it stirred ideas of a more sensible yesterday, or of fresh grain, or the relief when the milk was out of her swollen udder. She took an unwilling step toward the bars, and then came. There was no doubt. She had meant to all along.

Gram Sarah followed her into the barn and tied her up at the stanchion.

"Bag's most busted, you poor old slut," she said, sitting down with her milk-pail and leaning her head against the sweating nervous flank. "No wonder, it's way past milkin time. There, now. Ain't that better? There, now."

She carried the heavy pail into the house—at least, it seemed heavy tonight, though she found to her surprise on straining the milk that the cow hadn't given down very well.

"All that rantin round," she told herself. "Well, it's a good mess, considerin." Though, when she was a heifer and freshened, the cow'd given fifteen quarts a day.

Gram Sarah divided the milk into three containers. There was the bowlful for her breakfast. Set to rise in the cool milkroom, by morning it would be deep in heavy cream. There were the two milk cans full, one for Morgan's folks, one for

Sylvanus's. Emly wouldn't give it to the baby—oh, no, she wouldn't have that much sense. Seein she couldn't nurse him —and that was her own fault, too, traipsin off to a hospital where them doctors wouldn't know one namable thing about makin a woman's milk come right—Emly had new-fangled ideas about milk out of a can. But the good cow's milk was there, just in case she did come to her senses. At least, Phoebe didn't have no scruples about seein that Jacky got plenty of it.

Gram Sarah put on her shawl and picked up the milk cans. As she walked down the road in the dusk, she suddenly realized that she was more than middlin tired.

"Chasin that everlastin cow over them rocks and stumps, must be," she said. She'd go right home after she'd taken the milk around, and go to bed. No, she wouldn't, though. She hadn't seen Morgan for two days. She'd stay awhile and talk to him. Say he was there and not busy, she wasn't going to miss the chance to see him. He was as chirky as a ten-year-old, these days, since he'd made all that money. Just like Papa Jasper, he was now—reminded her so of him. Nearly nine thousand dollars, he'd made, all at one whack. She'd always known he'd be the one to amount to something.

Once she was settin down, the ache would quieten down in her back. Two-three times lately she'd felt that slippin-away, all-gone feeling. But it wasn't nuthin. Nuthin to speak of.

She went up Morgan's back steps and into the kitchen, setting her milk cans down on the cupboard. "I brought the milk," she said, and then, suddenly, unbelievably, she felt her knees let go . . .

. . . as if they'd turned to water, she thought. "Well, I ought t' know better, chasin round that pasture."

She was lying down. In a bed. Her eyes must be shut against a light, for all she could see was a mess of queer red-colored streaks. Funny her eyelids seemed so heavy. It was almost too much of a job to open them. But she did.

She was undressed, in a nightdress that wasn't hers. She was in Morgan's spare room, the one Emly had papered in a pattern of houses and trees that wasn't at all suitable for a bedroom. The morning sunlight was pouring through the window.

But it couldn't be morning. She had just set the cans with the night's milk on Morgan's cupboard.

My Lord, she thought with horror. I ain't sick. I ain't never been sick.

She'd get right out of bed and go downstairs and go home. But she couldn't make one of her legs move and her arm was lying as numb and heavy as if it had been turned to a cordwood stick. Something must have fallen on her and hurt her.

That sheet-rock ceilin in Morgan's kitchen—she'd always told him that one a them big sheets'd be down on somebody's head someday, that it warn't solid like good, old-fashioned plaster.

If that's all it is, she thought, I'll get right over it. It ain't as if I'd been took sick.

But she was off her feet. She was in bed and couldn't do for herself. A feeling of terrible shame swept over Gram Sarah.

UNCLE WHEAT felt bad. He certainly did feel bad about Sarah. One minute she'd been flippin round smart's a mosquito; the next thing, she'd had a shock and was in a coma. She was comin out of it now, they said, conscious and knowed people; but she'd never git up again.

That was the way it was, he thought sadly, sitting in the rocking chair in the sun on Mat's back porch. It was Sunday morning, a fine, clear, dry day, and his knees didn't feel stiff to amount to anything. But along the field by the back of the house the goldenrod ran like yellow fire; the asters were blue and dusty by the road. Signs of fall coming and after that winter. He could feel already the cold clinching about his bones. That was the way it was, for old people. Tomorrow might be his turn or Foley's. Foley wasn't well—he couldn't be, acting the way he was. Uncle Wheat shook his head, thinking very likely Foley wouldn't last out the winter.

Usually, when he felt blue like this, Uncle Wheat would have gone down aboard Frank Dalzell's lobster scow, and him and Frank and Foley would have had a game. But Foley kept to himself now—didn't act fit to lug guts to a bear. Ever since the morning Wheat had thrown the water over Whirligig, Foley'd been sore, and he wouldn't come out of it. It didn't seem possible that a grown man could act that foolish over a cat. Two-three times Wheat'd tried to patch things up, but all he got was grunts.

Mat said, from just inside the kitchen window, "No use to set there and sull, Pa. Whyn't you go down and see Foley—walk the shore line or somethin, the two of ya? It's too good a day just to set."

"I don't know but I will," Uncle Wheat said, as if the idea had just occurred to him. He wouldn't admit to himself that he'd had it in the back of his head all along. No, sir, Foley could come to him. He went into the house after his hat.

Mat had been using the leisurely Sunday morning to clean out her kitchen drawers. She'd taken all the odds and ends of string—she was a great string saver—and wound them all up into a neat ball. Now she was head and shoulders out of sight under the cupboard, rooting around among the pots and pans. The multicolored ball of string was on the table. Uncle Wheat saw it and, grinning, he scooped it up and put it in his pocket. Mat wouldn't miss it, now she knew she'd saved it, and it was just the thing, maybe, to make a little joke with on Foley. A little jab, right now, might bring Foley round.

Down at the shore, he launched his punt and rowed off aboard the scow. Frank would be there, for a few of the lobster boats, making use of the fine weather, had gone out even though it was Sunday. Foley was there, too, sitting on the deck with his back against the house and stretching his legs out in the sun.

Frank said, "Hi, Wheat. Come t' hev a game? We was waitin for you."

That sounded good. Uncle Wheat felt better at once. He said, "Hi, Frank. Hi, Foley."

Foley didn't say anything.

Grievances for a long time back had been working up in Foley. It wasn't alone Wheat's throwing water on his cat, though for two or three days after that Whirligig'd been so nervous Foley couldn't get anywheres near her. The thing was, Foley was just good and plain fed up with the way Wheat had always made fun of his rig. Foley figured that a man's boat and the way he kept her was his own business. He hadn't known that he was jealous of Wheat's good boat and gear—he didn't admit it now, even to himself. But it had been going on for years, backing up; the water-throwing incident and Wheat's crack about the Friendship being a floating fishhawk's nest had finally tipped it off.

A fishhawk keeps the worst house of any known creature; there were some that said you could smell it to wind'ard. And a good lobster fisherman will swallow an insult to his wife easier than he will one to his boat.

Foley was about ready to make it up with Wheat, though. That is, he was ready to jump either way. Life was kind of dull without Wheat's company; matter of fact, it was lonesome. But Foley wasn't going to take anything. Wheat could come to him.

So when Wheat dropped the ball of odds-and-ends of string into his lap, intended for the peace offering of a little joke, Foley sat for a moment regarding it with narrowed eyes.

The old son was at it again. It couldn't mean a thing except that Foley was to use the string to patch up his already patched-up engine. That, of course, was exactly what Uncle Wheat had intended it to mean; he'd thought a little joke like that would put things back, between him and Foley, to the way they'd always been.

Foley jumped up and bounced the ball of string, hard, off of Uncle Wheat's head.

Uncle Wheat would see the day when any man could heave a ball of string at him. He went for Foley and Foley went for him. They had each other down, rolling over and over on the deck of the scow before Frank could jump between them. It took him five minutes to pull them apart, and when he did, Foley, without a word, went over the side of the scow into his punt and Wheat went over the other side into his. They rowed away in different directions, Foley to his boat and Wheat ashore, leaving Frank with a scratched nose and as astonished as he'd ever been in his life.

"YOU go see Gram Sarah," Phoebe said. "It ain't decent you ain't been at all." She looked across at Theo who was absently eating breakfast, but Theo didn't glance up from her plate.

"Theo!" Phoebe said.

"What, Ma? Oh, I will, but I can't today."

"What's the matter with today, I'd like to know? It's Sunday and you've gut all kinds a time."

Theo reluctantly brought her thoughts back from the place where they were wandering. "Oh, Ma, I haven't got *any* time."

"Oh, sakes," Phoebe said. "You've got as much time as the rest of us, I guess. Besides, there might be somethin you could do to help Emly. She's got her hands full, goodness knows, and a baby to take care of, besides."

Phoebe's patience was short this morning. It had been ten days since Gram Sarah had had the shock. They'd all thought she was going to die. She was so old. But on the morning of the third day, she'd recovered consciousness, and she'd been getting better ever since. Though she was partially paralyzed in her left side, she was rational now most of the time—a double handful to take care of, as Phoebe and Emily were finding out. Phoebe had been sitting up with her on alternate nights to take some of the load off Emily. Last night had been Phoebe's night, and she was tired. When Theo didn't answer her again, she had to take hold of her temper to keep from snapping right out.

"I know you've got Sunday plans made," she went on, more gently than she would have if she hadn't been holding onto herself. The way Theo was acting these days, though, you wouldn't be able to find out with a hammer and a chisel what those Sunday plans were. "But it won't take long. Gram Sarah'd probly like to see you."

"She never did want to see me. Why would she now?" Theo was thinking, Howard may come today. He never had come to see her when she was at home, but he hadn't turned up last night at Leon's when he'd promised to, and surely he wouldn't wait until Monday to explain why he'd been detained somewhere. He knew where she lived. It was just possible he might stop by. She meant to be home—lying in the grass out front, reading or something, when—if he came. Because he might just drive by the house hoping to see her. He might not want to come in and ask where she was.

Phoebe was going on talking. "That don't mean a thing. Gram Sarah never was a one to show how she felt down deep. Of course, she thinks a lot of you. After breakfast, I want you to go up and see her."

Theo's mouth set in a stubborn line. "I don't want to."

"Well, you're goin to!" Phoebe blew up at last. "And you can stop actin as if I was to one end of the town and you was to the other. I don't know what ails you lately, Theo, but I'm sick 'n' tired of it and so's your pa. I'll be some glad when you git through over to Leon's and school starts and you come down to earth again. If there's anything the matter, you better tell me, but if the ain't, you can snap out of it, miss lady!"

The scolding, Phoebe realized, was one that had been backing up in her for quite a long time. She'd meant, for a while back, to have a talk with Theo, though not in a cross way. Leon had an idea she was mixed up with some fellow over in Bellport; though Phoebe didn't think so or she'd seen more signs of it. No fellow'd been hanging around over here, anyway, and Theo didn't seem to be unhappy. Just absent-minded.

But a home was something more than a place for a girl to come to sleep nights, and her folks were people just as much as any of her friends were, who were taking up so much of her time. It seemed, lately, as if they at home were just something Theo had to put up with, for all the interest she took.

The way she was sitting over there now, looking at her plate as if all it was, she was waiting for her mother to get through. What was being said wasn't making one mite of an impression.

Theo was thinking, School. It starts the Monday after Labor Day and that's next week. And soon after Labor Day, the boat Howard works on is going to be hauled up for the winter, and he will go away. He hasn't said he'll take me with him.

Phoebe said, "Well, there isn't, is there?"

"Isn't what?"

"There you are, you don't listen, and it makes me so mad I could fly! There isn't anything the matter, is there?"

"No." She looked over at her mother.

Phoebe noted the quiet face, the clear eyes. "Well, then, you take yourself up and see your gra'mother. You stay a little while, too. And you find out if Emly's got anything you can do."

Theo got up and started for the door.

"Theo—"

"What, Ma?"

"Leon says the's a boy—kind of a no-account . . ." Phoebe began doubtfully.

"Leon's an old maid. He thinks if a customer asks you for an extra teaspoon, he's trying to make a date. For heaven sake, Ma!" Theo went on out the door.

Well, there. She'd mentioned it and there wasn't anything in it. Phoebe got up from the table and started to stack the dishes.

Jacky was sitting, round-eyed and sober, as she always did when her mother raised her voice to someone, and Phoebe stopped to pat her on the head. "Come on," she said, putting a saucer in Jacky's hand. "You help Mama pick up the dishes."

Jacky took the saucer and started for the sink with it, but on the way she noticed that the saucer had a sprig of colored flowers. She sat down in the middle of the floor.

There now, she'd be entertained for the next hour, Phoebe thought. Jacky was such a comfort. In some ways, she wished the rest of the children were more like her . . .

My soul! Phoebe caught herself up with a feeling of startled shock. Of course she didn't, anything of the kind. Such a thing would never have come into her head, if it wasn't that she was so tired this morning and didn't want to deal with problems. She'd known before she started that she wasn't going to find out what went on inside Theo's head. When they were little, or like Jacky, they didn't worry you so much, that was all.

Le's see. The little boys were out in the boat with their father. Wes was over at his job, Jacky was here. Theo was on her way up to Morgan's to see Gram Sarah. Phoebe knew where each one of them was.

Theo's always been a good girl, Phoebe said to herself, pouring hot water into the dishpan. Never give me one minute's worry.

Emily was very glad to see Theo. "You haven't been up here in a long time," she said, giving Theo a kiss.

Theo hadn't; she hadn't, in fact, been to see Emily since the baby was born. It seemed to her that Emily wouldn't be able to look her in the face after that night. *She* certainly didn't want to see Emily.

But Emily didn't seem to mind. She looked lovely, too, her hair brushed into a misty fluff and her cheeks round and pink. She had on a crisp blue gingham dress with a frilly apron. The dress, together with the weight she had put on since the baby came, was becoming to Emily. And she had a look in her face of sweetness and contentment that Theo didn't recall seeing there before.

"Oh, yes," Emily said. "Do go up and see Gram Sarah. She hadn't ought to be left alone for long, because she's always trying to get out of bed. She can't, of course, but you know her. I'd be up there, except I've got to feed the baby."

Emily did, indeed, have her hands full with Gram Sarah. The old lady couldn't do anything for herself, and she resented having it done for her. She had a deep sense of modesty; being bathed or going to the toilet on a bedpan outraged her. Emily did the best she could.

She'd thought at first, it was going to be awful. But suddenly, she found herself understanding that Gram Sarah was the one things were awful for—living alone so long and being so independent and bossy, and now helpless. Emily didn't know how it was she came to understand this. Except, she told herself, I'm so happy now I've got Jamie, I can feel sorry for anyone who isn't.

Just at first, she'd been afraid she wouldn't know how to take care of a sick person, and she'd asked Morgan if he didn't think they'd better have a trained nurse. He could surely afford it, with all the money he'd made. Emily hadn't the slightest idea how much it was, for Morgan had put it all away in a bank somewhere, and their lives hadn't changed in the slightest. Morgan just said that he guessed his mother's own folks could take care of her. Emily hadn't pressed the matter. His face had begun to look all closed-up like; and when it did that, it wasn't any use to argue.

She understood better about Morgan, too, now. He was funny—very funny—about money. But, aside from that, he was a good husband, steady and dependable, and he was crazy about Jamie. She didn't love him the way she had when they were married. That was all gone. But she felt contented and safe with him; maybe it was better . . . to be sure you'd be taken care of, no matter what happened, and to know that Jamie would, too.

So far as taking care of Gram Sarah was concerned, Phoebe and Sylvanus helped a lot, and the neighbors were kind. Emily hadn't realized how kind they were until she had sickness in the house. She didn't know what she'd have done without Uncle Wheat. He stopped by every day and did odd chores for her—the ones Morgan didn't find time to do, he was so busy. Quite often Uncle Wheat helped her look after Jamie. He adored Jamie. He said a baby was a godsend to him these days for company, now he didn't have Foley. He and Foley had quarreled about something and weren't speaking.

Oh, Foley was just being an old fool, Uncle Wheat said. He'd get over it someday, but in the meantime, Uncle Wheat was blue.

Looking at Emily, Theo thought, You wouldn't think she had a horrid time at all when she'd had Jasper . . . Jamie, she called him. It was hard to remember to say Jamie, when everybody else in the family said Jasper.

Jasper . . . Jamie was a lovely fat pink baby. He lay now in his bassinet, regarding the world with wide sober blue eyes, while Theo looked back at him doubtfully and with skepticism.

"He smells so good," she said, won over at last. You *couldn't* not like Jamie for any reason in the world.

Emily laughed. "He didn't a minute ago. Just after I'd bathed and dressed him, too! He hasn't any sense of timing. Jamie," she said, putting her finger on his cheek. "Jamie, smile for Theo. He smiled for me this morning. I'm sure he did, but his pa said it was only gas." She gurgled richly, and it did seem to Theo that Jamie changed his expression a little, as if he had caught some of Emily's laughter.

"There!" Emily said. "See that? Gas! He already had his burps up, nice big ones, didn't you, Jamie?" She picked the baby up and popped the nipple of his nursing bottle into his mouth. "You know, they say you hadn't ought to pick them up to feed them, Theo, but I always do. Why, if I didn't hold him, how would he know I loved him so? He doesn't understand English." She laughed again, nestling the soft head in the crook of her arm.

No, you couldn't say that having Jamie had left any mark that was bad on Emily. Jamie was nice.

"Gram's better," Emily went on. "Oh, Theo, what an old Tartar! You know, awhile back, if anyone had told me I was going to have to take care of her the way she is now, I would have fell right over on my face."

"I know I would. Oh, Emily, it must be awful!"

"It's awful for her, poor thing, lying in bed like that."

"Oh, for you, I mean. Just to have to *see* her—"

"Why, that's not so bad." Emily glanced at Theo a little puzzled. "She's just the same. Oh, you mean because she don't like me. Well, she don't, of course, and it's dreadful for her to have to be sick in my house and me to take care of her."

"I expect I'd better go up," Theo said reluctantly.

"You do."

"Oh, dear, what'll I say to her?"

"My goodness, it's hard to think of anything that don't make her fly off the handle. At least it is for me. I'll never learn I guess, either," Emily said ruefully. "This morning Uncle Wheat stopped in and I told him to go up and see her. She let out a squall you could have heard a mile, and told him to march right out of her bedroom. You'd thought he'd come in there for . . ." Emily giggled ". . . for immoral purposes. Oh, dear, I mustn't laugh, it isn't a bit funny, but he did look so shocked. He said he felt as if a gull had flew into his hair."

Theo laughed, too. It was just like Gram Sarah.

"Maybe she won't notice you at all," Emily said. "Sometimes she just talks to herself."

But Gram Sarah's eyes were as bright as two buttons and they began taking Theo apart as soon as she came through the door.

"You hadn't ought t' wear them pants, now, Theo," she said.

Theo had tiptoed in, expecting to find her looking awful. She had steeled herself to meet the sight of dreadful sickness. But Gram Sarah looked much the same. She was lying in bed, of course, and her sparse old hair was in two pigtails, one on each side of her neck.

Theo felt her back go right up, the way it always did when she was around Gram Sarah. "They're not pants," she said. "They're just a pair of old slacks. All the girls wear them."

"Well, they hadn't ought to," Gram Sarah said. "And you hadn't ought to, either. Your tail's too big."

Theo went over and sat down in a chair, which she first pulled back a little so it wouldn't be so near the bed.

"Why didn't you bring Jacky?" Gram Sarah demanded. "Or don't none of you care whether a little girl ever sees her gra'mother?"

Oh, dear, Theo thought, I won't be here five minutes before I have her as mad as a hatter. She tried to think of some excuse why Jacky hadn't come.

"She wasn't through her breakfast."

"Breakfast! My Lord, it must be eight o'clock. What's your mother thinkin of! Not through breakfast!"

"Well, it's Sunday." It was nearer eleven than eight o'clock. Gram Sarah must be a little sick, if she was that much mixed up on the time.

"All the more reason t' be up 'n doin, on the Lord's day. Some of you's got to tend out on my gardin, make sure nothin don't go by before I can git up 'n round again to can it. Them string beans is just prime," the old lady said. "I was goin t' pick them yistiddy, but it rained and the's new ones comin on. I mustn't take no chances rustin my bean vines."

"The beans are all tended to," Theo said. She had heard Phoebe say that Uncle Wheat had gone over and picked Gram Sarah's beans and that Mat Dawes had put them up for her.

The jars were now on the shelves in Gram Sarah's preserve cellar.

"They are *not* all tended to," Gram Sarah said. "Don't you tell me whether I've picked and canned my own beans or not." A flush of excitement came into her face. "There'll be just time . . ." Her voice faded and paused, and Theo, glancing at her, saw that Gram Sarah's eyes were looking out past the foot of the bed, as if they saw something far away.

". . . before Ernest and the boys git in from fishin." The old voice came out again strongly. "I'll take that busted bushel basket, it's the handiest, if it'll hold together."

Ernest, Theo thought, startled. Why, that was my grandfather, the one I never saw. And the boys—they must be her father and Uncle Morgan. Gram Sarah's hands, moving delicately on the fold of the bed quilt, were picking a bean crop of a bygone day.

"Them's good beans," Gram Sarah said. "I knowed they'd be, when I see how big the blossoms was. The sun was pretty on them lavender blossoms. I'll hev that t' think about next winter when the snow's blowin. I'll open up a jar of these beans and I'll think, the sun come down through them green leaves and feathered out on the blossoms, just so."

She's awful sick, Theo thought. She's so sick she's out of her mind. Gram Sarah never stopped to notice anything pretty, like the sun on lavender blossoms. The same crawling sense of fear and shame Theo had felt the night Jamie was born started to come up from somewhere in the middle of her stomach. Oh, why did people ever have to be hurt or sick? Why did she have to be around to see them?

The unyielding old voice went on. ". . . when I woke up this mornin, the green tea bird was singing. *Green tea, sweeten it, sweeten it.*"

It was a white-throated sparrow she was talking about. Theo'd heard him often. "Sam Peabody," some called him, because they said his song was *Sam . . . Peabody, Peabody,*

Peabody. The old people, though, called him a swamp robin, or the green tea bird.

But this green tea bird Gram had heard was dust many years ago, his tiny skeleton cracked up by sun and frost. He was the one who had sung in the lilac tree on the morning when she stood there and watched Ernest come walking down the hill with a bokay of white lilacs in his hand. For she had gone still deeper back into time, and the morning she was talking about now was the morning Ernest had asked her to marry him.

". . . a grown man luggin around a bunch of posies. But they're pretty and they smell sweet. I guess he thinks they'll do some courtin for him. He's comin now over the hill and he's a good man. I feel about him the way a girl ought t' feel. He's goin t' ask me, and I'm goin t' take him."

Funny, you never thought about Gram Sarah—Gram Sarah of all people—ever being a girl—a girl with a man in love with her.

". . . I'll marry you, Ernest, but don't ask me if I love you, because I can't talk soft, and anyway, you know I do."

Oh, Gram. It happened to you, too.

Theo stared hard at two small shapeless blobs on the floor, keeping her eyes wide open, because if she winked it would let the tears come.

The two blobs, she realized, were Gram Sarah's shoes, set side by side under the edge of the bed. They were old shoes, beginning to crack, the soles worn paper thin even along the sides. One of them had a round knob on it, where the leather had stretched around Gram Sarah's bunion. She thought suddenly of how far these shoes had come—not these very ones, but all Gram Sarah's shoes—stepping back and back into time for over eighty years. And for a moment, Theo saw, not clearly but as if something blind were groping out of a sheath, what Gram Sarah's life was—rich and completed and, somehow, wonderful.

It was too bewildering to think of long. Because all Gram

Sarah had ever let you see was the seamed and crusty surface, and the person who lived under it was somebody you didn't know. You knew, too, that that kind of life was something you'd never, never want for your own. You had to go find what *you* wanted. Things better . . . lovelier . . . different . . .

But maybe that was how it was with everyone underneath, in the part that didn't show. Emily . . . would Emily trade whatever it was that made that look come on her face for anything Theo could find somewhere far away?

She felt the bewilderment grow. Oh, dear, you couldn't seem to think anything out and nobody ever helped you.

Theo was suddenly aware again of the bright, dark, fierce eyes.

"They've hurt Gram Sarah's baby," said the old lady. "They better not."

"Oh, Gram," Theo said. "I can't think what to do." She put her face down beside Gram Sarah into the bedclothes.

"I can't neither," Gram Sarah said. She touched her hand against Theo's hair, the bony hand as light as the brush of a wing. "Folks can't, sometimes, when things is bad." She snatched the hand away. "Hang on tight and do the best you kin. Howlin wun't help nuthin, I know that much."

WES was fascinated. He'd filled two or three sheets of tablet paper trying to figure out how much money Uncle Morgan must have made out of his haul of herring. Some said he'd taken nine, some ten, and some eleven thousand bushels out of the Cove. Nobody knew for sure but Uncle Morgan—he'd sold them to different boats at different prices. But Wes knew the price on any of them hadn't been under eighty-five cents a bushel. He calculated Uncle Morgan had made eight thousand dollars anyway and maybe nine or ten.

The season wasn't half over. No knowing how much it might be by the time Uncle Morgan had to take his net off the weir in late November. Wes couldn't get out of his mind the deep sense of exultation and importance he felt because some member of his family had made money.

Well, there it was. It could be done. The Sewells didn't have to stay as poor as salt cod forever. Uncle Morgan had proved it. Wes found himself wanting to hang around Uncle Morgan, get him to talk—oh, about anything, but mostly about the weir business, if he would. Wes even dropped in at his house quite often, a thing he seldom did, but he passed it off by saying he'd come in to see Gram Sarah. Uncle Morgan would talk, all right—he had a heck of a lot to say about the weir business. Wes would sit, full of admiration and interest, taking it all in. He'd catch himself thinking, If Uncle Morgan can do it, I can.

Wes was more than ever up in the air about his future. Neither Mrs. nor Mr. Beacon had said another word about a city job. Now, already, they were talking about going away. Felix and Jane were packing—they had to get back to school right after Labor Day. Their parents were staying on for another week of the fine September weather and to make sure the servants closed up the house properly. Wes had about decided he was going to ask Mr. Beacon outright if he knew of a job for him.

So far, though, Wes hadn't been able to make up his mind. Seemed if Mr. Beacon had anything at all to suggest, he'd have mentioned it before this. And another thing—this surprised him—something in the back of his mind was beginning to question a little the idea of going to the city and working for Mr. Beacon.

Oh, it'd be nice, *if you could find a good job*. But you'd have to get into something in a small way and work up. Felix had told him once what the jobs in his father's factories usually paid—twenty-five, thirty dollars a week. When you got right down to thinking about it, there was Luke, the chauffeur. He'd worked for Mr. Beacon for sixteen years, and he was getting under two hundred a month—found, of course. It didn't look to Wes as if Mr. Beacon was likely to offer anyone more than that to start in with—if he made any offers at all. What could you find anywhere, where you'd make eight thousand dollars or more in less than ten days?

It had been a pretty rotten summer. After Ken Murray left, Felix had had another friend to visit, and later on two more. The first one hadn't known anything about boats or the water, so Wes got to run the speedboat a lot while he was there. But the last two were like Ken—their folks had summer places on the ocean. They had speedboats of their own at home. Felix went off a lot with them—or he did at first, until the three of them got into trouble and Mr. Beacon put his foot down about their always taking Wes with them.

The three had gone out one day in the Chris-Craft, leaving Wes behind. Felix was steering, and he thought he'd be smart and circle around Foley Craddock, who was hauling traps in his old Friendship just outside the Hook. Felix never had any sense about distance, anyway. He'd circled too close and the big bow wave from the Chris-Craft had rolled right in over Foley's washboard, half filling his boat. And then, instead of stopping to see what damage they'd done, the crazy fools had gone right along, leaving Foley waving his arms and hollering.

Wes sure didn't think much of that. Oh, Foley, by the skin of his teeth, had got out of it all right, with nothing more than a good soaking. He'd pumped his boat out and gone ashore. The thing was, it could easily have been a pretty bad accident. It was a living wonder the Friendship hadn't rolled right bottom up.

Foley'd been madder than a hornet, and not to be blamed. He'd laid for Felix and his two pals when they came ashore, had caught one of them and had licked him good and hard before some of the fellows down around the shore could stop him. He'd been going to lick the other two—swore he would before the week was out. But Mr. Beacon had gone down to see Foley and, Wes guessed, had given him some money. Anyway, Foley cooled off.

Mr. Beacon'd been plenty mad, too. He told Felix it was too damn bad someone had interfered before Foley got around to him. He said if Felix touched the speedboat without Wes along, for the rest of the summer, it would be sold the next day, and that was that.

Having to take Wes along didn't suit Felix at all. For a while, he treated Wes like a hired deckhand right in front of the other two boys. Wes guessed he could see through a hole in a wall. He felt bad, but he was getting fed up with it. While they were kids, he and Felix had been swell friends. Now they were older, it didn't need a spyglass to tell that Felix didn't think Wes was good enough for his swanky school chums.

Today Wes had hung around the boathouse all day, while Luke had driven the other boys over to the movies in Ferriston. On account of something Mrs. Beacon had said, Wes had kind of taken it for granted he was invited. He'd even put on his new slacks and a dark jacket, getting ready to go. But they'd just piled into the car after lunch and gone without him.

Wes took off the fresh clothes and put his dungarees back on. He felt plenty sore. There wasn't even any work to do—Mrs. Beacon had gone off to tea somewhere without suggesting any jobs for the afternoon, because she must've thought he was going with Felix. He swept out the boathouse and then spent the rest of the afternoon lying on the pier in the sun, thinking.

Along about five o'clock, he heard Mrs. Beacon drive in—she'd taken Mr. Beacon's car today—and he went around front to put it away for her.

"Why, Wesley," Mrs. Beacon said. "Back so soon? Where are Felix and the others?"

"I didn't go," Wes said.

"You didn't? But I thought—" She stopped and bit her lip.

She started into the house while he got into the Lincoln, but at the doorway she turned and said, "Oh, Wesley. Will you come into the living room after you put the car away."

There it was—the nice, polite request—not a command the way it sounded, but you knew darn well it was one, all the same.

Wes put away the Lincoln, closing down half of the rolling door on the garage, leaving half of it open for the Cad to come in. He went back along the walk to the back door and in through the kitchen. Lena, the cook, was fixing cocktails on a tray—two glasses, he saw. Must be one for Mrs. Beacon and one for Jane. Not that there was any reason why she should give him a cocktail; but it would be nice if she did, once, just to show she thought of him as a little more than a hired hand.

She was sitting in the big chair by the window, looking out on the garden, and Jane was sprawled on the window seat. Wes tried to catch Jane's eye. After all, at that last dance, they'd had a swell time together. But Jane didn't look at him.

"Well, Wesley," Mrs. Beacon said. "Summer's nearly over, isn't it? I was thinking, looking out there at the garden, how wonderfully well you've done this year with the flowers."

"Thanks," Wes said. "They did do pretty well, but it was your work as much as mine, Mrs. Beacon."

"Oh, my, no. I just fritter around with the weeds. You did all the spading and anything that amounts to anything in these front beds. Mr. Beacon and I were talking about you this afternoon, Wesley. We've decided we can't get along without you."

Wes blushed. Well, here it was. It certainly looked as if this was it.

"Luke is leaving us, you know," Mrs. Beacon said.

"Luke . . . is?"

She nodded.

"But, *Luke*—he's worked for you so long. I didn't know . . . I thought—"

"That's just the trouble, Wesley. He's worked for us so long I suppose he feels privileged—you know, like one of the family. And that's not a good thing."

"No," Wes mumbled. He turned fiery red. "I don't suppose it is."

"And Sam and I—Mr. Beacon and I have felt for quite a while that we'd rather have somebody younger."

"You mean," Wesley said, in a thunderstruck voice, "you're offering me *Luke's* job?"

"Why, yes. Oh, you mustn't worry about that, Wesley. Mr. Beacon will see to it that Luke gets another."

"No, that's not it—I mean, of course I wouldn't want to take Luke's job away from him, but—"

She looked at him a little doubtfully. "Mr. Beacon will talk to you about the wages, Wesley."

A chauffeur. That was what they thought of him. She'd made it clear, too, that a chauffeur shouldn't think of himself as a member of the family.

He was glad, now, that Jane wasn't looking at him. She was apparently absorbed in something outside the window. Wes almost laughed out loud, thinking of the air castle he'd put himself to sleep with one night not long ago, about sometime falling in love with Jane and marrying her along with, of course, all that money. He wasn't in love with her now, of course, nor she with him. He was just woolgathering against the future. But they'd had some good times together.

It wasn't the job—a chauffeur had a swell time, with car engines and driving and all. The ones he knew were good guys —Luke was a heck of a good guy. Wes thought, suddenly, No, he didn't look down on the job.

It was just that knowing the Beacons so long, ever since you were a kid, running in and out of the house playing with Felix and Jane, and later on, going on parties with them, you didn't feel like a servant, but like a friend.

Lena came in carrying three cocktail glasses and a shaker on a tray.

"Oh, thank you, Lena," Mrs. Beacon said. "Gino not back yet?"

Gino was the houseboy, the one Wes and Felix and Jane called "Gizmo." Today was his afternoon off.

"He's just come, Ma'am," Lena said. "He was a little late, so I thought I wouldn't keep you waiting on the cocktails."

"I see. Speak to Mr. Beacon, will you? I think I just heard him go into the den. Well, Wesley? It's settled, I hope."

Mr. Beacon had come in, then. Wes had thought, just for a moment, seeing the three glasses—

"I—I guess I've got to think it over," he said feebly.

Mrs. Beacon looked astonished. "Why, Wesley! I didn't think you'd hesitate."

Wesley said, "There's another job I've been considering."

Mr. Beacon came in from the den. "Well, Wes, Mrs. Beacon made you a proposition, has she?" He picked up the shaker, poured the three glasses full, and picked one up. "Certainly glad to have you work for us winters, too, boy."

Mrs. Beacon said in a displeased voice, "He says he's considering something else, Sam."

"Oh. That so?" Mr. Beacon sipped his cocktail, regarding Wes. "What's that?"

"I'm thinking of going into the weir business with my Uncle Morgan," Wes said.

He realized now he had been. He just hadn't made it definite in his mind. He thought, with an inward grin, it sure was going to be news to Uncle Morgan.

"Morgan?" Mr. Beacon said. "Oh. That's the fellow made the killing with the big haul of herring, isn't it? Well, it's natural you should be beguiled by that, I suppose. But you want to remember, Wes, it was mostly luck. Wouldn't happen again in a hundred years."

"Why, I'm not sure—"

"Look around you at these fellows—some of them run a weir year in and year out and don't make expenses. Mrs. Beacon and I will pay you a—a hundred and fifty a month, that's all found." He had started to say a hundred and thirty-five, but thought that under the circumstances, he'd better up it a little. "Steady money every month. I'd advise you to think it over."

"I will."

"Good night, then." Mrs. Beacon was sore, Wes could tell from the tone of her voice. "You'll let us know your decision in the morning."

"Er—yes, I will. Good night, Mrs. Beacon."

Jane turned around as he went out and reached over after her cocktail. Wes glanced at her, but he let his grin freeze and die on his face. It seemed in the last ten minutes there'd been some changes made. He went out through the kitchen and along the walk to the boathouse to get his cap.

"Well, I must say, I'm surprised," Mrs. Beacon said. "After all we've done for that youngster."

"He's just playing hard to get," Mr. Beacon said. "Wants a little more money, probably. He'll come around."

"I hope so," she said. She sat thoughtfully gazing out into her flower beds, her face set in lines of worry. Felix was so unstable, now, so unmanageable, and Wesley had always been such a steadying influence on him. She'd racked her brain, wondering what would be the right thing to do. Letting Luke go had been a wrench; and Luke, even with the promise of another job, was hurt and angry. But Luke was useless where Felix was concerned. Felix just walked all over him. When they went on excursions, like the trip to Ferriston today, Felix would park Luke and the car somewhere, and then he'd be off on his own harum-scarum schemes. If Wesley had been along, she wouldn't have had to worry. Not so much.

She and Sam had considered carefully what kind of a job to offer to Wesley. Because he was such a nice boy and so capable, it didn't seem right for him to be left here in Granite Hook to grow up just a fisherman, like his people. And in the factories, Sam said, a country boy with no more preparation than Wes had for existence in the city would be lost. You had to take into consideration a boy's aptitudes; Wesley was wonderful with cars. They'd both thought he'd jump at the chance to have Luke's job. He'd always seemed so fond of her and Sam and the children.

Well, there it was—everyone was out for what he could get out of people who had money.

When Wes came out of the boathouse with his cap, he saw that the Ferriston expedition was back—Luke was just putting the Cadillac into the garage. Luke saw him, but instead of waving a high sign as he usually did, he merely turned his back and started for the stairs—he lived in the two rooms there over the garage.

He knows already, Wes thought. Mr. Beacon must've told him.

He quickened his step and caught up with Luke. "Hey, Luke—" he began.

"You ain't got nothing to say to me," Luke said. "I ought to tear you in two."

"Oh, gee, Luke, I never asked for the job. I've only just heard about it."

"How d'ya like that?" Luke said. "I've watched you undermining me for three years, you little punk."

"No," Wes said. "I haven't, Luke, I—"

"Ah, shut up. It's a good job and I had it a long time, and I got two kids. But if you want it that bad, you can have it and welcome." He turned and went up the stairs. Just before he went out of sight through the door, he spat with a resounding smack down on the concrete floor.

"Oh, my gee," Wes said. All of a sudden he realized how much he'd always liked Luke.

Felix came tearing around the corner of the boathouse and up the walk to the garage. "Where've you been, Wes? I've been out on the pier looking for you. I've left my leather windbreaker out aboard the boat. Row out and get it, will you?"

Wes said, "Row out and get it yourself."

Felix's jaw dropped. "Why . . . you—just who do you think you are?"

"I ain't your old man's chauffeur," Wes said.

"No? I had an idea you might feel a little bit too nice."

"Slapping me right back where you think I belong, aren't you?" Wes said, eyeing him. "From now on, you don't get the chance."

"Well, I'm glad of it. Maybe I can go somewhere, once in a while, without you nosing in so you can report back to Mother."

Wes reached over and put his hand on Felix's face; he was going to shove, but the soft nose was too tempting. He gave it a good twist first.

Felix spun backward with a squeal and sat down hard on the concrete floor.

"And you know what you can do with your lousy job," Wes said. "You and your whole tribe." He scooped up his cap and started out the door. Seeing Luke's amazed and grinning face at the top of the stairs, he made him a high sign before he went out of the garage for the last time.

Now, he thought, he'd have to do some darn fast talking to Uncle Morgan. But shucks, if Uncle Morgan wouldn't take him on, something else would turn up. All at once, Wes felt good.

He went down the white gravel road bordered with clipped grass and rhododendrons, past the stone gateposts with the terse black-and-white sign, PRIVATE ROAD. He thumbed his nose at the sign and trotted up the macadam whistling.

Sylvanus said, "You done *what?*" His surprise, above his newspaper, and the reading glasses on the end of his nose, gave him an owl-like look, and Wes grinned.

"I told ya. I chucked up my job."

"Warn't that a little mite brash? I kind of run of an idea you and Mr. Beacon had the future all planned out."

"*He* did," Wes said.

"Didn't suit?"

"Nope."

Sylvanus folded the paper. He laid it down and took the glasses off his nose before he said any more.

You'd have thought that losing his job with the Beacons would have knocked the pins out from under Wes, but here he was way above himself and looking as if somebody'd made him a present.

"You don't seem no ways broke up about it," Sylvanus said at last.

"Nope." Wes grinned again. "I pulled Felix's nose."

Sylvanus said, "Hah!"—a short sharp little bark of pleasure. "Give it a good yank?"

"A dandy."

"Bout time somebody did." Sylvanus looked at Wes with considerable approval. "Well, what now? Leaves you kind of hangin and rattlin, don't it?"

"Uh-huh. You think Uncle Morgan might take me into the weir business with him?"

"M-m. No."

"I don't know why not. He told me the other night he'd run a full gang of traps this fall if he had somebody to tend weir for him. I figured if I did that, he could haul his traps, except days when we had herring."

"We?" Sylvanus looked quizzical.

Wes didn't even look dashed. "Oh, sure, I know what you mean—Uncle Morgan wouldn't consider it unless there was something in it for him. Well, the way I'm going to put it to him, there will be."

"He might hire ya—day-by-day wages. I d'no's I'd count on any share basis, 'f I was you."

"I don't. Not at first. Might come a time when things'd be so it'd be worth his while to let me in on shares."

"Could be," Sylvanus said, blinking. "Why don't you put it up to him?"

"I plan to. Right now. I was thinking—a man doesn't need to limit his business. Uncle Morgan and I could run more than one weir. We might build two or three."

"So you might."

Wes flushed a little. "In the end, I mean. I didn't mean to sound as if I planned to start right in building tomorrow. Heck, Pa, Uncle Morgan ain't the only one in the family's got a head on him. I bet we could make more money working together than he could alone. Want to bet he'll see it that way?"

Wes didn't wait for an answer, but went clattering up the stairs to his room.

Sylvanus picked up his paper again. For a while, he sat thoughtfully twirling his glasses around on his finger. In a way, he'd have liked it if Wes had come to him—if the boy'd wanted to go in lobstering with him instead of weiring with Morgan. Sylvanus could see, though, why he hadn't.

He grinned a little ruefully, and then caught himself heaving a sigh of relief as he settled back in his chair. Himself, he'd always enjoyed working alone. He thought the world and all of Wes, but darned if he wanted to have to talk to him aboard a boat all day.

If this dust-up with the Beacons were permanent and Wes really intended to buckle down, he could be worth quite a lot to Morgan. Just at first, he'd take a beating on the money end of it, but, Sylvanus thought, his grin widening, not for long.

FOLEY, Uncle Wheat saw, was out shifting traps. He had pulled them up from the ledges around the Whirlpool, and he had on a heavy load, headed for deep water. Nobody else seemed to be shifting traps that day.

He's doin it just to be contry, Uncle Wheat decided. Hopes he'll scare me into shiftin mine, doin a lot a extra work for nothin.

The weather looked all right. He guessed *he'd* know if it was comin on to storm.

Nevertheless, he worried, keeping an eye on Foley. Foley was pretty smart about weather sign. He wasn't likely, even to be contry, to do a lot of heavy work when he didn't need to.

By midafternoon, the sky had mackereled over and a brisk wind was blowing. It was northeast, meeting the ebb tide flowing off the land, making mean moiling water. Most of the boats gave up hauling and went in.

Foley, though, still hung her tough. He was done shifting, but he was tied up to a lobster buoy, handlining. Uncle Wheat be damned if he was going to quit before Foley did. The old son, trying to outlast *him* in a little mite of a no'theast chop. Why, he'd been out in some blows that would curdle Foley's blood, times when he took them vessels up and down the coast. Maybe his joints were a little stiff, but he was still as much of a man as that shrimp.

Uncle Wheat put down a handline of his own. The minute Foley started for home, he meant to open up wide open and pass him. But all at once, Foley chucked over his anchor and went up on the bow to make it fast. Then he came down and stuck himself, all but his rear end, into his engine box.

Why, the old fool wasn't tryin to outlast anybody. He was havin trouble with his engine.

That was all Uncle Wheat needed. He wasn't one to let bygones be bygones, either.

"Havin trouble, Foley?" he bellowed, as he slid alongside.

Foley stuck his head out past the sprayhood. "No," he said. "I ain't."

"Hatchin an aig, maybe?"

Foley said nothing.

"Well, heave up anchor. I guess my nose can stand it t' tow ya in, seein's the wind'll be quarterin."

"I wouldn't take a tow from you if this was hell and you was a angel flyin straight to heaven," Foley said.

Uncle Wheat picked up a coil of heavy, new rope—twenty-four-thread—that he'd bought just so as to have aboard a stout anchor road if he needed it. He held one end in his hand and tossed the coil to Foley. "It's comin on t' blow," he yelled. "And I could raise a chop in a pot that would sink that thing."

Foley hauled on the twenty-four-thread until he had it all except about a fathom and a half, chopped it off with his fish knife and threw it overboard.

"If I'm goin t' sink," he said, "I'll sink decent, not tied up by no Atlantic cable to no waterlogged ole flounder."

The quality of these insults wasn't lost on Uncle Wheat.

A flounder was a fish that lived on bottom; also, in Foley's opinion, thus made clear, twenty-four-thread was too bulky for everyday purposes. He couldn't have said any plainer that Uncle Wheat was an overcautious, inexperienced landlubber.

It was true that Uncle Wheat was sometimes inclined to make his gear too stout, owing to having been so long aboard a vessel where you needed big rope. Foley had twitted him about it before.

"Sink, then! Set there and sink in your goddamned old punkinseed!" Uncle Wheat roared.

"I'd ruther set out a no'theaster in this *punkinseed,*" Foley said, "than tow home behind goddlemighty's yacht full a hot air."

Uncle Wheat made as if to go aboard of Foley, but with the cross-chop running, he found this impossible. He started up his engine, headed for home and left Foley sitting where he was.

By the time he got home, he was so roaring mad he couldn't eat his supper. He sat in his rocking chair with his stocking feet in the oven and wouldn't say a word. Mat thought he was sick.

"Well, go to bed, why don't you, Pa?" she kept saying.

Finally she gave up and sat down by the reading lamp with her magazine. By and by it would come out what was the trouble with him.

The night had come on pitch black, blowing a gale northeast and raining. Uncle Wheat sat rocking, glowering at the stove.

About nine o'clock, somebody walked up on the piazza and came into the entry, slatting the rain off a hat.

Mat said, "Now, who can that be, this time night? Oh, it's you, Wes."

"Ayeh," Wes said. "Phew, what a night!" He was in yellow oilskins, glistening with rain.

"Nothin t' be out in," Mat said. "Anything wrong, Wes? Your gra'mother's all right?"

"Oh, sure," Wes said. "Uncle Morgan and I was down seein to the moorins on the weir dories and boat just before dark. We saw Foley hadn't got in from haulin."

"The old fool," Uncle Wheat burst out. So far, he hadn't glanced around from the stove. Now he got up, paced twice across the kitchen floor and sat down again.

Wes looked puzzled. "Ayeh, Uncle Wheat, but it's a bad night—the storm came up so quick, must've caught him out. We was down again just now, and he ain't on his moorin."

Uncle Wheat, with great dignity, got up from his chair. He brushed by Wes, went into the entry and began hauling on his oilskins.

"Hey," Wes said, startled. "I didn't mean go after him. We just thought you might have some idea where he was. It's black's your hat and raining like a fool. You can't see ten feet."

"What'd you fresh-water sailors need to go out in?" Uncle Wheat demanded icily. "High-noon of a start-calm day?"

"Why, no," Wes said. "But now's no time. Unless we get Pa to go."

Uncle Wheat stamped his feet to settle his rubber boots and started for the door.

"Pa!" Mat said. "You stop it. Don't you do nothin foolish."

Uncle Wheat turned, holding the entry door ajar, so that raindrops swirled into the room. His sou'wester was jammed so far down that he had to tilt back his head to glare.

"I spose you think it was daylight when I sailed them vessels through some no'theasters I could name. I spose none a you around here's ever heard of a compass or dead reckonin. Well, it wan't, and you ain't."

He slammed the door behind him so hard that Mat's dishes rattled in the cupboard.

"Heaven sake," Wes said. "What ails the old gentleman?"

Mat groaned. "I wish I knew, Wes. He's been crossgrained's a bear all evenin. I wish you'd go after him so's he don't hurt hisself."

"Well, I will," Wes said dubiously. "But I ain't going to get close to him."

Mat sat up and read till eleven o'clock. She was worried, but knowing how her father felt about Foley, she supposed he'd stay down around the shore waiting for Foley to get in. If anybody went out in a boat tonight, after Foley, say he had been caught outside, of course they'd get Sylvanus or someone.

At eleven, she took her magazine to bed and read until twelve. She was just getting up to dress and go out and find what on earth had happened to Uncle Wheat, when she heard somebody blow into the house literally on a gust of wind. It was her father, all right, and somebody else was with him.

As she finished dressing, she heard a great touse coming up from the kitchen through the open register—a rattle of stove covers and the fire roaring up the chimney; a slapping sound as of wet clothes being flung down; and then a clashing of bottles and tumblers. She started to go downstairs, but knowing her father, she thought maybe she'd better peek down the kitchen register first. She ducked back with an outraged gasp.

Uncle Wheat and Foley, naked as jaybirds, were sitting in front of the stove drinking out of tumblers.

"I was comin alone," she heard Uncle Wheat say, "but that Wes, he jumped int' the punt, just as I was shovin off. He tried t' git me not to go, but after I started cussin him out for comin, he couldn't git a word in aidgeways. I guess he was sorry afterwards he come, because I scairt the livin daylights out a him."

There was a pause, while Uncle Wheat took a hefty pull on his drink.

"It was so rough *in the harbor*, that by the time we gut off to my boat, we was a-settin in six inches of water."

Foley said, "Sure t' wan't eight?"

"No, you damn fool. Eight would of sunk the punt. When we gut aboard, I lit the lantern I gut rigged up just right t' shed the light on my compass. Then I started the enjun and sent that Wes up on the bow t' cast off. He like to went ass over teakittle int' the drink before he gut her clear a the moorin chain. Said he never knew how he used both hands for that and still hung on."

"Beat hell, didn't it," Foley said.

"I took a bearin with the compass and the time from my watch. That's a chronometer watch, Foley. Then I opened up the throttle and sent her down the channel wide open. Wes he says to me, 'I never would dast t' put her into it like this.'"

"Neither would I, wide open."

"'T ain't foolish, if you know what you're doin. We drove down the channel for thirty-three minutes and thirty seconds. Thirty-three minutes and thirty seconds," he repeated. "I says t' Wes, I says, 'If Foley ain't gone adrift, this is where he ort t' be.' Wes says, he never'd believed it if he hadn't see it with his own eyes."

"Anybody could of done it," Foley said. "Maybe not Wes, but his pa could of, with his eyes shut."

"Not by a chronometer, by Jesus," Uncle Wheat said. "Blacker'n the inside of an old maid's placket hole, an thick rain. We lit the big lantern and waved it out and hollered, an' there, by darn, Foley, you *was!*"

Foley said, "Ayeh."

"Now, Foley, that line you hed for a tow rope warn't strong enough. The third time your boat busted loose, we never hed enough slack t' work with and I like to never gut you made fast again. Caught my thumb between the line and the cleat, too. Jammed it. Might of lost a hand . . ." There was a pause and a horrified silence.

"By God, Foley," Uncle Wheat said. "Look at that. My thumb's gone."

"Thunder 'n' lightnin," Foley said. " 'T is, ain't it?"

"Tore clean off," said Uncle Wheat. "An', by God, Foley, you done it."

"That's right. Did, didn' I?"

Mat let out a squawk and started down over the stairs.

But when she got there, the kitchen was deserted. Not a living thing was in sight except Foley's cat, Whirligig, who sat, wet as a drowned rat, on the rug by the stove, industriously washing and drying off her damp-scraggled fur. Whirligig didn't even glance up.

Mat said, "Pa! If your thumb's tore off, you come right out here and let me do it up."

There wasn't a sound. The kitchen closet door was wedged tight shut, though.

Mat stood outside it, expostulating. After a while, she glanced over at the table, on which sat Uncle Wheat's bottle of rum that he kept in the cellarway, a package of butter and the sugar bowl, and two big empty tumblers. She shut her mouth tight, went back upstairs, undressed, put out the light and got into bed.

If my father's thumb were tore off, you'd hear more ducks quackin than that, she told herself.

From downstairs, the conversation resumed as if there had been no interruption whatever, drifting up through the hot-air register in the kitchen.

"If I'd a hed that *Atlantic cable* you throwed overboard this afternoon, it wouldn't a happened. I wisht I hed that rope's end now. I'd lay it onto your hide, Folcy."

"Well, you ain't gut it."

"I'd a damn sight ruther lost you than lost that thumb."

"You'd hev your damn thumb, it 't hedn't been so soft it broke off like a pep'mint stick. I was out there longer'n you was, and I never lost nuthin. *Did* I? I ain't even lost no traps, Wheat. I d'no but you're liable t' lose some, Wheat. A few."

They were still at it when Mat finally gave up and went to sleep.

She saw, with little surprise, in the morning, that Uncle Wheat's thumbs were both on his hands—one of them was wrapped up in a dirty handkerchief, though, and she made him let her put on a clean gauze bandage. Perhaps an eighth of an inch of skin and fingernail were gone, and the remaining nail was black and blue, that was all.

But she was really horrified when she saw her pound of butter. She never would have believed two men could have used so much of it just by putting a little into a drink.

PART FIVE

September

HOWARD called up at six o'clock and said he was sorry he couldn't keep the date—his boat was going out on a Labor Day week-end cruise. But just before quitting time at eleven, Johnny Fleming and the other member of *Wanderlust's* crew, Dick Jones, came into Leon's for hamburgers. When Theo waited on them, she said, trying to make it very offhand indeed, "Haven't gone out on the cruise yet?" and Johnny said with a grin, "No more cruises this year. The boss and his wife went home."

Theo said, "Ketchup, Mr. Fleming?" and Johnny said, "Yes, please," and she got a bottle from another table and set it down at his elbow. "Somebody said you'd be sailing until the fifteenth," she said.

"Yare, Mr. Grover planned to, but he got called back to Jersey on business. Have some ketchup, Dick?"

She lingered on the pretext of glancing over the table. "Got everything you need, Mr. Fleming?" She wanted terribly to ask him if he knew where Howard was tonight, but the words wouldn't come.

"Uh-huh. Thanks."

"I guess you'll be laying the boat up soon."

Johnny glanced up, puzzled. "She's up now," he said. "We finish dismantling her for the winter tomorrow."

"Then you're all through?"

The crew member called Dick stepped lightly on Johnny's toe under the table. A light dawned on Johnny and he said, "Get me another cup of coffee, will you, kid? I think this one came out of the bottom of the urn."

"Howard," Dick said, when she had gone with the half-empty cup, "had better hop it out of town."

Johnny grunted. "Howard ought to get a boot in the place where it'd do the most good," he said.

Well, he was going sooner than he'd planned to. And he hadn't let her know. Theo waited numbly until the two men had finished and then carried their dishes to the kitchen.

Biff said cheerfully, "One more day of slavery for ya, eh, Theo?" and Theo found herself saying casually, as if nothing had happened, "That's right, Biff. One more day."

For after Labor Day, she was leaving Leon's to go home and get ready for the opening of school.

In the dressing room, Polly was at the mirror combing her hair.

Theo changed into street clothes and hung her uniform in the closet. She was putting on her coat, when Polly said suddenly, "Theo, lamb." Her mouth was full of hairpins, Theo could see in the mirror, but that wasn't the reason she sounded so funny. Polly, of all people, was crying.

"He ain't worth it," Polly said. "He's kid stuff, Theo—he ain't never growed up. Oh, I'm a fool to bawl, but I can't help it, please be awful careful what you do—" Polly stopped, mopping busily with her handkerchief.

"Who—what are you talking about?" Theo said woodenly.

But Polly didn't say any more. She just sat rubbing away with her handkerchief, and presently Theo turned and went out the door.

Outside the night was cool, with a winy smell of fall in the air. The street lamps seemed very bright. They gleamed even on the dusty fenders of Johnny Fleming's old car, parked in front of Leon's, and for an instant Theo's heart gave a jump. Of course Johnny was uptown tonight—he was using the car himself, not Howard.

Some other cars were parked along the curb between Leon's and the bus stop. One of them was Mr. Drummey's, she noticed, and he was sitting at the wheel.

It seemed a long time since she had seen Mr. Drummey. She couldn't remember having missed him. But as she came abreast the car, with a little run she ducked out of the brightly lighted street and into the seat beside him as if it were a haven.

"Hello," he said, in his deep, quiet voice.

Theo couldn't say anything; but as he backed the car away from the curb she tried to remember her manners. "I haven't seen you," she managed, at last.

"No," Roger said. "I haven't been here for a long time."

He wasn't offering to let her drive, but tonight she didn't care.

How far away and long ago it seemed when having a car just to drive it had been the only thing, almost, on earth. Now you wanted one, but it wasn't just a want. It was something fierce and terrible within you that told you you would do anything—you would pay anything you had. Because the difference now between having and not having a car was the difference between having and losing Howard. That was what he had said. She could see his face, recall the very tones of his voice.

"If we had a car, we could drive south, get married on the way, but—"

He loved her, she knew that. People like Polly and Leon and Henry tried to make him out different from what he was. They didn't know him, that was all. She was as sure of him as of all the sure things—the sun rising, the tide coming up and going down among the ledges twice a day. It was money—the car and things like that—holding him back. He was afraid he couldn't take care of her.

As if that mattered! There were plenty of ways for them both to make money. A car would have convinced Howard and driving south to the good job with Uncle Oscar . . .

Theo pulled herself up. She was thinking of Uncle Oscar as if he were real. For a time, he had been. He had to be. Because, if you let yourself look beyond the time when you and Howard were married, all you saw was a slow blacking-out.

What would happen then?

No. It wasn't a blacking-out. It was a dim light growing, shining on something not, after all, very beautiful. Something that made her lie. That made Howard lie. So that, however much you told yourself you were, you really weren't sure of anything.

You just went around and around inside like swirling water.

Mr. Drummey was slowing down the car. They were at the Granite Hook turn already. If she went home now, the house would be dark and lonesome; or somebody would be up and she'd have to talk, which was just as bad.

It was almost as if he had read her thoughts. "Can you take a ride tonight?" he was saying. "Or do you have to go home?"

His voice sounded tired or something, and suddenly she realized that all the way from Bellport he hadn't said a word, which wasn't like Mr. Drummey at all.

"Oh, yes," Theo said. "I was hoping you'd ask me."

"That's good," Roger said, and something in the sound of the two words told her that he had wanted her very much to go.

He put the car in gear and started her down the highway. Actually, when he had started out tonight, he had had no intention of driving Theo home or anywhere. He had only thought, I'll park in the shadows and see her go by when she comes out to go home.

For Roger had made desperate plans, and if he did catch a glimpse of her tonight, he knew it would be for the last time. He had meant to sit quietly in the car. But she had seen him and had come over and had got in. And she had been glad to see him.

The car whispered sweetly along the concrete—on one side, black pyramids of spruces between indefinite tan patches that were the open fields; on the other, the dark sea. Even this late, the coast highway was jammed with beginning holiday traffic; headlights showed up a long way off, glared brighter and went tearing by. For the tense machinery of work had stopped as if Labor Day were an iron bar jammed into its wheels; its servitors were roaring along the road to freedom.

After a while, Roger turned off on a side road. "Mind?" he asked. "The traffic's terrible on the main drag tonight."

"No," Theo said.

Watching the highway ahead, she had been thinking, We're headed south. Suppose it had been Howard driving, not Mr. Drummey and they had been going away. *Away*. But where was that? For now—*now*, not sometime in a distant starry future, would be the time when she would have had to tell Howard . . .

Roger had thought he knew this road, a graveled stretch that had once been part of the main highway, little used now that the new concrete had been laid farther back from the shore to iron out some dangerous curves and hills. But as the track narrowed down to a single lane winding among low hedges and big, tended trees, he saw he'd mistaken the turn. This must be a private way, leading through the grounds of some big estate. Yes, there was the house, closed and dark, windows and doors shuttered for winter. The road ran into a wide, white driveway, ending in a little park with a retaining wall above the ocean.

"Dead end," Roger said. He realized his voice sounded hollow and tried to make it a little more casual. "H'm, I thought this was the old coast road. We'll have to turn around."

The headlights slashed across the electric green of trimmed grass, picking out an iron bench turned bottom up to shed the coming weather; the neat, cemented edge of the wall; and beyond it, a black, illuminated patch of heaving water.

"It's the Westerly place," Theo said. "They've gone away."

"Yes. So they have," Roger said. He sat still, his hands on the wheel, looking out at darkness veiled on the edge of the light.

He was thinking, It would be as good a place as any. Sometime, I'll come back here. Soon.

Tonight? something in his heart asked, and stood back watchfully, waiting for the great empty throb of fear. But fear only stirred a little and then quietened. After the turmoil that had gone on in the past days, fear was not, it seemed, an emotion greatly to be dreaded.

"It's nice here," Theo said. "Nice and quiet after all the racket everywhere. Couldn't we sit here awhile, Mr. Drummey?"

"Of course."

He cut the engine and snapped off the lights. For a moment, night closed in, then beyond the wind screen, the sea began to grow, stretching away vast and empty to the indistinct line of lightening darkness where it met the sky. The moon was high, but it was blurred over by the faint film that would mean fog or rain before morning.

"Have you been sick, Mr. Drummey?"

Roger was suddenly aware again of the warmth in the seat beside him. He turned back to it as one turns back from a far journey.

"A little." He thought grimly of his latest visit to the doctor into which he had been forced by Evelyn. "But I'm just bad company tonight. Are you cold, my unicorn?"

"Oh, no." He wasn't at all like himself, she thought. He was sitting here remote, hardly speaking, and it was as if the last peg of all were being pulled away. Somehow, you forgot about Mr. Drummey; but seeing him again, you suddenly realized that here, if anywhere, was a rock. Only, now, he wasn't a rock. He wasn't anything.

"I've been working," Roger said suddenly. "Would you think I were a crazy man if I told you I'd been working at writing poetry?"

"Why, no, I wouldn't." She went on with an effort. "I expect I'd be proud of it, if I'd been trying to write some myself."

He laughed. Not a laugh, really. "I'm not. My state of mind, of course, is one about which very great poems have been written. You'd think I'd be content with some of those. But under the circumstances, other men's words have a hollow sound. You see, when reality at last grips you by the throat, all you have left is your own."

"What do you write about?" she asked.

"Sadness. Things ending. You wouldn't like it."

What did he know, she thought, a lump coming into her throat, about things ending? He was old. He *sounded* old.

He was like all the other old people who talked to you like that; the ones who never thought you were anything or that your feelings were ever worth thinking about. You saw them all around you, living their lives and disregarding yours; and they *had* everything. Their hands were hooked around all the things, like claws, when if only, *if only*, you had a fraction of what they had, your life wouldn't be dead and finished.

Roger was saying, "But perhaps it's just the kind of poetry the very young would like. Shall I tell you some?"

"Oh, if you want to," she said listlessly.

He said:

"The small brown birds are going, and the oak
Lets down its leaves and frosty fields are bare;
The days of summer they were less than smoke,
Less than a flight of sparrows in the air."

The first lines she hardly heard, but the last two, in his good, clear voice, dropped into her mind like a stone into water.

The days of summer. They had been less than smoke. They had been smoke disappearing into the sky and now they were gone.

"Light as the bird's wing, softer than her breast,
First snow, for gound the frost has rent apart,
O lovely snow, fill up the ruined nest,
You cannot heal disaster in my heart."

His voice went low, so that she missed some.

". . . creep up the bending bough,
And cradle deep the melancholy leaf,
No one but I remembers summer now,
Scattered in time and lost beyond belief.
Kindness on stone, on seed and stubble row,
But not upon my heart, O lovely snow."

She said in a thickened voice, "Stop. Oh, please, stop," and he jerked up his bowed head to look at her.

"What is it?" he said in bewilderment. "Theo! What is it?"

She had put her hands over her face and was sobbing into them like a little girl.

He leaned over and took hold of her wrists, trying to pull them away from her face, and the touch of the thin, childlike wrists sent a pang to his heart. "Please tell me what's the matter," he said shakily.

She said wildly, "It's nothing. It isn't anything. Oh, yes, it is. Please help me. Someone's got to help me."

"Of course," Roger said. He slipped his arms gently around her and let her burrow her wet face against his coat. "Tell me what it is and I'll help you if I can."

But it was minutes before she could, and meanwhile he sat staring out over her head into the darkness beyond the wind screen.

What a bleak fool I am, he thought, with my mind full only of myself. Trying to unload my own pitiful troubles. I'm sorry, he said to her silently, feeling under his chin the innocent parting in her smooth hair, it was only because for a moment I didn't see how I could manage them alone. Old people are like that, too, as well as the young, sometimes.

"Better?" he said aloud, after a few minutes. "Then tell me, and let's see what we can do."

"I want to marry a . . . a boy," she said slowly. "I can't because we haven't anything." Her voice went out of control and Roger sat, growing slowly cold with horror, thinking, She's in trouble. She's probably going to have a child by that thug and, if she is, what on earth can I tell her to do?

"He's . . . he's going away. We could get a job in Florida, if only we had a way to get there. He says he'd marry me, if only we had a car."

Roger said in a remote voice, "Have you got to marry this boy?" and she answered him with a full heart, never thinking how it would sound. "Oh, yes. I have. I've *got* to marry him, Mr. Drummey."

Roger felt the old bitterness surge over him, the sense of irreparable loss. The balance was set on the side of the cold and ugly hearts, the senseless boots that tramped their way over the defenseless and the young. That was the wedge that split apart the timber of his life and had from the beginning.

Long ago, he thought he had proved to his own satisfaction that compensation was due to every man—that the price exacted from him he could, if he chose, make up by other considerations, so that in the end his spirit suffered no robbery. But now he knew that no restitution could be made to mankind for some things that were taken away—taken away not in reason but in wantonness and irresponsibility.

"You mean," he said slowly, jerking his attention back to the halting sentences, "that this . . . this boy says he will marry you if you get him a car?"

Put that way, it sounded awful! "Oh, dear, no, he didn't put it like that . . . he's just afraid he can't take care of me if he doesn't have a job . . . I—I'm afraid, I—"

"Don't be," Roger said. "You can have this car. I shan't be needing it any longer."

Theo drew a quick breath. "Please don't kid about it. I can't stand it if you kid me about it."

"Nonsense." His voice was firm. "I'm not kidding. I was going to . . . turn this car in on a new one. The difference won't mean a lot to me. I've got plenty of money. Let me help out that much."

"I can't, of course, but it's nice of you. Thank you, Mr. Drummey, but I wouldn't have any way to pay you back." She didn't believe him, and he didn't blame her.

It's no solution, he told himself, but what else can I do? You can't tell them to reason about the future. Not when they were sure the end of the world had come. If she went away with Howard Thurlow her life would not be much; but what would it be if she stayed at home here and had his child without him? What wise man could judge between the two evils? Not he.

Roger took a deep breath. "I mean it about the car," he said. "What I am going to tell you now, is to convince you that I do. You see, I'm not a very wise man nor a strong one. I haven't known how to handle a beautiful and terrible thing that has happened to me. It's inappropriate, I know, and perhaps will seem ugly to you, but I have fallen in love with you."

He sensed the quick startled tension in her and went on quickly. "You understand," he said carefully, "it wasn't a thing I meant to happen. I was very lonely. When it did happen, out of a clear sky, I was frightened and bewildered."

"Oh," Theo said. "Yes." A great many things about Mr. Drummey began to be explained. She hadn't believed him about the car; but she believed what he was saying now.

"Please don't think," Roger's voice went on steadily, "that I could do anything, in any way, to harm you. Perhaps you don't even understand these things, you're very . . . young. I thought at first I wouldn't try to explain, but now I see I must. You must let me help you, because any man owes a debt to the woman he loves . . . however unrequited he may be." The steady voice strained and grated over the words. "For I think she gives him an essential beauty to take with him wherever he goes . . . whatever happens to him. Or to her. Do you see?"

"I think so," she said in a low voice.

"I don't think you do," he said, "but never mind. If you need such a thing as a car, my unicorn, to smooth out your way where you're going, take mine and welcome. Please take it now and go quickly."

"If there were only something I could do for you," she said. "I never saw anyone so kind."

"Kind?" Roger said. "No. It's a great cruelty to you, really, but I can't think of anything else to do. Someday you'll know that it's a cruelty, making it possible for you to go away with this boy. But now is an emergency. Neither you nor I can think as clearly as we could if our mind's weren't clouded with emotion. I think it would pay me back if you would remember that, when . . . when the time comes and you . . ." He stopped.

After a moment, he leaned down and switched on the dash-light. He took a small notebook from his pocket and a fountain pen. "This is my personal book," he said, "with my name printed on the cover. It has a few notes in it, nothing important. But here in the middle fold, I'll write you a . . . well, I guess you could call it a kind of bill of sale, in case anybody disputes the fact that you own this car."

He wrote rapidly for quite a long time, then closed the book and handed it to her. He got out of the car and stood for a moment with his hands on the door over the rolled-down window.

"For once in my life I've remembered to be practical," he said. "If my wife makes trouble about the car, you'll have the book to show. It's in my handwriting and ought to be legal, though I don't know. Witnesses would be better, but we haven't got any."

"But, Mr. Drummey, you could say . . . Where will you be?"

"I'm not very well," he said slowly. "I haven't told you that, but I expect I'll have to go away pretty soon and . . . and get cured."

"I can't leave you here. Please get back in the car."

He leaned in the window and looked at his wrist watch in the light of the bulb on the dash. "Quarter to one," he said. "In fifteen minutes, the bus comes past on the highway."

"I don't think there's a bus—"

"There is. I'm going up to the highway and take it. But for ten minutes, I want to look at the sea. This is as good a place as any."

"Please ride up to the highway."

"Nonsense. It's only a step. Good night, my unicorn. Be happy."

He stepped away into the darkness, and even though she put

the headlights on, she couldn't see him. She called, but he didn't answer. Presently, she put the car in gear and drove up the road to the highway.

In Bellport, Howard's rooming house was dark, but in answer to repeated rings of the doorbell, his landlady at last put her head out an upstairs window.

"Who is it?" she demanded. "What you want?"

"I have to see Howard Thurlow."

"Howard? Well, things is to a pretty pass, when the wimmen come runnin here after him at two o'clock in the mornin. Wait a minute."

The head was withdrawn from the window, but shortly it was thrust forth again.

"Howard ain't here. He's out."

"He—he hasn't gone for good, has he?"

"No. All his stuff's here. He's just out. When he's gone this late, he ain't never home before mornin. You better git back to your Ma." The landlady banged the window down.

Theo climbed back into Roger Drummey's car and drove away down the street. What now? she thought. Where to?

Ever since she had left Roger in the little park by the water, things had seemed strange—moving too fast, as if pictures were flicked across a screen.

Just get to Howard, had kept going through her mind. Just get there and everything will be all right. He'll take over from then on.

But Howard wasn't there.

She'd better go home and wait until morning. There wasn't anything else to do.

She drove slowly along the highway, turned down the road to Granite Hook. At the edge of the woods, just before they opened out into the village, was a deserted shed. A few years ago, Alton Curtis had had the idea of damming up Hardhack Brook to make an ice pond, and he had built the shed to store his ice in. But he hadn't found it a paying proposition—after the war, everybody broke their necks to buy electric iceboxes. Now the shed stood there empty, its door creaking in the wind. In the early morning before daylight, it was a ghostly and lonesome place; but it would hide the car until tomorrow. Until she found Howard and could know what to do.

HOWARD had spent the night with Jo Brown. They had gone in Jo's car to a dance at Ferriston, and on the way home had found an overnight cabin just outside the city. It had been quite an evening with plenty to drink; Howard woke up about noon with a head like a well-beaten dinner gong. Jo's wasn't much better. It took them awhile to get straightened around. What with one thing and another, he didn't get back to the Grovers' private pier, where Johnny Fleming and Dick were dismantling *Wanderlust,* until nearly three o'clock.

The job was finished by then except for odds and ends. Dick and Johnny, in paint-stained dungarees, were taking a well-earned break in the boathouse, before they put on the shutters and locked up for the winter. Empty coke bottles were on the floor beside them and Dick had his portable radio connected to an overhead outlet.

"Look who's here," Dick said. "The Duke himself. Come down to see how the help was makin out, did you?"

Johnny said, "Where in hell you been?"

"Got stuck," Howard said. "Car broke down."

"Woman broke down, you mean," Dick said, grinning.

"I got kind of tangled up, Johnny," Howard said.

Johnny, he could see, was plenty sore.

"Yare," Johnny said. "Well, you can get tangled up with the boathouse shutters. Dick and I's done our share. We're knockin off for the day."

"Okay, Johnny." You didn't give Johnny any lip, not if you wanted to go on working for Mr. Grover.

"There's the paint brushes and can to clean out, and I want

the place swept. It better be a good job, too. Goddammit, for two cents, I'd fire ya. I would anyway, if it wasn't for old lady Grover. None of the rest of us'd feel any loss."

Johnny had it in mind to say a few words to Mr. Grover, when he got back to Jersey. He very much doubted if Howard would spend another season on *Wanderlust*, but no sense making an issue out of it now. Better let Mr. Grover hand out the bad news. Johnny was a decent, peaceable soul.

He got up and went into the lavatory to clean up, leaving Howard standing, flat-footed, in the middle of the boathouse floor.

"He's pretty sore," Howard said to Dick.

"Sure is." Dick stretched his legs luxuriously. He was tired and the boathouse shutters were heavy—he was glad *he* didn't have to put them on alone. If it had been anybody but Howard, Dick would have stayed, though, and helped him. But the heck with him. "Y'ought of got back here, Howard. It was a hell of a job unstepping them masts, just the two of us. Johnny's been roaring about it all day." Dick reached to disconnect the radio, then paused with his hand in midair. "Hey, listen. There's some more about that Drummey guy disappeared."

Howard was pulling on his heavy work overalls, buckling the straps over his shoulders. "Drummey? The little guy? What happened to him?"

"Nobody knows. Seems he never come home last night. They been broadcasting that ever since noon."

The radio was saying, "1947 Plymouth sedan, dark green, white sidewall tires. License plate number—"

"His wife suspects foul play," Dick said. "He was in the habit of riding around picking up hitchhikers."

"They'll probably find him under a clamshell somewhere," Howard said. "Where's the screws for the shutters?"

"Tin can back on the shelf in the rope closet." Dick disconnected the radio, tucked the light case under his arm. "So long, Howie."

"And to hell with you, too," Howard said. He turned to with

a will, hoping Johnny would come back and see how hard he was working, but when Johnny came out of the lavatory he put on his hat and stalked by without a word or a look.

Oh, well, Howard thought. After today, no more sweating for a while. Tonight, after he got paid off, he and Jo Brown were lighting out of town in her car. She was a right-minded gal, if he ever saw one—hadn't said a word about getting married. Like him, she had no entanglements and wanted none. She had some kind of a family in Kansas that she never saw, and a job in Kansas City that she could keep or leave. Right now, she was keen to drive down with him to Congo Key and see whether old man Sewell really did have a decent job for a young couple.

Howard whistled, wrestling with the boathouse shutters.

THEO worked all day at Leon's, because she didn't dare not to. Until she caught up with Howard, she couldn't let anyone get suspicious, either Leon or the folks at home. She had got up as usual and had taken a scolding from Phoebe, managing, she hoped, to look as though getting in so late last night was just an ordinary escapade that she was sorry for and wouldn't do again.

Phoebe eyed her sharply and didn't make the scolding very bad.

"I'm certainly glad you're getting through over to Leon's today," she said. "You look tuckered out, Theo, and that's a fact. After school starts, no more gallivantin around, and my goodness, I'll be thankful."

Maybe Phoebe suspected something wasn't just as it should be, or maybe she'd stopped because she didn't want to make Theo late for the bus. Whatever it was, Theo couldn't help it—she was doing the best she could.

She took the bus to Bellport, because it would have looked odd if she hadn't. Chandler Warren drove the bus—he'd have thought it very strange indeed if she'd got out on the outskirts of the village and gone off into the woods; he'd be sure to tell somebody about it, seeing he'd promised Leon to keep an eye on her for Sylvanus. But she had a plan. As soon as she talked with Howard, she'd take a bus back and get the car. They ran every hour. As near home as that, headed the right way, she could think up some kind of a story to satisfy Chandler.

The pictures were flashing past fast on the screen again, bright and unreal; they did all day at Leon's, which was a madhouse with the Labor Day trade. Everybody from everywhere, it seemed, wanted to eat at Leon's. There was no time to think.

Theo did manage through the day to call Howard's rooming house twice. The first time, in the morning, he hadn't got back yet. The second time, he'd been and gone—was down working on the Grovers' pier, the landlady said. She thought he might be home around suppertime.

But at suppertime, Leon's was jammed, with a line waiting for tables. You might lie and walk out on people in an emergency like this if they hadn't been your friends. But this was Polly and Leon, not just anybody. No waitress, not even Polly, could handle a mob like this alone. Polly was tired, too, and in the kitchen Biff and Henry were going crazy.

So Theo told herself; but something else, unbidden, had crept into the back of her mind, where it lay like a shadow. As long as she stayed at Leon's, her mind and body drugged with work, she didn't have to think. She didn't have to do anything strange or unfamiliar. Once she stepped outside the door, closing it behind her, she would close another door on all the places and all the people she had known. She must go to Howard; she had to. But the bright lights and familiar faces at Leon's seemed, just for a time, so homely and so safe.

At early dark, the crowd began to thin out. It was raining, settling in for a steady downpour. People began to hunt cover early, in the movies, in hotels and rooming houses and overnight cabins. A good many were starting out for the long, dismal ride in the rain and on jam-packed highways, back to the cities whence they had come.

Theo went to Leon and told him she guessed she'd strained her knee. It was hurting and swelling and she'd had about all she could take. Leon said, sure, he could manage now, and didn't she want Henry to go out and help her on the bus. He rang open the cash register behind the fountain and pulled out two ten dollar bills.

"Bonus," he said gruffly. "You done damn good, Theo. I hope you'll work for me next summer."

She couldn't even say thank you. She just took the bills and squeezed Leon's hand. Because if she had tried to talk, she would have started crying right in Leon's face. He was so nice.

She went into the dressing room and changed; and Polly found time to come in and tell her that Old Hoss Liniment was the best thing in the world for a pulled ligament.

Leon said, "Somethin more ails that kid than a bum knee, Pol."

Polly said rudely, "You don't say. You got eyes like a tack."

"You peek out and see she gits on the bus all right, will ya?"

And Polly said, "What d'you think I gut my coat on for?"

So Polly walked out with Theo and helped her on the bus; and all the way she didn't say a word. She stood for a minute in the rain looking after the bus, as it pulled out, and when an inoffensive stout tourist, hurrying past in a mackintosh, accidentally jostled her a little, she turned on him and shouted in a voice that curdled his blood, "If all the men in the world was sunk in concrete, I'd be glad of it!"

The stout tourist scuttled on by, thinking, Heavens! Drunk, and was glad when he got around the corner.

Leon was satisfied; he'd seen Theo himself through the window, as the bus pulled past the restaurant.

At the edge of the woods, on the Granite Hook road, Theo pulled the cord to get out, and Chandler looked at her to see if she'd made a mistake.

"Ain't you a little previous, Theo?" he asked, as she went past him.

"Oh, no," she said airily. "I lost my best handkerchief along the road here Sunday. I thought I'd have a look, see if I could find it."

"Pretty dark, ain't it?"

"Oh, it's a white handkerchief—it'll show up, if someone hasn't found it. Don't worry, Chandler, it's only a step down home from here."

She made believe search in the tall weeds along the roadside until the bus was out of sight. Then she ran through the darkening woods to Alton Curtis's shed and backed out the car.

HOWARD hadn't got back to his room until nearly dark. The work Johnny had laid out for him had taken him the rest of the afternoon. Then, when he was through, he'd had to hunt up Johnny at his room to get his pay. Ordinarily, Johnny was around the boathouse on pay day. Tonight, he wasn't.

Howard was tired and sweaty. He made straight for the bathroom and cleaned up, rolling his soiled work clothes into a ball and chucking them into a corner. It would be quite a while before he needed anything like that again. His landlady could make what she wanted to of it—he wouldn't be here.

He put on his best dark blue uniform and then he packed his bag. Everything he had worth taking would go into one suitcase—travel light, that was his slogan. He was snapping the catches shut when his landlady called up the stairs that there was a girl down there to see him.

Jo had said she'd wait till he phoned her at the hotel to say he was ready—he'd had an idea Johnny'd keep him late. She'd probably got tired of waiting. He caught up his cap and his bag, cast a hurried look around the room to see if he'd forgotten anything—holy smoke, there was his billfold on the dresser with his whole season's savings in it. Wow, suppose he'd forgotten that!

He went over to pick it up, and through the window caught a glimpse of the car standing by the curb under the street lamp. That wasn't Jo's car.

Howard set his suitcase down. He snapped off the light and leaned silently out the window, peering down through the clematis vine that grew up the front of the house. He saw Theo, waiting on the doorstep under the porch light.

Howard said, "Oh, Jesus." He stood for a second indecisively, then hc tossed his cap onto the bed. Might as well have it over. He went quickly down the front stairs and opened the door.

"Hi'ya, babe. What's with you?"

Theo said, "Oh, Howard. I'm so glad you're here." Relief at seeing him was like a wave over her head, and she leaned against the doorjamb looking at him.

"Listen," Howard said. "I—"

"Oh, Howard, I've got a car for us. Uncle Oscar . . . he sent us a check to buy it. Now we can go."

"No!" Howard stared, the wind completely taken out of his sails. "You mean the old boy actually sent you *money?*"

"Yes, and I bought us a car." No time to explain how she had really got it, go through with all that talking. Later, it could all be told, not now. "It's second hand, but almost new. To go to Florida in. Come and see it, Howard."

By the Judas, it *was* a car, and a honey. He went down the steps, drawn to it as a moth to a flame.

"Plymouth," he marveled. "This year's. Wow!"

"Get in and try it, see how lovely it drives." She ran around to the other door and got in herself. "Oh, do get in, Howard!"

He got in, running his hands lovingly around the smooth plastic of the wheel. "Holy smoke, I don't need that pillow," he said, sending Roger Drummey's cushion flying into the back seat.

Theo thought, wonderingly, I don't either, but I hadn't even noticed it was there. "The man who owned the car was short," she explained. "He had to have it, but of course you don't, Howard."

"My gee! What a pip! Say, Uncle Oscar must be a prince. That must've been some check he sent you."

"It was."

"How'd you happen to run across a new one? Nobody can get a new one, unless he's lined with dough."

"Oh, it was a man's that comes into Leon's. I heard him say he was going to turn it in. I knew him quite well, Howard—sometimes he took me home from work nights and let me drive. So I . . ."

More practical considerations were filling Howard's mind. After all, Jo's car was a '39 Ford, and she didn't let him have any doubts as to who owned it. This one . . . well, the way the kid felt about him, anything that was hers could easily be his.

"You get the registration fixed up?" He switched on the dashlight and leaned down to read the card in its leather holder on the steering-post.

"*Roger Drummey!*" he said. "Why, he's—"

A cold finger seemed to lay itself on the back of Howard's neck and draw around the line of his hair. He looked across at Theo, in the light of the dashbulb. He hadn't had a really good look at her before. She was white as a sheet. *What went on here?*

"You're all hyped up," he said slowly.

"Who wouldn't be? Howard . . ."

"Theo, where'd you get this car?"

"I told you. Roger Drummey—I knew him. I went driving with him."

"Oh," he said. "You went driving with him."

They'd been broadcasting ever since noon: "1947 Plymouth sedan, dark green, white sidewall tires . . ."

The state cops thought Roger Drummey might be dead.

They were looking for this car. There might be a prowl car on its trail this very minute.

Howard let go the wheel as if it were hot, opened the door and jumped out on the sidewalk. Whatever this was, Howard Thurlow sure as hell wasn't going to get mixed up in it.

"Okay, babe," he said. He felt the line of sweat start around his clean white collar. "You wait here while I pack my bag. Be back in fifteen minutes."

He must want to go terribly, she thought, to go tearing into the house like that.

Howard went straight to the phone booth in the hall. He sweated while he waited for the operator to ring Jo's hotel and for her to answer her phone.

"Jo?"

"I wondered if you'd run out on me, you lug." Her voice, husky and amused.

"Look, can you meet me on the corner of Elm Street in five minutes?"

"Five minutes! Your past catching up with you?"

"A dame," he said succinctly. "You know where Elm Street is, next street above the one I live on, runs parallel."

"Mm-hm. I know. I'll be there."

"And, Jo . . . step on it, huh?" He didn't wait for her to hang up.

He got his cap and his bag from his room, came down the front stairs and went out through his landlady's kitchen.

She was sitting at the table over a newspaper, but he didn't doubt she'd been listening to his phone call. As she looked at him, all neat and clean and dressed up, carrying his suitcase, one of her eyebrows twitched and crept upward slowly toward the roots of her hair.

"Owe you some room rent, Mrs. Jackson," he said. He handed her a couple of bills.

"I'll hev t' go upstairs and git change," she said. "I don't keep none down here."

"Ne' mind," he said hastily. "Keep it to remember me by.

Mind if I use the back door? So long, Mrs. Jackson. Take it easy."

"I don't mind if I do," she said, looking after him as he closed the door. After a while she got up and went into the dark front room, peering out from behind the curtains.

Yes, there she was, the poor little thing, out there a-waiting. No more'n a high school girl by the looks of her. Somebody ought to do something, but it warn't none of Mrs. Jackson's mix. She sat down in the dark by the window and watched avidly until at last the girl got out of the car and came slowly up the walk.

Why was he so long? He'd said fifteen minutes and the clock on the dashboard had marked half an hour. That was his room on the corner—no light there. It came to her that since he had gone in there hadn't been any light there. It hadn't been turned on.

The front door opened at once before she had a chance to ring the bell. Howard's landlady said, "You better go home, miss. He's gone."

"But—he can't have gone. He was coming right back after he packed his bag."

"He's a liar," the woman said. "I'm sorry t' hev t' be the one t' tell ya, but it ain't the first time. You better go home."

The words were like blows that you took in your face, even while you tried to understand them.

"But he . . . we were going . . ."

"Listen. He come in here just now, and he calls up this girl. He says to her, he says, a dame is ketchin up with me, and would she meet him at the corner a Elm Street. He took his suitcase. Look, honey, you go home."

Theo went back down the walk to the car. Mechanically, she started the engine, engaged the gears and pulled away from the curb.

You would go down the coast highway, headed south, over the smooth concrete, the car whispering along; but you would not go far. At the Granite Hook road, you would turn down the hill, hide the car in the shed and go home.

No. You would follow Howard, blindly, go alone on the long road to Florida. You didn't even know what kind of a car he was riding in or where he was going.

Oh, Howard, which way did you go?

But suppose, by chance and luck, you overtook him, what then? He didn't love you. He had gone away with someone else.

The traffic light ahead was red. The cop was holding up his hand.

Joe Cambrini, the night traffic cop who had just come on duty, knew Roger Drummey's car, even if he hadn't, earlier in the afternoon, memorized the license number. He also knew something which the general public did not—that just before dark, Roger Drummey's body had been found washed up on the rocks below the Westerly cottage just off the state highway.

PAUL SEAVEY, the county attorney from Ferriston, had been born and brought up in Bellport. He knew various members of the Sewell family; as a boy growing up he had known Roger Drummey well. The job of investigating Roger's death was made both simpler and more complicated because some of the people concerned were his friends.

Through the years Paul had held his office, he had refused to be toughened by his job; and he held certain convictions about the application of the law, that, for one thing, it was a process essentially human. Since Ferriston was a factory town, he had seen plenty of delinquent kids, and he knew they seldom ran to a pattern. Unless you could call their parents a pattern, if they had parents. Sometimes nice kids, from sober law-abiding families, went off haywire for no reason that showed on the surface. You sometimes could find the reason —if you could get below the surface.

"That's the story, as much of it as we've got," he said. "The youngster's dazed and I think there's a lot of it we haven't. Apparently she was going around with one of the young fellows off the yachts—"

"Who says so?" Sylvanus said.

"Her friends— Polly Gerrish, who works with her at Leon's, told us quite a bit."

"I didn't know it. Her mother didn't."

Parents weren't often a great deal of help, Paul thought, looking across the desk at Sylvanus. Nor could you say they were to blame, either. Few of them ever thought of sixteen-year-olds as people in their own right; or felt that a youngster's inner life was anything serious—his emotions, sometimes, more terrible than they ever might be again. A good many parents thought of their children as children until the day—hour or minute, perhaps—when they could be pronounced "grown up." What marked that moment, Paul couldn't say. He did know that at times, in his job, he ran across a youngster in the transition period, half-child half-adult, under circumstances that curdled his blood.

He thought of the seventeen-year-old who had shot a gas station attendant because he wanted a tankful of gas and hadn't the cash to pay for it. That kid had an emotional drive that even an adult wouldn't have known how to manage; at the same time, he had an undeveloped understanding of pain. The boy of five who pulled the wings off a fly or squeezed a kitten too hard usually learned as he grew older about other feelings besides his own; how much he learned depended on a lot of things. This kid hadn't learned—he combined callousness with unchecked adolescent hungers and wants; it was a bad combination. Sometimes, Paul thought, glancing again at Sylvanus, it led to murder.

"This young fellow—this Thurlow—led her on all summer, it seems, and then went off and left her. Various people tell me he was an old hand at that kind of thing. I think she wanted the car pretty badly—maybe to follow him," Paul said.

"You tryin to tell me she wanted a man's car bad enough t' kill him for it?" Sylvanus said. His face was heavily flushed and he had a blind look around the eyes. "A kid like that?"

"M'm," Paul said. "We don't know. We're trying to get the story."

"She'll tell you, won't she?"

"She won't talk about Thurlow. She says Roger Drummey gave her the car. It doesn't make sense."

"No," Sylvanus said. A man wouldn't be likely to give away a brand-new car. But the other made no sense either. The other made so little sense to Sylvanus that he couldn't take in the possibility.

"On the other hand," Paul said, "Roger Drummey was an idealistic man. It's just possible—" He stopped. "We'll be a lot more sure of ourselves than we are before we bring any charges. Of course, we've got to satisfy Drummey's wife. She's convinced her husband was murdered."

Sylvanus merely sat staring at him. Drummey's wife couldn't think it was Theo who'd done a thing like that.

"She swears Roger was meeting some girl somewhere nights. She thinks the girl was Theo."

"Good God!" Sylvanus burst out. "When does she think it was? Theo was home most nights—her mother kept an eye on her. When does anyone think she had time for all this—this runnin around?"

"That's what we're trying to find out." Paul got up from behind the desk. "Let's see if your wife has made any progress. I figured Theo might tell her mother things she didn't want to tell me." He turned and went through the door that led to the inner rooms of the police station.

Sylvanus and Phoebe had been in Bellport all night, leaving Wes at home to look after Jacky and the boys. They hadn't either of them believed, when the police car stopped at the house in the evening, that the girl who'd been arrested in Bellport was Theo. All the way to Bellport, they'd both insisted there was some mistake. They hadn't believed it until they'd come into the room at the police station and seen with their own eyes that it was Theo.

She was sitting there, white and dazed, and Phoebe had gone right up to her and put her arms around her. She'd said, "What happened, honey?"

Theo said, "Something awful, Ma. They think I killed Mr. Drummey and stole his car. Oh, but I didn't—he took the bus, he said he was going to take the bus. I didn't know . . . Oh, Ma, he was such a kind man, I didn't know he meant to kill himself."

They had the story now, Sylvanus and Phoebe—or as much of it as Mr. Seavey said Theo had told. Mr. Drummey had said he was going to take the bus home. He was going away for his health soon. He didn't need his car any more, so he'd given it to her. Yes, she knew him quite well. He'd driven her home from work a number of nights; once or twice they'd taken a ride together. Nearly always he'd let her drive, so that he knew how much she'd liked the car. That was all there was. That was all there was; he didn't want the car any more, so he'd given it to her. He'd given her a bill of sale written in his notebook. They couldn't find the notebook, and they didn't believe her. But he had.

Phoebe believed the story from the beginning.

She said, "You ain't lyin, anywhere, Theo?" and Theo said, "No, Ma."

But Sylvanus didn't know what to think—it was certainly a thin yarn. Still, it might be just thin enough to be true—a bright kid, if she wanted to make up a story, certainly could have thought of a better one. He didn't believe for a minute that she'd killed anybody.

That fellow, that Thurlow, Sylvanus thought, waiting for Mr. Seavey to come back, I'd like to get my hands on him. What if there was something more to it, what if Theo—

Sylvanus said something under his breath, and his big fingers clenched, and Phoebe, coming in through the door with Mr. Seavey, glanced at him with a scared look on her face.

"I d'no b't you better go home, Syl," she said. "Somebody's got to be with the kids. I'm worried about them." The truth of the matter was, she was more worried about Sylvanus. He'd better be at home where he could find something to do with his hands than sitting there looking as if he'd been hit over the head. Or as if he were going to hit somebody over the head, which was almost worse.

"She said any more?"

"She's said all there is to say," Phoebe said, looking at him. "That man liked her and give her his car. She don't know what happened after she left him down by the shore. Mr. Seavey, she thinks he killed himself. She says he gave her a little book tellin how he'd given her the car."

Paul thought, And that certainly sounds like something a sixteen-year-old made up. But he merely nodded.

"Things will take a lot more looking into," he said. "We can't do anything till we know more. There's not likely to be anything new until afternoon, Mr. Sewell, if you'd like to go home."

"You go, Syl," Phoebe said. "I'll stay here."

He saw she really wanted him to go, so he went.

He walked up the street to the bus stop, feeling as if everybody in Bellport were staring at him, but he saw nobody he knew. He had a feeling he'd never had before in his life—as if he wanted to get under cover somewhere, out of sight. On the bus, Chandler Warren looked as if he were bursting to say something, but Sylvanus didn't catch his eye. He sat staring out the window until the bus pulled into Granite Hook.

At home, nobody was in the house, but looking out the kitchen window he saw Wes and the three kids playing some kind of ball in the back lot, so he guessed they were all right. He didn't call them, but went upstairs and took off his sober best suit and the black shoes that creaked a little, that he'd put on in a hurry when the cop said he and Phoebe'd have to go to Bellport last night. He'd have to see the kids soon enough and talk to Wes. Right now, he didn't want to talk to anybody. His work clothes felt good.

But when he came downstairs, he saw that Emily had come in and was sitting in the chair by the bay window.

She said, "I saw you get off the bus, Syl. Is . . . They're saying on the radio that man was . . . was murdered."

Sylvanus felt his face go hot with rage. God damn it, they were havin it over on the radio, were they? What kind of a cussid thing was that to do with people's private affairs? He held himself in, saying shortly, "It ain't so. What the police think is, he committed suicide."

"Oh-h." Emily's breath was a long-drawn one of relief. "Will Theo . . . will she be all right?"

"I guess so."

She saw he didn't want to talk about it. "Send the kids up to my house to meals, Syl, till Phoebe gets home," she said, and went quickly away.

He sat down in his own chair by the window and stared at the radio as if it were an infernal machine about to blow up in his face. Once he put out his hand to turn it on, then snatched it away.

Someone else was coming in—through the kitchen. He half got up, thinking, I'll git out a sight till whoever it is is gone; but it was only Jacky, come in from the back lot. Jacky always had a kind of sixth sense that told her whenever her father was in the house. She came over and stood beside him, her eyes watching him, big and sober, and Sylvanus took her up onto his lap.

Kids, he thought. You think you know what's going on and how they feel, and all of a sudden you find you don't know nothin. All that, inside of Theo's mind, and he nor her mother ever suspected a thing. He realized suddenly that he never had known any more about Theo than he did about Jacky, who was sitting there now, looking at him with her soft, bright, meaningless little smile.

But what more could I have done? he thought miserably. Kept them fed and clothed and a roof over their heads—took care of them. What more could any man do?

He sat rocking Jacky gently back and forth, and she put her head down on his big chest. She was going to sleep, he realized.

Well, he wished he could. He was done in—more tired than he'd ever been after the biggest day's work of his life. He rested his head against the comfortable back of the chair. Presently, his eyes dropped shut, and he went sound asleep.

THE police had been going over Roger Drummey's car for signs of violence, or anything else that might throw some light on what had happened. It was Joe Cambrini who found the notebook, where it had slid down behind the seat cushion. He brought it in to Paul along with some other odds and ends that didn't seem to mean much and dumped the lot on the desk.

"There y' are," he said.

Paul poked at the pile. There was a safety pin and a powder compact, a handkerchief—he smelled of the handkerchief and the reek of verbena almost knocked him over.

"Pu!" he said.

Joe grinned. "That must be his wife's," he said. "Anyway, I danced with her one night and that was what she smelt of."

"Oh, she went dancing, did she?" Paul said, absently thumbing through the notebook.

"Sure. Evelyn and Roger always went to the dances."

"Funny. Roger used to hate dances when I knew him. You look at this notebook, Joe?"

"Didn't take time—just grabbed up the lot and brought it along."

"Have a look at this."

He creased the notebook at its middle fold and handed it over.

"H'm," Joe said. "I'll be damned."

The page read, in the minute, up-and-down handwriting:

> This is a codicil to my last will and testament, which is in my wife's safety deposit box at the Bellport Trust Company. Being in my right mind and conscious that death is drawing near me, I give and bequeath to Theoline Sewell my 1947 automobile.
>
> (Signed) Roger Drummey

EVELYN DRUMMEY was dressed to go out. In all her extensive wardrobe, there was nothing that could be put on for sober mourning; she wore a red felt hat encircled with cherries and a mustard-colored suit of woolly tweed.

"I'm sorry to bother you again, Mrs. Drummey," Paul said. "But there are certain things I need to know."

Upright and stony, she stood in her front door and stared at Paul and Joe Cambrini.

"I don't know what more you need," she said. "That's certainly the girl I saw him dancing and drinking with at the Dream Hill Pavilion. He's been sneaking off nights to meet her and there's no doubt in my mind that she pushed him off the rocks and stole his car. Well, come in," she went on, moving aside unwillingly.

"I'm afraid it isn't quite that simple," Paul said. He sat down uncomfortably in a straight chair in her living room and held his hat on his knees. "Where did he meet her, Mrs. Drummey? Who saw them?"

"They'd take pretty good care no one did see them, wouldn't they?"

Paul sighed. "Mrs. Drummey, had Roger been under any kind of a strain?"

"No more than any old fool is who's traipsin after a girl of sixteen."

Wow! Paul thought. Nails and ice. You'd think she'd show a little feeling for the poor guy, but not a sign. Well, perhaps it was understandable, if she thought he'd been chasing. But though Paul had planned to handle her gently, he felt his hackles going up.

"Things may seem open and shut, Mrs. Drummey," he said. "But the Sewell girl is only sixteen, as you say. She seems to be a decent enough kid and her folks are nice folks. We don't want to make any mistakes."

"Look, Mr. Seavey. You can't tell me anything about sixteen-year-old kids. I run overnight cabins." For an instant her hatred of everything young showed in her eyes.

Paul eyed her. "Are you telling me you've been renting your cabins to sixteen-year-olds, Mrs. Drummey?"

"I am not. I'm saying that young kids are capable of anything. My husband's been murdered. I want the law to do something about it."

You had to hand it to her for nerve. Paul was well aware of the reputation of her cabins, but neither he nor his predecessor had ever been able to catch up with her.

"The girl tells a fairly straight story," he said. "She says your husband drove her home from work sometimes. They took a couple of rides together. That was all."

"So she says he gave her a car, too."

"She was in love with a young fellow—not your husband."

"Then she was working him for what she could get out of him. Roger was an easy mark."

"She says she doesn't want the car now. She wants to return it."

"Return it!" Evelyn said indignantly. "I should think so."

"I told you there was more to this than meets the eye, Mrs. Drummey. This is Roger's notebook?" He held it up. "It was found on the seat of his car."

"What are you askin me for? Got his name on it, hasn't it?"

"You identify it?"

"Certainly. He had those little books made up by the dozen"—he caught the faint sneer in her voice—"to write down his ideas in."

"And this is his handwriting?"

He opened the book to its first page, jotted with random words and phrases.

Fire and lilies.
Fire and a rope of sand.

"That's Roger, all right." She might have said in much the same tone, "That was Roger for you."

"It's his handwriting?"

"Yes."

"The bank also identifies his writing and his signature. Will you read this?" He handed the open book to her without further comment.

"Nonsense!" Evelyn said, staring at it. "A thing like this isn't legal."

"In his handwriting, it's a holograph will."

"She wrote it herself."

"Would she have known where his will was? It *is* in your safety deposit box?"

"He probably told her. Don't ask me how she worked it."

"Mrs. Drummey, we aren't interested in just sending people to jail. We're interested in the truth and punishment if the truth warrants it. Aren't you?"

"I want that little slut sent up for killing my husband," Evelyn said.

"Suppose she didn't. Suppose he gave her the car, as this"—he tapped the notebook—"as this indicates, because for some reason she needed it, and then committed suicide?"

"Give away a new car? Are you crazy?"

"I knew Roger pretty well, when I was a kid growing up here," Paul Seavey said. "Do you honestly think it was out of character for him to have given away anything he had if he thought the occasion warranted it?"

Her hesitation was only a flicker of her heavy-lidded eyes, but it was hesitation. "Yes, I do. He wasn't *that* much of a fool. And as for committing suicide . . . Look, Mr. Seavey. You don't want to forget that I knew Roger pretty well, too. He was so weak-kneed he couldn't kill a fly. The idea of killing himself would have made him faint dead away."

"That's why I ask you if he'd been under any kind of strain."

"I answered that once."

"Will you let me look through his private papers?"

"No. I don't think it's necessary."

"I'm afraid I'll have to insist."

She shrugged. "All right, if you're bound to nose around. His stuff's in that little back room there, he called his 'study.' If you want to look at his shirts and collars, they're upstairs in his bureau drawer. I can't waste any more time. I've got to go over to the Cabins."

"I'm sorry, Mrs. Drummey."

She gave him a brief, icy stare before she turned and went silently out the door.

But at the foot of the front steps, before she went out across the driveway, Evelyn stumbled a little. She put out a hand to the white-painted rail to steady herself.

Roger was dead. He had been a fool of a little man, more like a baby than a man around the house, and he'd been next to no good as a husband. She'd been ashamed of him and ashamed of herself for never having found, or wanted, someone better.

Torture would never have wrung from her an admission to the world that she had thought anything of him. But she had. She had loved him and her heart was as bleak and blackened as if it had been swept over by fire. She tightened her lips and pulled straight her mustard-colored skirt before she went out into the bright, sunlit drive.

"Pleasant, ain't she?" Joe Cambrini said, mopping his face with his handkerchief. He hated an assignment like this, which meant nosing into someone else's business. Usually, he didn't get one, since he was mostly on traffic; but he had been available this afternoon, and, after all, the Bellport police force wasn't large.

"M'm," Paul said. He was looking ruefully at the mess of papers strewn around Roger's desk and wondering what, after all, he'd hoped to find. "Looks hopeless, Joe. If he left any kind of a suicide note, she's probably found it. I have an idea, the way she feels, she'd have disposed of it, too. She doesn't want to think he committed suicide, Joe." He sat down at the desk, pulling out a drawer. "And she doesn't want us to think so."

"D'you think he did, Paul?"

"Sure. Don't you?"

"I d'no. That will business could've been faked, maybe."

"Just possibly. Not beyond reasonable doubt, eh, Joe?"

That was the rub. In his own mind he was sure now, partly from the note in Roger's notebook, partly from talking with the girl. There were a few illogical points, though, not tied up with a neat string on them. The thing was, in cases of this kind, to close them up with as few ends dragging as possible, and as little publicity. No sense leaving a doubt in anybody's mind or a shadow to tag after a youngster for the rest of her life. What he needed now was something to convince good sound family men, like Joe Cambrini, that there might be a circumstance that would make reasonable a man's giving away a brand-new car. Forty banks or forty handwriting experts could swear to Roger's signature and his handwriting; but there'd always be some, like Joe, who'd wonder if anybody's writing couldn't be copied—close enough.

"Take the bottom drawer and work up, Joe," he said. "I doubt if we find anything."

They worked in a silence broken only by the rapid rustling of paper and, once, the eruption of a gilt cuckoo clock on the wall, which, without warning, burst into full cry.

Joe jumped and then looked foolish. "Jeest," he said, "if Drummey had a state a mind, I d'no's I blame him. I would, myself, in a room long with that thing. This stuff is funny, Paul. Looks like he copied down every poem was ever written."

"Looks like he wrote some of his own," Paul said. "Not bad stuff. I wonder what a publisher would say to it."

"You mean anybody'd ever *want* to read it?"

Paul chuckled. You couldn't exactly call Joe a literary man. Still, if a simple, good-hearted guy like Joe could get the ideas into his head without having to *read*—if he could get over his antipathy to the medium—he'd probably enjoy some of this stuff of Roger's.

They went on for a while turning over papers, and presently Joe, from his seat on the floor, let out a strangled croak. He had found a fat black notebook, whose pages were filled with the neat, meticulous handwriting. He was reading it, with his face turned purplish red, his eyes bulging, and a line of sweat along his upper lip.

"Kuh-rist!" Joe said.

"Found something?"

"His diary. Here, take it. I don't want t' read no more of it. All you need is them lines on the last page. The pages before it'll tell you why." He began, methodically, as a police officer who knew his job should, to put the scattered papers back into the drawer.

Paul read the final four pages of the diary, the testament of Roger Drummey's last days with his wife. It ended:

> "And so I have come to the place where I know I can no longer bear to live. Evelyn has my gratitude, for, without her, I should never have the courage to kill myself."

Paul closed the book and slipped it into his pocket. "That's all we need, Joe. Something, isn't it?"

Joe, he could see, was shocked to the marrow of his bones. He was a kind and decent man, who loved his wife and enjoyed marriage.

"She's gut a hell of a nerve," he said, "to accuse anybody else of murderin her husband."

THEO couldn't help liking Mr. Seavey. He was a grave man, but even when he had thought she'd done all those awful things, she had sensed behind his gravity a steady kindness. She wished she could have talked to him, as he wanted her to do; but when it came to telling about Uncle Oscar and . . . and Howard, the words seemed to coil up in a bunch in her throat and wouldn't come out. How could you ever tell anybody such things as that?

"The suicide note we found in Roger Drummey's study will be published in the newspapers," Mr. Seavey said. "It's already gone out to the public over the radio. His wife's given us a statement, too. She understands now that he killed himself."

Theo thought, He's kind, but oh, I wish he wouldn't talk about Mr. Drummey. Perhaps he wouldn't, if he knew everything.

But she couldn't tell him. She stared at the floor.

"I won't say much," Paul said, as if he had read her mind. "Before you go home, I want you to know that you aren't in disgrace—nobody thinks so. A man offered you a ride home from work and you took it, supposing he would take you home. It wasn't your fault that he happened to be going through a tragic crisis in his life."

It was, too, her fault, she thought, staring miserably at the floor.

"The worst people can think of you," he went on, "is that you were a little foolish."

Now he was going to lecture her, the way they all would, she thought exhaustedly. She waited for him to get it over.

"I don't think you were," he said. "You don't want to tell everything that happened, and I don't blame you. I shouldn't, in your place. Everybody does things that look right at the time and afterwards may seem humiliating and foolish. Particularly, when they're so upset they can't think." He grinned suddenly, and it was startling in so grave a face. "I do, myself. But I don't tell anyone stuff that's better forgotten."

He was, she thought, wonderingly, talking to her as if she were a human being, not a child to be lectured and disciplined.

"So you keep under your hat the story about Howard Thurlow," he said, and saw her flinch a little at the name. "It's nobody's business but yours. You feel bad about him, and no wonder. Well, listen. If he told you anything about his life, see if you can't figure out how circumstances ganged up on him to make him what he turned out to be. Things that happen to people sometimes do that—if someone is weak or hasn't any particular reason to care about his integrity."

The poor little devil, he thought, I'm opening it all up, saying all the wrong things, I don't doubt. But he had to go it blind, and things couldn't be left the way they were.

"There's one more thing," he said. "You may worry, thinking you caused Roger Drummey's death. You didn't."

That must be it, he thought, with relief. Or part of it. Her dull gaze swerved upward from the floor and came to rest, hopefully, on his face.

He took Roger's diary out of his desk drawer. "The whole story's in here," he said. "He was unhappy at home; so unhappy he may have been a little out of his mind."

"No," Theo said. "He wasn't crazy, Mr. Seavey."

Well, at least, he'd got her to say something.

"I don't mean crazy," he said. "I mean something that might happen to any sane person, after a long time trying to think what to do. I'm in no doubt about Roger. He had a fine mind—it might have been a great one, if someone had helped him a little. If circumstances hadn't ganged up on him, and if he hadn't been sick. He was sick, you know. He'd just found out he hadn't very long to live."

"Oh," Theo said. "No. I didn't know."

The words sounded merely casual and polite, and Paul glanced at her curiously.

Now what went on there then? he thought, puzzled. How in thunder could you ever tell, with youngsters?

She sat looking at him now as brightly attentive as if he were giving her a tennis lesson, or something of equal emotional value.

He handed her the diary. "There are three pages in there marked with paper clips," he said. "They are about you. I want you to read them. I'll have to ask you not to look at any of the other pages because they tell about his unhappiness, and no one should see them."

He watched her while she read the three pages. He said nothing when she turned back and read them through again. She handed the book back to him, her face expressionless.

"You see?" Paul said. "Far from harming him, you gave him a great happiness. The poor devil hadn't had much of that."

She nodded.

Well, Paul thought, if she were thirty, she might have understood that that was the real thing, written there on those pages: that it wasn't something you came across every day.

Actually Theo was not seeing him at all. She seemed to hear a strained voice say, ". . . because any man owes a debt to the woman he loves . . . however unrequited he may be. For I think she gives him an essential beauty to take with him wherever he goes . . ."

"Good luck," Paul said. "Go home now with your Pa and Ma. They ought to be out there waiting." He shook hands with her.

Theo said, "Oh, thank you, Mr. Seavey." But that was all.

Her throat was clenched tight with sorrow, the look on her face that puzzled him a mask for the naked shame the very young feel when a thing like sorrow starts to show.

IT seemed at first to Theo that once she was alone with Sylvanus and Phoebe, she wouldn't be able to look them in the face. But, somehow, it wasn't hard at all. Sylvanus didn't take them home on the bus—he hired a taxi to drive them back to Granite Hook; and on the way over, Phoebe put her hand, in the old black glove that was her best, though it was faded rusty and mended along the seam, down over Theo's and kept it there. But after a while, she snatched it away and impatiently hauled off the glove, turning it wrong side out.

"Thank heavens, there!" she said. "I can't stand gloves. They don't let your hands breathe."

It was funny and at the same time endearing—just like Phoebe. Theo thought, through her numbness, with a little sense of wonder, Awhile ago, I would just have felt she was acting countrified, when she said she hated gloves. I'd have been kind of ashamed of her. But the thing was, she really *didn't* like gloves—not liking gloves was a part of Phoebe.

Well, she wasn't ashamed of Phoebe now. Nor of Sylvanus.

They're the ones to be ashamed—of me.

They were quite people, Sylvanus and Phoebe. She'd watched them answering Mr. Seavey's questions—if she went out nights, and all. They had been quiet and dignified and simple, and it stuck out all over them that they loved her. That look of outrage Phoebe'd had, when Mr. Seavey'd mentioned the fact that Theo might have been going wrong behind their backs—nobody had any doubt in his mind as to what Phoebe thought of that!

The way Phoebe's face had looked from the beginning had said to Theo, "I love you and I'll stand by you no matter what happens." You were sure of it, even if neither of you said anything.

And you were sure of Sylvanus, too, even though you knew he was thinking you were a damned little fool.

It wasn't bad when she got home. Even Wes was nice. The kids were quiet and didn't ask questions. They just seemed glad to see her, and Jacky put up her face to be kissed.

They were all three worn out. Even Sylvanus lay down on the couch to have a nap. Theo went up to her room to rest. She'd thought she wouldn't ever be able to sleep again, but as soon as she was on the bed she knew she was going to. The next thing she knew, a light had come on in the room. She turned over and saw that the window was dark; Phoebe, coming in, had snapped on a reading lamp by the bed. She had a glass of milk and some sandwiches on a plate.

She said, "It's ten o'clock. I thought I'd see you had a little something before you settled away for the night."

Theo sat up. She sipped the milk and looked at Phoebe, her eyes big over the rim of the glass. "Aren't you going to scold me, Ma?"

"No," Phoebe said. "My heavens, there, it's a time for being thankful, child, not for scoldin." She sat down on the foot of the bed. "We don't hev t' talk about it," she said. "We're all here and all in one piece. I guess that's what's important."

She said speculatively—and it was a part of Phoebe that to save her life she couldn't leave it at that—"Theo, he must have been a dreadful wicked boy, that Thurlow boy."

"No, Ma. He wasn't. I mean, he was. But—" She couldn't explain, her eyes said. "It was his shoes."

"His shoes?" Phoebe said in bewilderment. "You go to sleep now, Theo, and get rested. You'll feel better in the morning."

She snapped out the light and went away.

It was a part of Phoebe, too, that she hadn't cried at all while the trouble was going on. Now she went alone into the spare room and cried for an hour; and nobody knew that she had cried at all.

Theo tried to nestle her head into the pillow. Maybe Phoebe would have understood about Gram Sarah's shoes meaning what she was, the shoes with the thin leather and the bulge around the bunion, stepping back through time. And Howard's shoes, the gay, dancing ones, they had stepped back, too—carrying him past the war, and the saloons, and the rousting times along the waterfronts that he had told her about, past the faces of women and their tears, and the oyster boats in Chesapeake Bay, to the time when the tough lonesome little boy hoed lettuce on his brother's farm.

Oh, he had told her a lot, he loved to talk about his life. You couldn't blame him now, if he wanted things easy and to have fun—not to be tied by anything; any more than you could blame Gram Sarah if she couldn't bear to lie in bed, all her hard work taken away. It was strange to think how Gram Sarah had made her understand about Howard.

Thinking of Howard, she felt the familiar pain come sharp and blinding. It would come for a long time whenever she thought of him or saw someone with dark red hair or an officer's blue tailored uniform. But if what Mr. Drummey had said were true about the one you loved leaving you beauty she should have something more when she thought of Howard. Howard hadn't left any beauty at all—only a feeling of shame and a crawling, humiliating ugliness. Because no matter what fairy tales you made believe to yourself, it ended up the same—she hadn't been smart enough or pretty enough and Howard hadn't wanted her at all.

I guess I'm not much, any way you look at it, she thought, feeling behind her eyelids the familiar sting of tears.

She got out of bed, fumbling for the light switch by the bureau and stood forlornly before the mirror. And then, suddenly, she leaned forward and stared at herself dumbfounded.

She saw a face heart-shaped, like Phoebe's, with Phoebe's humorous, tip-tilted nose and wide-apart, gray eyes. The forehead was broad and smooth, with a tawny widow's-peak growing down, the mouth firm and generous—Sylvanus's nice mouth, his pointed, stubborn chin.

For the first time in her life Theo saw her face as it really was. It wasn't beautiful, but it wasn't any face to be ashamed of either.

And even if it were, she told herself, I'd better start learning how to put up with it, not try to make myself out something I'm not. That's kid stuff.

For a moment it was hard to meet the steady gray eyes looking back at her out of the mirror.

I lied to Howard and I chased him, she said. I guess I must've known deep down all the time he didn't really want me.

Something stood up in her mind and said, clearly and coldly, You were lucky. You were lucky you didn't marry him.

For Howard was kid stuff too. He wasn't grown up and he very likely never would be. As long as he lived, he would never have in his heart a fraction of what, simple and agonizingly beautiful, Roger Drummey had had in his, the night he offered her his princely gifts and she had accepted the very least of them.

So long as you knew that such a thing had been in the world and might be again, you would be wary until you found it, taking no substitutes, however lovely the faces they might wear. You would know that no one was a princess enchanted in a tower, nor needed to be; for if the light of common day were uglier than the soft shine of dreams, you had the sense now to know that a time might come tomorrow, when it could shake your heart and blind your eyes with beauty.

THE weather built up for the line storm a week earlier than usual, on the twelfth of September. It was more a feeling in the air than any perceptible change in the sea or sky. The sun shone out of clear blue, and islands on the southern horizon, ordinarily misty with distance, stood out in clear black outlines. But to breathe out of doors was like breathing in an old powder house; the air felt dead and woolly and seemed, almost, to give off a musky smell.

In the afternoon, on that day, Sylvanus went to see his mother. She had sent word by Morgan for him to come up —Morgan didn't know why.

"I was in a hurry," Morgan said, "so I didn't stop to ask questions. But I think she wants to see ya quite bad, Syl."

"All right," Sylvanus said. "I'll go up right now. She probly wants to bawl me out."

He set out from the house, walking with Morgan, but shortly found himself forced out of his leisurely stroll, keeping up with Morgan's pumping legs.

"Where's the fire?" Sylvanus said, at last. "You'll bust, one a these days, Morg."

Morgan didn't slow down. "Wes and I are overhaulin seines," he said. "Kind of like to get through this afternoon, before it rains."

"How you and Wes makin out together?"

"Fine," Morgan said. "Saves me a lot in time and money, Wes does."

"I thought he might," Sylvanus said, grinning.

Morgan turned off down the road that led to the shore. "If you're going up to the house, you might tell Emily I'll be late," he called back over his shoulder. "Tell her she may have to milk."

Sylvanus nodded.

Morgan had thought, at first, that they ought to sell Gram Sarah's cow; but the old lady'd made such a touse that everybody was afraid she'd make herself sicker than she was, so the cow had been kept on in Gram Sarah's barn. Morgan usually milked her, but sometimes he was late getting home at night; after a while, he'd shown Emily how. At first she'd been as scared as a rabbit; now she didn't seem to mind. Sylvanus gave her Morgan's message. She merely nodded.

"Jamie and I'll go over, if Morgan isn't back in time," she

said. "Jamie won't like it, though. Would you believe it, Uncle Syl, he's scared of Gram Sarah's cow?"

"Takes after his ma," Sylvanus said, grinning. He liked Emily. There was a lot more to her than met the eye.

"Not now, I'm not," Emily said, blushing a little. Of course, Syl would think it was foolish ever to have been afraid of a cow.

"I'll milk for ya tonight," he said, as he started up the stairs. "Might's well, I've got time."

"Oh, *would* you?" Emily said in a heartfelt voice.

Syl paused on the landing. "I guess you don't like to much, eh?"

"Well, no, I don't. Not much. But I had to because Morgan doesn't always have time, and he said he'd have to sell the cow. It seemed too bad, your mother felt so about it, so I told Morgan I'd learn to milk. Now I'm kind of proud I can."

"Well, I'll do it tonight," Sylvanus said, and went on into his mother's room.

Gram Sarah was propped up in the bed on a couple of pillows. She looked horribly thin and shrunken, but her fierce old eyes were as bright as ever.

"Well," she greeted him. "You don't break your neck comin t' see me when I'm cast, no more'n you ever did, do ya?"

"I planned to," he said. "But—"

"If plans was rattlesnakes, you'd be bit to death, Sylvanus Sewell," she said.

He supposed he'd heard that from her a thousand times in his life. "Ayeh," he said. "I'd be swelled up out of all reason. Morgan says you want somethin, Ma."

"Well, I do. I want t' git up out a this bed."

"Look, if there's anythin within reason you want, just ask me and I'll try to git it for you."

"Well, there is. I want some hash."

"Sure," he said. "I'll tell Emly."

"That mackerel-chum she makes ain't hash. What I want, Sylvanus, is some *hash*, like your Pa knew how t' put together.

And I want it cooked on my own stove and to eat it in my own kitchen."

"Well . . ." Sylvanus opened his mouth to explain why he couldn't manage that for her; then he closed it again. After all, why not? The doctor'd already said Gram Sarah'd never be any better. She'd never get up again under her own steam. It must be hell, lying in that bed all day.

Sylvanus glanced at her and saw she was looking at him shrewdly. He laughed outright.

"You knew Morgan wouldn't," he said. "You could argue all day with him. But you knew darn well I'd be just fool enough. Well, come on, then. I spose it's liable t' kill ya . . ."

He wrapped her up like a cocoon in blankets he took off the bed, until nothing was visible out of the bundle but her bird-like old head. Then he scooped her up gently in his arms and started down the stairs.

Emily appeared in the door as he went through the living room, her eyes popping.

"It's all right," Sylvanus said. "Ma and I's goin on a little picnic, that's all."

He carried her down the front steps, out along the walk and into the grassy path that led to her home.

"My soul and body," Gram Sarah said. "September, ain't it? Look at them asters, Sylvanus."

"Fall, all right," he said.

"The year could roll right over you in that blarsted bed and you never know. Buildin up for a storm, it is. The weather smells mean."

As they passed Mat Dawes's house, Uncle Wheat, sitting on the front porch, batted his eyes and then came down the front walk at a limping run.

"Well, Sarah," he said heartily. "It's the best sight I ever had come before my eyes to see you out."

"You mind your own business, you lechin old fool," Gram Sarah said. "And don't come buttering round me now. I ain't forgut that drunken orjus you tried to start with me the night Morgan's baby was born."

Uncle Wheat looked foolish. He beat a hasty retreat to the house.

"That's tellin em," Sylvanus said, grinning over the top of her head.

"The old goat," she said indignantly. "I been layin up a few things t' tell him, soon's I thought I could handle my tongue."

Sylvanus carried her all around the farm—out through the garden where the late vegetables were ripening, through the barn and hen house, past the pasture bars, so she could see the cow placidly feeding at a distance.

"The old besom," Gram Sarah said. "Hadn't been for her, I'd been on my feet today. But if 't hadn't been her, 't would likely been somethin else. I'd been feelin for a long time, Sylvanus, like a fog comin down." She recovered herself quickly. "I wisht you'd do the milkin of her, Sylvanus. Morgan's been, but he never had a light milkin hand."

"Ayeh, I'll try to, Ma."

He finished by carrying her around front, so she could see how her flower beds were doing.

"Some a the kids might come up and pull a few weeds for me," she said. "Things goin t' rack 'n ruin."

"I'll tell Phoebe. You seen all the things now, Ma? Say what you want now, and don't tear my head off when I git you back to Morgan's."

"I want t' go down suller," she said. "See my preserve closet."

It was something of a trick to get the door open and get her down the narrow cellar stairs, but he managed it. Poor old soul, he thought, she can't weigh more than fifty pounds.

Gram Sarah looked with complacency at the preserve closet, the consummation of so many summer hours before she'd been took sick. But she let out a yell of indignation, when they came to the shelf on which stood the string beans, which Uncle Wheat had picked for her and Mat had canned.

"My God, she's used them snap-top jars!" Gram Sarah said. "I *never*, in all my life, used anything but a screw-top jar. Sylvanus, you tell Phoebe and Emily to start usin them beans right away, for they wun't keep a month. Wouldn't you know that fluppit'd do some kind of a foolish trick like that!"

"Better take up a jar a mustard pickles t' go with the hash, hadn't we, Ma?" Sylvanus said.

"If you'd le' me git my good hand out a these cussid blankets, I'd carry it, Syl. The idea, wrappin anybody up like a mummy. I'm bout roasted."

He loosened the blankets and managed, after some digging, to release her hand. The pickle jar was hard for her to hold; he changed the angle of his arm, so that when he carried her up the stairs, the weight of the jar rested against her body.

In the kitchen, he put her down on the old horsehair sofa between the windows, threw up the sash and let the sun stream in on her through the screen.

"M-m," Gram Sarah said.

He saw, as he rattled the covers off the stove, beginning to redden a little with rust, that she had dropped off to sleep, still holding the pickle jar.

Phoebe and Emily, when they had closed up Gram Sarah's house after she'd been taken sick, had taken care of the perishables in her supply closet, but neither of them had had time since to do any more. Sylvanus found salt pork, laid away in a crock, and a can of corned beef on the shelf in the cellarway. He cut up a piece of salt pork in Gram Sarah's smooth, seasoned old frying pan, and set it on the stove to try out, while he went down cellar to see if there were any potatoes in the potato barrel. There weren't and there weren't any onions. Maybe Mat had some. If she had some cold boiled potatoes, it would be better for hash—save him the trouble of cooking some and waiting for them to cool. He glanced at Gram Sarah, but she was still sleeping, so he slipped out the back door and across the yard to Mat's.

Mat had onions and she had cold boiled potatoes on hand. She also donated a half-loaf of fresh homemade bread, some butter and two wedges of apple pie.

Sylvanus carried the lot back to his mother's kitchen. The pork was tried out, nice and brown, and Sylvanus sniffed with appreciation. He could use some of that hash himself.

Gram Sarah was awake when he pulled down the big white bowl, cracked in fine lines from many warmings-up in the oven, and dumped into it the browned hash, crisp on both sides and soft in the middle. He grinned at her, sliced the bread into thick slices, put it on a plate and set the plate on the table. He set two places with knives and forks, plates and cups and saucers, and reached a long arm for the jar of pickles, which he opened and shook out into a bowl. He poured two cups of steaming tea. Then he went over to her.

She was lying contentedly, her eyes wide open and moving over and over the things in the room.

"I'm home," she said, looking at him. "I'm home, ain't I, Sylvanus?"

"Ayeh," he said. "You want t' sit up to the table?"

"Of course I do," she snapped. "What's the matter with you, Sylvanus? You never had a brain in your head anyway."

He pulled her Boston rocker up to the table and padded it with pillows. Then he braced the rockers forward with a couple of sticks of stove wood from the woodbox, so that when he put her into the chair, she'd sit high enough and steady.

Between them, they ate all the hash and bread. They very nearly finished up the pint jar of mustard pickles. They each drank three cups of tea and topped off with the wedges of apple pie.

Gram Sarah was nodding by the time they finished, and he picked her out of the chair and put her on the sofa again, while he cleaned up the dishes. She slept soundly when he carried her back to Morgan's house; but when he laid her down again on the bed in the spare room, she opened her eyes.

"I'm glad I went t' sleep, not to see myself leavin home again," she said.

"Well, we'll do it again sometime, Ma."

"That was a good hash, Sylvanus. You warn't never my best, you never had the brains Morgan's gut, but you was always a good boy." She stopped. "But you was aggravatin as a carbuncle from the day you was born."

He grinned at her, the cocky, derisive and half-secret grin for which she had whipped him when he was a boy.

"There you go!" she said indignantly. "I git my hands on you, Sylvanus Sewell . . . Sylvanus . . . Syl . . ." She fumbled after the words. "There was something I had to tell you. I can't remember."

"Go to sleep, Ma."

"Look after your girl, Sylvanus. That was it. She's in some trouble."

"I know about it, Ma. She's all right now, she's back to school. Go to sleep, Ma."

How in the devil, he thought, did she know about that? Well, if they *had* succeeded in keeping something from her, it would be the first time in their lives.

He was a little scared at what he had done. That slug of hash, he told himself, would kill a mule. Already, in his own midriff, he was feeling the slight rumblings of beginning indigestion.

But the feast hadn't hurt Gram Sarah. When she woke up at suppertime, she was as bright as a ribbon.

It was on the second night of the line gale that Gram Sarah woke up and found she could move her left hand. Her leg was all right, too. She could almost wiggle it. Slowly, like an old animal that obeys inborn, subconscious, stubborn instinct, she pushed back the bedclothes and sat on the edge of the bed, holding with her good hand to the bedside table.

She couldn't think where her clothes were. That fool Emly

had hung them away; but she knew her shoes were under the edge of the bed. She slid down to the floor, found them and tugged them on.

It seemed she couldn't move her hand and her leg as much as she'd thought at first. But she had moved them a little, which was a sure sign, must be, that they were starting to get better.

She managed after a while to crawl over to the window, which Emily had left cracked open for ventilation. That Emly never opened the window wide enough, as she very well knew. Gram Sarah'd told her so times enough. After a long time, bracing and pushing upwards from the floor, Gram Sarah got it a little wider open.

The wind sweeping out of the east from over the sea a long way away, caught her in the face with a mighty gust; but she clutched the window sill.

"You're givin us another storm, God, I see," she said. "Well, hev it and git it over, so's we can live again. Thank you for makin me well, so's I can move my arm and my leg. I'll outlive any of em," she said, and tasted the raindrops that were salty with spray but still sweet in her mouth.